Angelica

The Burkes: Book 1

by

KIMBERLY RAE
JORDAN

THREE**STRAND**
P R E S S

A CORD OF THREE STRANDS IS NOT EASILY BROKEN.

A man, a woman & their God.
Three Strand Press publishes Christian Romance stories
that intertwine love, faith and family. Always clean.
Always heartwarming. Always uplifting.

ANGELICA/ Kimberly Rae Jordan. -- 1st ed.
ISBN-13: 978-1-988409-88-7

I can do all things
through Christ who strengthens me.

Philippians 4:13

CHAPTER ONE

"Angela!"

Angela Reynolds was startled at the sound of her name, which was followed by a rush of familiar tension. She wanted to keep walking. To ignore the man who was trailing after her.

She took a breath and forced her shoulders to relax. Then, she turned to face the man, hoping her expression didn't show how she truly felt about him.

"What do you want, Craig?" Angela asked.

The tall, stocky man stopped a few paces away, a smug look on his face as he crossed his arms. Fear curled inside her as his gaze wandered over her.

He may have had the role of brother by virtue of them having been adopted by the same people, but she had never considered him that. Just like she didn't like to think of Jim Reynolds as her dad.

"Dad wants you back at the farm," he said. "You need to help with the garden."

Angela shook her head. "I can't. I have to work."

Craig's expression hardened. "Your job is at the farm. Not here."

Here was the small town of Briar Hollow in central Kentucky. The homestead was located about half an hour to the northwest of the town, though she wished it was on the other side of the country. Or maybe even on the other side of the world.

Unfortunately, they hadn't been able to get very far away when she and her sister, Kiara, escaped the homestead. That meant that at least once a week, Jim or Craig would track them down and insist they return to the homestead.

The homestead where she'd been raised was the last place on earth she wanted to be. It had been their world for so long, giving them barely a glimpse of anything beyond the boundaries of the homestead as they'd grown up. And had the people she'd lived there with been different—kinder—it might have been an idyllic life. Unfortunately, it had been anything but.

Angela wrapped her arms around herself. "Kiara and I both have jobs here. Our home is here now."

"You both are ungrateful little brats," Craig spat out. "You owe Dad everything."

Angela's insides trembled. "We have helped him plenty. Now it's our turn to have lives of our own."

Her words sounded braver than she felt, but she had to stay strong. For her sake, and for Kiara's.

There was a reason Jim and Craig always approached her and not Kiara. If one of them was going to cave under the pressure, it would be her.

Angela didn't like to admit that about herself, but the reality was that she wasn't as strong as Kiara.

"We're not coming back," Angela said firmly as she lifted her chin. "You and Dad have to accept that."

"Not sure that we do," Craig said, glancing around the street where they stood. "Watch your back."

As he ambled down the sidewalk to the old pickup truck parked in front of the hardware store, Angela wasn't sure if what he'd said was a caution or a threat.

Not wanting Craig to catch her watching him, Angela swung around and rapidly continued in the direction she'd been headed before he'd stopped her.

She tugged her coat more tightly around her body as she hurried toward the grocery store. A brisk late November wind cut through to her bones, though she wasn't sure it was all the wind. The interaction with Craig had left her shivering.

A bell chimed as she stepped into the store. The place wasn't very big, but it carried all the basics, along with a few specialty items. From what she'd heard from others in town, the prices weren't very cheap, but she and Kiara had no choice but to shop there.

They'd never gone beyond the homestead or Briar Hollow, so she'd never shopped at the bigger grocery stores where prices might be more reasonable.

"Good afternoon, Angela."

Angela turned to smile at the older woman behind the front counter. She and her husband were the owners of the store, and she'd always been friendly to Angela.

"Good afternoon, Mrs. Martin. How are you doing?"

"Just fine, hun. And you?"

"I'm fine too."

"Do you have plans for Thanksgiving?"

"Nothing too fancy," Angela said. "We're just having a small dinner."

"A small dinner sounds lovely. I'll be cooking dinner for almost thirty."

Angela couldn't imagine a gathering of that many people. "I'm sure they'll appreciate your efforts."

"I certainly hope so," the woman said with a laugh. "They'll be bringing some food as well, so it won't all be on me."

The bell chimed again, and Mrs. Martin turned to greet the entering customer. Pulling out the paper with the list she and Kiara had made the night before, Angela got one of the small wheeled carts and made her way down the nearest aisle.

There wasn't much variation in what they bought from week to week, so it didn't take her long to gather everything on the list. She also had a small list for their landlady, so she added those things to her cart.

Once everything was in the cart, she took a couple of minutes to add up the total of everything on the paper. After a brief hesitation, she headed to the candy section.

She picked up a package of gummy bears for Kiara and a plain milk chocolate bar for herself. Kiara would probably tell her she shouldn't have wasted the money, but she'd still eat the candy in one sitting.

There was one other customer standing at the register when Angela approached it. Knowing that no one ever rushed when Mrs. Martin checked them out, Angela stood looking at the magazines in the rack beside the checkout.

She and Kiara hadn't been raised knowing anything about celebrities. There had been no television for them, and the books they'd been given to read had all been historical.

It wasn't until they'd gotten older and started coming into town periodically with Jim and Sandra that they'd realized that there was so much more to the world than the homestead surrounded by gardens and trees.

Kiara had memories of the time before she'd been adopted, but Jim had gotten angry with her whenever she'd tried to talk about the shows she liked on television. Eventually, she'd stopped talking about any of it.

Now, though, Kiara loved to read all the magazines about movie stars and professional athletes. Her favorite thing was to look at pictures from fancy events to see the red carpet looks. Kiara also liked to watch movies, shows, and even sporting events on their old laptop.

"Did you find everything, hun?" Mrs. Martin asked as Angela shuffled forward with her cart and began to unload it.

"Yes, thank you."

Mrs. Martin deftly rang up each item, giving Angela a wink when she got to the candy. When she told her the total, Angela frowned and looked down at her paper.

Had she done her math wrong? Thankfully, she'd erred on the high side, so the bill was lower than she'd expected.

Math had always been a weakness for her. As a baker, she had to know measurements and how to adjust recipes, but she always double and triple-checked her figures.

"There are a few things on sale this week that I haven't gotten around to changing the price tags for yet," Mrs. Martin said.

"Really?" Angela had a hard time believing that, but she was grateful. "Thank you."

"You're welcome, hun."

Once Angela had paid for both orders, she thanked the woman again, then picked up the bags. The door swung open as she approached it, and a middle-aged man stepped back to hold it open for her.

She gave him a smile and a nod before stepping out into the chilly air. Cold had swept in that week, a reminder that winter was on its way.

It took her fifteen minutes to walk from Main Street to Hawthorn Avenue, where she and Kiara rented a basement suite from an elderly woman.

After living in the apartment above the bakery for over two years, they'd had the opportunity to move somewhere else. And just a couple of days prior, they'd transferred their meager amount of belongings into the basement apartment.

It was small and dark, but it was safe and affordable. Best of all, they didn't have to worry about Patty, the owner of the bakery, her boss, and their landlady, walking into their space whenever she felt like it.

There hadn't been a lot of options for rentals in the small town, but they hadn't had a way to get somewhere bigger. That hadn't bothered Angela too much, as she'd been wary of living in a more densely populated city, even if it was farther away from Jim and Craig.

Before going down to the apartment, Angela knocked on the door to the main part of the house. Hearing Miss Ida call for her to come in, Angela opened the door and stepped into the kitchen.

Miss Ida approached from the living room, her steps slow. She was a vibrant woman, but her body was beginning to fail her. Arthritis had settled into her joints, especially her legs and hips, making it difficult for her to walk.

"Are you okay, my dear?" she asked as she approached the bag Angela had set on the counter. "Darlene called to say she saw that man harassing you again."

"Yeah, Craig stopped me, but I'm fine." That was basically the truth, especially since she was safely in the security of her own home.

"I still think you should talk to the sheriff about him."

Angela could only imagine the hell that would rain down on her and Kiara if she called the cops on Jim and Craig. That wasn't something she wanted to chance.

"For now, they're mainly just a nuisance," Angela said as she helped Ida unload the groceries into the fridge.

"How's that new project coming along?" Ida asked.

"I'm stuck," Angela confessed. "I've had to rip out stitches several times. I'm ready to give up."

"Why don't you come up after dinner and let me have a look at it?" Ida suggested. "I'm sure we can figure it out."

"I'll do that," Angela said. Ida was a master knitter, and when she'd discovered that Angela also knitted, thanks to Sandra's tutelage, she'd invited her to the knitting group she was a part of. The women were mostly from the church where Ida, and now Angela, attended.

"Thank you for doing the shopping for me," Ida said. "I sure appreciate the help."

"You're welcome." Angela approached Ida and brushed a kiss on her soft wrinkled cheek, getting a whiff of the light lilac scent the older woman favored. "I'll see you later."

Leaving Ida, Angela carried her bags down the steps that led to the door into their suite. After she let herself in, Angela went to the small kitchen and unpacked the groceries.

She was switching over their laundry when she heard the door open, and slam shut.

"Angie!"

Poking her head out of the laundry room, she frowned at Kiara. "What? Why are you yelling?"

"I saw something today." Kiara dropped her bag and coat on the floor by the door and hurried to Angela with a piece of paper in her hand.

"What did you see?" Angela asked as she shoved the damp laundry in her hands into the dryer.

"This." Kiara held out the paper. "You have to look at this."

Angela turned the dryer on before taking the paper. She looked down at it to see a picture printed on it. A large picture. Of... her?

"What is this?" Angela asked. "Are you practicing with graphics programs at the library?"

Kiara shook her head. "No. I printed this from the internet. It was slow at work today, so I was looking through my go-to celebrity gossip site. One of them had pictures from a gala that was held in California, and one of my favorite basketball players attended. She was his date."

"What?" Angela looked at the paper again. "But... that looks like me."

"It does, doesn't it?" Kiara came to stand next to her and looked down at the paper with her. "She could be your twin."

"Only with nicer clothes, jewelry, and hair."

"Yeah." Kiara laughed, but it didn't last long. "Seriously, though. She looks *just* like you."

Angela peered more closely at the picture. The woman's hair was up, but from what she could see, it was a similar shade of light brown to Angela's. The woman looked to be the same height as her as well.

Was it possible?

She knew nothing about her birth family. Only what Jim and Sandra had told her, which had been that her birth parents hadn't been good to her, and they'd taken her to give her a better life.

"Do you really think it's possible that I have a twin sister, Kiki?"

"I don't know," Kiara said as they left the small laundry room and went into the suite. "But maybe she was given up for adoption too."

"Why wouldn't they have adopted both of us?"

"I don't know," Kiara admitted. "And I'm not sure I want to ask Jim."

Angela didn't want to ask him either. The last time she'd pressed for information on her birth family, it hadn't gone well.

"What am I supposed to do with this information?" Angela asked as she sat down at the small round dining table that was just big enough for the two of them. "How am I supposed to find more information? Did the article give her name?"

"Nope." Kiara got a glass of water, then sat down across from her. "But maybe we could phone the office of the team Cole Halverson plays for to see if we could get in contact with him."

Angela wrinkled her nose. "I don't like talking on the phone."

"I know," Kiara said. "So I'll phone and pretend to be you. I doubt they'll forward us on to him right away. They'll probably just take a message and pass it to him."

"I guess if that's what you think we should do…" Angela wasn't sure how she felt about this new bit of information.

She'd resigned herself to never finding out about her family, considering she'd thought her only source of information was Jim.

"Maybe you just have a double," Kiara said. "But then again, maybe you have a sister. A twin."

"Were there more pictures?" Angela asked.

Kiara pulled out her phone, and after a few swipes, she handed it to Angela. The picture on the screen was another one of the couple, only this time, they were looking at each other instead of facing forward.

The tall, handsome basketball player had his arm around the woman, and he was looking down at her with clear adoration. The woman had a shy smile on her face, but no less affection, as she gazed up at him.

They weren't looking directly at the camera, so Angela didn't know if the woman was even aware that her picture had been taken.

"They look like they're in love," she murmured, feeling a pang of longing. Whoever this woman was, she'd found someone who adored her.

"Yes," Kiara agreed. "But there's been no mention of Cole dating anyone recently."

"You've kept up with his dating life?"

"Hey. You know I'm a fan of basketball and football. He's one of the best, so of course, I follow news about him. Just like I follow news about my favorite quarterbacks."

Kiara spent the next little while trying to find a contact number for Cole. As soon as she did, she placed the call.

Angela listened as Kiara asked the person on the other end of the line if she could pass a message to Cole Halverson. It seemed that the woman was agreeable because Kiara gave her Angela's name and number.

"Do you think he'll call me?" Angela asked.

Kiara shrugged as she set her phone down. She removed the scrunchy from her hair, shook her head, then gathered her curly brown hair back into a ponytail.

"If he doesn't call back within a few days, I'll call again. And then again."

"I don't want to bother him."

"But don't you want answers?"

Angela pressed a hand to her stomach. Did she want answers? If they were by some wild chance actually twins, it was clear the other woman moved in a completely different world than the one Angela lived in.

If Kiara was correct in the things she'd said, Cole Halverson was wealthy. Very wealthy. Which meant that this woman was used to moving in socially elite circles.

Angela certainly wasn't.

She'd never even graduated from high school. It was only recently that she'd managed to get her GED. The same with Kiara. Neither of them even had a driver's license.

Jim had only made the effort to get Craig his license, insisting that the girls hadn't needed one. Even now that they'd gotten away from him, they still hadn't been able to get their licenses.

The small town where they lived didn't have a DMV, and they had no way of getting to the nearest one. So they had to make do with walking everywhere. Which wasn't a problem, since the town wasn't big. But it kept them trapped in the area, even though they'd managed to leave the homestead years ago.

It had taken far too long for them to work up the nerve to leave. Actually, it had taken *her* far too long. Kiara would have left as soon as she'd turned eighteen if it hadn't been for Angela and, to a lesser degree, Sandra.

Instead, it had taken almost ten years—and Sandra's death—before they'd left. Once they'd settled into life in Briar Hollow, Angela wished they'd done it sooner. Kiara's response to that had always been that the important point was that they *had* done it. Better late than never.

Now Angela was looking at another possible change in her life. Would finding a sister mean she and Kiara could have a life beyond Briar Hollow?

She wasn't sure what she wanted the answer to be.

As the days and weeks passed, without hearing any response to Kiara's call, Angela tried to put it out of her mind. Kiara, however, wasn't ready to give up so easily.

"This will be my last call," Kiara said on New Year's Eve, nearly six weeks after that first phone call. "If they don't respond to this one, I'll stop calling."

"You said that before every other call you've made," Angela reminded her.

She put the sandwich she'd prepared for Kiara on a plate and handed it to her, before making one for herself.

"I know." Kiara set the plate down on the table, then sat in her chair. "But this time for sure."

Angela joined her at the table. "Why this time for sure and not all the other times you've said it was the last time?"

"New year, new project," Kiara replied with a shrug. "And if they have no interest in who you might be, their loss."

Recalling the beautifully dressed woman on a handsome athlete's arm, Angela wasn't so sure they had lost anything by not getting in contact with her.

Over the past few weeks, she couldn't help but wonder—if they really were siblings—why they'd been separated. Why whoever adopted the woman in the picture hadn't wanted her too. Why Jim and Sandra hadn't wanted Angela's sister.

Though they had questions—well, Kiara had questions—Angela had felt a growing certainty that maybe it was best not to know about her past. Maybe God didn't want her to know. She'd been praying about it and was willing to accept that perhaps that knowledge was not God's will for her.

Sometimes she wished she remembered things about her life before the Reynolds the way Kiara and Craig did. But perhaps it was better that she remained clueless. Just forget about the past—both before her adoption and afterward—and focus on the future she and Kiara were striving for.

One far, far away from Briar Hollow and her adoptive father's reach.

CHAPTER TWO

Jude tapped his phone to accept the call, then put it on speakerphone before setting it on his desk. "Hello, Mom."

"Darling!" His mother's voice filled the air. "Happy New Year's Eve!"

"Same to you."

"Do you have any special plans?" she asked.

Jude stared through the window at the towering evergreens outside the cabin he called home on the Burke Estate. "Nope. Nothing special. I probably won't even be up until midnight."

"That's such a shame," his mom said with a sigh. "You should have someone special in your life by now. You're forty, you know."

"Thirty-eight, Mom. I'm thirty-eight," Jude corrected, his tone flat. He leaned back in his chair, pinching the bridge of his nose.

"That's still too old to be alone on New Year's Eve." The concern in her voice was genuine, even if her methods were intrusive. "I worry about you, sweetheart."

"You don't have to, Mom. I'm fine. Really." Jude glanced at the security monitors on the wall of his home office that displayed various angles of the Burke estate. All quiet, as it should be. "The job keeps me busy."

"Too busy." There was a hard edge to her voice. "Your father was the same way. Always the job first."

Jude's jaw tightened. Though not surprised at the direction their call had taken, he wished that, for once, they could have a conversation without his mom venting her frustration about her marriage to Jude's dad.

The man had been dead for most of Jude's adult life, and his parents had been divorced for decades. His mom had even remarried and had more kids. So, as far as Jude was concerned, she needed to let her frustration go.

There wasn't a day that went by that Jude didn't miss his dad. He'd done a lot for Jude, including taking on the sole task of raising him after his mom had left them.

And even though he'd had good reason to turn Jude against her, his dad had never done that. Instead, he'd encouraged Jude to build a relationship with her.

It was only because his dad had made that request that Jude had continued to answer any of his mom's calls following his dad's death. Now, they had a relationship that was good, for the most part, but he could never really let himself open up completely to her.

She'd left his dad, angry that he wouldn't give up his low-paying, dangerous job as a cop. The irony was that because she'd abandoned them, his dad had ended up quitting his job. Since he'd viewed himself then as a single parent with a co-parent who wasn't around, his dad had decided he had to work at a safer job for Jude's sake.

He'd eventually ended up employed by Duncan Burke, ultra-wealthy business tycoon. It had ended all too soon, however, with his dad dying of a heart attack when Jude was just twenty-one years old.

Jude had carried on working for the Burkes, eventually taking over as head of security. The job his dad had held at the time of his death.

"The job is important."

"More important than having a life? Than finding someone to love?" There was a pause. "I just want you to be happy, Jude."

"I *am* happy." The words came automatically, rehearsed from countless similar conversations.

His mother's laugh told him she wasn't convinced. "At least tell me you're not working tonight."

"I'm on call." He was always on call.

Jude's eyes drifted to the framed photo on his desk—the only photo he had in his house. His dad stood with his arm around Jude's shoulders, a proud expression on his face. It had been taken shortly after Jude had begun to do work around the estate as part of the security team. He'd been just seventeen years old, but already willing to do what he could to prepare for the career he wanted in the future.

"You're always on call," his mother said with a weary sigh. "When was the last time you took a real vacation? Or even a weekend off?"

Jude couldn't remember. The Burke family's safety was his responsibility, and that didn't take breaks. He had plenty of downtime. Plus... "I like what I do."

"That's not what I asked." Her voice softened. "Honey, I know you think I don't understand your dedication, but I do. I lived with it for years with your father. I just don't want you to wake up one day and realize you've missed out on everything that makes life worth living."

The familiar knot in Jude's chest tightened. "Dad didn't miss out on anything."

"Didn't he?" The question hung in the air between them, heavy with his mom's bitterness. "He died alone in that office, Jude. Working late. Again."

Jude's hand curled into a fist on the desk, wishing he'd never told her the details of that evening. "He died doing what he loved — working to keep the people he cared about safe."

"I'm not saying he was wrong for how he lived his life. I just want better for you." His mother's voice cracked slightly. "You deserve more than just duty and obligation."

Except that duty and obligation were something he could depend on. Something that had never hurt him in the years since he'd joined his dad on the employment path that provided security for a wealthy family.

"I'm just not sure it's healthy for you to still be single," she said. "I mean..."

Jude understood her implication, but he wasn't interested in justifying his life decisions. His father had instilled in him the belief that a man should transcend his basic instincts, exercising self-control and overcoming the temptations of the flesh.

He hadn't been perfect, especially in the time following his dad's death. But when his grieving had lessened in intensity, and he'd been able to think about his dad without drowning in pain, he'd straightened up and done his best to live an honorable life. Glorifying to God.

Daniel Kessler had lived that way, while also leaning heavily on the belief that he couldn't do it on his own. He'd become a Christian after his wife had left him, and each day, he'd reminded Jude that God gave them strength and wisdom to deal with the situations they faced.

"I'm fine, Mom," Jude said. "I *am* happy with my life. I'm content and fulfilled."

"Can you really be fulfilled when you're all alone?"

Before Jude could respond, his phone vibrated on the desk with an incoming message. He pulled it close, tuning out his mom's continued attempts to make him dissatisfied with his life, and read the message.

D. Burke: *Please come to my office. ASAP*

Jude frowned. Though he'd told his mom that he was on-call, he hadn't anticipated needing to do anything. The whole Burke family was at the estate, and there had been no plan for them to leave the property until the next day.

"Sorry, Mom. I've got to go," Jude said as he got to his feet.

"See? Always duty."

Ignoring her jab, Jude said, "Have a happy new year, Mom. And give my regards to Robert and the kids."

He didn't know Robert well, but he'd gone to their wedding. And his dad had done a background check on the man, just to be sure he was a good person.

Since the marriage, his mom and Robert had had two kids. A boy and a girl. There was a significant age gap between him and them, with the kids just barely out of their teens, so he didn't know them at all either.

Putting thoughts of his mom's family from his mind, Jude strapped on the weapons he always wore when out of the house, then headed for the door that led to his garage.

Once through it, he ignored the twenty-five-year-old truck that had once been his dad's pride and joy, as well as his own shiny, newer, bigger truck. He went straight to the rugged UTV that he used for driving on the estate.

After firing up the engine, he pressed the remote to open the garage. Bright late afternoon sunlight poured into the space, sparkling off the snow that lay on the ground and making him squint until he lowered his sunglasses over his eyes.

Within a couple of minutes, Jude was pulling the UTV into the brightly lit garage at the back of the security building. But rather than go further into the building, he exited it the same way he'd driven into it, through the large opening. He used his phone to close the garage door, then headed in the direction of the main house.

The cold air had him pulling up his collar, then shoving his hands deeper into the heavy coat he wore. He'd stupidly left his gloves back at the house. Thankfully, the walk from the security building to the main house didn't take too long.

He let himself into the mudroom, then peeled out of his jacket and hung it on a hook near the door. After stamping his feet a few times to shake the snow from his combat boots, Jude ventured deeper into the mansion.

Stopping by the kitchen, he quickly greeted the housekeeper and her daughter before he headed down the hallway that would take him to Duncan Burke's office. It was a walk he'd made countless times over the years since Duncan had moved his kids—and his entire life—from New York to Idaho.

The door stood open, so Jude stepped through the doorway.

"Good afternoon, Duncan," he said, trying not to wince at the use of the man's first name.

For too many years, he'd been Mr. Burke. It had only been when he'd been promoted to head of security that Mr. Burke requested Jude call him Duncan. And though it had been several years since that had occurred, Jude still wasn't completely comfortable with the familiarity.

"Good evening," Duncan said as he looked up from his computer screen. He gestured to the chairs opposite him at the desk. "Please sit down."

A knot formed in Jude's stomach. After knowing the man for as many years as he had, he could read him quite well.

But right at that moment, he had no idea what was going on. Duncan's emotions were hidden behind a wall of stoicism, which didn't bode well.

"What's happened?" Jude asked, wondering if Duncan was unhappy with something he'd done.

Of late, his two younger children—one an adult, the other in high school—had been rebelling more than usual against the restrictions their father had put on them. Jude had loosened their security a bit, but only after having a discussion with Duncan about ways to make things a little less restrictive for Benji and Annie.

Had something happened that had led him to change his mind?

"As you know, Cole Halverson is arriving shortly," Duncan said as he sat back in his chair.

"Has something happened to him?"

"No. However, he sent me an email a few minutes ago detailing a phone call he'd received."

"A phone call? Was it threatening Annie?"

"No, though it did have to do with those pictures that showed up online of Annalisa and Cole. Someone saw the photo and recognized Annalisa."

There was one explanation that came to mind for Jude, but was that even possible?

"Angelica?" he asked.

"Well, her name is Angela Reynolds, but she thinks she might be related to Annalisa."

"And she reached out to Cole with this information?"

Duncan nodded. "I guess it was the only way she knew to get in contact with her."

"So you've spoken to this Angela person?" Jude asked.

"No. I thought it would be best to get some verification before we revealed who we are."

Jude nodded, agreeing with that completely. "How do you want me to handle it?"

"I sent the info to the tech guys so they can look a bit further into her to see what info we can get before we decide on our next move."

"And if it's really her?"

"Then I think I want you to initiate a meeting with her. As a representative of our family... without telling her who we are. At least not until we're sure of who she is."

"And to make sure that the people who kidnapped her aren't still in her life," Jude added.

Duncan sighed. "Yes. We must make sure that there is not an ulterior motive behind her reaching out. Either because of the people who kidnapped her, or because of the type of person she is."

Jude frowned. "Do you really think she might be seeking you out with evil intentions?"

"I wish I didn't have to be so skeptical," Duncan said. "However, I've learned not to take people at face value. It is far better to be safe than sorry. I learned that lesson a long time ago."

Jude remembered when the kidnapping of Duncan's twin girls had occurred. His dad had been part of the security team, though not the head of it yet. His promotion had come after Duncan had fired the previous head for bungling the security checks that should have been done on the pair who'd abducted Annalisa and Angelica.

Duncan's gaze darkened as he looked at a framed photo on his desk. Jude knew without seeing it that it was the one of the twins as toddlers, taken just weeks before the kidnapping.

"I won't make the same mistake again," Duncan said quietly. "Not with Annalisa."

"Of course not," Jude agreed. "I'll handle this with the utmost caution."

"I know you will."

When his computer beeped, Duncan shifted forward to look at the monitor. "Here's an email from our team with an initial report. You should have a copy too."

Jude pulled out his phone and opened his email program. Sure enough, there was an email from the head of the team that Duncan used to follow any leads on the kidnappers.

For years, there had been nothing substantial. It was as if the kidnappers had disappeared off the planet.

Now, however, they had something to work with. And wow, had they run with it.

"She lives in Briar Hollow, Kentucky," Duncan read. "Small town, population under a thousand. Works at a bakery called Sweet Nothings. No criminal record. Limited digital footprint.

Most of which has been over the past couple of years. Nothing really before that."

Jude leaned forward. "I would have thought they'd include a picture. Visual verification would go a long way to helping us plan our next step."

"I'm sure that as soon as they get their hands on one, they'll forward it."

This tech team had never been under Jude or his father's responsibility. They'd reported directly to Duncan, but they had always updated Jude, at Duncan's request.

He'd questioned his dad about why details of the kidnapping hadn't been released to the public. Or why the cops hadn't been brought in. His dad's explanation had revealed to Jude just how wealthy Duncan really was. And not just wealthy, but influential. More influential than most in the world.

And with power and influence backing him, Duncan made the choice to keep from letting the world know what had happened in order to prevent the rest of his family from becoming targets. He'd also been able to hire people who were more skilled than anyone who worked for the police department, and some of them were willing to step into the gray areas in order to get information in their search.

A second beep from Duncan's computer sounded just as another email showed up in Jude's inbox.

"Pictures," Duncan murmured.

Jude's heart pounded as he clicked to open the attachment. It felt almost surreal to be at this point. Twenty-four years of dead ends. Of no leads. Of losing hope.

Jude glanced up at his boss and saw that the wall hiding his emotions had dropped. There was now a wealth of feeling on the man's face as he stared at his monitor.

Looking down at his phone, Jude found himself looking at a familiar—and yet completely unknown—face. "Oh, wow."

"Yeah..." Duncan's voice trailed away. "Wow."

The picture looked like a selfie. One taken to use as a profile picture on social media. There was no denying that the woman in the photo was Annie's twin. However, there were subtle differences.

Annie's hair was long and straight, while Angela's was shorter and had some curl to it. Annie had a ready smile and a confidence to her that it seemed like the woman in the photo lacked.

Even though it was a selfie, Angela looked uncertain, almost shy, her shoulders slightly hunched. The photo radiated awkwardness, which made Jude even more curious about her.

Jude studied her face more carefully. The resemblance to Annie was uncanny—same delicate bone structure, same blue-green eyes—but there was a wariness in Angela's expression that Annie had never shown.

"It's her," Duncan said, his voice thick with emotion. "After all these years..."

Jude nodded. "The resemblance is undeniable."

"What do you make of her?" Duncan asked, gesturing at his monitor.

Jude considered the question carefully. Reading people was part of his job, and even from a photograph, he could see aspects of the woman's personality.

"She looks... cautious. Wary," he observed. "Which isn't exactly the expression of someone planning to exploit a connection to your family."

Duncan rubbed his jaw, eyes never leaving his screen. "Unless that's exactly what she wants us to think."

"Possibly," Jude conceded. "But my gut says otherwise."

He scrolled through the additional photos that had been sent. These included another woman, and Angela looked more relaxed in those.

Jude lingered the longest on the one that had the two women sitting with their heads pressed close together, smiling at the camera. From the angle of the picture, he assumed that the other woman had taken the snap, which may have explained why Angela looked more relaxed.

"The team gave another update, along with the photos," Jude said, scrolling through the rest of the email. "According to this, Angela lives with someone named Kiara in an apartment in Briar Hollow. Both work minimum-wage jobs. It seems neither have a license and there are no vehicles registered to either of them. I'm sure we'll know much more in another twenty-four hours."

"The money I pay to have the best computer specialists working for me has been worth every penny," Duncan murmured.

"So where do we go from here?"

"I want you to go to Kentucky and meet with them."

Jude wasn't surprised to hear that that was Duncan's plan. The man trusted him to be discreet and to make sure that Angela was safe. He'd played a role in the safety of Duncan's family for most of his adult life, and that wouldn't be changing anytime soon.

He opened the attachments again and swept through them, pausing on the selfie photo once more. Something shifted within him as he studied the woman.

Her world was going to be turned upside down. Going from a minimum-wage existence to life with one of the richest men in the world was going to be shocking.

How would she handle that?

And how would everyone handle her return?

Jude was well-versed in human physiology to know that this wasn't going to be an easy process. Each person would have a different struggle with Angela's reappearance in their lives.

But at the end of the day, Duncan would have his daughter back. Annalisa and Julian would have their sister back. And Elizabeth and Benji would meet Angela for the first time.

Jude's role in everything would be the same as it had always been. He'd protect Duncan and his family in any way he could.

CHAPTER THREE

Angela dumped the dough out onto the stainless steel work surface in the back of the bakery, then hefted the large metal bowl back to the mixer standing next to the wall.

Returning to the table, she used a dough scraper to portion out the dough, weighing each piece on the scale. It was work she did six days a week now and had done for many years before that but on a smaller scale. The familiar movement was calming.

Sandra might not have left her with many happy memories, but the woman had equipped her with knowledge that had enabled her to get a job after leaving the homestead.

If only her boss wasn't such a not-so-great person.

When the ringing of her phone interrupted her thoughts, Angela hesitated before answering it. She knew Patty wouldn't like it if she chatted too long during work hours.

However, ever since Kiara had been making phone calls trying to get hold of Cole Halverson, Angela had answered every call. Regardless of whether she recognized the number or not.

She wiped her hands on her apron, then pulled her phone from the back pocket of her jeans.

"Hello?"

"Good morning." The man who greeted her had a deep voice that resonated through the phone, rich and commanding, with a hint of gravel that made her picture someone tall and broad-shouldered standing at military attention. "Am I speaking with Angela Reynolds?"

"Uh... yes. I am she... uh, I'm her." Angela rolled her eyes at her own stupidity. "I am Angela Reynolds. How... how can I help you?"

"Did you phone Cole Halverson wanting information about his date for a gala?"

Technically, it had been Kiara, but Angela had been there for each conversation. "Yes. I think I look a lot like her."

"Is there a reason you'd automatically think you might be related to her instead of just seeing an uncanny resemblance in a stranger?"

Angela sank down on one of the stools in the bakery's kitchen, wishing that Kiara was there.

"I'm adopted," she said. There didn't seem to be a reason to not be honest about that. "So I thought maybe I had a sibling somewhere."

"Would you be willing to take a DNA test to confirm whether or not you are related to her?"

"I suppose." Angela hesitated. "Are you related to her?"

"No, I'm a friend of the family. They asked me to make contact, just in case it really is simply a coincidence. They don't want to get their hopes up until they have confirmation."

Hope flared in her heart. Had they been looking for her? "Oh. Okay. That makes sense."

"I'd like to meet with you in person, if possible."

Angela hesitated. "Um... sure."

"And do you have a couple of minutes to answer a few questions?"

She glanced toward the doorway that led to the front of the bakery. Patty wasn't there, but her niece was manning the shop, and she reported everything back to her aunt.

"I'm at work at the moment, and I... uh... shouldn't be on the phone for very long."

"That's understandable," the man said, apparently not upset by her putting him off. "When would be a better time for us to talk?"

"Maybe around four?" If he agreed to the time, Kiara would be there when he called.

"Four would be fine. I'll give you a call then."

"Um... what's your name?" Angela hoped he'd answer her question because she knew Kiara would want that information.

"I'm Jude Kessler," he said readily enough.

Angela immediately began formulating an image in her head. She wished he'd told her a bit more about himself. But all that she really needed to know was that the woman with Cole Halverson had trusted Jude Kessler enough to send him to check her out.

"I'll talk to you later," Jude said.

When he cut off the call, Angela stared at the phone for a long moment before getting back to her feet. Sliding the phone into her pocket, she made her way over to the sink to wash her hands before returning to her dough.

Once she had the dough all prepped for baking the next morning, she slid the pans into the baking racks in the refrigerated room. The bakery had become well-known for the cinnamon buns Angela made, so it was something she did every day.

"Are there more muffins, Ang?" Jenn asked as she stepped through the doorway.

"Yep." Angela helped her carry a couple of trays of muffins to the bakery cabinet in the front.

Angela made note of other things that were running low, then went to the back to get what they had. Making the cinnamon rolls was the last thing she did each day. The bakery was open until three, but since she started at four each morning, Angela only worked until noon.

It was New Year's Day, but Patty had insisted they still open. Kiara was also working at her cashier's job at the gas station, so she wouldn't be home until three.

The walk from the bakery was frigid, and Angela was glad to step into the warmth of the house. She popped in to check on Miss Ida, then made her way down to the apartment.

She shed her coat and hung it on a hook near the door, shivering as she rubbed her arms. The basement apartment was never truly warm, but after the biting cold outside, even the slightly chilly air felt like a blessing.

Angela checked her phone—still three hours and forty minutes until Jude would call back. Three hours and forty minutes to prepare herself. To figure out what she wanted to say. She needed Kiara's advice, but that would have to wait.

Moving to the kitchenette, Angela filled the electric kettle and switched it on.

As she waited for the water to boil, she went into the small bedroom to change out of her work clothes and into a pair of sweatpants and a sweatshirt. She also pulled on a pair of thick fluffy socks since her feet were always cold.

When she returned to the kitchen, the kettle had already clicked off. She began to prepare the tea. Selecting her favorite mug, dropping in the tea bag, pouring the steaming water. The familiar movements calmed her. She cupped the warm mug between her palms as she settled onto the couch.

She picked up her journal from the end table and opened it to where she'd put the printout of the photograph of the woman.

Carefully unfolding it, Angela gazed at the elegant woman in the photograph, so poised and confident on the arm of a famous athlete. How could someone like that be related to her—a girl who'd never even finished high school properly? Who lived in a basement and worked for minimum wage?

But what if she doesn't want me in her life? What if I'm not good enough for her world?

The questions swirled in her mind like the steam rising from her tea.

Angela folded the paper and put it back in the journal, then closed it and set it aside. The waiting was going to drive her crazy.

She spent the next hour tidying their already spotless apartment, then tried to read, but the words blurred together on the page. Every few minutes, she found herself checking her phone for the time.

When the door finally opened and Kiara burst in, stamping snow from her boots, Angela nearly jumped out of her skin.

"You look like you've seen a ghost," Kiara said, unwinding her scarf. "What's wrong?"

"Someone called," Angela said, her voice barely above a murmur. "About the picture. About... her."

Kiara froze, one boot half off her foot. "What? When? What did they say?"

"It was a man. He said his name was Jude Kessler. He's a friend of the family." Angela twisted her hands together. "They want me to take a DNA test."

"Oh my goodness, Angie." Kiara kicked off her remaining boot and hurried over, dropping into the chair across from Angela. "Tell me everything. Word for word."

Angela recounted the conversation as best she could remember, watching Kiara's eyes grow wider with each detail.

"They're taking this seriously," Kiara said when Angela finished. "If they're willing to pay for a DNA test, they must think there's a real possibility you're related."

"Or they just want to hand me definitive proof that I'm not the woman's sister."

"Angie." Kiara reached across the table and squeezed her hand. "Don't do that. Don't assume the worst before you even know what's happening."

Angela looked down at the time on her phone. "I guess I just don't want to get my hopes up, you know? So it's better to just assume the worst."

"Angie, this might be your chance to get out of here."

Angela shook her head. "What about you?"

"What do you mean?"

"You said that this was *my* chance to get out of here. That's not going to happen if I have to leave you behind."

Kiara slouched back in her seat. "Let's cross that bridge when we get to it."

"I'm not leaving here if it means leaving you behind," Angela said again. "We're already at that bridge, and I'm telling you that this is how we're crossing it."

Kiara gave a huff of laughter, and sat forward to lean her arms on the table. Her hazel gaze sparkled with love, something that Angela felt for her as well.

It was why she refused to consider any future without Kiara at her side. They might not be biological sisters, but Angela couldn't imagine her life without Kiara. They'd been through a lot together, and Angela wasn't sure she would have made it through so well if it hadn't been for Kiki.

"We'll figure it out together," Kiara said softly. "We always do."

The clock inched its way to four o'clock with infuriating slowness. Kiara made grilled cheese sandwiches that neither of them had much appetite for, while Angela paced between the kitchen and the living area, checking her phone every few minutes.

At exactly four o'clock, the phone rang.

Both women froze, staring at the device on the table. On the second ring, Kiara nodded encouragingly at Angela.

"Hello?" Her greeting sounded weak, so she cleared her throat, then repeated it before she tapped the screen to put it on speakerphone.

"Good afternoon, Angela. This is Jude Kessler."

His voice was just as she remembered—deep and steady, with a quality that somehow made her feel like he could be trusted. "Hi."

"Do you have a few minutes to talk now?"

"Yes." Angela sank into her chair, and Kiara immediately moved closer. "Um, my sister is here with me. Is that okay?"

"Of course."

Angela felt a rush of relief that he had accepted Kiara's presence so easily. "Thank you."

"I'd like to ask you some questions about your adoption, if that's all right."

Angela's stomach clenched. "Okay."

"How old were you when you were adopted?"

"Two or three."

"Do you remember anything from before that time?"

Angela glanced at Kiara, who nodded encouragingly. "No. Nothing at all. I've tried, but it's all blank."

"That's not uncommon," Jude said, his deep voice gentle. "What about your adoptive parents? Are they still alive?"

"Sandra, my adoptive mother, passed away a few years ago. My adoptive father..." Angela hesitated, not sure how much to reveal. "We don't live with him anymore."

"I see." There was a pause, and Angela could hear what sounded like typing in the background. "Were you told anything about your birth family? Given any details about why you were available for adoption?"

Angela swallowed past a growing tightness in her throat. "Not really. Just that... that my birth parents weren't good. That they couldn't take care of me properly."

"Angela, I need to ask you something, and I want you to know that whatever you tell me will be kept in complete confidence." Jude's voice became more serious. "Were you happy with your adoptive family?"

The question hung in the air. Angela looked at Kiara, whose expression had grown concerned.

"I... I was sometimes. Sandra was okay most of the time but..." Angela hesitated, wary of revealing the truth. "But my adoptive father, Jim, isn't a very... warm man."

The silence on the other end of the line stretched for several seconds. When Jude spoke again, his voice had a controlled quality to it that hadn't been there before.

"Are you safe now?" The question was direct, his tone leaving no room for evasion.

"Yes," Angela said, gripping Kiara's hand. "We got away. We live in town now, and he's out at the homestead. But he still comes looking for us."

"I see." The sound of more typing came through the speaker. "Would you be comfortable meeting in person? I'd like to arrange for that DNA test we discussed, and I think it might be easier to talk through some of these details face to face."

Angela bit her lip, looking at Kiara, who nodded vigorously.

"I would, but..." She hesitated. "We don't have a car. We're kind of limited to Briar Hollow."

"That's not a problem. I can come to you." Jude's response was immediate.

"Do you want to meet at the bakery?" Angela asked.

"I had considered that, but I think it might be better if we could meet somewhere privately? I'll be bringing someone to do the DNA test, and it would probably be best not to do it sitting in a restaurant."

That made sense, but as Angela glanced around their small apartment, she wasn't sure she wanted him there.

"You could use one of the study rooms at the library," Kiara suggested. "I'm working there until one tomorrow, so I can make sure a room is available for you."

"That sounds like a good idea," Jude said. "Would that work for you, Angela?"

Angela appreciated that he was checking with her, and it would definitely work for her. Mainly because it meant that Kiara would be there if she needed her.

"That would be fine. I'm at the bakery until noon, so meeting anytime after that would work."

"We'll aim to be there around one."

"Do you need directions to the library?"

Jude chuckled, a lovely deep sound that washed over her, making Angela smile, even though she was still in knots over the whole thing.

"I'm pretty sure I won't get too lost in Briar Hollow," he said. "And I can look up the address of the library."

"Okay. Sounds good."

"See you then," Jude said. "Take care, Angela."

"Uh... you too."

When the screen of her phone went black, Angela stared at it.

"Well, this is exciting," Kiara said as she leaned to loop her arm over Angela's shoulders.

"Is it?" Angela glanced over at her sister. "I find it a little scary."

Kiara sighed, then shifted her chair so she faced Angela directly. "I know the unknown can be scary, but you're going to get some answers."

"Maybe I don't want answers."

"Why not?"

"Jim and Sandra always said that they rescued us from terrible circumstances. I'm not sure I want to know what they might be."

"I don't think you're going to be finding out about your birth family," Kiara said. "The only thing that makes sense is that you and the woman in the picture were put up for adoption separately, so her adopted family might not have known there were two of you."

"Why wouldn't they try to keep siblings together?" Angela asked.

"I don't know," Kiara said as she rested her arms on the table. "But I have a feeling we're going to find out."

Angela still wasn't sure that she wanted to go forward. Suddenly, the unknown loomed large, like a dark entity, waiting to deal her a harsh blow.

"What if they don't like me?" The question slipped out before Angela could stop it.

Kiara's expression softened. "Angie, how could anyone not like you?"

"I'm not exactly..." Angela gestured vaguely at herself. "I'm not sophisticated or educated or anything special."

"You're plenty special," Kiara insisted, squeezing Angela's hand. "And if they can't see that, then they don't deserve to know you."

Angela appreciated the sentiment, but doubt still gnawed at her. She tried to imagine meeting this woman, who looked so much like her but seemed to inhabit an entirely different world. What would they even talk about?

"I should probably figure out what to wear," Angela said, trying to focus on practical matters.

They spent the evening talking through various scenarios, Kiara's enthusiasm balancing Angela's apprehension. By the time they went to bed, Angela had almost convinced herself that tomorrow might bring something good.

Sleep, however, proved elusive. Angela tossed and turned, her mind racing with possibilities both wonderful and terrible.

When her alarm went off at three, Angela quickly shut it off so it wouldn't wake Kiara. Just like they always had, they shared a room, though unlike their younger years, when they'd also shared a bed, they now each had their own twin bed.

The only downside of sharing space was their different schedules. They'd had to learn to be quiet as they moved around when the other was sleeping.

After getting dressed, Angela braided her hair. She hoped to have time to come home and change before meeting with Jude and the DNA person. She didn't really want to meet them sweaty and mussed from work.

Her stomach was a mess of knots, and she was thoroughly distracted throughout her shift. But thankfully, she didn't make any mistakes in her baking. Patty would have been livid if she had.

Once her shift was done, she hurried home to take the quickest shower ever and then change into the blue sweater Kiara had suggested along with a pair of black slacks. Once dressed, she unwound her hair from its braid so that it lay just past her shoulders in loose waves.

The walk to the library was cold and blustery. They didn't get much snow that stuck around through the winter, but she still hated the cold, damp days. She'd hated them on the homestead, and she hated them in Briar Hollow. There were times when she felt like she could never get warm.

When she reached the library, Angela saw a large black SUV in front of it. There were other cars parked on the street, but that one stood out in a town where most vehicles were dusty trucks.

Her steps came to a halt as she stared at the fancy SUV. She glanced at the heavy wooden and glass doors that led into the library and took a step back.

What was she getting herself into?

If Kiara hadn't been at work, and was even now waiting inside with Jude Kessler, Angela would have turned around and left. In that moment, her fear of the unknown was far greater than her desire for answers.

But she had no choice. From the moment she'd agreed to Kiara calling Cole Halverson, she'd started on a journey of no return.

Clasping her hands together, Angela headed to the library entrance. She'd just reached out to grasp the handle of the door when it swung open.

She stepped back, preparing to let whoever was coming out to exit first. Only the man holding the door open with his outstretched arm didn't exit. It seemed he was holding the door open for her.

"Angela," he said with a nod, his voice familiar.

It wasn't a question. It was as if he knew exactly who she was.

"Uh... are you Jude?" she asked as she stepped past him into the foyer of the library.

"I am." He stepped to the side and held out his hand. "It's a pleasure to meet you."

Angela stared at his large hand for a moment before taking it. His grip was strong, and the warmth of his hand felt good against her cold fingers. He didn't prolong the contact, releasing her hand after a gentle squeeze.

"Likewise," Angela murmured, finally looking up. Her breath caught slightly as her gaze met his.

He was tall—taller than she'd expected—with dark hair that was neatly trimmed and a shadow of stubble along his firm square jaw.

His shoulders and chest were broad beneath the black wool coat he wore, but it was his eyes that captured her attention. They were a striking light blue, framed by thick dark lashes, and they seemed to take in everything about her in one swift assessment.

"Your sister is waiting for us in one of the study rooms," Jude said, gesturing toward the interior of the library. "Dr. Reeves is with her as well. She'll be handling the DNA test."

Angela nodded, trying to find her voice. "Thank you for coming all this way."

"It's no trouble," he replied, his tone neutral but not unkind.

As they walked through the library, Angela was acutely aware of Jude beside her. He moved with a quiet confidence that made her feel even more uncertain about herself. His presence filled the space around them, and she found herself stealing glances at his profile.

"How long have you lived in Briar Hollow?" he asked, his voice low to respect the library's atmosphere, even though it was empty at the moment.

"Just over two years," Angela replied, wrapping her arms across her waist. "We moved here after we left the homestead. About a year after Sandra died."

"Was she good to you?"

That was such a difficult question to answer. Had Sandra been better than Jim? Yes. Had she been as good as the mothers in the books Angela had been allowed to read back then? No.

"She took care of us," Angela said. "She taught us many practical things. It was because of what she taught me that I was able to get a job in the bakery."

They reached a small study room where Kiara sat across from an older woman with silver hair pulled back in a neat bun. The woman wore professional attire and had kind eyes behind wire-rimmed glasses.

"Angie!" Kiara stood immediately, her relief evident. "This is Dr. Reeves."

The older woman rose and extended her hand with a warm smile. "Angela, it's so nice to meet you. I'm Dr. Patricia Reeves. I'll be handling your DNA collection today."

Angela shook her hand, realizing at that moment, she had passed the point of no return.

CHAPTER FOUR

Jude fought to keep control of his emotions as he sat down across from Angela... Angelica. If he'd had any doubts about whether she was Annie's twin, they'd been dispelled when he'd laid eyes on her in person for the first time.

Though there were a few differences, Angela's similarity to Annie was overwhelming.

The last time he'd seen Angelica had been right before she'd been kidnapped. He'd been fourteen, and she'd been three. The jump from that little girl to this woman in her late twenties would have been jarring, had he not seen Annie transition through those years.

The resemblance to Annie was uncanny—from the delicate curve of her cheekbones to the unique blue-green of her eyes. Even the way she tucked her hair behind her ear mirrored Annie's habit.

But where Annie carried herself with the confidence that came from a life of privilege and security, this woman seemed to fold inward, as if trying to take up as little space as possible.

"This procedure is quite simple," Dr. Reeves explained, opening her case. "Just a cheek swab that takes seconds."

Angela nodded, her eyes flicking briefly to Jude before settling back on the doctor. That brief glance held wariness, and Jude wondered what her life had truly been like with Jim and Sandra.

He supposed that he'd always hoped that because Sandra had been Angelica's nanny, she would have cared for her with love and concern. Jim... well, he'd been a brash, often cocky, man when they'd worked together.

As he watched Angelica, he got the feeling that his hope that she had been in a loving, stable home had been misplaced.

"After we collect the sample," Jude said, keeping his voice gentle, "we'll rush the analysis. We should have the results within forty-eight hours."

"That fast?" Kiara asked, leaning forward with interest. "I thought these things took weeks."

"We have... connections to expedite the process," Jude replied carefully.

Dr. Reeves efficiently completed the DNA collection, sealing the sample in a sterile container.

"All done," she said with a reassuring smile. "I'll have this to the lab within the hour."

Angela touched her cheek. "What happens now?"

"Now we wait," Jude said, studying her carefully. Even sitting still, she radiated nervous energy, her fingers twisting together on the table. "But while we're here, I'd like to ask you a few more questions, if that's all right."

"Of course."

Dr. Reeves packed up her equipment. "I'll see myself out. Angela, it was lovely meeting you."

After the doctor left, silence settled over the small room. Jude could see Angela's shoulders tense further, and Kiara reached over to squeeze her hands.

"You mentioned that your adoptive father still comes looking for you," Jude said carefully. "How often does that happen?"

Angela's jaw tightened almost imperceptibly. "At least once a week. Sometimes Craig comes instead."

"Craig?"

"Jim's other adopted child," Kiara explained, her voice holding an edge.

Jude's protective instincts sharpened at the tone in Kiara's voice. "Other adopted child?"

"He's older than us," Angela said quietly.

"Jim and Sandra adopted him after they adopted Angie," Kiara said. "He was ten at the time. They adopted me when I was eight, and by that point, Angie was five, and Craig was twelve."

"And he helps your adoptive father try to convince you to return?"

Angela's fingers twisted together more tightly. "He can sometimes be very aggressive about it."

The carefully controlled words told Jude everything he needed to know. His jaw clenched, but he kept his expression neutral. "Aggressive how?"

"He just..." Angela glanced at Kiara, who nodded encouragingly. "He follows me sometimes. Makes comments about how we owe Jim everything. He keeps telling me that at some point we'll be back there, whether we want to be or not."

Jude's blood ran cold. The idea that someone was threatening Angelica—Duncan's daughter—made every protective instinct he possessed roar to life. He wanted to load the pair up into the SUV and drive right out of Briar Hollow.

But he couldn't do that or reveal the truth yet. Not until they had official confirmation.

"Has he ever hurt you?" The question came out rougher than he had intended.

Angela shook her head quickly. "No. Not physically. He just... intimidates."

"What about your adoptive father?"

The silence stretched too long. Angela's gaze dropped to her hands, and Kiara's expression darkened.

"Jim believes in discipline," Angela finally whispered. "He had very strict rules about everything when we were growing up. How we dressed, what we said, when we could speak."

"And your adoptive mother?" Jude prompted. "How was she?"

"She wasn't as strict," Kiara said. "But she carried out Jim's wishes."

"Do you know anything about their lives before they adopted you?"

Angela shrugged. "Not much. Jim mentioned working as a cop and then doing private security, and Sandra said she was a nanny. They decided to move to the homestead so that they could live self-reliant lives and raise us the way they wanted to, without schools or other people interfering."

Jude was a bit surprised that Jim had revealed the truth of their past. "Did he talk about how they came to adopt you, Angela?"

"They always just said that they took each of us from bad situations," Angela said.

"And you don't remember anything from before they adopted you."

Angela shook her head, her expression growing more troubled. "I've tried so many times to remember something—anything—but there's just nothing there. But it's probably just as well since I didn't have a good family before they adopted me."

Jude's chest tightened. He could picture three-year-old Angelica in Duncan's arms, surrounded by the love of her family. She'd had the very best family, and hopefully soon, she'd see that for herself.

"What about you, Kiara?" Jude asked, turning his attention to the other young woman. "Do you remember anything from before your adoption?"

Kiara's expression hardened. "More than I wish I did. My parents were hateful people. I was happiest when they would completely neglect me."

"I'm sorry," Jude said, meaning it. The stark contrast between the two young women's experiences before adoption spoke volumes, even though they weren't aware of the details of that disparity.

"Don't be." Kiara shrugged, though her eyes remained hard. "I survived. And now I have Angie."

Angelica smiled faintly at her sister, and Jude noticed how her posture relaxed slightly at the mention of their bond. The connection between them was palpable—forged, he suspected, through years of shared hardship.

"How did the two of you manage to leave?" Jude asked. "From what you've described, it doesn't sound like Jim would have simply let you walk away."

Angela and Kiara exchanged glances before Angela spoke. "After Sandra died, things got... worse. Jim became more controlling, and Craig..." She trailed off, shaking her head slightly.

"We planned for months," Kiara continued when Angela faltered. "When Jim and Craig went on a three-day hunting trip, we packed what little we had and just... left."

"We had to walk," Angela added softly. "We don't have driver's licenses, and there is no public transportation around here. This was as far as we could get."

Jude nodded, mentally cataloging every detail. "So you found jobs and a place to live?"

"Angie got a job first," Kiara said. "The bakery was willing to hire her after she baked a batch of cinnamon buns for them, proving she really knew what she was doing. Patty, the bakery owner, also let us rent the apartment over the bakery as part of Angie's salary. I found a job working at the gas station, then I got a job here at the library a couple of months later."

"Are you still living above the bakery?"

"No, we just moved a few weeks ago," Angela said. "It wasn't a good arrangement."

"Why is that?" Jude asked, wanting to have all the information he could gather about their lives.

Duncan wanted to protect his family, so Jude knew that he needed to be able to give the man a well-rounded picture of the life his daughter had been leading.

Everything was telling him that Duncan had nothing to worry about. That Angela wasn't out to harm him or his family.

"We didn't realize until recently that the rent Patty was charging us was quite high compared to other places. Also, we didn't like that she'd come into the apartment whenever she liked."

"Without notice?"

"She never gave us any notice," Angela said. "And there was never a good reason for her to be there."

"So where are you living now?"

"We've rented a basement apartment from a woman Angie met at the bakery," Kiara explained. "She's elderly, and we help her with some things around the house in exchange for a small discount on the rent. Plus, it was furnished, which is what we needed."

"Do you have a plan for your future?" Jude asked, curious how that might gel with what Duncan wanted.

"We do hope that we'll be able to one day leave Briar Hollow," Angela said.

"But it's hard," Kiara chimed in. "First and foremost, we need to get our licenses, which is a challenge since the closest DMV is beyond walking distance."

"And no one would help you out?"

The women exchanged a look before Kiara said, "We haven't really made super close connections in the town. Angie knows a few people from the church, but they're all older. We just didn't feel comfortable asking people to help us."

"Most people view us as part of the crazy prepper homestead. They know that Jim especially is big into self-sustenance and keeping to himself. Also, some suspect that he is stockpiling weapons. They've made comments about that to us."

"But they actually have no idea how much he and Craig have stockpiled," Angela murmured. "They are preparing for the end of the world."

"And how do you feel about that?" Jude asked, more curious than anything. But the fact that Jim and his son were armed made approaching them a bit more of a challenge.

Angela shrugged. "I'm not going to say it's wrong to make some preparation. I mean, there are catastrophes that happen where people might benefit from having stockpiled food and water. Like storms. And I think it's a good idea to know how to plant a garden and be somewhat self-sufficient."

"But he takes it too far," Kiara said. "He's preparing to protect what he's stockpiled. In addition to the weapons, he's built walls around the homestead, and parts of the property are booby-trapped."

Jude's brows lifted at that revelation. So, it appeared that going after Jim was going to take some careful planning.

"Is there anything you can tell me about the woman in the photo?" Angela asked, clearly done with the discussion about Jim and his weapons.

Jude still had questions, but he was willing to put them aside for the time being. "Let me make a phone call to see how they want to move forward."

"We'll let you have the room for the call," Kiara said.

Angela looked from Jude to Kiara, then the two of them stood up. "Um... come get us when you're done."

Jude also got to his feet. "Will do."

He watched as Kiara led Angela from the room. As the door closed behind them, he pulled out his phone.

He spent a moment gathering his thoughts about everything he'd learned from the two women. None of it was a total surprise.

It made sense that Jim and Sandra would create a life for themselves and Angelica that was out of the public eye. Had he considered that the pair would turn into weapon's stockpilers preparing for the end of the world? No, that definitely hadn't crossed his mind.

But everything Angela and Kiara had shared revealed a level of paranoia that made sense for someone who had kidnapped a wealthy man's children and only returned one of them, and then absconded with a million dollars of his money.

Turning his attention to his phone, he placed the call to Duncan, then walked over to the narrow windows that looked out on the small patch of grass that lay between the library and the building next to it.

Duncan answered on the first ring. "How did it go?"

"It's her," Jude said without preamble. "No question about it. The resemblance to Annie is remarkable."

The silence on the other end stretched for several seconds before Duncan's voice came through, thick with emotion. "Are you certain?"

"Absolutely. We have the DNA sample, but I don't need it for confirmation. She has some of the same mannerisms, the same eyes."

"How is she?" Duncan's voice was low and full of emotion.

Jude turned away from the window, his jaw tightening as he considered how to answer. "Physically, she appears healthy. Emotionally..." He paused, choosing his words carefully. "She's been through a lot, Duncan. Jim and Sandra—Jim especially—weren't kind to her."

"Tell me."

"Not over the phone. But I will say this—she and another adopted daughter managed to escape the homestead two years ago, though they didn't get far. They're living in a basement apartment in Briar Hollow, not far from the homestead. Sandra is dead, but Jim and his adopted son are still harassing them to return."

Duncan's sharp intake of breath was audible. "Are they in immediate danger?"

"Hard to say. The threats seem to be for intimidation rather than actual physical violence." Jude ran a hand through his hair. "There's something else you need to know. Jim Reynolds apparently has turned into a survivalist."

"A survivalist?"

"It sounds like he's gone completely off-grid. He's stockpiled weapons and food, built walls around the property, and, according to Angela, booby-trapped parts of it. He's preparing for some kind of apocalyptic scenario."

Duncan was quiet for a long moment. "That explains why he's managed to stay hidden for so long. And why our investigators never found any trace of them."

"It also makes approaching him directly more complicated," Jude said, his voice grim. "We need to be strategic about this."

"What's your assessment of Angelica's state of mind? Is she ready to learn the truth?"

Jude considered the question carefully, picturing Angela's guarded posture, the way she seemed to look to Kiara for support.

"She seems... fragile, but I suspect she's stronger than she comes across. It seems that she's been conditioned to expect the worst, but I think there's still hope in her. The fact that she reached out at all tells me that at least a part of her wants to find her family."

"And the other young woman? Kiara?"

"Protective of Angela. Fiercely so, actually. I doubt Angela would go anywhere without her," Jude said. "And honestly, I don't think she should have to. From everything they said, they've been each other's lifeline."

"I wouldn't ask her to leave Kiara behind." Duncan's voice softened. "If Angelica considers her family, then she is family. What do you recommend for the next step?"

Jude moved back to the window, catching a brief glimpse of people passing by on the sidewalk at the front of the building. "We need to move carefully. Angela's been hurt by the people who were supposed to protect her."

"And let down by people who loved her but didn't protect her," Duncan said, a sad edge to his voice.

"I don't think she'll blame you for what happened." Though in all honesty, Jude didn't know for sure how she'd react to the revelations about her past.

"Do you think they'd be willing to leave the area? Permanently?" Duncan asked. "If they seem willing to leave their lives there, go ahead and tell them who we are."

"And if they're not?" Jude prompted.

Duncan sighed. "I don't really even want to contemplate that."

"I'll find out," Jude promised. "But I think we need to consider our approach to Jim Reynolds as well. If what Angela and Kiara say is true, he's potentially more dangerous than we realized."

"I agree. We'll need to involve law enforcement eventually, but I want to get Angelica safely away first." Duncan's voice hardened. "I've waited twenty-four years to get my daughter back. I won't risk losing her again."

"Understood." Jude watched as a few snowflakes began to drift past the window, dropping out of the gray clouds that hung heavy in the sky. "I'll call you after I speak with them again."

"Thank you, Jude." The gratitude in Duncan's voice was palpable. "For everything."

After ending the call, Jude took a moment to collect himself. There was a lot of emotion in the situation as a whole, and not just for Duncan and his family.

Jude's thoughts turned to his dad. He'd prayed every day that they would find the "little angel," as he'd called her. And Jude had continued with that prayer even after his dad's death.

Though his dad hadn't been the head of security at the time of the kidnapping, he'd still felt responsible since he'd been part of the security team. Who would have thought that it would take twenty-four years to finally get Angelica—Angela—back?

As positive as this was for Duncan, the weight of what he was about to do—potentially upending Angela's entire understanding of her life—settled heavily on Jude's shoulders. But there was no gentle way to deliver this kind of news.

He found Angela and Kiara sitting at a table in the reading area, heads bent close together in hushed conversation. They looked up simultaneously as he approached, their expressions a mixture of hope and apprehension.

"Can you both come back to the study room?" he asked quietly.

They followed him without question, and once they were seated, Jude closed the door firmly behind them.

"I spoke with my employer," he began carefully, sitting across from them. "And I need to ask you both something important before we proceed further."

"Okay..." Kiara said, suspicion on her face.

"If the DNA test confirms what we believe," Jude said, "would you be willing to leave Briar Hollow? Permanently?"

Angela's eyes widened, and she glanced at Kiara, who leaned forward with interest.

"Leave?" Angela repeated, her voice soft with apprehension. "You mean... just me? Or us together?"

"Together," Jude confirmed, noting how her first concern was for her sister. "Both of you."

Kiara's expression brightened immediately. "Where would we go?"

"Idaho," Jude said, watching Angela's reaction closely. "To a private estate where you would be safe."

"Idaho?" Angela's brow furrowed. "That's... far."

"That's the point," Jude said gently. "Distance from Jim Reynolds would be beneficial, don't you think?"

Angela wrapped her arms around herself, her shoulders hunching. "But our jobs... our apartment..."

"Those can be replaced," Kiara said, squeezing Angela's arm. "Angie, this could be our chance. Remember our plan? Getting away from here for good?"

"I know, but..." Angela's voice trailed off as she stared down at the table.

Jude leaned forward slightly. "Angela, I understand this is overwhelming. But I need to be honest with you now about why we're here."

She looked up, those blue-green eyes filled with wariness and a flicker of fear. "What do you mean?"

Jude took a steadying breath. There was no easy way to say this. "The woman in the photograph—her name is Annalisa. Annie. She's not just someone who looks like you. She's your twin sister."

Angela's face went completely white. Kiara's hand flew to her mouth, stifling a gasp.

"My... my twin?" Angela's voice was barely audible. "We wondered if that was possible, but we couldn't figure out why we weren't kept together."

"There's a reason for that," Jude said, hating that he had to completely upend her belief about her past. "Twenty-four years ago, you and Annie were kidnapped from your family's home in upstate New York by your nanny and her husband, a member of the security team. A ransom was paid, and Annie was returned to the family. You..." Jude's voice gentled. "You were never found."

The silence in the small room was deafening. Angela sat frozen, staring at him as if he'd spoken in a foreign language.

"That's impossible," she whispered finally. "Jim said my birth parents couldn't take care of me. That they were... that they were bad people."

"Jim Reynolds lied to you." Jude's voice carried quiet conviction. "Your birth father is Duncan Burke. He's spent the last twenty-four years searching for you. Your family never stopped looking, never stopped hoping to one day find you."

Tears spilled down Angela's cheeks. "I don't... I can't..."

Kiara moved closer, wrapping her arms around Angela's shoulders. "It's okay, Angie. Breathe."

Jude could see that Angela's hands were shaking as she pressed them against her mouth as if trying to hold back sobs. The revelation had obviously taken her totally off-guard.

He fought the urge to offer her comfort, knowing it wasn't his place. Plus, Kiara was there for her.

"I was... I was stolen?" The words came out broken, fractured by the weight of understanding. "You're saying that Jim... that Jim kidnapped me?"

"Yes." Jude kept his voice steady, hoping to help calm her. "Along with your nanny."

"Sandra was our nanny?" The words came out strangled. Angela pressed a hand to her chest. "But she... she was my mother."

"She was the woman who raised you," Jude corrected gently. "But she wasn't your mother. You were taken from your family, who loved you deeply. Who has never stopped loving you."

"But Jim said..." Angela's voice cracked. "He said they didn't want me. That they couldn't take care of me properly."

"He lied." Jude's voice carried a gentle firmness. "Everything he told you about your birth family was a lie designed to keep you from questioning your situation or trying to find them."

Kiara wrapped her arms around Angela, her own eyes bright with unshed tears. "Angie, this is good news. This means you have a family out there who wants you."

Angela pulled back slightly, looking at Kiara with panic in her eyes. "But what about you? If I have a real family, where does that leave you?"

"Hey." Kiara cupped Angela's face in her hands. "You're my sister, no matter what. That doesn't change."

Jude watched the exchange, struck by the depth of their bond. "Kiara would be welcome as well. Your father—Duncan—made that very clear. He understands that family isn't just about blood."

Angela's breathing was still coming in short, panicked bursts. "But why would they do this? Why would Jim and Sandra take me away from my family?"

"Money," Jude said simply. "Your father is a wealthy man. They demanded a ransom of a million dollars for the return of both you and your sister."

"But they only returned Annie," Kiara said, her brow furrowing. "If they only wanted the money, why would they keep Angie?"

"We think the money was for Jim, and you were for Sandra."

Jude could see how lost Angela felt at the news and wished he could do something to help her. She called to the part of him that made him so good at his job. His desire to protect. He wanted to shield her from the pain this revelation was causing her, but there was nothing he could do. She needed to have this information.

"We believe that they used the money to establish their homestead," Jude continued. "By staying off the grid and isolating them and you, they made it difficult for us to trace them."

Angela shook her head, tears still streaming down her face. "All these years... I thought no one wanted me. That I should be grateful that Jim and Sandra took me in."

"That's what they wanted you to believe," Jude said, his voice softening. "It made you easier to control." Jude hesitated, then reached into his pocket and pulled out his phone. "Would you like to see some photos? Of your family?"

Angela stared at him for a long moment, then nodded slowly.

Jude opened an album of images Duncan had sent him and passed the phone to her. "That's your father, Duncan Burke. Your twin sister, Annie. Your brother, Julian. Your stepmother, Elizabeth, and your half-brother, Benjamin."

"And my birth mother?" Angela asked as she stared down at the phone.

"She left your dad when Annie was around five years old." Jude hesitated to reveal more. It wasn't his place to give those details, but Angela deserved to know at least a little about the woman who had given birth to her. "She had a hard time with the fact that they hadn't been able to find you. Jill will be very happy to hear that you're alive and well."

Jude wasn't sure how that reunion would go, but really, at the end of the day, all that mattered was getting her back to the safety of Duncan's estate.

That was his job. And even though he felt emotionally invested in what was happening with Angela, his only responsibilities were to secure her safety and get her back to her family.

CHAPTER FIVE

Angela looked around the small bedroom, a knot of sadness in her stomach. This had been the first place she had been able to truly call home. A place that had offered her safety and security.

It may have been small and a bit dingy, but it had been theirs. She and Kiara had made some happy memories there, even though they'd lived there only a month. And during that time, they'd added little touches to make it their own.

But now, it was back to just being a dingy basement apartment. They'd taken down all the things that had made the space their own.

It was hard to think about leaving it all behind, even though that was what they'd been hoping to do one day. Now that the day was upon her, Angela felt sad and more than a little anxious about leaving it all behind.

She pressed her hands against her stomach and blew out a breath, glancing up as Kiara came into the room.

"Ready to go?" she asked.

"No." Angela sank down onto the twin bed that had been hers while they lived there. "I'm worried."

"Everything is going to be fine," Kiara said as she sat down next to her.

Angela wasn't so sure about that. Everything was rushing at her like a tsunami, threatening to overwhelm her. To drown her.

In the couple of days since the meeting with Jude at the library, everything had changed. Even before the preliminary DNA results came in, plans were underway for her and Kiara to depart Briar Hollow.

At Jude's insistence, they weren't telling anyone about their plans to leave. He'd told them that he'd make sure that their landlady was compensated for them vacating the premises so abruptly.

Angela had written out a letter to Ida, letting her know the basics of their sudden departure, but not going into detail. She was going to miss the spritely older lady.

Kiara felt bad about leaving the library and the gas station in a lurch, but Angela wasn't as concerned about the bakery. While she'd enjoyed the work, she hadn't enjoyed working for Patty.

The woman had been demanding, forcing her to work long hours for more days in a row than she should have. But Angela had put up with it because there weren't a lot of job options around the area. And she didn't exactly have any other skills to fall back on.

Patty had been the baker before she'd hired her, so as far as Angela was concerned, she could do it again.

"Jude said he'd be here at seven, so we need to have everything ready."

Angela looked at her phone.

6:55

Just five short minutes until she left everything familiar behind. Again. Her stomach quivered with nerves.

"Let's go," Kiara said as she got to her feet. "There's nothing left in here."

Angela watched her sister leave the room, wishing she had the same level of confidence that Kiara had. Maybe Kiara would feel differently if it was her family they were meeting.

With a sigh, Angela got up and left the bedroom, hitting the light switch as she walked by it. They didn't have much to take since the apartment had come furnished with plenty of mismatched dishes and silverware and well-worn furniture.

They'd never bothered to buy things to replace any of it, choosing instead to save their money for the future. Now, it made walking away from Briar Hollow even easier.

A pair of large suitcases and three large boxes sat by the door. They each had a suitcase, but only one of the boxes belonged to Angela. Kiara had needed two to contain all her books.

Angela's box held some books too, but unlike Kiara's collection of fiction, they were cookbooks. Though she loved reading fiction, she tended to read whatever Kiara had around.

The box also contained her journals and a binder that held all of Sandra's handwritten recipes. Even though she was angry at the woman, she hadn't wanted to leave that behind.

Only a couple of minutes passed before there was a light knock on the door. Kiara rushed over to open it.

"Good morning, Kiara."

Jude's deep voice didn't rush the greeting, and the timber of it washed over Angela, settling something inside her. She didn't know what it was about the man, given he was virtually a stranger, but having him around made her feel safer.

That could be because of he had revealed that he wasn't just a friend of the Burke family, he was the head of their security team. The man obviously knew a thing or two about keeping people safe.

And though he was bigger in stature than Craig and Jim, Angela didn't feel any fear in his presence the way she did when she was around those two.

"Good morning, Angela," Jude said when he spotted her.

Angela attempted to give him a smile, but it felt like a weak imitation. "Good morning."

"Is everything ready to go?" Jude asked, looking around the room.

"Yep. We just have these suitcases and boxes," Kiara said, motioning to the stack by the door. "Is it too much?"

"Not at all," Jude said. "I rented a small trailer to take everything to the airport."

It didn't take long for them to carry their belongings out into the cool, early morning air. Jude stacked the boxes and suitcases into the trailer with ease.

Kiara told Angela to take the front seat next to Jude in the SUV. Angela thought she probably should have insisted Kiara sit in the front because Angela wasn't sure she'd be able to hold any kind of conversation with Jude.

Still, she took some comfort in his nearness as he competently drove the SUV and trailer out of Briar Hollow. Angela couldn't help but look back over her shoulder as the town's lights slipped into the distance behind them.

"How are you doing today, Angela?" Jude asked.

She glanced over at him, taking in the man's chiseled profile. "I'm fine."

It was clear that she was going to have to fake it until she made it. She couldn't cower her way into this meeting with her family. She had to meet them with a confidence that she didn't feel.

She'd always struggled with confidence and with having a backbone. In recent years, with Ida's help, she'd been learning to lean on God, especially in those times when she felt like she wasn't strong enough.

Philippians 4:13 had become her life verse. *I can do all things through Christ who strengthens me.* She'd been reciting it many times since that first meeting with Jude.

"It's okay if you're not fine," Jude said. "I'm sure everyone involved is feeling a little apprehensive about this."

"Really?" Angela asked, angling her body toward his. "You think they're a little anxious about meeting me?"

Jude nodded. "I'm sure they hope you'll accept them."

"Why wouldn't I?" Angela asked with a frown. "It's more likely that they won't accept me."

"Not gonna happen." Jude glanced over at her, his eyes shining in the morning light. "You didn't cease to be part of the family just because you'd been taken from them."

"I don't know how to be in that world," Angela said, giving voice to just one of the many worries she had.

"You're very fortunate in that Duncan has kept his two younger kids—Annie and Benji—out of the spotlight. They've lived a fairly normal life, all things considered."

Angela hoped her skepticism wasn't too apparent on her face. She didn't know how normal a life people could lead when their father was extremely wealthy, the way Duncan Burke was.

"Okay. I realize that perhaps that sounds ridiculous," Jude said. "But honestly, Annie and Benji are very down-to-earth people. Benji goes to the local high school and plays on the basketball team. Both of them attend church in Serenity Point."

It wasn't long before Jude pulled the car into the lot of a private airport. "You two can go ahead and get on board the plane while I supervise the loading of your things."

"I've never been on a plane before," Angela said as she stared out the window at the jet that sat parked nearby.

"Well, you're getting introduced to the best way to travel for those who can afford it," Jude said as he opened his door. "You'll never want to travel commercially after this."

"I can't wait," Kiara said as she got out when Jude did.

Angela moved a little more slowly. But soon, she and Kiara had been escorted on board the luxury private jet. A woman wearing a dark blue pantsuit with red trim greeted them with a friendly smile.

After they'd settled into a pair of soft leather seats, the woman asked them what they'd like to drink. Since they hadn't even had breakfast yet, Angela asked for a cup of coffee.

"Once we're in the air, I'll have your drinks and some breakfast for you."

After she'd left them, Angela turned to the window and stared out at Jude as he directed the men moving the boxes and suitcases from the trailer to the plane.

A man wearing a thigh-length black coat approached Jude, and the two men talked for a couple of minutes before Jude handed the man something. They shook hands, then the man went to the SUV and slid behind the wheel.

Jude stood watching as they loaded the last box into the plane, then he turned and headed for the stairs that led up into the jet. Angela watched as he disappeared from view outside, shifting her gaze to catch him as he walked into the area where they were seated.

"Everything is loaded," Jude said as he took off his black wool jacket. After laying it on an empty seat, he sat down in the chair facing Angela. "We're ready to go."

Angela wasn't sure that she was ready to go yet, but that decision had been taken out of her hands.

I can do all things through Christ who strengthens me.

"This is so exciting," Kiara said as she buckled her seatbelt. "How long is it going to take to get to Idaho?"

"Should be about three hours or so once we get in the air," Jude said. "We'll have to transfer to a helicopter to fly from Coeur d'Alene to the estate."

Angela's stomach clenched. "A helicopter?"

"Wow," Kiara said. "We're getting all the new experiences in one day."

Jude chuckled as he buckled himself into his seat. The flight attendant came back into the cabin of the plane, greeting Jude with a familiar smile.

"We'll be taking off shortly."

"Thanks, Tanya," Jude said.

Tanya moved away from them and sat down in a seat near the cockpit. She'd barely buckled her seatbelt when the plane jerked into motion.

Angela gripped the arms of her seat, trying to prepare herself for the next few minutes. She didn't know if she had a fear of flying, but she had a feeling she was about to find out.

"It'll be fine, Angie," Kiara said, her hand landing on top of Angela's. She gave Angela a reassuring smile as she squeezed her hand. "Don't worry."

Famous last words. Angela had a tendency to worry, and in her mind, there was good reason to worry about her current situation.

She took a deep breath as she looked away from Kiara, only to find Jude watching her with a furrowed brow.

"Kiara is right," Jude said, his low voice gentle and almost lost to the sudden roar of the plane's engines. "It'll be fine."

Angela nodded, then took a quick breath as the plane gathered speed. All too soon, it catapulted down the runway. When the plane lifted into the air, Angela could have sworn she had left her stomach on earth.

She closed her eyes, then opened them again when she felt Kiara lean across her. Automatically, she turned to see what Kiara was looking at. And wished she hadn't.

The earth was dropping away from them at an alarming rate, and Angela felt as if her connection to everything she'd ever known was disappearing as quickly.

Kiara, however, was entranced by the view, remarking on how incredible it was. She had always been the more adventurous of the two of them.

Angela closed her eyes and tried to imagine being anywhere but on that plane, winging its way across the country to where her family waited. Would it be her new home?

No one had mentioned specifically what would happen once they got there. Would they have a home of their own? Would she and Kiara be able to find jobs nearby?

"I'm actually going to sit over there," Kiara said, making Angela open her eyes to see what was going on.

The attendant stood next to their seats with a tray in her hands.

"Why are you moving?" Angela asked.

"I want to sit next to the window," Kiara said as she undid her belt. "Plus, I'd like to read while I eat."

Angela didn't try to keep her from moving. She just watched as Kiara settled into a seat that was a short distance in front of the area where Angela sat on the opposite side of the plane.

Tanya showed Kiara how to lift a tray into position before she set her drink on it. Looking at Jude, Angela saw him doing something similar.

She felt totally out of her element as she struggled to get her own tray into position.

"Here, let me help you." Jude had moved his tray and removed his seat belt and was now down on one knee in front of her.

With practiced ease, he had her tray out of the armrest and lowered into position in front of her. He gave her a quick smile as he got back to his feet and returned to his seat.

"Thank you," she said. Both to him and to Tanya, who held out her cup of coffee.

Angela took a tentative sip of the hot beverage, her eyes widening as the taste of it filled her mouth. She and Kiara were both coffee drinkers, but they'd always settled for the cheapest brand they could find.

This was clearly *not* the brand they usually used. That had a bitterness to it that never completely disappeared after the first sip, even if she added some chocolate milk to it.

This one, however, had a more balanced taste and a velvety feel. And the flavor was incredible, with distinct notes that she'd never tasted in coffee before.

If this was the type of coffee she was going to get to drink as a result of being part of the Burke family, Angela had just found the first positive of her life's upheaval.

"This is amazing," Angela said as she watched Jude pick up his cup. "I've never tasted anything like it."

The skin at the corners of Jude's eyes crinkled as he smiled, softening his stern expression. He took a sip from his mug, then said, "Duncan insists on having the best coffee available anywhere he might drink it."

"I can see why he'd want that."

Tanya returned with large plates containing their breakfasts.

When Tanya set a plate down in front of her, Angela stared down at the plate in wonder. Fluffy scrambled eggs, perfectly crispy bacon, golden hash browns, and fresh fruit artfully arranged on fine china. It was more elaborate than any breakfast she'd ever been served, and certainly more elegant than anything she'd ever made for herself and Kiara.

"This looks incredible," she murmured, picking up the heavy silverware.

"Once again, only the best," Jude said. "Duncan would have wanted you to have a delicious meal on the trip to Idaho. You'll find that his motivation for most things is what is best for his family."

Angela didn't know how that would relate to her, but she had a feeling it was important since Jude had mentioned it. The man had dropped little tidbits here and there about life in Idaho, mainly about Duncan and the other members of the family.

She'd tucked away the bits of knowledge, assuming they'd come in handy at some point. But while the man had been willing to share information about the Burke family with her, he hadn't shared much about himself.

"You said that you live on the estate," she began. At his nod, she continued, "Does your family live with you?"

He froze with his forkful of scrambled eggs halfway to his mouth. His eyes narrowed for a moment before he said, "No. My only family is my mom and her kids, and they don't live in Idaho."

Angela couldn't explain why she felt so relieved when he revealed he wasn't married. That didn't mean he didn't have a significant other, however.

It shouldn't matter, but she found herself curious about the details of his personal life in a way that surprised her. She figured it had to do with him being the one connection between her old life and new.

He also knew so much about her, it only felt fair to balance that out with her knowing about him. But realistically, she knew she was looking for a distraction.

"What about you?" Jude asked, turning the question back on her. "Any significant relationships you're leaving behind in Briar Hollow? Although I guess it's probably a little late to be asking about that."

Angela felt heat creep up her neck. "No. There's not. I've never really... I mean, there isn't anyone I'm really close to. Just Kiara." She took a bite of the eggs, hoping to hide her embarrassment behind the act of eating.

The eggs were as delicious as everything else on the plate, but she barely tasted them as she waited for Jude's response.

"That's probably for the best," he said simply. "It would have made this transition more complicated."

Angela glanced over at Kiara, who was absorbed in her book while she ate, completely oblivious to the conversation happening behind her.

"Can I ask you something?" Angela said, setting down her fork.

Jude nodded, his gaze focused on her with an intensity that made her stomach flutter.

"Why you? I mean, why did Duncan send you specifically to meet with us?"

Jude was quiet for a long moment, and Angela wondered if she'd overstepped somehow. Then he leaned back in his seat, his expression thoughtful.

"I've been with the family for a long time," he said finally. "Duncan trusts me to handle sensitive situations. And meeting with you... that was one of the most important things he's ever asked me to do."

"When did you first meet them?"

"My dad took a job working on the security team for the family in New York when I was around nine years old. At the time, Duncan was still married to Jill, your mom. They only had Julian when Dad first started working for them, but a couple of years later, you and Annie arrived."

"So you knew me back then."

Jude nodded. "I was almost fifteen when you were kidnapped, and I saw the huge toll it took on everyone. Duncan fired the man who'd been the head of his security team and promoted my dad to the position. It was the one he held until he died when I was twenty."

"And then you took over?"

Jude shook his head. "No. I didn't have enough experience for that. But Duncan kept me on and gave me every opportunity to gain the knowledge and experience I would need to one day lead the team myself. I've been in charge of the family's security for around eight years now."

That explained a lot to Angela. It did give her a bit of pause, however. If there was a time when Jude had to choose what she wanted or what Duncan wanted, which way would he go? Something told her that his decision would not be in her favor.

She'd already sensed that he was devoted to his job and to the Burke family, but now she had confirmation of it.

With his latest revelation about his life, she'd come to realize that Jude was at least eleven years older than her.

"Angela?"

She blinked as she realized she'd zoned out thinking about the man seated across from her. "Yes?"

"Are you okay?"

Angela felt her cheeks warm. "Sorry, I was just thinking about everything you told me." She took another sip of her coffee, using the moment to gather her thoughts. "It's a lot to process."

"I imagine it is." Jude's voice carried a gentleness that made something in her chest tighten. "If you have other questions, I'm happy to answer them."

She wanted to ask him more—about himself, about what it had been like growing up with her family, about what he thought of her. But the words stuck in her throat, familiar hesitation holding her back.

"What are they like?" she asked instead. He'd told her bits and pieces about all of them, but she wanted more. Even though it was overwhelming. "Duncan and... and the others?"

Jude set down his coffee cup, considering her question. "Duncan's a good man. He's made mistakes, but he loves his family fiercely. After you were taken, he never stopped looking for you. Never stopped hoping you'd come home."

The words hit her harder than she expected. She'd always assumed that her parents had been glad to let her go. That they had probably forgotten her as soon as Jim and Sandra had taken her. And yet, the opposite had been true.

All this time, she'd had people who would have loved and cared for her. Protected her.

"Annie is probably the one you'll connect with most easily," Jude continued. "She's got a gentle spirit, kind of like you."

Angela hadn't spent much time thinking about Annie. Her twin. The person who'd been returned to live her life in the lap of luxury, with a father who loved and treated her well. While Angela had ended up with the opposite.

"And Julian?"

"Oh." Jude frowned. "Well, Julian is... complicated. He rebelled against his father's attempts to protect him. He indulges in alcohol and women a bit too much for Duncan's liking."

It was weird to think that these people who were related to her were total strangers. She hoped that they liked her... and that she liked them too.

If they didn't, she had no idea what she'd do with her life now that she'd fled Briar Hollow.

CHAPTER SIX

Jude watched as Angela's expression closed off when Tanya let them know they'd be landing soon.

For most of the trip, he'd told her about the Burkes. He was trying his hardest to give her the information she needed in order to feel at least somewhat prepared for the upcoming meeting.

She'd had questions. Lots of them. But they hadn't just been about her family. She'd asked about him and his life too.

Jude wasn't surprised that she wanted to know more about him. He knew that he was the bridge between her old life and the new one that awaited her, so he didn't mind her questions too much.

It had just been odd to talk about himself. Sure, his mom asked him questions about his life. But Angela was asking more than how his week had gone.

Perhaps it had just been a way to keep her mind off all the changes she was facing. Focusing on his life might be easier than focusing on hers.

"We'll be landing in about fifteen minutes," Tanya announced as she collected their empty plates. "Please make sure your seats are in the upright position and your seat belts are fastened."

Angela nodded mutely, her fingers fidgeting with the edge of her sleeve. The curious woman who'd been peppering him with questions throughout the flight had retreated, replaced by someone who seemed determined to hide her emotions.

He didn't like the idea of her closing herself off. How would he know if she needed something if he couldn't read her expression?

He was better than most at reading people. His dad had reiterated over and over how important that skill was when dealing with potential threats.

However, there were moments when Angela's face went completely blank. He was coming to realize that those moments were usually when she felt the most vulnerable.

Given what he now knew about her past, it didn't surprise him that she'd learned to hide the softest parts of herself. The environment she'd grown up in had almost guaranteed that would be the result.

"Hey," Jude said softly, leaning forward. "It's going to be fine."

She met his gaze, the vulnerability missing from her expression was clear in her eyes. "You keep saying that."

"Because it's true." He wanted to reach across and take her hand, but held back. That wasn't his place. "Duncan has been waiting for this moment for over twenty years."

"What if I'm not what they expect?" The words tumbled out in a whisper. "What if I'm not... enough?"

The question hit Jude in an unexpected place. He'd spent years proving himself worthy of his position, worthy of Duncan's trust. The man had given him a chance, a life after his dad had died. Jude understood the fear of not measuring up better than most.

"You're exactly who they want to meet," he said firmly. "Just you. You're perfect as you are."

Angela's eyes widened slightly at his intensity, and Jude realized he'd let more emotion into his voice than he'd intended. He cleared his throat and sat back, composing himself.

"Thank you," she murmured, a hint of pink coloring her cheeks.

The plane began its descent, and Angela's knuckles turned white as she gripped the armrests. Jude wanted to reassure her again, but he also understood that some fears couldn't be talked away.

Unfortunately, all he could do was sit across from her and offer his verbal assurances.

When they landed with a gentle bump on the runway, he watched her exhale the breath she'd been holding. Her sister turned around in her seat, grinning widely.

"That was amazing!" Kiara called back. "Did you see how small everything looked from up there?"

Angela managed a tight smile. "I didn't look out the window."

After they taxied to a stop, Tanya informed them they could unbuckle and prepare to disembark. Jude stood, reaching for his jacket and slipping it on with practiced ease.

"The helicopter is waiting for us," he explained. "But we have time if you need a moment."

Angela shook her head, squaring her shoulders. "No. Let's keep going."

Jude admired her determination. Many people would have been overwhelmed by now, but she kept pushing forward despite her obvious anxiety. It spoke to a strength that perhaps even she didn't recognize in herself.

As they stepped off the plane into the bright Idaho sun, Angela lifted her hand to shield her eyes.

"This way," Jude said, placing a gentle hand on her back to guide her toward the helicopter that sat waiting on the tarmac.

The helicopter was painted a deep blue with gold and red accents. The pilot in a crisp uniform stood beside it, checking something on a clipboard.

"Mr. Kessler," the pilot said as he lifted his head at their approach. "Good to see you again."

"Marcus," Jude replied with a nod. "How's the weather looking for the flight to the estate?"

"Clear skies all the way. Should be a smooth ride."

Kiara was already approaching the open door of the helicopter with enthusiasm, but Angela remained rooted to the spot.

"Second thoughts?" Jude asked quietly, moving to stand beside her.

"It's just... small," she said.

The irony was that the helicopter was actually one of the larger luxury models. But next to the jet, it did look a little smaller.

"Marcus has been flying for the family for over a decade. He's one of the best pilots I know. And Duncan would only ever have someone flying his aircraft that he trusted."

Jude hoped his words would reassure her. However, he didn't know if her reluctance to board it had as much to do with the aircraft as with what waited at the end of the flight.

"C'mon," he said, placing a hand on her back and once again gently urging her to follow her sister onto the helicopter.

Finally, she approached the steps leading up into the body of the helicopter. Jude waited until she'd climbed inside before following her up the steps.

The seats were configured with three seats facing two, which were then backed by another two, facing three. Kiara had taken one of the two seats, choosing the one closest to the window.

Angela had also chosen a seat, but rather than sit across from her sister, she'd chosen the middle seat of the three facing her.

Jude was left with the options of sitting beside Angela, beside Kiara or by himself in the other section of seats behind the pilots.

Knowing how Angela felt about flying, Jude couldn't bring himself to sit far away from her. Turning, he settled into the seat beside her, closest to the door.

"This is a more complicated seatbelt," Angela said as she tried to get herself strapped in.

"Here." Jude helped her loop the straps over her shoulders and across her hips before snapping them all into the center buckle.

"Thanks."

A man checked in with Jude to make sure that everything was okay and to let him know the luggage had all been transferred to the truck that Jude had arranged for since there wasn't room for that amount of cargo on the helicopter.

As the door was shut and secured, Jude strapped himself in, then glanced at Angela. She sat with her hands gripped tightly in her lap, her posture ramrod straight.

"How long is this flight?" Kiara asked, her eyes alight with excitement. She was definitely showing herself to be someone who embraced new experiences.

"We should be at the estate in about twenty-five minutes."

"So soon," Angela murmured.

When the engines spooled up with a deepening whine, Jude handed headsets to Angela and Kiara, then put a set on himself.

Outside the window, the five-blade rotor began to turn, sluggish at first, slicing the crisp morning air with a rhythmic *whump-whump* that quickened into a blurred disc overhead.

"This is so cool," Kiara said, her voice clear in Jude's ears.

"That's one word for it," Angela said. "I didn't know it would be so loud."

"It's a bit different from a plane," Jude explained. "So wearing these just makes it easier to communicate."

"Does the pilot hear us too?" Angela asked.

"No, they're on a different frequency, though they can switch to ours in cases of emergency."

"Emergency?"

Jude wanted to slap his forehead. That wasn't the best thing to reference when he had a nervous flyer on his hands.

As the helicopter lifted off, a gentle shudder rippled through the cabin, the seats vibrating beneath them.

Jude wasn't surprised when Angela reached out and grabbed his arm. He covered her hand with his as the helicopter tilted forward slightly, beginning the short journey north to the estate.

"Look at all the snow, Angie," Kiara said, her face pressed close to the window. "It's so beautiful."

Mindful of how cold it would be in Idaho compared to Kentucky, Jude had had Duncan's assistant order and overnight deliver winter wear for both women to the hotel where he'd been staying. She'd sent heavy coats, scarves, boots, and mitts. Otherwise, they wouldn't have been prepared for the weather that had greeted them once they'd arrived in Coeur d'Alene.

"I'll take your word for it, Kiki," Angela said, keeping her head pressed back against the seat, her gaze straight forward.

There was a bit more sway to the helicopter than there had been to the plane, and Jude could tell that Angela felt it because her fingers tightened on his arm.

He always enjoyed riding in the helicopter and turned to watch the evergreens standing tall above a carpet of snow. It looked like they had gotten more snow in the few days that he'd been gone. Or maybe he'd just forgotten how much had been there after spending time in a place without any.

Jude didn't interact much for the remainder of the flight, just listened as Kiara tried to convince Angela that she was really missing out by not looking out the windows. Angela's responses were short and to the point.

She wasn't going to give in to her sister's attempts to get her to look out the window.

The nearer they drew to the estate, the more it settled on Jude that his part in this family reunification was nearly over. His job had been to verify Angela's identity, and then get her safely back to the estate.

He'd done both of those things, and soon he'd be turning over the care of Angela and Kiara to Duncan.

And though he'd still see them, he wouldn't be dealing with them directly, for the most part. He wouldn't be responsible for Angela. Anything she needed would be taken care of by someone else now.

The thought shouldn't bother him so much. It was just a job. A mission completed successfully.

Yet as the helicopter began its descent toward the estate's helipad, Jude found himself oddly reluctant to let go of the connection he'd formed with Angela.

In just a few days, he'd watched her world turn upside down, had been there as she'd said goodbye to her old life. He'd watched the shifting emotions cross her face as she processed what was happening. Had seen her strength even as she struggled.

He might witness more of her adjustments, but it would be from a distance. Just as it should be.

"We're landing," he said, his voice gentler than he'd intended.

Angela's eyes flew to his, wide and anxious. "Already?"

"Already," he confirmed, nodding toward the window where the Burke estate was coming into view.

The main house stood proud against the backdrop of mountains, its stone exterior dusted with snow. It wasn't as large or lavish as one might expect someone of Duncan's financial status to own, but it would still be awe-inspiring to the average person. Especially someone who had just recently been living in a one-bedroom basement apartment with her sister.

Smoke curled from one of the chimneys, a welcoming sight in the winter landscape. The helipad was situated a short distance from the main house, with a road leading to it.

"Oh my goodness," Kiara breathed, pressing her face closer to the window. "It's like something out of a fairy tale."

Angela finally turned to look, her hand still gripping Jude's arm. He felt her fingers tighten even more as she took in the sprawling estate.

"That's... where they live?" she whispered.

"Yes, that's the home Duncan had built when he moved his family from New York to Idaho."

"You said your house is on the estate too?"

"Yep." Jude pointed out the opposite window. "My cabin is over there. Annie has a cabin as well, but hers is a bit closer to the main house."

"Is that where we're going to stay?" Kiara asked.

"Definitely." Jude couldn't imagine a scenario where Duncan wouldn't want them close. "They have plenty of room."

Angela looked away from the window and bent her head. As she tucked a strand of hair behind her ear, Jude had a momentary reminder of who she was.

Annie's twin.

It seemed strange not to have that be uppermost in his mind every time he looked at her. Instead, her relationship to the family formed in his mind as Duncan's daughter. Not as Annie's twin.

But now he was reminded that Annie was waiting down below, along with Duncan.

He thought about what Duncan would feel when he saw his twin daughters together for the first time in over two decades. Though they might be identical at the DNA level, they were also different.

Both had a gentle air about them, but Angela's came with the addition of vulnerability. Annie, however, didn't have that same vulnerability. She would go head to head with her dad—and, to Jude's dismay, even with him—when she felt she had to, without fear of anything happening to her.

Annie knew that regardless of what they might argue about, her dad loved her and Jude cared for her. Something told Jude that Angela had never had that sense of security.

Jude prayed that would be something that Angela came to understand as well.

The helicopter began its descent toward the large helipad near the main house, and Jude felt Angela's grip tighten further.

"Almost there," he said, keeping his voice soft.

As they hovered over the landing pad, the snow swirled in miniature cyclones beneath them. Marcus brought them down with practiced precision, the skids touching ground with only the slight-est bump.

"We've arrived at the Burke Estate," Marcus announced through their headsets. "Please remain seated until the rotors have stopped completely."

Jude watched as Angela took rapid breaths. Her eyes were closed, her lips moving slightly as if in prayer. When the rotors finally slowed to a stop, she opened her eyes and met his gaze.

"You did it," he said.

A small smile flickered across her face. "I survived."

"More than survived. You were brave."

She looked down at where her hand still clutched his arm, quickly releasing it. "Sorry."

"Don't be," Jude said, unbuckling his harness. "That's what I'm here for."

He took their headsets and returned them to their storage spot, then helped both women with their harnesses. When the door opened, the crisp mountain air rushed in, carrying the scent of pine and wood smoke. Angela remained in her seat, and Jude under-stood why.

On the edge of the helipad stood a group of people. His quick glance over the group showed him that all the Burkes were there except for Benji.

He climbed out of the helicopter, then turned to offer his hand to Angela. After a brief hesitation, she grasped it and took cautious steps down the small flight of stairs. She held onto his hand tightly for a moment before letting go and stepping to the side.

Kiara also took his hand, but she released it as soon as she was on the helipad.

Angela glanced at him briefly, then she walked towards the group. At first, her steps were tentative, but as Kiara joined her, they grew steadier.

Jude wasn't part of this reunion, so he stayed where he was, watching.

He had expected Duncan to be the one to approach Angela first, but it seemed Angela's attention was on Annie. Since he'd stayed at the helicopter, he was too far away to hear anything that was said.

But it seemed that introductions were made, even without his help. There were, however, no attempts made to hug Angela, which Jude thought was perhaps a good thing. They were still strangers to her.

Thankfully, she had Kiara at her side. She wasn't alone.

Jude struggled with the position he currently found himself in as he watched Angela meet her family.

For years, he'd been perfectly content to live his life on the sidelines, keeping watch for anyone or anything that might harm the members of the Burke family.

It had always fulfilled him to continue in the position his father had once held. He'd followed the advice the man had given him, both personally and professionally. And it had always brought fulfillment.

Until that moment.

There was an ache in his chest as he realized that in the current situation, he was no longer needed. He would be expected to step back. To fade into the shadows once again.

And he would do it.

But for the first time, he felt a strange reluctance to take that step back.

Which was probably why it was a good thing he had to. Being there to support her through such a challenging time in her life had felt good, and he'd gotten closer to Angela than was probably wise.

Now that she was back with her family, it was time for him to get back to his life. Such as it was.

Spotting a UTV approaching from the direction of the security building, Jude moved toward it. As he passed the group, his gaze caught Annie's.

He could see the strain on her face and realized that perhaps this reunion wasn't all sunshine and roses for her either. Giving her a small nod, Jude hoped that somehow, the two sisters would find some common ground on which to build a relationship.

They'd been close at one time. Inseparable as toddlers. Now, they were strangers with no memory of each other.

Sharing a bloodline didn't necessarily mean people loved each other or got along. Julian and Annie were proof of that.

But Annie was a warm and friendly person, so Jude thought she might try to get along with her twin, even if they might feel like they had very little in common at first.

Jude just hoped that Angela didn't get too overwhelmed by everything and everyone.

CHAPTER SEVEN

Angela clung to Kiara's hand as they walked toward the waiting black SUV. Her stomach was a mess of nerves, and she was afraid she was going to be sick.

Glancing over, she saw Jude striding toward a waiting UTV. They'd had something similar at the farm, though it hadn't looked nearly as nice as this one.

As he passed them, he looked toward their group. His gaze didn't land on her, however. It went to Annie. Her twin.

Angela felt a swirl of something dark inside her. Jealousy?

How was that possible?

Without a thought, she took a step in his direction. It was only Kiara's grip on her hand that kept her moving toward the waiting vehicle.

Jude swung himself into the UTV, where another man waited behind the wheel. As the UTV moved away from the helipad, Angela tore her gaze from Jude, trying to ignore the sense of loss she felt as he disappeared from sight.

She hadn't realized how much she'd come to rely on him over the past several days. And now he was walking away from her. Leaving her to face this new life on her own.

Even though Kiara was still at her side, Angela felt adrift. As if her anchor in this new reality had been taken away. Jude had been the one who'd helped her feel like she wasn't going into her new life completely blind. He was an important connection, a steadying presence in the upheaval of her life.

But no one else seemed to realize that. Or maybe they just didn't care.

It was a short trip from the helicopter to the house. The mansion. It was so much more than a house. It was huge. Bigger than any home she'd ever seen before.

"Wow..." Kiara murmured as they climbed from the SUV. "This is..."

"Yeah." She figured that Kiara didn't have any more words than she did to describe what they were seeing.

The exterior was made of glass, timber, and stone. It fit in well with the surroundings, but lacked the modern look that Angela had assumed it would have.

"Welcome home," Duncan said as they walked through the large doors leading into the foyer of the mansion.

Angela unwound her scarf, then unbuttoned the peacoat that Jude had given her. She hadn't wanted to accept it at first, but he'd insisted, telling her that the weather in Idaho was much colder than in Kentucky. Knowing she didn't have anything warm enough for that, she'd finally accepted.

Once their coats were hung in the closet, Angela clasped her hands, taking in the foyer with its towering ceiling. Everywhere she looked was an understated elegance.

A lanky teen appeared in an arched doorway not far from where they stood, his eyes widening as his gaze went from Annie to Angela and back again.

"Wow," he said. "That's... incredible."

"This is Benjamin," Duncan said, placing a hand on the teen's shoulder. "My youngest."

Angela smiled tentatively at him. "It's nice to meet you."

"You can call me Benji," he offered. "Everyone but my dad does."

"Why don't we go into the living room," Duncan said, gesturing to the doorway where Benji had appeared.

As she followed the other family members, Angela took in the lavish surroundings—the high ceilings, the artwork, the expensive furnishings. She tried her best to keep her awe from showing on her face, but it was hard. She was overwhelmed as she observed everything.

"Please make yourselves comfortable." Elizabeth, Duncan's wife, gestured toward an arranged seating area where some refreshments had been laid out on the coffee table.

Angela sat down on one of the sofas with Kiara, drawing strength from the press of her arm. A reminder that she wasn't alone. She noticed that Duncan was occupied with his phone, but soon he slid it into his pocket and looked at her.

"I imagine you have questions," Duncan said once everyone was seated.

"A lifetime of them," Angela replied softly, trying not to shift under Duncan's intense gaze. "But I hardly know where to start."

"Perhaps with how we found each other?" Duncan suggested.

Angela nodded, her hands clasped tightly in her lap. "I saw Annie's photo from the charity gala." She glanced at Annie. "It was like... looking in a mirror. I knew immediately we had to be related."

"You're identical twins," Duncan said. "Born three minutes apart."

"I don't remember anything from my life... before," Angela said, feeling the need to apologize for that lapse in memory. "I'm sorry."

"There's no need to apologize," Duncan said. "You were young."

"I don't remember anything from that time either," Annie said.

Before Angela had a chance to respond, Jude walked in, and something inside her relaxed. He met her gaze for a moment, then took a seat not far from Duncan.

Kiara shifted slightly, and Angela's hand found hers, squeezing gently. Over the next few minutes, she answered questions from Duncan about her past and their life in Briar Hollow. She would have thought he already had all that information from Jude, but she went ahead and gave him the details he asked her for.

Through all of it, the other members of the Burke family and Jude remained silent. It made Angela shift in her seat, wondering if there were wrong answers. Could she say something that might make them change their minds about her and Kiara being there?

Or could it be that they were asking her to tell her story again in order to see if she would give the same details?

Neither option sat well with her, and her nervousness increased. She glanced at Kiara, then at Jude. When their gazes met, he gave her a slight smile and a nod of his head as if to offer encouragement. She stared at him for a long moment, then took a little breath before looking back at Duncan.

All she could do was be honest and hope that they would understand that she wasn't there to take advantage of them.

Throughout the conversation, Annie didn't show much emotion, leaving Angela to wonder how she was feeling about everything. She'd had the benefit of knowing she had a twin, unlike Angela, who was still in shock over the revelation.

Still, she wanted to get to know Annie. Kiara would always be her sister. The one who'd endured the same challenges growing up. But there was always room for another sister. If they could find some common ground.

Annie had grown up in the lap of luxury, while Angela had lived a life of hardship. She bet that her sister didn't have calluses on her hands the way Angela did. She'd probably never had to spend hours hoeing a garden until her hands had weeping blisters.

But even though they didn't appear to have much in common, Angela found that she wanted to find some point of connection. So she figured the best place to start was with asking if Annie would be willing to show her around the estate.

"Annie?"

Annie glanced around. She apparently hadn't been paying attention to the conversation.

"I'm sorry." Annie smoothed a hand over her sweater. "What was the question?"

"Angela was asking if you'd show her around the grounds later," Duncan said.

"Oh. Of course." Annie smiled, but Angela could see that it didn't quite reach her eyes.

Angela studied her, head tilted slightly. "We don't have to if you're not comfortable."

Annie's eyes widened briefly, then she said, "No, it's fine."

An awkward silence filled the room until Elizabeth gracefully intervened. "Perhaps some refreshments first? Our cook prepared quite a spread."

When the platter loaded with delicacies reached her, Angela looked them over carefully before choosing a lemon tart.

"So you work in a bakery?" Julian asked, speaking for the first time since they'd all sat down in the living room.

Angela nodded, relaxing slightly at the change of topic. "For a couple of years now. I love it."

"She's being modest," Kiara interjected. "She practically runs the place. Her cinnamon rolls are famous in three counties."

Heat filled Angela's cheeks. "Baking is just something I enjoy."

They talked a bit more about her and Kiara's jobs as they ate the pastries they'd each selected, then Duncan set down his coffee cup. "Angela, I hope you understand that we never stopped looking for you. Not for a single day."

The raw emotion in his voice silenced the room.

"Jude explained some of what happened," she said softly, her gaze flicking to him briefly. "It's still hard to process. All these years thinking I was someone else..."

"You're still you," Kiara said firmly. "Nothing changes who you are."

Angela gave her sister an affectionate and appreciative smile. Kiara had been there for her when no one else had, and Angela hoped they'd always have that bond. They might not share blood, but they shared a deep, deep bond.

Over the next little while, the others asked her questions, and through it all, Jude remained a silent, steady presence.

"Would you tell us more about your life?" Elizabeth asked gently. "Whatever you're comfortable sharing."

Angela looked at Kiara, who gave an encouraging nod.

"We lived on a homestead outside a small town in Kentucky," Angela began. "It was... simple. Sandra homeschooled us throughout our school years. Kiara is three years older than me." She smiled at her sister. "She's always looked out for me."

"That's what big sisters do," Kiara said, bumping Angela's shoulder affectionately.

"How did you come to be part of the family, Kiara?" Duncan asked.

"They got me when I was eight," she said. "Jim said my parents couldn't afford to raise me, so they offered to take me in. I'm not sure that I was legally adopted, to be honest. But I don't think I was kidnapped. What little I remember of my biological family makes me think they were happy to see me go. "

"Perhaps we can help you get more information about your family if you're interested in it," Duncan offered.

Kiara shook her head. "Since I do remember my life before I ended up at Jim and Sandra's, I know it's nothing I want to revisit."

"So, life with them was better?"

Kiara and Angela exchanged another look. Angela didn't really want to get into all the nitty-gritty details. "In some ways."

The cryptic answer had Duncan looking at Jude again, but they didn't press for more details. She hadn't told Jude everything about their time at the homestead, but Angela figured that time would come. She was just glad it wasn't right then.

When the silence got heavy again, Elizabeth filled it once more. "Why don't we show you to your rooms? Maybe you'd like to have some time to yourselves."

Relief filled Angela. "That would be nice. Thank you."

Everyone stood when they did, and Angela wanted to go to Jude. To speak to him and see how he felt the reunification was going.

But he remained standing directly behind Duncan, hands in his pockets. It was a stark reminder that Jude's loyalties were, first and foremost, to Duncan.

When their gazes met briefly, Jude's expression softened with a slight smile, and Angela took strength from that. As she left the room with Kiara, Annie, and Elizabeth, Angela hoped that she'd be able to talk to him again soon.

Leaving the men behind, they walked up a sweeping staircase to a long hallway lined with beautiful paintings on the wall.

"Here we go," Elizabeth said as they approached a couple of doors that stood open opposite each other. "You each have a room, but we'll let you decide which one you want."

Angela had never not shared a room with Kiara. She wasn't sure that she was ready to do it for the first time in a totally new place.

"Your things have been brought up here already," Elizabeth said as she stepped into one of the rooms. "But if there's anything you need, please let me know."

"Thank you," Angela said. "We appreciate everything you've done for us."

The smile Elizabeth gave her was gentle. "We're just so glad to have you home. And to have you here as well, Kiara."

Annie remained silent as she stood beside Elizabeth. Angela wondered about their biological mom. Jill. So far, she hadn't spoken with her, and Jude hadn't had a lot to say about her either.

"We'll leave you to rest," Elizabeth said. "I've put a card with our cell phone numbers on each desk. Feel free to call us if you need anything."

After Elizabeth and Annie had left, closing the door behind them, Angela felt an overwhelming desire to cry.

Kiara wrapped her arms around her, and Angela hung onto her desperately.

"It's okay," Kiara whispered, stroking Angela's hair. "I know it's overwhelming."

"I don't know if I can do this," Angela said, her voice muffled against Kiara's shoulder. "Everything feels so... foreign. Like I'm pretending to be someone I'm not."

"You're not pretending. You're just discovering another part of who you are." Kiara pulled back to look at her. "And you don't have to figure it all out today."

Angela wiped her eyes with the back of her hand. "Annie seems... distant. I thought maybe we'd have some kind of instant connection, but it feels like she doesn't want me here."

"Maybe she's as overwhelmed as you are," Kiara suggested. "Think about it—she's had her whole life turned upside down too. She probably doesn't know how to act any more than you do."

Angela nodded, though she wasn't entirely convinced. She glanced toward the window, where she could see the forest stretching out toward distant mountains. Somewhere out there, Jude was going about his business, probably already moving on to whatever security matters needed his attention.

The thought made her chest tighten and her heart ache.

"What is it?" Kiara asked, following her gaze.

"Nothing," Angela said quickly, then sighed. "It's just... Jude. I got used to having him around. He made everything feel less scary."

Kiara raised an eyebrow. "You like him. Don't try to deny it. I saw how you looked at him downstairs."

"It doesn't matter," Angela said quietly. "He works for Duncan. His loyalty is to this family."

"You're part of this family now."

"Am I?" Angela wasn't so sure.

Kiara placed her hands on Angela's shoulders, giving her a gentle shake. "Of course you are. You heard Duncan downstairs—he never stopped looking for you. That doesn't sound like someone who's going to turn his back on you now."

Angela moved to the window, pressing her palm against the cool glass. The view was breathtaking—snow-covered mountains in the distance, tall pines swaying in the afternoon breeze, and the kind of natural beauty she'd only seen in magazines. But it felt like looking at someone else's life.

"I keep waiting for someone to tell me there's been a mistake," she admitted. "That I don't actually belong here."

"The DNA test doesn't lie, Angie."

"The DNA test proves I'm related to them. It doesn't prove I fit in." Angela turned back to face Kiara. "Do you see this place? The way they dress, the way they talk? I'm a baker who has nothing to her name but the very basics. What am I supposed to contribute to all of this?"

Angela sank down onto the loveseat by the window.

"I feel like I'm caught between two worlds," she admitted. "Part of me wants to embrace all of this, to finally have a real family. But the other part keeps waiting for something to go wrong. For them to decide I don't belong here after all."

Kiara joined her on the loveseat. "That's the farm talking. Jim and Sandra made us believe we had to earn our place, that love was conditional. But look around, Angie. This isn't the same thing."

Angela hoped that Kiara was right. If only she could talk to Jude. To get his thoughts on what he thought her place in this new world might be and how she'd done so far.

Getting up, she went to the desk and picked up the card that Elizabeth had left there. She skimmed over the names and numbers written in precise handwriting. Everyone was listed there but Jude.

She had Jude's number because he'd given it to her in Briar Hollow. However, the list seemed to make it clear that the family members were the people Angela should contact for help. Not Jude.

Straightening, Angela took a deep breath. Was she strong enough to do this? To try to fit into this world that was so very different from what she'd known? From what she was comfortable with?

"So, are we sharing a room still?" Kiara asked as she joined her at the desk.

Angela glanced over at her. "What do you want?"

She felt like she'd already made too many demands of Kiara in leaving their life in Kentucky.

"Let's give staying in separate rooms a try," Kiara said. "And if it doesn't work, then we'll bunk up."

Angela nodded, though her stomach sank at Kiara's suggestion. It would be weird, for sure, but if it was what Kiara wanted, she'd do it.

"Let's go look at the other bedroom," Kiara suggested. "Then we can decide which one we each want."

Angela trailed Kiara out of that bedroom, across the hall and into the one opposite it.

This room was a mirror image of the other in terms of the positioning of the furniture. However, it was decorated in shades of blues instead of sage green and cream.

The bed was just as large, the furnishings just as elegant, and the view equally stunning.

"They're both beautiful," Kiara said, running her hand along the carved wooden headboard. "I can't believe this is real."

Angela moved to the window, noting how the afternoon light filtered through the trees differently from this angle. She could see a narrow road winding through the snow toward what looked like smaller buildings nestled among the pines.

"I wonder where Jude's cabin is," she murmured without thinking.

Kiara shot her a knowing look. "Angela..."

"I know." Angela pressed her forehead against the cool glass. "I know it's complicated. I know he works for Duncan. I know I shouldn't even be thinking about him that way."

"But you are."

"But I am." The admission felt heavy on her tongue. "Which is ridiculous. I barely know him."

"Sometimes it doesn't take long," Kiara said gently. "And he was good to you. To both of us."

Angela turned from the window. "It doesn't matter. He's already stepped back. Did you see how he positioned himself downstairs? He's making it clear where his priorities lie."

"Maybe he's just being professional."

Angela wanted to believe that, but the way he'd looked at Annie instead of her when they'd first arrived still stung. It was selfish and stupid, especially since Jude had said he'd known Annie since she was born. Of course, he would be worried about how she might be doing with the changes.

She shook her head, trying to push the selfish hurt away. "I should focus on getting to know my family. That's why I'm here."

"That's one reason you're here," Kiara said. "But it's not the only reason you're allowed to be here. You don't have to prove yourself worthy of existing in this space, Angie."

Angela managed a weak smile. "When did you become so wise?"

"Someone had to balance out your tendency to overthink everything." Kiara grinned. "So, which room do you want?"

"This one," Angela said, gesturing around the blue-toned space. "The view is... peaceful."

"Perfect. I'll take the green room then." Kiara moved toward the door, then paused. "Are you going to be okay? I can stay if you need to talk more."

"I'm fine. I think I just need a few minutes to process everything."

After Kiara left, Angela sat on the edge of the bed and looked around the room that was now, apparently, hers. Everything was so pristine, so carefully arranged. She was almost afraid to touch anything.

Her suitcase sat at the foot of the bed, looking worn and shabby against the elegant surroundings. She unzipped it and began pulling out her few belongings, hanging them in the spacious closet that was larger than the bedroom she'd shared with Kiara back in Briar Hollow.

Her clothes looked lost in the vast closet, a meager collection that highlighted just how out of place she felt. Angela ran her fingers along the wooden hangers, wondering what Annie's closet looked like. Probably filled with designer clothes and shoes that cost more than Angela had made in a month at the bakery.

Sighing, she closed the closet door and turned her attention to unpacking the box. At the bottom lay her most precious possessions—her journals and Sandra's recipe book.

Despite everything, she couldn't bring herself to leave Sandra's book behind. Those recipes represented the only good memories she had from her childhood. The times when Sandra would let her help in the kitchen, teaching her to measure flour and knead dough.

Angela placed the books carefully on the nightstand before trying to figure out where to put everything. It didn't take long. Twenty minutes later, everything she owned had been put away, and the empty suitcase and box were stored in the closet.

Angela organized her few toiletries on the marble vanity in the ensuite bathroom, trying not to compare them to the luxury products already arranged there, apparently for her use. She caught sight of herself in the mirror—same face as Annie's, but somehow different. Less polished. Less sure.

The silence in the room felt oppressive. Back home—no, not home anymore. Back in Briar Hollow, she and Kiara had always shared space. There had always been the sound of Kiara turning pages or humming softly while she read. Now there was just... nothing.

Angela moved to the window again, watching as the afternoon sun began its descent toward the mountains. Movement caught her eye—a figure walking along one of the paths below. Even from this distance, she recognized Jude's confident stride.

Without thinking, she pressed her palm against the glass as if she could reach out to him. He paused on the path, turning to look toward the main house.

For a moment, she thought he might be looking directly at her window. But then he continued on his way, disappearing into the trees.

Angela stepped back from the window, wrapping her arms around herself. The loneliness felt overwhelming in a way she hadn't expected. She'd thought that finding her family would fill the empty spaces inside her. But instead, it seemed to highlight how adrift she truly felt.

All she could do was hope that the more time she spent there, the more at ease she'd feel. With or without Jude by her side.

I can do all things through Christ who gives me strength.

She had to remember that and not get too reliant on others to help her through all the changes she was sure to encounter in the days ahead.

CHAPTER EIGHT

Jude pushed back from his desk and got to his feet. Grabbing his leather jacket from the back of his chair, he shrugged it on, then left his office.

"I'm going to the main house," he said to the members of the team present in the security room.

Duncan had summoned him a short time ago, and Jude figured it had something to do with Angela and Kiara. They'd been there for just twenty-four hours, and Jude was a bit surprised that it had taken Duncan this long to call him for a meeting.

The cold air greeted him like a slap in the face as he left the security building. He strode across the distance between it and the main house, feeling no need to linger in the fresh air.

As he approached the back door, Jude wondered if he'd get the chance to see Angela. He wanted to know how she was adjusting to life there in Idaho, but things had shifted between them with their arrival at the estate.

He was no longer responsible for everything where she and Kiara were concerned. Now that she was back with her family, Jude was only responsible for her safety.

"Good morning, Jude," Duncan said when Jude reached his office.

Jude returned the greeting as he took his usual seat across the desk from the man. He wanted to ask how Angela was but bit his tongue. Duncan would tell him what he wanted Jude to know.

Duncan leaned back in his chair, fingers laced across his stomach. "I figured we need to have a discussion about Angelica and Kiara."

Jude nodded. "Is everything going okay so far?"

While he might have wanted specifics on Angela, he'd settle for some general info.

"It's an adjustment," Duncan said, his brow furrowing. "For all of us."

"I'm sure that's true."

"I hope that I'm handling this correctly for everyone, but there are some things we need to get going on, regardless." Duncan sat forward and flipped open a file on his desk. "I've made a list of all the things we need to do for the two of them."

Jude took the paper that Duncan held out to him and read it over.

- *Set up bank accounts*
- *Set them up with health insurance*
- *Get them driver's licenses*
- *Set up security for them*
- *Training for personal defense*
- *Weapons training*

Not everything on the list was Jude's responsibility, but several of the items were.

"I want you to take charge of helping them learn to drive, in addition to the security training," Duncan said. "Oh yes, I also want new phones for both of them with all the same apps you put on Annalisa and Benjamin's."

"And the trackers too?"

Duncan hesitated before he nodded. "Yes. For now, anyway. Until we have a better handle on Reynolds and his intentions."

Because his job was making sure the members of the Burke family were always safe, Jude believed in utilizing whatever was necessary to keep them that way. And while he felt that Annie and Benji were pretty well equipped to participate in keeping themselves safe, the same couldn't be said for Angela and Kiara. At least not yet.

"I want you to put Angelica and Kiara through everything An-nalisa and Benjamin have been through. In fact, it might be good to put those two through a refresher as well."

Jude nodded. It would probably be good for Angela and Kiara to see Annie doing what he was asking of them. Just to show them that all family members went through the same training.

"Do you have any concerns I've missed?" Duncan asked.

"What is your plan with regards to Angela and Kiara long-term?" Jude asked.

Duncan tapped his pen on the desk. "I'd like for Angelica to stay here on the estate."

"And Kiara?"

"I hope she stays as well. We need to consider her as part of the family," Duncan said, surprising Jude just a bit. "Clearly, she's been there for Angelica when we couldn't be. In Angelica's eyes, she's her family more than we are."

Jude agreed with that assessment, and he was glad that Duncan himself had seen that. It was good that the man hadn't been so blinded by Angela's return that he didn't take into consideration the life and relationships she'd built over the past twenty-four years.

"Will you build a place for them?" Jude asked.

He had a cabin of his own, as did Annie. And he had a feeling that since they'd struck out on their own in Briar Hollow, Angelica and Kiara wouldn't want to live with Duncan and Elizabeth. At least not forever.

"Yes. I think it's the only way to keep them here."

One of the things Jude appreciated about his job with Duncan was how often the two of them were on the same wavelength. It made it much easier for him to carry out his boss's wishes.

"I've got a call in to my architect," Duncan said. "He's coming here in the next week to meet with us. In the meantime, I plan to tell the girls... ladies to think of what they'd like in a home of their own."

"Maybe Annie could show them her place to give them an idea of what's possible."

Duncan nodded. "I'll see if she's willing to let them look around her cabin."

As much as Jude wanted this reunion to be successful for Angela, he was also aware of the impact it must be having on Annie. He was glad that Duncan wasn't trying to force a relationship between the twins.

"When do you want me to start the training?" Jude asked, setting the list back on Duncan's desk.

"As soon as possible. I'd like you to begin with the self-defense, but also I'd like you to get them behind the wheel of a car soon. Both of them need to be able to get around independently." Duncan paused, his expression growing more serious. "I just hope... Well, I feel like we need to handle Angelica carefully."

Jude thought he knew why the man thought that, but he needed him to voice the reason. "What do you mean?"

"She seems... fragile in a way that Annalisa never was. I can see it in how she carries herself, how she responds to direct questions. Whatever happened to her during those years away from us, has left marks." Duncan's jaw tightened. "I don't want to push too hard and risk her running."

The protective instinct that had been simmering in Jude's chest since he'd first met Angela flared to life. "Has she said something?"

"Not directly. But Elizabeth noticed she barely touched her dinner last night, and she asked three times if she was allowed to use the kitchen." Duncan's voice carried a note of pain. "My daughter asked permission to go somewhere in her own home. I feel like she's not viewing this as her home, which means she won't feel obliged to stay."

Jude's hands curled into fists, wishing Jim were within striking distance.

The picture Duncan was painting aligned with his own observations about Angela's behavior. The way she'd apologized for gripping his arm on the helicopter. How she'd seemed to brace herself whenever someone asked her a direct question.

"I'll be gentle with her," Jude assured him, not letting on how easy that would be because she'd already triggered his protective instincts. "But I can't be too easy with the training because we need to make sure they're prepared. I'll have to get them to understand the importance of it, and I think they'll be on board."

"Good thinking." Duncan rubbed his temple. "There's something else. I want you to be the primary point of contact for both of them during this transition period."

Jude's pulse quickened, though he kept his expression neutral. "Sir?"

"You're the one person here they already trust. Angelica especially seems comfortable with you." Duncan's gaze sharpened slightly. "I noticed how she looked for you yesterday when we were talking. And how she relaxed when you entered the room."

Heat crept up Jude's neck. Had that really happened? "I was just doing my job, bringing them here safely."

"I know that. But the fact remains that you've established a rapport with her that the rest of us don't have yet." Duncan leaned forward. "I'm not asking you to overstep any boundaries, Jude. I'm just asking you to help ease her transition by being available when she needs guidance or has questions."

The assignment should have felt like any other task Duncan had given him over the years. But the thought of spending more time with Angela, of being the person she turned to when she needed help, sent something warm spiraling through his chest.

It was an unfamiliar feeling. He'd never felt this way about any part of his job with the Burkes. He held a certain amount of affection—and possibly even love—for the Burke family.

But this felt... different, and he wasn't sure he liked it.

"Of course," Jude said. "Whatever you need me to do. I'll make sure she has the skills to protect herself if Jim decides to come after her."

"Just maybe nothing too intense at first. Let her build up her confidence."

"What about Kiara?"

"She seems more... resilient. Less guarded. You can probably push her a bit more." Duncan closed the file. "But they're a package deal, Jude. Whatever happens to one affects the other."

Jude understood that more than Duncan realized. He'd seen how Angela looked to Kiara for reassurance, how she drew strength from her presence. "I'll keep them together for the training."

"Good." Duncan stood, signaling the meeting was ending.

As Jude left Duncan's office, he headed toward the back of the house. The sound of quiet conversation drifted from the kitchen, and Jude paused in the hallway.

Through the partially open door, he could see Angela standing at the large island, her hands dusted with flour. She was explaining something to Kiara, who sat perched on one of the bar stools, chin propped in her hands.

"The key is to knead it until you get it to this smooth and satiny texture," Angela was saying, her voice more animated than Jude had heard it before. He liked the sound of it. "You've got to put your back into it."

Kiara laughed. "Pretty sure Sandra told me all this already, and it didn't stick. We both know you're the baker in this family."

"Only because you didn't want to do it," Angela retorted, but there was warmth in her tone. "Besides, it's therapeutic. Helps me think."

Jude found himself lingering in the doorway, drawn by the sight of Angela in her element. Her shoulders had lost their rigid tension, and her movements were confident as she worked the dough.

It was the first time he'd seen her look truly comfortable since he'd met her.

"Good morning," Jude said, stepping into the kitchen.

Both women looked up. Kiara offered a cheerful greeting, but Jude's attention was on Angela. Her eyes widened as her hands stilled on the dough.

"I hope it's okay that we're using the kitchen," she said quickly. "We didn't know where Elizabeth was to ask her, but Mrs. Stevens said it would be alright."

"Of course it's okay," Jude said, keeping his voice gentle. "This is your home now. You don't need permission to use anything here."

Angela's shoulders relaxed slightly, but Jude noticed she still had that cautious look in her eyes—the one that appeared whenever she wasn't sure of her footing.

"I wanted to make something to thank everyone for their hospitality," she explained, her flour-dusted fingers returning to the dough. "I thought cinnamon buns would be a good start."

Jude moved closer to the island, careful not to crowd her. "I'm sure they'll taste great. You worked in a bakery after all."

"She was the star there," Kiara interjected. "Patty took all the credit, but Angela was the one who kept that place going with her baking. People in the town loved it."

Angela shot her sister a look. "Kiara exaggerates."

"I really don't," Kiara said with a grin before sliding off her stool. "I'm going to check out the library. Will you be okay without me for a bit?"

The question wasn't directed at Jude, but at Angela, who hesitated before nodding. "I'll be fine."

After Kiara left, silence settled between them. Angela focused intently on rolling out the dough.

"Duncan asked me to talk to you," Jude said finally. "About some practical matters."

Angela glanced up. "Like what?"

"Well, things that will help you both get acclimated to life here," Jude explained. "That includes teaching you to drive, getting you familiar with the security protocols, and some self-defense training."

Angela's hands stilled again. "Self-defense?"

"Nothing too intense at first," Jude assured her. "Just some basics that everyone in the family needs to know."

"Is that really necessary?" Angela asked, her voice smaller now.

"Unfortunately, yes," Jude said, noting the way her knuckles had gone white when she gripped the rolling pin. "Given Duncan's high profile and the situation with Jim, it's important that you're able to protect yourself if necessary."

Angela's gaze dropped back to the dough. "I don't know if I'm cut out for that kind of thing."

Jude stepped closer, close enough to catch the scent of vanilla and cinnamon that seemed to envelop her. "You're stronger than you think, Angela. You survived over twenty years in a situation that would have broken a lot of people."

She looked up at him then, something vulnerable flickering in her blue-green eyes. "That's different. That was just... enduring."

"Sometimes enduring is more difficult than fighting back," Jude said quietly.

The words hung between them, and Jude saw something shift in her expression. Recognition, maybe. Understanding.

"Would you..." she started, then stopped, shaking her head. "Never mind."

"What is it?" Jude prompted.

Angela kept her gaze focused on her task. "Would you be the one teaching us? The self-defense, I mean."

"If you're comfortable with that."

"I am. I trust you." She lifted her head and gave him a quick smile. "I'm sure it's not a surprise that I feel safe with you."

That simple statement hit Jude like a physical blow. He'd spent years protecting the Burke family, but he'd never had one of them tell him that he made them feel safe. Not the way Angelica just had.

"That's what I'm here for," he said, his voice gruffer than he intended.

Angela nodded, returning her attention to the dough, but Jude caught the small smile that tugged at the corners of her mouth. She began spreading butter, then sprinkled cinnamon and sugar across the rolled surface with practiced ease.

"When would we start?" she asked.

"Soon. Duncan wants you to at least have a basic understanding of self-defense as soon as possible." Jude watched her work, noting the confidence in her movements when she was doing something familiar. Something that she liked. "We could begin with the driving lessons if you prefer. That might be less intimidating."

"I've never driven a car," Angela admitted, carefully rolling the dough into a log. "Jim said that it was only important that Craig knew how to drive."

Another piece of the puzzle that was Angela's past clicked into place for Jude. Their isolation had been complete—no television, no car, no connection to the outside world beyond what Jim and Sandra had allowed.

"It's not as hard as it looks," he said. "And I'm also a pretty patient teacher."

Angela began slicing the rolled dough into even portions. "Kiara's excited about learning. She's been talking about driving for years."

"What about you?"

She paused, knife halfway through the dough. "I'm terrified I'll crash into something expensive."

Jude couldn't help but smile at that. "We'll start on the roads here on the estate. No traffic, no pressure." He watched as she sliced the log into perfect spirals, each one uniform in size. "You have good hands for detail work."

Angela glanced up at him, surprise flickering across her features. "Thank you."

"Do you think you'll miss working at the bakery?" Jude asked, watching as she lined up each spiral on a baking tray.

"I don't know." She covered the filled tray with a white cloth, then set it to the side. "I love to bake, but it wasn't always fun at the bakery. Patty could be... demanding."

"Well, now you can choose where and when you want to bake."

A small smile tugged at the corners of her mouth. "Yes. I suppose I can."

The kitchen was filled with the warm scent of yeast and cinnamon as Angela moved to wash her hands at the sink. Jude found himself reluctant to leave, though he knew he should get back to his office.

"There's something else," he said, pulling out his phone. "Duncan wants you and Kiara to have new phones. With GPS tracking and some other security features."

Angela dried her hands on a towel, her expression growing uncertain again. "Tracking?"

"It's standard for everyone in the family," Jude explained quickly. "Just a precaution. If something happened, we'd be able to find you quickly."

She nodded, though he could see the wheels turning in her mind. "Like if Jim tried to take us back?"

"That's one scenario, yes." Jude wished he could soften the reality of it, but Angela needed to understand the potential threats. "Duncan takes the safety of his family very seriously."

"His family," Angela repeated quietly, as if testing the words. "It still doesn't feel real."

"It will," Jude said. "Give it time."

Angela leaned against the counter, her arms crossed over her chest. "Can I ask you something?"

"Of course."

"Yesterday, when we arrived... Annie seemed..." Angela appeared to struggle for the right words. "Do you think she resents me? For coming back?"

Jude considered his answer carefully. He'd noticed Annie's reserved behavior too, the way she'd seemed to keep her distance. But he also knew Annie well enough to understand the complexity of her feelings.

It was hard because, surprisingly, he'd developed a bond with Angela. He also had a bond—albeit completely different from the one he shared with Angela—with Annie.

Because of the gap in their ages, Annie had always been like a little sister to Jude. He'd been in her life since her birth, so he knew her, and he knew that this would be hard for her.

"I don't think she resents you," Jude said finally. "Though Annie doesn't remember you, she's always known *about* you. She grew up with your pictures around, hearing stories about her twin sister. But knowing about you and suddenly having you here are two different things."

Angela nodded slowly. "I just don't want to make things harder for her. For any of them."

"That's not your responsibility," Jude said, his voice gentle but firm. "You didn't ask to be taken from your family."

"It's just..." Angela trailed off, her fingers fidgeting with the edge of the towel. "I feel like I'm intruding. Like I've disrupted this perfect life they had."

Jude moved closer, though he was careful to maintain a respectful distance. "Their life hasn't been perfect without you, Angela. There's been a hole in this family for twenty-four years. Duncan never stopped looking for you, never stopped hoping."

Her eyes met his. "And Annie?"

"Annie's complicated," Jude admitted. "She's grown up with this ghost beside her—the sister she was supposed to have but didn't. That's a lot to process. Give her time."

Angela's shoulders relaxed slightly. "I just want to be somewhere... safe. To feel like I belong."

"You do belong," Jude said, his voice quiet. "More than you realize."

The kitchen fell silent except for the gentle hum of the refrigerator. Angela looked up at him, her eyes holding questions that she didn't ask.

"I should let you finish your baking," Jude said, taking a step back. "We can start the self-defense stuff tomorrow, after we get you and Kiara set up with your new phones. Just to put Duncan a little more at ease."

"Okay," Angela said, tucking a strand of hair behind her ear. "Though I'm still not convinced I won't be terrible at all of it."

"You'll do fine," Jude assured her. He was fairly confident in that assessment since Annie had picked it up quickly.

"Thank you." Angela glanced at the covered tray of cinnamon rolls. "Would you like to stay? They'll be ready in about an hour."

The invitation surprised him. "I should get back to work, but maybe I'll come back later."

A soft smile spread across Angela's face. "I'll save you some."

Jude was more pleased with that idea than he should have been. And much like the warmth he'd felt earlier, the feeling wasn't familiar.

When his one and only serious relationship had imploded in his early twenties, he'd decided that he didn't have the time or emotional energy to deal with another breakup.

Now it felt like the doorknob to the room where he'd shoved his capability to feel things like that had begun to slowly turn. He knew that he couldn't allow it to fully open.

Because feeling even just the beginning stages of those emotions was opening himself up to something that wasn't a good idea. He never wanted anything that distracted him from his job or blurred the line between his work and his personal life.

But emotions were stirring inside him that he couldn't seem to suppress, and there was a part of him that didn't want to.

"I've got to get back to work," Jude said. "I'll talk to you later."

Angela nodded, and the smile she gave him lingered in his mind after they said goodbye.

As he walked back to the security building, Jude found his thoughts drifting back to a time he never revisited if he could help it.

He'd tried his best to ignore that period of time. Back when he hadn't been so protective of his heart. When he'd viewed the women who'd walked away from his dad and Duncan as the exception, not the rule.

Unfortunately, he'd discovered over the years that maybe they'd been the rule. Even though Duncan had gone on to find love again with Elizabeth, Jude wasn't one hundred percent certain it would last. Though he hoped it would for Duncan's sake, and because he did really like Elizabeth.

He needed to keep in mind that he had a position with Duncan Burke that others would kill for. And while that position might require him to spend time with Angela, there were lines he shouldn't cross.

He was pretty sure Duncan wouldn't be on board for anything of that sort.

And he shouldn't be either, Jude reminded himself. He had to remember where his time and attention needed to be.

CHAPTER NINE

Although disappointed, Angela wasn't really surprised when Jude didn't return to sample the cinnamon rolls later that day. She had to remember that she was just another person whose security was his responsibility.

Anything he did with her was at the behest of Duncan. Her... father.

With a sigh, she sank down on the loveseat next to the window in her room and stared out at the forest around the mansion.

The trees swayed gently in the late afternoon breeze, their stark branches creating dancing shadows across the snowy lawn. The sun would soon be gone for the day, since the winter days in Idaho were short.

Angela traced her finger along the windowpane, feeling the cool glass against her skin. How strange to think that not that long ago, she'd never seen a house so grand. Never seen so much snow that lingered. Never known she was a Burke.

She picked up the worn, leather-bound book beside her. She'd found it in the kitchen, and Mrs. Stevens had said she could look through it. The book contained the handwritten recipes of Mrs. Stevens and her mother, going back several decades.

But she couldn't focus on the words. And it wasn't because she needed to concentrate to make out the words written in a spidery scrawl.

Her mind kept drifting back to Jude's serious expression, and the way his blue eyes had softened slightly when she'd asked him if he wanted to stick around for a cinnamon bun, even though he'd said he couldn't.

There had been something there, hadn't there? Or was she imagining a connection where none existed?

"You're being silly," she whispered to herself.

A man like Jude wouldn't be interested in someone like her—someone who barely understood the world she now found herself in. Besides, he worked for her father. There were probably rules about that sort of thing.

The sound of footsteps in the hallway made her heart quicken, even though she knew it wasn't likely to be Jude. In fact, it was Kiara, and when she stepped through the doorway, Angela straightened.

"Hey, Sis," Kiara said as she plopped down on the loveseat next to Angela. "What've you been up to? I smell the cinnamon rolls, so I assume they turned out okay."

"I think they did," Angela said. "They looked like the ones I made at the bakery."

"Do you miss it?" Kiara asked.

"Not the early mornings or Patty," Angela told her. "But I do miss all the baking I did."

"Cinnamon rolls weren't enough?"

"Just felt different." Angela shrugged. "But it will be fine. How about you? Do you miss your jobs?"

"Not the gas station," Kiara said with a laugh. "But I miss the library."

"What are we going to do here?" Angela rubbed her fingers on the leather cover of the recipe book. "Just... nothing?"

"Good question." Kiara sighed, and her easygoing attitude slipped away. "I don't know what we're supposed to do. Have you talked to your... to Duncan about it?"

"No. I don't know how to broach it with him."

"What about Jude?"

Warmth threatened to flood her cheeks, but she hoped that Kiara didn't notice. "What about him?"

"Have you talked to him about it?"

"Not about jobs or anything," she said. "But he did mention that he was going to be helping us learn self-defense."

"Self defense?"

"Yep, and driving."

Kiara's eyes glowed. "I'm excited about that."

"Also, we're supposed to be getting new phones."

Kiara looked down at her phone. They each had the cheapest model they could get, so the prospect of an updated one was appealing.

"Do you think we'll get the latest versions?"

"I don't know," Angela said. "They'll probably just give us whichever ones the tracker works on."

"Tracker? What tracker?"

"Oh. Well, Jude said they'll give us phones with tracker software on them so that if we're ever abducted or need help, they know right away where we are."

Kiara frowned. "I'm not sure I like the idea of that."

Angela understood Kiara's hesitation. The idea of being constantly monitored felt suffocating, even if it was for their protection. "I know what you mean. But after everything that's happened..."

"You're right," Kiara said, though she still looked uncomfortable. "I guess I'm still adjusting to the idea that we need that level of security."

They sat in comfortable silence for a moment, watching the shadows lengthen across the snow. Angela found herself thinking about how different their lives had become—from scraping by paycheck to paycheck to living in a mansion where their every move was monitored for their safety.

"Can I ask you something?" Kiara's voice was quieter now.

"Of course."

"Do you think we'll ever feel like we belong here? Like, is this really our life?"

Angela closed the recipe book and turned to face her sister fully. It was a question that had been weighing on her own heart. "I don't know. When I was baking earlier, it felt almost normal. But then I remember where I am, and it's like I'm playing dress-up in someone else's life."

"Exactly." Kiara pulled her knees up to her chest. "Everyone here—Duncan, Elizabeth, even the staff—is all so kind. But I feel like I'm waiting for the other shoe to drop."

"What do you mean?"

"Like they'll realize we don't fit and send us back to our old lives." Kiara paused, rubbing her hand against her heart. "Or maybe they'll just send me back to our old life."

An icy fear wound its way through Angela. She shook her head almost frantically. "No. I won't let that happen."

She couldn't imagine a worse scenario. If they truly thought that she'd stick around if they sent Kiara away, they were in for a rude awakening.

"We're a package deal, Kiki," she said.

Kiara shrugged. "We don't have to be. Maybe you'd rather have your new family."

"I want it all," Angela said. "I want you and my family." *And Jude,* a small voice in her head said. "But I've lived a lifetime without the Burkes. I wouldn't want to live the rest of my life without them, but I would. For you."

Kiara gave her a tremulous smile. "We might have had a bad childhood, but it brought us together. I don't want to lose you."

"You're what got me through that time." Angela shifted over to lean against Kiara's shoulder. "I can't imagine life without you."

"Well, hopefully we never have to experience that." Kiara reached up to pat her cheek. "We'll be fine."

It wasn't the first time Kiara had said those words to her, and Angela had believed them each and every time. They *would* be fine.

Because as long as her expectations were never too high, everything would be okay.

The next morning, she and Kiara left the mansion and made their way to the security building. The rural setting was similar to where they'd grown up, just on a much grander scale.

The homestead had had a rambling farmhouse with several outbuildings. However, they hadn't been anywhere near as well-kept as the buildings here. So far, in addition to the mansion, they'd seen a rec center that had a pool and basketball court, as well as a weight room.

This was their first visit to the security building, and Angela found her pulse was beating faster in anticipation of seeing Jude again. She tried to keep her steps slow and measured to match Kiara's, but inside, she wanted to rush along the road and through the door.

Soon enough, they reached the building. Kiara opened the door and held it for Angela.

"Hello."

"Hi," Kiara said, smiling at the woman who had greeted them.

"You must be Kiara and Angela," she said, holding out her hand. "I'm Dawn."

"Are you a bodyguard?" Kiara asked as they each shook hands with her.

"Yes." Dawn led them through a door into a large space where there were large monitors on the wall and several more people. "I provide security for Annie."

Before she could respond to that revelation, Jude came through a doorway on the opposite side of the room. He wore a white button-down shirt tucked into a pair of black slacks.

"Good morning, ladies," Jude said with a nod. "Let me introduce you to the rest of the team."

There were two women and four men present, though Jude mentioned that several more were scattered around the estate.

Some of the ones present in the room were bodyguards for the other members of the Burke family.

Angela wondered if she and Kiara would be assigned bodyguards of their own. It was weird even to consider.

"Come on through to my office," Jude said. "I've got your phones there."

Angela followed Jude into the room, trying not to notice how the crisp white shirt stretched across his broad shoulders or how his dark hair curled slightly at the nape of his neck.

His office was meticulously organized—a large desk dominated the space, with several monitors displaying what appeared to be security camera feeds from around the property. A bookshelf stood against one wall, filled with books, but Angela couldn't read their titles.

"Have a seat," Jude gestured to the two chairs facing his desk. As they settled in, he reached into a drawer and pulled out two sleek boxes, then slid them across the desk. One to each of them. "These are yours."

Kiara immediately opened hers, her eyes widening at the sight of the sleek device. "This is the latest version. We could barely afford phones from four years ago."

Angela hesitated before opening her box. "Thank you," she said softly, meeting Jude's eyes. "About the tracker—"

"It's standard protocol for all family members," Jude interrupted, his voice professional but not harsh. "The tracking app is only used in emergency situations or if you press the panic button. Your privacy is still respected."

He looked directly at Kiara as he said this last part, making Angela wonder if he'd somehow overheard their conversation from yesterday.

"Is the tracking always on?" Kiara asked, voicing what Angela was thinking.

"Yes," Jude said without apology. "It's non-negotiable for all Burke family members. Even Duncan has it on his phone."

"So you know where everyone is all the time?" Angela asked as she gripped the box.

Jude's expression softened almost imperceptibly when he looked at her. "Not personally. The system keeps track of all of the locations, and we only access that information if we absolutely have to."

Angela nodded, trying to understand this new reality where her movements would be monitored, even if it was just by a computer.

"There are other security measures as well," Jude continued, his voice low and steady. "The phones have encrypted communications, and a direct line to our security team." He tapped the screen of his own phone, demonstrating. "One button, and we know where you are."

Angela's fingers traced the edge of her box, still unopened. The technology felt foreign in her hands—not just the expensive phone, but what it represented. Protection. Surveillance. A tether to this new family she barely knew.

"What if we go somewhere without our phones?" Kiara asked, already exploring the device's features.

Jude's expression didn't change, but something in his eyes hardened. "Don't."

The simple command hung in the air between them. Angela felt a chill run through her at the seriousness in his tone.

"That's it? Just 'don't'?" Kiara pressed, her brow furrowing.

"For now, yes." Jude leaned forward slightly. "Your safety isn't something we take lightly. Not after what happened to Angela and Annie."

Nodding, Angela finally opened her box, carefully removing the sleek device. It felt substantial in her palm, nothing like the cheap phone she'd been using. "So we're basically prisoners here? Just with nicer accommodations?"

Jude's jaw tightened. "No. You are family members who need protection."

"And you don't think if one of us is kidnapped that the first thing the kidnappers will do is get rid of our phone?" Kiara asked.

"That's why we're also in the process of getting you each some jewelry—most likely a watch—that will contain trackers."

Angela looked up at Jude with wide eyes. "You're not messing around."

"No, Duncan isn't taking any chances with his family," Jude said. "His increased wealth has only made him more of a target. I'm sorry if you feel this is suffocating, but it's just how things are when you're part of the Burke family."

"And we don't have the option of *not* being part of the family," Kiara said dryly.

"Well, *you* do," Jude told her. His words might have felt a bit harsh, but his tone wasn't. "Unfortunately, Angela has an undeniable connection to the Burkes now. And though Duncan has managed to keep Annie hidden for a lot of years, because of Cole, she's been resisting being kept secluded recently. So it seems that perhaps the revelation of that connection is inevitable."

Angela felt like she had gone from a small pond to an expansive ocean, and she couldn't see the shore. Her new life was huge and complex, and she didn't know if she'd ever figure out how to live as the daughter of such a wealthy man.

Did she wish that she'd never allowed Kiara to make that phone call to Cole Halverson? Did she wish she'd never gotten the answers she'd thought she wanted?

Looking at Jude, she wasn't so sure. So far, meeting him had been the highlight of everything.

Sure, she had ended up with a family. A good family, by all accounts. But she didn't feel connected to them yet.

In fact, she still felt very much like she was an outsider. And if she felt that way, she could only imagine how much more Kiara did.

"When do we start the self-defense training?" she asked, wanting to change the subject.

Jude's eyes met hers, and for a moment, Angela thought she saw something flicker there. But it was gone so quickly she might have imagined it.

"We can start tomorrow morning if that works for you both. Nine o'clock in the gym at the rec center."

"That's fine," Kiara said, still engrossed in exploring her new phone.

Angela nodded her agreement, trying not to think about what self-defense training with Jude might entail. Spending time together. Her cheeks warmed at the thought.

"There's something else," Jude said, his voice lowering slightly. "Duncan wants me to teach the two of you how to shoot."

Angela felt her mouth go dry. "Shoot? As in guns?"

There had been plenty of weapons around them growing up, but the only ones allowed to touch them had been Jim and Craig.

"Yes." Jude's expression remained neutral, but his eyes seemed to track her reaction carefully. "Firearms training is part of the security protocol for all family members."

Kiara looked up from her phone, suddenly interested. "I've never even held a gun before. Jim wouldn't let us touch them. Probably figured we might be tempted to turn one on him."

Jude's expression darkened for a moment before clearing again.

"We'll start with safety fundamentals and work our way up," Jude said. "The indoor range is in the basement of this building."

Angela pulled her arms close to her sides as she clutched her phone in her hands, feeling a chill that had nothing to do with the temperature. "I don't know if I'm comfortable with that."

Jude's gaze softened almost imperceptibly as he held hers. "It's not about comfort, Angela. It's about being prepared."

The way he said her name made something flutter in her chest, despite her unease about the subject.

"When would we start that?" she asked, trying to keep her voice steady.

"After you've had a few self-defense sessions. No rush. Take today to get familiar with your new phones. Dawn can help with any questions about the features."

"And we're going to have driving lessons?" Kiara asked.

"Yes, we'll start those soon too."

"So much to learn," Angela mused, once again feeling overwhelmed.

"It's a lot," Jude agreed. "But we'll take it one day at a time."

As they rose to leave, Jude cleared his throat. "Angela."

She paused, heart quickening as Kiara continued toward the door.

Jude glanced toward the door that Kiara had disappeared through, then back to Angela. "The cinnamon rolls yesterday—I wanted to apologize for not coming back. I got caught up in a security briefing that ran late."

Relief flooded through her, followed quickly by embarrassment at how much his explanation mattered to her. "Oh, you don't need to apologize. I understand you're busy."

"I'd like to try one sometime, if the offer still stands."

Angela felt her cheeks warm. "Of course. I could make a fresh batch anytime."

"Good." His lips quirked up in what might have been the beginning of a smile. "And Angela? In the training we're going to do—if you ever feel uncomfortable or need to take a break, just say so. This isn't about pushing you past your limits. It's about helping you get comfortable defending yourself."

The gentleness in his voice made her chest tighten. "Thank you. That means a lot."

For a moment, they stood there looking at each other, and Angela felt that same flutter of connection she'd experienced the day before. Then Jude stepped back, and Angela realized she might very well be alone in feeling that connection.

"I'll see you tomorrow morning."

Feeling a little sad, Angela nodded and hurried to catch up with Kiara, who was examining the security monitors with Dawn.

"Ready to go?" Kiara asked, pocketing her new phone.

"Yes," Angela said, then followed her sister out of the security building.

Crisp winter air greeted them, a welcome relief from the warmth that had flooded her cheeks during her conversation with Jude.

"So," Kiara said as they walked back toward the mansion. "What did Mr. Tall-Dark-and-Serious want to talk to you about?"

"Nothing important," Angela replied, trying to sound casual. "Just apologizing for missing the cinnamon rolls yesterday."

Kiara shot her a knowing look. "Mmhmm. And that's why you're blushing."

"I'm not blushing."

"If you say so." Kiara looped her arm through Angela's. "But for what it's worth, I think he likes you."

"Don't be ridiculous," Angela said, though her heart skipped at the suggestion. "He's just doing his job."

"His job is to apologize for missing pastries? Interesting career choice."

Angela couldn't help but laugh. "Stop it. He's just being polite."

They continued to walk in silence, their boots crunching on the snow-dusted path. The mansion loomed ahead, grand and imposing against the winter sky.

Would it ever feel like home? Would its beautiful walls feel less like a prison one day?

She'd wanted a home. A place of safety. She wanted to believe this could be that for her and Kiara.

Jude's handsome face came more sharply into focus in her mind.

She'd never had much interest in men. It probably wasn't too surprising, considering the type of men she'd been around for much of her life.

But now she'd met men who seemed to be completely different from Jim and Craig. Even Julian, whom she hadn't spent a lot of time with yet, seemed to be a decent man.

A father and brother in direct contrast to the father and brother she'd been raised with.

And then there was Jude. A man unlike any she'd ever known before. A man of quiet strength, who could easily hurt someone, and yet she was confident he would never hurt her. She felt completely safe with him.

It was foolish, she knew, to even look at Jude as anything but a man who worked for Duncan... her father.

But there was something about him that drew her to him. She didn't have anything to offer him, however. Of that, she had no doubt.

Still, the yearning of her heart for things she'd never had before was stronger than it had ever been.

Safety.

Security.

Peace.

Love.

Please, God, help me to not set my heart on something that isn't your plan for me.

CHAPTER TEN

Jude closed his Bible and the devotional book he'd started at the beginning of the year and set them aside. Each year, he tried to find a devotional that would guide him through his daily quiet time.

He'd chosen this particular study because it was for men and offered insight into the things he was trying—with God's help—to pursue in his life.

Self control. Discipline. Humility.

They were all qualities his dad had not only impressed upon Jude, but he'd strived to live them out in his own life. Jude knew that part of why he'd pursued those specific qualities was to honor his dad. But his dad had always told him, "Don't do it for me. Do it for God."

So that was the reminder that played in his mind as he went through each day now: *Do it for God.*

And because of his desire to honor God, his favorite verse was Colossians 3:17. *And whatsoever you do, in word or deed, do all in the name of the Lord Jesus, giving thanks to God and the Father by Him.*

Some might say his life was stark and too rigid, but it was what worked for him. His focus, of course, was on his job, and he wanted to do his best and never give Duncan a reason to question his decision to give him the job of head of security.

Now, his focus was on Angela and Kiara. At Duncan's request, of course. He needed to remember that.

After he finished his breakfast of bacon and eggs with a side of avocado, he took a few minutes to clean up the kitchen before he headed to the security building.

The morning was cold, and the UTV barely had time to warm up before he pulled into the garage of the building.

"Morning," one of the men in front of the monitors greeted him. Andrew was Benji's primary bodyguard and would be leaving shortly to take the teen to school.

"Good morning," Jude replied. "Any updates?"

He already knew that nothing major had happened, because if there had been a significant issue, he would have been called. He was never truly off duty.

"All good," Andrew reported. "We need to check a couple of the perimeter cameras, though. They've been flickering."

Jude frowned. "Someone trying to hack them?"

"We did a scan, but nothing showed up," one of the other men present stated.

"Where are they on the maintenance schedule?"

"They're due for maintenance in the next round."

"Move that up," Jude said. "I want to make sure that they're operating as they should."

"Will do."

Jude went to his office and put his duffel bag on a chair. It contained the clothes he'd change into for the self-defense training. Shrugging out of his wool peacoat, he hung it on the coat rack in the corner of the room.

He rolled up the sleeves of his long sleeve button down as he settled into his chair. The first thing to do was check his email for a report from the people he'd hired, at Duncan's request, to keep an eye on Jim and Craig.

Finding the expected email, he skimmed over it. His gaze snagged on a portion.

Vincent went to a bar where Craig was hanging out and made contact with him. The more Craig drank, the more he talked, expressing great frustration that his sisters had disappeared. It seems at this point that he doesn't know where the women are.

We're hoping that Vincent will be able to continue the contact. He gave subtle hints that he was interested in the same things as Jim and Craig — weapons, homesteading, living off the grid.

Jude allowed a rare smile to cross his face. It was good to hear that they seemed unaware of where Angela and Kiara were. Jim probably had a good idea of who they were with, given Annie's recent appearance in public. Hopefully, he didn't know *where* she was.

Jim wasn't dumb. He'd proven that when he'd worked on the security team. But he lacked Duncan's resources, so it was possible he hadn't figured out where Angela and Kiara were.

The best-case scenario would be if Vincent could strike up a friendship with Craig that would give them an insight into what was happening with the two men. So far, Jim hadn't been spotted off the homestead—the fortified homestead—and Jude was sure that was because the guy was lying low.

The question was... would he hunker down on the homestead? Or would he go on the run?

They were working with the police and the FBI to see about having Jim arrested for kidnapping. Given that he had kidnapped a minor and never released her, there was no statute of limitations.

He had a feeling that the feds would also be interested in pressing weapons charges.

Jude didn't care about that. He just wanted to make sure that Jim was behind bars for the rest of his life.

If Jude had his way, Jim would just... disappear. There was no question about his guilt. As far as Jude was concerned, there was no *innocent until proven guilty* in Jim's case. He was guilty. End of story.

But he wouldn't take things into his own hands. That went against everything he believed in.

However, if Jim somehow ended up dead as a result of his interactions with law enforcement, Jude wouldn't shed a tear.

Craig, he didn't have much of an opinion on. He hadn't been involved in the kidnapping. However, from the little Angela had said, the man hadn't treated her or Kiara well, so maybe he needed to disappear as well.

Jude took a moment to type out a reply, then forwarded the email to Duncan to keep him updated.

Though Jude was responsible for the guys currently down in Briar Hollow, Duncan had taken the lead with the authorities.

He took a few minutes to read through the reports for the night, then checked over the schedule for the next two weeks.

"Morning, Jude."

He glanced up to see Annie in his doorway, her dog Nyla at her side. Getting to his feet, he gave her a smile. "Good morning, Annie. How are you doing?"

"I'm fine."

The smile she gave him was small, and he thought that perhaps she'd just lied to him.

"Have a seat," he said, gesturing to the chairs across from him.

He waited until she'd taken a seat, then settled back in his chair. "Thank you for being willing to help with the self-defense training. I think Angela and Kiara will be able to picture it better with you and Dawn also doing it."

Annie nodded. "That makes sense."

"Are you sure you're okay with this?" Jude didn't want her to feel obliged, especially since he sensed that she was really struggling with things.

He thought about probing a bit more, but it really wasn't his place. Yes, they'd known each other for a long time. However, he'd never been a close confidante of hers.

In fact, recently, they'd been at odds more often than not. The older Benji had gotten, the more Annie seemed willing to push against the security restrictions that had been placed on her and Benji.

"I'm fine to help," she said, though she didn't look completely happy about it.

Jude wasn't sure if that was because she was struggling or just her general feelings about the self-defense classes he'd forced on her.

Before Jude could say anything more, he spotted Kiara and Angela approaching his door.

"Are we interrupting?" Angela asked, her gaze going from him to Annie and back again.

"Not at all," Jude assured her. "Just talking to Annie about helping with the self-defense training."

"We're all ready," Kiara said, spreading her arms. "Dressed per your instructions."

"Good. Then we might as well get to work."

When Jude got to his feet, so did Annie. He grabbed his jacket and then picked up his duffel bag.

"We're heading over to the rec center," Jude told Dawn. "Are you joining us?"

"I sure am," she said. "I'll drive over with Annie."

Jude nodded, then led the way to the garage. He, Angela, and Kiara got in his UTV, while Dawn and Annie got in one of the other smaller ones.

If the weather had been nicer, they could have walked. But since Angela and Kiara weren't used to the colder weather yet, it was better to take the UTVs.

As they drove the short distance to the rec center, Jude found himself acutely aware of Angela sitting in the passenger seat beside him. She was quiet, her hands folded in her lap, and he could sense her nervousness about the upcoming training.

"You okay?" he asked, glancing at her briefly before returning his attention to the narrow road ahead.

"Just a little nervous," she admitted. "I've never done anything like this before."

"That's normal," he said, his voice gentler than usual. "We'll start slow."

From the back seat, Kiara leaned forward. "Will we be learning the same things Annie did?"

"Yes," Jude replied. "That's why I've asked her and Dawn to come help out."

When they reached the rec center, Jude parked the UTV and led them inside. The gymnasium where Benji spent a lot of time practicing basketball was spacious with high ceilings and polished wooden floors. Mats had already been laid out in the center of the room.

"First things first," Jude said, setting down his duffle bag. "We're going to talk about awareness. The best defense is avoiding dangerous situations altogether."

He waited for Dawn and Annie to join them, then left Dawn explaining situational awareness while he went to get changed in the changing room. His plan was to let Dawn and Annie be the ones to physically work with Angela and Kiara as much as possible. However, he also wanted to show them that they were capable of taking down anyone, even someone of his stature.

Dawn and Annie had both set him onto his back more than once. Jude wanted Angela and Kiara to aspire to do the same.

When Jude returned to the gym floor in workout clothes, he found the women in a loose circle. For a brief moment, his gaze met Angela's, but then she turned her attention back to Dawn.

"The goal isn't to make you paranoid," Dawn was saying. "It's to make awareness second nature."

Jude stepped onto the mat next to Dawn, and at her nod, he said, "Awareness is crucial, but sometimes a situation escalates despite your best efforts to avoid it. That's when you need physical skills."

He positioned himself in the center of the mat. "Annie and Dawn are going to demonstrate some basic techniques. I'll be playing the role of the attacker."

Annie stepped forward, a determined look on her face. She was slight compared to Jude, which made her the perfect person to show that size wasn't everything.

"The first thing to understand is that your attacker will almost always have a physical advantage," Jude explained. "But you have other advantages—surprise, leverage, and targeted strikes."

He lunged toward Annie, reaching for her arm. In a fluid motion that happened almost too quickly to follow, Annie sidestepped, grabbed his wrist, and used his momentum against him. Before Jude knew it, he was looking up at the ceiling, the impact of hitting the mat knocking the wind out of him.

"Are you okay?" Angela asked, coming to look down at him.

"He's fine," Annie said as she stood on his other side. "This isn't the first time I've put him on his back."

"Really?" Angela sounded incredulous.

"Really. He made me practice over and over again until I was capable of doing that."

The women stepped back as Jude got back up to his feet. "Annie's correct. She has done it many, many times. And now, her reaction to me approaching her is second nature. Instinct."

"The most important thing about self-defense," Dawn added, "is believing you can protect yourself. Regardless of your opponent's size. Many attackers count on your hesitation or fear."

Jude nodded. "That's right. One of the reasons I asked Annie and Dawn to be here today was to show you what's possible."

He positioned himself in the center of the mat again. "Annie? Up for another demonstration?"

Annie stepped forward with the confidence of someone who'd been through the exercises many times before.

"An attacker will often grab you from behind," Jude explained. "I'm going to demonstrate, and then Annie will show you how to counter."

He placed his arms around Annie in a bear hug, pinning her arms to her sides. For a moment, he glanced at Angela. Her expression was a mixture of concern and intense focus.

"Ready?" he asked Annie.

She nodded, and in one fluid motion, she stomped her heel down on his instep, dropped her weight to create space, then twisted and drove her elbow back toward his solar plexus, stopping just short of contact.

Jude released her immediately. "Perfect. Again, we can see that despite her size, she has the ability to maneuver herself into a position where she has the opportunity to break free. The goal isn't necessarily to win a fight. It's to create enough space and time to escape." He looked directly at Angela as he spoke. "Run. Get to safety. Get help. That's always the primary objective."

Angela nodded, though her hands were still clasped tightly in front of her. The demonstration should have been reassuring for Angela and Kiara, but Jude could see the tension in Angela's shoulders. The way she held herself was as if preparing to flee.

"Let's start with some basic stances," Dawn said, stepping forward. "Angela, would you like to go first?"

"I... okay." Angela moved onto the mat, her movements cautious.

"Stand with your feet shoulder-width apart," Dawn instructed. "Good. Now bend your knees slightly. You want to be balanced but ready to move."

Jude watched as Angela adjusted her stance, noting how she seemed to shrink in on herself despite Dawn's encouraging tone. He'd seen this before—people who'd lived with fear for so long that the idea of fighting back felt foreign, almost wrong.

"Perfect," Dawn said. "Now, Angela, I want you to practice a simple palm strike. Target is here." She gestured to the center of the padded target she held in front of her. "Using the heel of your palm, drive up and through."

Angela hesitated, her hand barely making contact when she attempted the strike.

"Harder," Dawn encouraged. "Remember, this person is trying to hurt you."

Angela tried again, with slightly more force, but Jude could see her holding back.

"May I?" he asked, stepping closer.

Handing him the target, Dawn stepped aside as Jude approached Angela, keeping his movements slow and deliberate.

"I know this feels unnatural," he said, his voice low enough that only she could hear. "But think about Kiara. If someone was threatening her, what would you do?"

Something flashed in Angela's blue-green eyes—a protective instinct that Jude had been counting on.

"I'd do whatever it took," she said quietly.

"That's the mindset. This isn't about aggression. It's about protection. Yours and those you care about."

He positioned himself in front of her, holding up the padded target. "Try again. This time, think about creating distance between a threat and someone you love."

Angela took a deep breath, adjusted her stance as Dawn had shown her, and struck the pad with the heel of her palm. The impact was solid enough to mildly jar Jude.

"Good," he said, approval in his voice. "Much better."

A small smile tugged at Angela's lips, and Jude felt something shift in his chest—pride, but also something warmer he didn't want to focus on right then.

He gestured for her to try again, and then again. Each time her confidence inched up.

"Now it's Kiara's turn," Dawn called after a few minutes, gesturing for Kiara to join them on the mat.

Unlike her sister, Kiara approached with barely contained enthusiasm. "I've been waiting for this my whole life," she said, bouncing lightly on her toes.

"Glad to hear it," Dawn said with a laugh.

Jude gave the padded target back to Dawn, then stepped out of their way.

As Jude watched Kiara throw herself into the training with enthusiasm, he couldn't help but notice the stark contrast between the sisters. Where Angela approached with caution, Kiara seemed to have been waiting for permission to fight back her entire life.

"Whoa, easy there," Dawn laughed as Kiara's palm strike nearly knocked her off balance. "Save some for the actual attackers."

After a few more strikes, Dawn motioned for Annie and Angela to join them. "Let me show you both a technique that works particularly well for women. This is about using your opponent's weight against them."

For the next little while, Jude observed from a few feet away, arms crossed over his chest. Though Annie was participating in the training, she was definitely not her usual self. During the moments when Dawn was explaining things to Angela and Kiara, she was distracted, often pulling out her phone.

Jude was concerned, but he didn't know what to do to help her. He wondered whether he should have a conversation with Duncan about it.

But was that his place? Her aloofness obviously wasn't a security concern, but he really did view her more as a younger sister than just part of the job.

Annie wasn't the only one he was struggling to maintain a professional relationship with.

His gaze kept drifting to Angela and noticing the way she bit her lower lip in concentration. How her eyes widened when Annie demonstrated a particularly effective move. How at times she seemed to be talking to herself. Perhaps psyching herself up.

"Jude, we need you again," Dawn called, interrupting his thoughts.

He stepped forward, mentally chastising himself for his wandering attention. "What do you need me to do?"

"Go on the attack," Dawn said. "I think we need to practice breaking holds of someone larger now."

For the next hour, Jude played the role of attacker while Dawn and Annie taught Angela and Kiara various defensive techniques. By the end, their faces were flushed from exertion, but they looked pleased with their progress. Especially Kiara.

He was proud of Angela for continuing to engage in the training, even though it was clear that she wasn't entirely comfortable with it the way Kiara was.

"You both did well for your first session," Jude said as they took a water break. "We'll practice again tomorrow."

"Really?" Kiara asked, excitement clear in her voice despite her fatigue. "Daily lessons?"

"For the first little while, yes," Jude confirmed. "Then we'll scale back these practices and move on to something else. The more you practice, the more instinctive these movements become."

"Driving next, right?" Kiara asked eagerly.

"Yes, driving."

"I can't wait to learn," Kiara said.

Angela took a long drink from her water bottle, her gaze flicking between Jude and Annie. "Will you both be teaching us the self-defense stuff each time?"

"I should be here most of the time," Jude said, then glanced at Annie, who was checking her phone again. "Annie?"

She looked up, slightly startled. "Sorry, what?"

"Will you be able to help with training tomorrow?"

Annie hesitated. "Maybe." She slipped her phone into her pocket. "I need to go now, but I'll let you know later about tomorrow."

"I'll go with you," Dawn said.

"No need," Annie told her with a wave of her hand. "I'm just going home."

Dawn glanced at Jude, who just gave a single nod, accepting Annie's desire to be on her own. Since they were on the estate, she was safe.

Jude watched her go, making note again of her distance. Something was definitely going on with her.

"How did we do?" Angela asked as she approached him while Dawn and Kiara discussed a particular technique a few feet away.

Letting thoughts of Annie go for the moment, Jude gave Angela a smile. "Better than I expected for a first session. Especially you."

"Me?" Surprise colored her voice.

"Yes. I could see how uncomfortable you were at the beginning, but you pushed through it. That takes courage."

A flush spread across her cheeks that had nothing to do with exertion. "It doesn't feel like courage. It feels like... survival."

Jude was drawn to her strength. To the way she'd found the determination to fight back despite everything she'd endured. "Sometimes those are the same thing."

Their gazes held for a moment longer than professional courtesy would dictate, and Jude felt that familiar tightening in his chest. He needed to step back, maintain boundaries. But something about Angela made that increasingly difficult.

"We should head back," he said, his voice rougher than intended.

"Of course." Angela stepped away, the moment broken. However, Jude caught the flash of disappointment in her expression before she turned toward Kiara.

As they gathered up their things, Jude couldn't shake the feeling that his carefully ordered world was shifting in ways he hadn't expected. And he wasn't sure how to handle it.

Ignoring it seemed easiest, but he had a feeling it wouldn't be effective in the long run. The draw to Angela would just continue to grow.

The drive back to the mansion was quiet, with Angela staring out the window at the snow-covered landscape. Jude found himself stealing glances at her profile, noting the way her hair caught the winter light filtering through the windshield.

"Thank you," she said suddenly, breaking the silence. "For being patient with me today."

"I learned from training Annie, Elizabeth, and Benji that being patient is the best approach. This is important, so I'll do whatever is necessary to equip you to take care of yourself."

"Will Kiara and I have bodyguards like Annie has Dawn?"

"Yes." Jude wasn't sure who would have the job permanently yet, but they had enough staff to cover them temporarily.

"Do you bodyguard?"

"Not so much anymore," he said. "Before I became head of security, I was part of Duncan's security entourage. I was the leader of that team for about a year before he promoted me to head of all security. The only time I travel with him now is when he goes to certain parts of the world. For safety's sake, a bigger security team travels with him, and I'm usually part of that."

"He must really trust you."

"Yes." There was no doubt of that, since Jude knew that Duncan would never put someone in charge of his family's safety that he didn't trust completely. "And I don't take that trust for granted. He's been very good to me."

"Did you ever want to work somewhere else?"

"Nope. I saw my dad's love for his job, first as a cop and then working for Duncan. I wanted that same passion for whatever I did, and I've found that here."

Kiara had been quiet for the drive to the house, and when Jude glanced back at her, he saw she was focused on her phone.

Jude swung the UTV around so that the ladies could exit closest to the back door of the house.

"Thanks for the lesson," Kiara said as she slipped from the UTV. "It was a lot of fun."

Flashing him a quick smile, she headed for the door while Angela moved more slowly.

"I guess I'll see you tomorrow," she said as she stood outside the UTV.

"Yes. You will."

He wanted to ask her how she planned to spend the rest of her day, but he held his tongue. It was none of his business, he reminded himself.

Duncan had outlined what his responsibility was when it came to Angela, and it had nothing to do with chitchatting with her about what she was doing with her time. He had to remember that.

Her expression was serious as she gave him a little wave, then turned and headed for the back door. She didn't look back before disappearing inside the house.

Jude stared at the closed door for a long moment before turning the wheel of the UTV and heading for the security building.

Back in his office a few minutes later, Jude tried to focus on his work, but it was nearly impossible. His mind was caught up in Angela, and he couldn't figure out what it was exactly that drew him to her.

It wasn't a physical thing. Because if it was a physical draw, he would have been attracted to Annie, and that had never, ever been the case.

He'd never dwelt on what kind of woman might be his type, so he didn't have a checklist to hold up against Angela.

Maybe if she hadn't been his employer's daughter. Maybe if she hadn't been over a decade his junior. Maybe if she hadn't been in the middle of a huge upheaval in her life.

Maybe then he might have considered seeing where things might go because he had a feeling that she had some sort of draw to him as well.

But it was all irrelevant because she was all of those things, and nothing could change them.

He had to stay focused on his job, regardless of how drawn he felt to her. He was responsible for keeping her safe and equipping her with the skills that her father demanded she have in order to survive in his world.

Nothing more.

Maybe if he told himself that enough, it would eventually sink in sufficiently to squash the feelings for her that had taken root in his heart. Maybe... but he didn't think so.

CHAPTER ELEVEN

"We need to talk about your mother," Duncan said.

Angela blinked in surprise. Not much had been said about the woman since they'd arrived at the estate. From the little she'd been able to glean, Julian had a relationship with her, but Annie did not.

It was an odd situation, and she'd wanted more details but didn't feel like it was her place to ask.

She was still struggling to think of anyone but Jim and Sandra as her parents. Even Duncan, who had been beyond nice, didn't automatically come to mind when someone referred to her dad.

If she was being honest, Angela was glad to have just one new parent to deal with at a time. But it seemed that it was time for her to meet her other one.

Julian was currently sprawled in an armchair, nursing a glass filled with an alcoholic beverage. No one else seemed to drink, and definitely no one else got drunk the way Julian did.

He was a handsome man with tousled dark blonde hair. It was hard to see a likeness to him in her or Annie. Where they had a much more average appearance, Julian had high cheekbones accentuated by striking gray eyes and a dimple in his chin.

Benji had made frequent references to Julian and his many girlfriends, and Angela could see why he'd be popular with the ladies. She still hadn't really gotten to know him. But so far, he'd been kind in his interactions with her and Kiara.

"It's about time," Julian said. "It doesn't feel right to keep Mom in the dark about Angela coming home."

"I understand why you feel that way," Duncan said. "But I felt it prudent to give Angelica a bit of time to adjust to this change in her life before bringing your mother into the mix."

Duncan's expression was tight, and Angela got the feeling that he didn't like having to deal with his ex-wife any more than absolutely necessary.

"Do you feel prepared to meet her, Angelica?" Duncan asked. "I would like to respect your feelings in that regard."

It was curiosity more than anything that had Angela nodding. "I think I'd like to meet her."

"She wasn't nice to Annie," Benji blurted out.

Angela looked at him with a frown. "What do you mean?"

"Benjamin," Duncan cautioned.

"She deserves to know the type of person she is."

"It's none of your business, Benny. She's not *your* mother," Julian said, sitting forward in his chair. "So keep out."

Angela had noticed that Benji was very protective of Annie. More so than Julian.

Annie was absent from this conversation, and Angela wondered if that was because what Benji had said was true.

"What does he mean?" Angela asked, directing her question to Julian.

She didn't think the teen would say something like that without a reason. And if Julian didn't want Benji discussing it, then he could answer her question.

Julian stared down at his drink. "She had a hard time seeing Annie, knowing that you were gone. Annie was a reminder of what she'd lost."

Angela felt an ache sprout in her heart. "She rejected her?"

"Something like that." Julian sighed as he lifted his glass to take a drink. "But she's trying to make amends now."

"Too little, too late," Benji murmured with a scowl.

Angela looked at Duncan, curious to see if he'd add anything.

"When we divorced, the agreement for shared custody only applied to Julian. I was given sole custody of Annalisa."

The weight of this revelation settled over Angela as she tried to process what Duncan was saying—her birth mother had willingly relinquished custody of Annie while keeping Julian. The implication made her chest tighten.

She'd been missing from her family's life, but Annie had experienced a different kind of absence—a mother who couldn't bear to look at her. Both losses were painful in their own way.

"I don't understand," she said quietly. "How could a mother choose one child over another?"

Julian shifted in his seat. "It wasn't that simple."

"It seemed pretty simple to Annie," Benji interjected, earning a sharp look from his father.

Duncan cleared his throat. "Jill was... struggling after your disappearance. The grief affected her deeply. She couldn't look at Annie without seeing you, and it became too painful for her."

Angela absently traced the rim of her teacup with her fingertip. "So she abandoned her."

"She made choices that hurt people," Duncan said carefully. "People she should have protected."

Julian set his glass down with more force than necessary. "Look, Mom's not perfect. She knows that. But she's been trying to reconnect with Annie for years now."

"Annie doesn't want anything to do with her," Benji said. "And I don't blame her."

Angela's mind whirled with questions. What would it be like to meet this woman who gave birth to her but rejected her sister? Would she see herself in Jill's face? Would Jill look at her and see only the daughter she lost, or would she see Angela as she truly was now?

Before she could ask any further questions, there was movement at the entrance to the living room. Her gaze landed on Jude, and immediately, her heart clenched.

They'd spent time together over the past several days as they'd continued with the self-defense training, but he'd kept all interactions professional.

She hated how much it bothered her, because it wasn't like he'd ever led her to believe she was anything other than an assignment to him.

"Cole!" Benji jumped up from his chair and went to greet the tall man standing with Jude. She hadn't even noticed him. "We didn't know you were coming."

Cole rested a hand on Benji's shoulder. "Nope. I wanted to surprise Annie."

"Oh, nice! I'll go get her." Benji disappeared before anyone could say anything to him.

"It's good to see you again," Duncan said as he approached him with his hand out.

Cole smiled as he gave it a shake. "I hope it's okay that I showed up unannounced."

"It's perfectly fine," Duncan assured him. "Though you should have let me know to send the plane."

"I appreciate that," Cole said. "But I don't want to take advantage."

Duncan gave him a nod, then turned to the rest of the room. "Come meet Angela and her sister."

The tall, handsome man followed Duncan further into the room to where the women were seated. Cole gave Julian and Elizabeth a smile, then turned his attention to her and Kiara.

"Cole, this is Angela and Kiara," Duncan said. "Ladies, this is Cole Halverson."

Angela waited for some sort of reaction from Cole to the fact that she was his girlfriend's identical twin. His eyes widened briefly, but that was it.

"Nice to meet you," he said, holding his hand out first to Kiara, who stood closer to him, then to Angela.

"This is amazing," Kiara said, before proceeding to gush a little.

Before Cole could respond, there was a gasp from the doorway. "Cole?"

Angela looked over to see Annie standing in the doorway with Benji and her dog, Nyla. She would have expected Annie to be thrilled to see her boyfriend, but instead, she just stood there.

No smile. Only a strained expression as she looked from Cole to her, almost like she was afraid of how Cole would react to her twin.

Angela looked up at Cole and saw concern on his face. His attention had zeroed in on Annie, and it seemed that the rest of the people in the room had ceased to exist.

She watched as the man crossed the room to take Annie in his arms. And in a move she'd only read about in the romance novels Kiara loved, Cole swept Annie off her feet. Annie's arms went around his shoulders as she buried her head against his neck.

"Go to the theater room," Benji called out as Cole and Annie left the living room.

With their departure, the room fell into an awkward silence. Duncan cleared his throat. "Well, I think we've covered enough about your mother for now. We'll arrange a meeting soon, if you're still comfortable with that."

Angela nodded, though her mind was elsewhere. What was it about Cole's arrival that had caused such distress for Annie?

Jude shifted his weight, drawing Angela's attention. His eyes met hers briefly before he looked away, his jaw tightening. "I'll be in the security office if anyone needs me," he said, directing his comment to Duncan.

As he turned to leave, Angela felt an irrational urge to call him back.

Seeing how loving and caring Cole had been with Annie had stirred a longing within Angela. She'd never witnessed loving relationships like she had since coming to the estate.

Duncan might come across as stern, but Angela had seen that when it came to his family—especially to his wife—he let down his guard. Elizabeth seemed to be able to calm him like no one else could, and whenever he entered a room, he always looked for her.

And Cole... He'd clearly sensed that Annie needed him and had flown from LA to see her. If that wasn't love, Angela didn't know what it was.

Her heart longed for something like that for herself. Unfortunately, her heart had attached itself to a man who saw her as nothing more than a responsibility. An assignment.

She had no doubt that if she needed protection, Jude would be there in a heartbeat. Because that's what he was paid to do.

But would he ever sweep her off her feet because she needed more than just physical protection? No, he wouldn't.

"That was really romantic," Kiara murmured.

"Romance is highly overrated," Julian replied.

"I'm sad to say that you know nothing about romance, son," Duncan said. "And nothing about love."

"Maybe." Julian swirled his glass as he stared at it. "Or maybe it's more trouble than it's worth."

Angela wondered if Jude felt that way too. It seemed odd for a man of his age to be single. He'd said he didn't have a family, but she'd never asked if he had a girlfriend. So maybe he did.

The thought made her feel a little ill. And while she really didn't think he did, she knew she needed to find out.

In her mind, the only thing that could put a stop to her growing feelings and the hope she harbored in her heart would be if he was already in a relationship.

Over the next few days, her desire for something more in her life grew as she witnessed the love Annie shared with Cole. It seemed like her twin had come alive with his arrival.

The worry and strain Angela had witnessed from Annie since she'd arrived had disappeared, and for the first time, Angela felt like she was getting an honest look at the type of woman her sister was.

"We're supposed to have more training today," Kiara said from her bed. "But I feel awful."

Angela plugged in the heating pad, then handed it to her sister, where she was curled up under her comforter. Kiara had the misfortune of experiencing crippling cramps during the first day of her period each month.

"Did you take any meds?" Angela asked.

Kiara shook her head. "I ran out."

"I'll see if I can go get some more," Angela said as she smoothed an errant curl back from Kiara's face. "I need a couple of things myself, anyway."

"Can you pick up some other stuff for me too?"

"Of course. Send me a text with what you need."

Angela sank down on the edge of Kiara's bed and opened the banking app on her phone. The balance in her account was low since she hadn't had a paycheck in almost three weeks. She might have to dip into her savings, which, while not plentiful, would maybe tide her over for a month.

"We're going to have to look for jobs," she said.

Kiara sighed. "I know. But how are we supposed to apply or even get to work when we live so far out? There's no bus here, and walking would be terrible with the snow and cold."

"Maybe Jude or one of the security people could drive us."

"Or maybe we could get a place in Serenity. I've been looking at options."

"Is rent expensive?" Angela asked.

"Unfortunately, yes. But even if we have to get a studio and share a bed, it will be better than what we had in Briar Hollow."

"Is there a library in Serenity?" Angela asked, knowing that her sister's preference would be to work somewhere with books. "Or a bookstore?"

"It has both, but I don't know if either place is hiring."

Angela knew that there was a bakery in town, but like Kiara, she didn't know if they were looking for a baker.

If she couldn't get a job there, she'd have to settle for whoever was hiring because while they didn't currently have to pay rent, they still needed money for incidentals.

And there was no way Kiara wouldn't want a car now that she was going to learn how to drive. So, they would need to continue saving up for one.

Nothing had been said about their future, so Angela didn't want to presume that Duncan would want them to stay at the house. Of the Burke children, only Benji lived there full time. And while Annie was still on the estate, she had her own place. Julian didn't even live nearby.

"Okay. I'd better go." Angela bent to press a kiss to Kiara's head. "I'll see you in a bit."

After leaving the room, Angela walked down to the mudroom without seeing anyone, then got her wool coat and shoved her feet into her winter boots that had thick tread on them.

A frigid wind greeted her as she stepped out of the house. Angela pulled her knit cap down over her ears and lifted her scarf to cover her nose. She still wasn't used to the cold, and she wasn't sure she ever would be.

Hurrying to the security building, Angela was glad to reach its warmth.

"Hey, Angela." Dawn greeted her with a friendly smile. "What brings you here? I thought we were picking you up at the house."

"Actually, I was wondering if we could cancel the training today," Angela said. "Kiara isn't feeling well, and I need to run to the store to get her some stuff. Could you drive me?"

"I'll drive you."

Angela turned to see Jude coming from his office. "I don't want to interrupt your day."

"It's fine. I'm not dealing with anything pressing at the moment," he said.

That wasn't an enthusiastic reaction to the prospect of driving her to the store, but it wasn't surprising. The few glimpses of interest she'd thought she'd seen early on were nowhere to be found now. Which told her that perhaps her ability to read—and possibly convey—romantic interest didn't come naturally.

"Are you ready to go now?" he asked.

"Yes."

"Just give me a minute," he said, then disappeared back into his office.

"Is Kiara okay?" Dawn asked.

"Yeah. It's just... you know."

"Ah." Dawn gave a nod. "I do know."

"So I just need a few things for her because she's having a rough go of it."

"Poor girl."

When Jude reappeared, he was pulling on his black coat. She caught a glimpse of a gun in a shoulder harness, a clear reminder of who he was. And probably why he was going with her.

Down in the garage, Jude opened the front passenger door of a large black SUV. After she was settled in the seat, she pulled the seatbelt into place.

Jude slid behind the wheel, his presence filling the interior of the vehicle. He pushed a button to start it, and the dashboard lit up. It was the most luxurious vehicle she'd ever been in.

"I think it's best if we go to Coeur d'Alene," Jude said.

"Really?" She wasn't going to complain about having some extra time with him. Still, she was curious. "Why not Serenity?"

"Annie attends church in Serenity and has friends there, so there's a good possibility we'll run into someone who knows her. Since we haven't revealed anything about you and Annie to the public, it would be a potentially awkward situation if someone thought you were Annie."

"Oh. That makes sense." Angela pulled her knit cap off and ran her hands through her hair. "Do you think that will become public knowledge soon?"

"I don't know what Duncan is thinking," Jude said. "He has kept Annie and Benji out of the public eye for a couple of decades, so I'm sure he's in no rush to plunge them into the spotlight now."

"Could we somehow let people know about me without revealing the connection to Duncan?"

Jude glanced over at her. "Why? The longer we can keep your identity under wraps, the better. Especially with Jim and Craig out there."

"Kiara and I are going to need to get jobs soon," Angela said. "And since there's no bus and we can't drive, we'll need to move to wherever we can get work. We assumed that could be Serenity, but maybe it will have to be Coeur d'Alene."

"Wait. Hang on."

Jude guided the SUV to the side of the road and came to a stop. Shifting in his seat, he frowned at her, making Angela wonder what she'd done to warrant it.

"Has Duncan not spoken to you about the future?" he asked.

"Well, no." Angela rubbed her hand on her leg. "We just assumed we'd do the same thing we'd done in Briar Hollow."

"Which was?"

"I mean, get jobs. Find a place to stay."

"Why wouldn't you assume that you could stay on the estate and not have to work?"

This time it was her turn to frown. "Jim always told us that we'd have to work to earn our keep. That we weren't entitled to anything that we didn't work for."

Jude gave a humorless laugh as he gazed out the front windshield. "That's rich coming from him, considering his lifestyle is funded by a stolen ransom."

"Yeah. I suppose that is a bit hypocritical. But we never knew how he'd gotten his money, so the lecture resonated at the time."

"Well, I think you'll find that Duncan hopes that you'll stay on the estate."

"I don't feel right taking advantage of him."

"You're not taking advantage if he's offering it." Jude put the SUV in gear and pulled out onto the road. "Just don't make any final plans before you have a conversation with Duncan."

The idea didn't thrill Angela. She still wasn't sure how she felt about Duncan. Logically, she knew that he was her dad, and that he was a better dad than Jim had ever been.

But that was part of the problem. She didn't know how to relate to someone like Duncan. They'd never had a father who cared about them the way Duncan seemed to care about his children. Even Julian, who spent most of his evenings drunk.

So, she didn't know how to approach Duncan. And apparently he didn't know how to talk to her either, because aside from the brief discussion they'd had about her mom, they hadn't had any in-depth conversations.

"Do you know what Duncan really wants?"

Jude was quiet for a moment as he smoothly guided the SUV around the curves of the road that was flanked on either side by snowbanks and towering evergreens.

"I know he wants to get to know you," Jude finally said. "I know he wants to keep you safe and give you the life you were entitled to but have never had."

"I don't feel entitled to it," Angela told him.

"You're as entitled as Annie, Julian, or Benji. You're Duncan Burke's daughter."

"Is it wrong to say that maybe I'd rather not be?"

Jude shook his head. "It's not wrong. If it's how you feel."

"I suppose it doesn't make sense. Who wouldn't want to be related to one of the richest men in the world?"

"So why do you feel that way?"

Angela shifted to look at him, turning as much as she could with the seatbelt. "I just think it might make certain things easier."

She wondered if they'd met under different circumstances whether Jude would have let that flicker of interest she thought she'd seen early on grow into something more. Or had that just been a figment of her imagination? Wishful thinking?

As she observed his chiseled profile and his strong hands, Angela wondered what sort of woman he was drawn to. Was it a stumbling block that she looked identical to a woman he'd known since she was in diapers?

There were definitely a lot of things resisting the hope and love growing in her heart. What was she supposed to do with that knowledge, though?

As the SUV ate up the miles between the estate and Coeur d'Alene, Angela came to a realization. Everything that had brought her and Kiara to this point had required them to take things into their own hands.

If they'd waited around for someone to rescue them from the homestead, they'd probably still be there. If she'd waited for Duncan to find her, he might never have been able to.

They'd had to make the decision to leave the homestead and then follow through. They'd had to make that phone call to Cole Halverson. Not just leave the picture of him and Annie under a magnet on their fridge.

They'd had to be proactive, and Angela realized she needed to be proactive in how she felt about Jude. Those other times, it had been Kiara that propelled them into action. This time, it would be up to her.

I can do all things through Christ who strengthens me.

She had to believe that God would give her the strength to learn what was necessary in order to move forward. And if this path led to heartache for her, He'd give her the strength to deal with that too.

Before she dismissed her feelings for Jude as hopeless, she needed to know for sure. She needed to know if anything was even remotely possible.

If he had someone else in his life, she'd have to move on. No matter how much she didn't want to. So, she had to ask.

"You said you didn't have a wife, right?"

Jude's brows lifted as he shot her a quick look. As he focused on the road again, she saw his jaw tense.

Was he trying to decide whether to tell the truth or to lie in order to keep her at arm's length?

"No, no wife."

"Ex-wife?"

"No."

"Girlfriend?"

"No."

"Why not?"

Jude's gaze met hers for a moment. "Why do I not have any of the above?"

"Yes."

"My job is my life."

"So you've never wanted to have a wife and kids?"

"It's not that simple. Sometimes you can want something that just isn't meant for you."

The finality in his words struck deep inside Angela. She turned to stare out the window, wishing now that she'd never asked him any of her questions.

CHAPTER TWELVE

Jude tightened his hands on the steering wheel, wishing he'd been able to send Dawn with Angela instead of taking her himself. But Duncan had assigned Jude as Angela's bodyguard for the time being, so when she asked to leave the estate, he had no choice but to go with her.

He also knew that he was the best person to accompany her to Coeur d'Alene. He'd know how to handle the situation should they run into someone who knew Annie. Or if they ran into Jim.

What he hadn't expected was for Angela to grill him about his personal life. Though he supposed it wasn't a surprise. He'd sensed that Angela might be drawn to him.

He might not have a lot of dating experience, but he had learned over the years how to tell if a woman was interested in him. Some were blatant about it. Others were more subtle.

Angela was a curious mix of both. She wasn't blatant in a flirting way. But when they were together, he could sense her attention on him, and she seemed to gravitate toward him.

"Why do you feel like it's not meant for you?"

Another question that didn't surprise Jude. However, he didn't want to have this discussion with her. As long as he could ignore the little glances or how she moved closer to him when they were in the same room, he could pretend that Angela was just another responsibility.

"My job requires all of my focus," Jude said, keeping his eyes fixed on the road ahead. "A family would be a distraction."

But even as the words left his mouth, he knew they weren't entirely true. His father had managed both for years—until his mother couldn't take the riskiness of the job anymore. The memory of her leaving still stung, even after all these years. Especially since he suspected that his dad's job had only been an excuse to cover up her real reason for leaving.

"My father was a cop before he worked for Duncan," Jude said finally, keeping his eyes on the road. "My mother left us because she couldn't handle the uncertainty of never knowing if he'd come home at the end of his shift."

He gripped the steering wheel tighter, remembering the night his father had sat him down and explained why his mother wasn't coming back. He'd been eight.

"I chose a similar path. The people I protect are high-value targets. There's always risk involved." He glanced at her briefly. "It's not fair to ask someone to live with that kind of worry."

Although if he was honest, his specific position held less risk than others on the team. As head of security, he didn't do as much bodyguard work as he previously had. There were times Duncan required him to fill the position—like his current trip to Coeur d'Alene—but they weren't that frequent.

Angela was quiet for a moment, and Jude could feel her studying his profile. "But don't you get lonely?"

The question hit closer to home than he wanted to admit. "I've made my peace with it."

"That's not really an answer," she pressed gently.

Jude sighed. "Everyone gets lonely sometimes. But I have the team. I have my church and a few friends there. And the Burke family has always treated me like one of their own."

"It's not the same though, is it?"

No, it wasn't. But he'd learned to live with the hollow spaces in his life.

"Look, Angela, my priority is keeping the Burke family safe. That's what I was trained to do. That's what I'm good at." He paused, choosing his next words carefully. "Relationships require attention and can be a distraction. And in my line of work, distractions can be deadly."

"But everyone needs someone, don't they? Even you."

The sincerity in Angela's voice made something in Jude's chest constrict. He'd spent years building walls around himself, focusing solely on his duty to the Burkes. Telling himself that it was enough. That his purpose in life was to serve as protection for the Burkes.

His few friendships were enough to satisfy any need he had to socialize, and they'd accepted that he wasn't a super sociable person.

Now here was this woman—this Burke—trying to peek over those walls with innocent questions that cut straight to his core.

"We're almost there," he said, deliberately changing the subject as they approached the outskirts of Coeur d'Alene. "Do you want to go to one of the big-box stores? Or do you have somewhere else in mind?"

Angela seemed to understand he wasn't going to keep pursuing her line of conversation. She turned her attention to her phone, scrolling through something.

"Big-box is fine," she said after a moment. "I should be able to get everything there."

Jude nodded, grateful for a reprieve from the intensely personal conversation they'd just had. It was the most he'd talked to a woman—to anyone!—about personal stuff in years.

And he'd be happy not to have to do it again anytime soon. Hopefully, Angela had gotten whatever information she'd wanted, and now she'd just let the subject die.

As Jude pulled into the parking lot, he couldn't help but notice Angela's reflection in the side window. Her expression was drawn, almost sad.

He'd disappointed her with his answers. But what else could he say? That sometimes at night, alone in his cabin surrounded by trees, he thought about what it might be like to have someone waiting for him? That watching Duncan with Elizabeth and Cole with Annie made him wonder if that was something he could have?

Those weren't things he could admit—especially not to her. He didn't want to hurt her, but it felt like he had no choice. Regardless of whether he let her down now or later.

"I'll be close," he said as they walked toward the store's entrance. "Just in case."

The store was moderately busy for a weekday. Jude stuck close to Angela as she gathered what she needed, keeping his eyes moving, scanning for potential threats. This was what he was good at—being vigilant and focused. Not talking about feelings.

At one point, he noticed her comparing prices and always choosing the cheaper version. Knowing there was no need for it, he stepped up beside her and took the store-brand painkillers from her hand. He put it back on the shelf and picked up the brand name.

In that particular case, there probably wasn't much difference between the two products aside from price. But it was the principle of the thing. She didn't need to pinch pennies anymore.

Jude had no idea why Duncan hadn't addressed this with her yet, but he knew the man wouldn't want her worrying about money.

"Listen. Get the best," he said. "Your father would want you to."

Angela looked at him, worry in her gaze. "But I don't want to spend more, and then he says we need to take care of ourselves."

"Angela, he's not going to say that," Jude assured her. "Here. Let me ask him."

Pulling out his phone, he hit the button to call Duncan, then after making sure there was no one else too close to them, he put it on speakerphone so Angela could hear.

"Jude? Is everything okay?" Duncan asked when the call connected.

"Everything's fine," Jude told him. "But I'm here at the store with Angela. She needed to pick up a few things."

"Does she have enough money?" Duncan asked. "I haven't had a chance to talk to her about setting up accounts for her and Kiara."

"Should I just put whatever she needs on my credit card?" Jude asked.

"Yes. Whatever she needs. No limits."

"Okay."

"Thanks for taking care of her for me. I'll have a chat with her and Kiara soon."

After saying goodbye, Jude slipped his phone into the pocket of his jacket. "Do you feel better about spending money now?"

"Yeah." She sighed. "It's just so... weird. I feel a little overwhelmed."

"Well, for now, let's get what you need," Jude said. He wasn't a big fan of shopping and tended to buy what he needed online, but he dutifully stuck close to Angela.

She didn't rush, but she also didn't linger too long in the pharmacy and personal hygiene areas. After she had the painkillers, some hair care and personal hygiene products, she hesitated.

By that point, Jude was pushing the cart for her, and he slowed his steps when he realized she wasn't keeping up with him.

"Where to now?" he asked.

She hesitated a moment before she said, "Would you mind if I picked out a few clothing items?"

"Not at all. Lead the way."

Together, they walked to the women's section. When he realized she was headed for the lingerie section, he stayed in the main aisle with the cart.

He kept an eye on her while also glancing around to watch for threats. Not that he was expecting any, but he would never slack off.

They probably should have gone to a more upscale store, but he had a feeling that Angela wouldn't have known how to deal with that. Even he struggled with seeing fifty-dollar price tags on a simple black T-shirt.

When she walked over to where he waited, she had an armful of clothing.

"Do you think it's too much?" she asked as she placed the load into the cart.

"Nope. It's not too much. If you want it, get it."

"I bought some stuff for Kiara too," she said, lifting a hanger with a cozy-looking outfit on it. She ran a hand along the pants. "It's been so cold that I wanted something cozy for us. The pants are fleecy, and the top is so soft. I got me and Kiara each a set, plus some fuzzy socks."

Jude listened as she described the different items she'd picked up. Normally, he wouldn't have this type of conversation with someone he was protecting, but he couldn't bring himself to cut her off.

"Do you need new shoes or boots?"

"I think we're both okay with what we have," she said.

"Anything else?"

"Um... Can we go to the book section and then the candy aisle?"

Jude chuckled. "Sure."

In the book aisle, Angela went right to the women's fiction section. She picked up several books and read the blurb on the back before settling on two. After putting them in the cart, she went to the puzzle books and picked up a couple.

"Do you like to read?" Jude asked her as they headed toward the candy aisle.

"I do, but Kiara is a more voracious reader than I am," Angela said. "These books are for her, though I'll probably read them when she's done with them."

"Do you read eBooks at all?"

"Sometimes, but Kiara mainly picked up books from the thrift store, or she borrowed them from the library."

"I noticed you had a couple of boxes of books that you brought with you."

"The fiction ones are Kiara's, and the cookbooks are mine."

When they reached the candy aisle, Jude followed Angela as she searched among the sweets.

Finally, she approached him with a package of gummy bears and one of mini chocolate bars with almonds.

"You like chocolate?" he asked as she placed the chocolate bars in the cart.

"Yeah. But I'm mainly getting this for Kiara. When she's feeling like this, she likes to have sweets." She slanted a look at him. "How about you? Do you have a sweet tooth?"

"I do," he confessed. "But I try not to indulge in it too often."

"Do you like anything in particular?"

"Chocolate is always a winner," he said. "But honestly, if it's got sugar in it, I'd probably eat it."

"You don't look like you have a sweet tooth," she said, her gaze shifting away from him.

"Well, in addition to a sweet tooth, I also like to exercise, so they balance each other out."

"I'm not a big fan of exercise," Angela said with a grimace. "Jim was insistent that we be strong, so he would make us run laps on the dirt road that circled through the property. It was terrible."

Anger burned inside Jude as he imagined Angela trying to run to Jim's no doubt exacting standards. "Annie isn't big on exercise either. But she's put in the work so that she can defend herself."

"I should do that too," Angela said. "I already feel stronger with the training we've gone through."

"You've done a good job so far," Jude told her. "I appreciate that you've committed to the training, even though I'm sure you don't see the purpose in it yet."

"To be honest, I hope that I never understand the purpose in it."

Jude nodded. "I hope that too. Because understanding can come through experience, and I'd rather that none of you have the opportunity to use what you're learning."

"That makes two of us."

Jude gave her a quick smile. "Do you need anything else?"

She stared into the cart, then consulted her phone. "No. I think that's it."

Jude pushed the cart to the cashier at the front, then unloaded everything onto the conveyor belt. He was placing each bag into the cart as the cashier filled them when he noticed that Angela was staring at the cash register screen with a frown.

Moving closer to her, he bent to look at the screen himself, trying to ignore the light floral scent that surrounded her. "What's wrong?"

"It's just adding up really quickly."

Jude gently took her arm and moved her away from the screen. "Help me load the bags into the cart."

"But—"

"No buts," Jude said firmly. "Don't worry about the total."

When the cashier finished scanning everything, Jude paid with his credit card without even glancing at the screen. He could see Angela trying to peek around him to get a glimpse of the total, but he blocked her view.

After completing the transaction, he pushed the cart toward the exit with Angela walking beside him, still looking troubled.

"I feel terrible," she said once they were outside in the cold air. "That was so much money."

"Angela." Jude stopped walking and turned to face her. "You picked up basic necessities and a couple of books. Duncan Burke probably spends more than that on a single bottle of wine."

"But still—"

"Do you know what your father's net worth is?"

She shook her head.

"Billions. With a capital B." Jude resumed pushing the cart toward the SUV. "What you just bought wouldn't even register as a rounding error in his monthly budget."

They loaded the bags into the back of the vehicle in silence. Once they were both settled in their seats, Angela turned to him.

"It's going to take me a while to get used to this," she said quietly.

"I know. But you need to understand that Duncan wants to take care of you in the way he hasn't been able to for years. It's not charity—you're his daughter. This is what fathers do."

Angela was quiet as they pulled out of the parking lot. After several minutes, she spoke again.

"Can I ask you something else?" she said softly.

Jude tensed, hoping she wasn't going to circle back to his personal life. "What?"

"Do you think Duncan really wants us to stay? Or does he feel obligated because I'm his daughter?"

The vulnerability in her voice caught Jude off guard. He glanced over to see her staring down at her hands folded in her lap.

"He wants you to stay," Jude said without hesitation. "I've known your father for three decades, Angela. I've seen him make decisions based on obligation, and I've seen him make decisions based on love. This is love."

"How can you be so sure?"

"Because I've watched him grieve for you every single day since you were taken. There's a photo of you and Annie as toddlers on his desk that never got moved. His greatest wish was to have you back in his life. I think he would have given up his fortune to get you back."

Angela's breath hitched slightly. "Really?"

"Really." Jude navigated around a slow-moving truck. "Duncan Burke is a complicated man, but when it comes to his children, there's no question about his priorities. You are safe with him."

"What about with you?"

The question hung in the air between them. Jude felt his pulse quicken as he tried to interpret her meaning.

"What do you mean?"

"Am I safe with you?" Her voice was barely above a whisper.

"Definitely." Jude glanced over at her. "You are part of Duncan's family, and my job is to keep all of you safe." He hesitated, feeling compelled to let her know that she wasn't *just* a job to him. "That doesn't mean I don't view you as a person too. I view Annie and Benji the same way I view you."

It was all the truth, and at the same time, it kept some distance between them. He hoped.

This was the first time in a long time that he'd had a woman pique his interest, and he wasn't sure how to deal with it. The complication came from the fact that he couldn't just avoid her.

If a woman at church seemed interested in him, he could steer clear of her because the church was big enough. But that wasn't possible with Angela.

It was going to take all his mental fortitude to be able to interact with her without being drawn to her even more. There was just something about her that called to him.

A softness wrapped in strength. She was a survivor. She had faced difficult situations and pushed forward, even though she might not have wanted to. He was drawn to those qualities.

"I see." Angela's voice was flat, and when Jude glanced over, her expression had shuttered closed.

Even though he hadn't wanted to, he'd hurt her. The knowledge hit him like a punch to the gut.

But what else could he have said? That he thought about her more than he should? That seeing her smile made his heart race? That he'd started looking forward to any chance they had to interact?

He couldn't tell her any of that.

So instead, he'd hurt her with his answer. That hadn't been his intention, but maybe it was for the best. The last thing either of them needed was for her to develop feelings for someone who couldn't—wouldn't—reciprocate.

The silence stretched between them as they drove through the snowy landscape. Jude found himself stealing glances at her, noting the way she held herself so still, as if she was trying to disappear into the seat.

"Angela," he said finally, his voice softer than normal.

"It's okay," she said quickly, still not looking at him. "I understand. I'm just another responsibility."

"That's not what I said."

"It's what you meant." She finally turned to face him, and he was struck by the hurt in her blue-green eyes. "I'm sorry if I made you uncomfortable with my questions. I won't do it again."

The formal politeness in her tone was somehow worse than if she'd been angry. It reminded him of how she'd been when they first met—guarded and distant. He'd thought they'd moved past that.

"You didn't make me uncomfortable," he said, though it wasn't entirely true. She made him *very* uncomfortable, just not in the way she thought.

"It's fine, Jude. Really."

The rest of the drive passed in tense silence. Angela stared out her window, and Jude focused on the road, hating the tension that now filled the space between them.

When they arrived back at the estate, Jude carried the bags up to the house while Angela walked ahead of him, her shoulders rigid. In the mudroom, she kicked off her boots and hung up her coat without looking at him.

"Thank you for the ride," she said, her tone distant, taking the bags from his hands. "I can manage from here."

"Angela—"

But she was already walking away, leaving him standing alone in the mudroom with the echo of her footsteps fading down the hall.

Jude ran a hand through his hair. He'd handled that badly.

But what was the alternative? Tell her the truth? That she was becoming more than an assignment?

That wouldn't change anything for them.

She'd still be the daughter of the man who trusted Jude to protect her. And he also had a hard time getting past the nearly twelve-year difference in their ages.

With a sigh, Jude turned to leave the house. As he drove the SUV to the security building, he told himself this was all for the best.

His life wasn't conducive to a relationship. It was best he not have to answer to anyone but Duncan Burke. It meant that he could do his job to the best of his ability. He also liked not having to worry about a potential date using him to gain access to the wealthy Burke family.

Yeah, he definitely was happy that he'd decided not to get into a relationship. He just wished that his heart was as on board now as it had been when he'd first made that decision.

CHAPTER THIRTEEN

Angela felt the tension she'd been holding bleed out of her as Kiara wrapped her arms around her. They were seated on Angela's bed, both wearing the pajamas Angela had bought the previous day.

For the first time since coming to Serenity, they'd slept in the same bed. Both of them had needed the presence of the other, and the king-size bed was plenty big enough for them to share.

"Let's go get some breakfast and then see what Duncan wants," Kiara said. "Jude won't be around, so you'll be able to relax."

That should have been a good thing, but part of Angela wanted to see him. Regardless of how they'd parted ways after their shopping trip.

"Yeah. Until we have to practice driving this afternoon," she said.

"Oooh, right." Kiara straightened. "I can't believe we're finally going to be able to drive."

"Knowing how to drive won't do us much good without a car."

Kiara waved her hand dismissively. "They've got enough cars around here that we could probably just borrow one whenever we need to go somewhere. Maybe even to our jobs. And if we don't have to pay for rent and food here, we'll be able to save up enough money for our own car even quicker."

Angela hadn't told her about the conversation she'd had with Jude, nor about the phone call he'd made to Duncan in her presence. She still needed some clarification before she told Kiara that they might not have to work.

"Let's get dressed," she said, getting to her feet. "And maybe we need to dress a little nicer since we're meeting with Duncan."

It was a bit odd to dress up to go see the person who was her dad, but it felt like the right thing to do.

Kiara nodded, then headed for the door. "See you in a few."

Alone, Angela headed to her bathroom to begin her morning routine. Picking out what to wear was a bit of a challenge. For her whole life, she'd dressed for practicality or comfort. However, she didn't think she should show up to a meeting with Duncan in a pair of leggings and a sweatshirt.

Though she didn't have a lot to choose from, it still took her a few minutes to decide which of her sweaters she'd wear with black slacks. After she was dressed, she curled her hair and put on a little makeup.

Kiara poked her head into the bathroom. "Ready?"

"As I'll ever be."

As they walked down the hallway to the stairs, the aroma of coffee grew stronger the closer they got to the kitchen. They found Julian still in the breakfast room when they got there.

"Good morning," Angela said when she spotted him.

Julian looked up and blinked at them blearily. The man had clearly over-indulged yet again the night before. "Morning."

Angela moved over to the buffet, where there were warming dishes containing their breakfast options. She still wasn't used to having so many choices for breakfast.

"How are you this morning, Julian?" Kiara asked as she sat down across from him with her plate.

Angela set hers down at the seat next to Kiara, then went to get them coffee. She carried the carafe back to the table.

"Do you want a top-up?"

"Sure." Julian lifted his mug toward her. "Thanks." He glanced at Kiara. "I'm doing... fine."

Kiara looked skeptical, which Angela definitely understood. She had no idea why Julian was such a heavy drinker, when no one else in the family drank much at all. And if he had a problem with alcohol, why did Duncan keep it in the house?

"What do you do to fill your days?" Kiara asked, bolder than Angela was when it came to starting a conversation with her newly found brother.

"Work."

"You can work remotely?"

"A lot of the time." His gaze shifted to Angela. "Are you excited to meet Mom?"

"Um... I guess? To be honest, I don't really know how I feel."

"She's excited to see you."

"Does she wish that Annie was with us for the meeting?"

Julian paused, his gaze dropping to his mug. "I think she's just focused on you right now. There will be time with Annie later."

Angela was unsettled by the thought that Jill—she still couldn't think of her as Mom—could put aside her desire to see Annie just because Angela was back. Had their mom played favorites when they were little?

"What happens if I'm not really interested in having a relationship with her?"

Julian's features tightened for a moment, then he sighed. "Nothing, I guess. I just hope that you'll tell her that to her face. I'm tired of having to be the middle person. It's been that way with Annie. I don't need it with you too."

Angela couldn't imagine anything worse than having to tell Jill that she wasn't interested in a relationship. But this was something she couldn't rely on Kiara to do.

She knew it probably wasn't fair that she was going into this meeting with the woman already thinking she didn't want a relationship with her. But given how she'd treated Annie, Angela had a hard time believing that she'd be the sort of woman she'd want for a mother.

"Don't forget you have a meeting with Dad this morning," Julian said as he got to his feet.

"I won't," Angela assured him.

"See you later." With that, Julian left the room, coffee cup in hand.

"That's a tortured soul if I ever saw one," Kiara said when it was just the two of them.

Angela figured that was a good description of the man. He had an edge to him that was lacking in Duncan and Jude.

Neither of them talked as they finished their breakfast, then left the room to go to Duncan's office for their ten o'clock meeting. It was weird to think that she had an appointment with her father, but she knew he was a busy man.

"Come in," Duncan said when she knocked on his office door.

The space was decorated just as she'd expect of a powerful man. It was all leather and polished wood with a large stone fireplace at one end of the room. A wall of glass looked out on the snow-covered lawn, which faded into the trees that filled the estate.

"Good morning," Duncan said as he got to his feet. He started to come around the desk to them, then seemed to check himself. Instead, he smiled and gestured to the cluster of chairs that grouped together near the fireplace. "Let's have a seat over there."

It was definitely more comfortable than sitting opposite him at the desk. Yet Angela couldn't seem to quell the nerves that were fluttering in her stomach.

"How are you doing?" Duncan asked, his gaze on her. "Is everything going okay?"

"Everything is fine. Thank you."

"Good." He reached for a couple of files that sat on the end table next to him. "I suppose you'll be seeing Jill soon."

Angela nodded. "On Wednesday."

"I believe you're meeting her at the resort?"

"Yes. Julian said that's where she's staying."

"I want Jude to go with you," Duncan said. "The resort should be safe enough, but I'd feel better if he was there."

Angela couldn't deny that, despite the tension of their last conversation, she'd feel better too. But she kept that to herself.

"Are you going too, Kiara?" he asked, turning his attention to her.

Angela exchanged a glance with Kiara. They'd talked a lot about it. Kiara wasn't sure it was her place to go, but Angela was adamant that she wanted her there with her.

"Yes, Angie wants me there."

Duncan nodded. "I think that's a good decision."

"You do?" Angela asked.

"Yes, I do. Kiara is an important part of your life. It's best Jill knows that right from the start."

From what she'd heard about Jill, Angela wasn't sure she'd feel the same way.

"Don't let Jill manipulate you into anything you don't want," Duncan said. "I've never interfered with her relationships with the children we share, but I also have no problem stepping in when necessary."

"Have you done that with Annie?"

"Yes. Annie has had difficulty in the past with expressing how she feels about her mom. She's better now, but since this is your first time meeting her, if you have trouble expressing yourself, I'm prepared to step in and help you communicate with her."

Relief filled Angela. "Julian said he didn't want to be caught in the middle."

"And I don't want that for him either," Duncan said. "Unfortunately, Jill has put him in that position frequently by asking him to get Annie to meet with her. She should have been talking to me about Annie, but she knew that I wouldn't guilt Annie into talking to her like she could get Julian to do."

"I don't know how I feel about her."

"I know it probably isn't easy to reserve judgment since you've already heard how she treated Annie," Duncan said. "But going into your meet-up with no expectations might be helpful."

"I'll keep that in mind."

"Good." Duncan gave her a smile that crinkled the corners of his eyes and made them shine. There was a kindness that radiated from him that she'd never experienced with Jim. "And now let's talk about something more pleasant. I realized that I have been remiss in helping the two of you settle into life here by making things clear."

Angela glanced at Kiara, wondering what they were about to hear.

"Like my other three children, you will receive a monthly allowance. You are free to spend it as you wish. We've set up bank accounts for you as well as debit and credit cards." He looked from Angela to Kiara. "This also includes you."

Kiara's eyes widened. "Me? But I'm not one of your kids."

"No, you're not a biological child. However, you are Angela's sister in all the ways that count, and because of that, I consider you a daughter as I do her."

"Really?"

Angela slipped her arm around Kiara's shoulders and leaned her head against hers. She knew Kiara would be moved by Duncan's declaration, and Angela was more grateful than she could say.

"These have all the information about the allowance and the debit and credit cards," Duncan said as he held out a folder to each of them. "Also, if you have a need that this money doesn't cover, don't be afraid to come talk to me about it."

Angela couldn't keep the gasp from slipping out as she opened the folder and caught a glimpse of the kind of money Duncan was talking about. He was offering her more in a month than she'd made in a full year at the bakery. It was ridiculous how much their lives had changed.

"What are we supposed to do?" Kiara asked.

Duncan's brow furrowed. "What do you mean?"

She lifted her folder. "This kind of money means we don't have to work. What are we supposed to do with all our time? I can't imagine just sitting around all day, every day."

"You can do whatever you'd like. Travel. Take online college."

"You wouldn't let me go to an actual college?"

Duncan stared at her for a long moment. "Is that what you'd like to do?"

"I don't know," Kiara admitted. "But I'll need to do *something.*"

Angela agreed with her. It had been nice not to have to work after working so hard on the homestead and in Briar Hollow. But having nothing to do moving forward didn't hold much appeal.

"Why don't the two of you talk it over, then we can meet again to discuss your options."

"Okay," Kiara said. "We can do that."

"Moving onto the second purpose for this meeting," Duncan looked toward the window as the sound of a helicopter approaching the estate reached them. "I have an architect joining us this morning to help you formulate ideas of what you'd like for your home."

"Our home?" Angela asked.

"You are more than welcome to live in this house for as long as you'd like, but I thought perhaps you'd like your own space here on the estate. Annie has her own home, and Julian has a home in New York. So, I'd like to offer you the opportunity to work with an architect to design a home for the two of you."

"That's... amazing," Angela said. She'd never imagined she'd one day have a place to call her own, though it had been a fervent wish.

"It's up to you if you'd like to share a home, or if you'd rather have two separate houses."

"We've never really talked about something like that," Kiara said. "I guess we figured we'd live together until one or both of us got married."

"That can still be the case," Duncan said. "The architect I've hired for this project is very good, and he'll be able to turn what you'd like in your home into reality."

Angela's head was spinning, and she felt a bit like she had to be dreaming. This couldn't possibly be true.

How had she gone from her struggling life in Kentucky to this lavish life in Idaho? It didn't seem like it was actually real.

And yet the pinch she gave to her arm told her that it was. She was wide awake and getting ready to design her dream home. Whatever that was.

When the architect walked through the door a few minutes later, he had Jude with him. Angela had been trying her best not to think about the man since she'd stormed away from him after their shopping spree. He'd made his feelings abundantly clear, and she'd known that she had to keep her distance as best she could.

But she couldn't deny that something settled inside her at the sight of him. The spinning of her head and the fluttering nerves quieted when her gaze landed on him, even as her heart beat faster.

"Welcome, Garrett," Duncan said as he held out his hand to the only stranger in the room. "I'd like to introduce you to Angela and Kiara. They are the people you'll be designing for."

Garrett was a handsome man with styled light brown hair and hazel eyes. He looked to be in his late thirties. Maybe around Jude's age.

"Nice to meet you," he said as he shook their hands in turn. "I look forward to working with you."

"I've also asked Jude to be present to give his input on the security of the building."

Jude held himself stiffly. And though he nodded at both of them, there was no smile in his greeting. He was probably angry with her for how she'd acted.

She lowered her gaze to her hands. It hadn't been the most mature way to handle their interaction, she knew that. But it had been difficult to be rejected. And she'd felt stupid and like he was just tolerating her because of his job.

"Why don't we go into the boardroom?"

Duncan led the way through a door into a space that was decorated similarly to his office, but with a large table surrounded by chairs dominating the space. The room was bright because, like his office, one wall was essentially all glass.

"Have a seat," Duncan said as he sank down into the chair at the head of the table.

Jude sat next to Garrett, while Angela and Kiara took seats opposite them. There were rolls of white paper on the table between them.

Garrett pulled a tablet out of his briefcase and set it on the table in front of him.

"So, I have the blueprints here for Annie's house and also for Jude's." Duncan looked at Jude. "Hope that's okay."

"It's fine."

Duncan stared at Jude for a long moment before reaching for the rolled papers. "These will give you an idea of what we've already done for the homes on the estate."

"Do you have a location already picked out for this?" Kiara asked.

"Yes, there's a suitable spot halfway between Annie's and Jude's. But there is plenty of forest between all the sites, so you can't even see the other cabins."

Angela watched as Duncan unrolled the paper and used some coasters to hold down the corners. There had been some mention of them going to see Annie's home, but it hadn't happened, so she was curious to see what it was like.

"Annie's home is two stories," Duncan said, then went on to describe its layout, pointing to the papers as reference. It seemed like a nice place for her sister. "Now Jude's place is bigger, as it was built with a family in mind."

Jude cleared his throat as Duncan moved on to the other set of rolled papers. "My dad and I moved in there when we came to Idaho."

"Yes. And it became your home with his death."

Angela saw again that Duncan viewed Jude as more than just another employee. She wondered whether Jude was aware of that.

She was curious about his home, so she listened more intently when Duncan described it.

"It has four bedrooms, with the master on the main floor. There's also a space that could be used as a study or a nursery."

Angela lifted her gaze to find Jude watching her. When their eyes met, something flickered across Jude's expression before he looked away, his jaw tightening. Angela felt heat rise in her cheeks and forced herself to focus on the blueprints spread across the table.

"So," Garrett said, opening his tablet and pulling up what looked like a questionnaire. "Let's start with the basics. Are you thinking of sharing one home, or would you prefer separate residences?"

Angela glanced at Kiara, who shrugged. "We've never really had the option of choosing before."

"What do you think would work best for you?" Duncan asked gently.

"I think... maybe one home?" Angela said hesitantly, glancing at Kiara. "At least for now. We've always been together."

Kiara nodded. "But maybe with our own separate wings or something? So we each have privacy when we want it?"

"That's definitely doable," Garrett said, making notes on his tablet. "What about size? How many bedrooms are you thinking of?"

"I don't know," Angela admitted. "This is all so overwhelming."

"Why don't we start with what you each like to do?" Garrett suggested. "That will help me understand what kind of spaces you'd each want."

Angela felt her cheeks warm. "I like to bake. And read."

"So maybe a really nice kitchen? And a cozy reading nook?"

"That sounds amazing," she said softly, still unable to believe they were actually giving their input into a home that would one day be theirs.

"I love to read too," Kiara added. "And I'd like space for puzzles and maybe crafts. Oh, and a space for lots of plants."

"A sunroom would be perfect for plants," Garrett said, his stylus moving across the tablet as he took notes. "And we could design built-in shelving for books. What about entertaining? Do you see yourselves hosting family gatherings?"

Angela looked around the table uncertainly. She'd never hosted anything in her life. "I... I'm not sure."

"Maybe start with a nice dining area that could accommodate the immediate family," Duncan suggested. "You can always expand later if needed."

"That makes sense," Kiara agreed. "What about outdoor space?"

"Definitely," Garrett said. "Four season sunrooms are popular, and with the right design, you could have outdoor dining and seating areas that would be usable all year."

Angela found herself getting caught up in the excitement of planning. "Could we have a garden? I'd love to grow my own herbs and vegetables."

Not all of the things they'd done on the homestead had been horrible. In fact, Angela was quite grateful for a lot of the skills she'd learned growing up there.

"Of course," Duncan said with a smile. "We can have the landscaping team help design that for you."

"What about security considerations?" Garrett asked, turning to Jude.

Jude had been quiet throughout most of the discussion, but now he straightened in his chair. "Same protocols as the other residences. Security system integrated with the main house, reinforced entry points, fireproofed walls, and automated protective blinds."

Garrett nodded as he made notes. "I'll have to get more information about what was used on the other houses since I wasn't the one who worked with you on those security precautions."

"I take the protection of my family very seriously," Duncan told him. "There is never any expense spared when it comes to keeping them safe."

"We will definitely come up with something that meets Angela and Kiara's needs, but also satisfies the need you have for their security."

"Thank you," Duncan said. "How long until you have some preliminary sketches that the girls can look at?"

"Not long." Garrett flashed him a smile. "Your project is at the top of my list."

Duncan's money probably helped to make that the case.

"How long does it usually take to build a house?" Kiara asked.

Duncan looked at Garrett, obviously deferring to him.

"Normally, it could take anywhere from twelve to eighteen months," Garrett said. "However, since Duncan has expressed his desire to have this done quickly with no regard for cost, we'll probably have it done in eight months."

That seemed like a long time. Where would she and Kiara be in eight months? Would they have settled in on the estate? Would they have found things to do to fill their time?

Most importantly, Angela wondered how she'd feel about Jude in eight months' time. Would her heart still race at the sight of him? Would she still long to be something more to him than just a job?

Or would she have accepted the inevitable and tried to move on from her feelings for him?

One thing she was fairly certain of was that they wouldn't have any type of relationship beyond a professional one. It hurt her heart to think about that, but it was a reality she'd need to accept sooner than later.

CHAPTER FOURTEEN

Jude wanted to bail on the driving lessons he'd promised Duncan he'd give Angela and Kiara. There was a tension between him and Angela that caused him to hurt in ways that made no sense.

How had he allowed this to happen?

Ever since his one serious relationship had ended years ago, he'd gone out of his way to make sure he didn't get close enough to a woman to fall in love.

Had he been attracted to women over the years? Sure. However, he'd kept his distance from them, so it never developed into anything more. And that had worked... until it hadn't.

With Angela, he'd failed completely. Every time he saw her, he felt that pull toward her—that desire to protect her that went beyond his job description. His efforts to keep his distance from her had been pathetic and ineffective, because even when he wasn't with her, he was constantly thinking about her.

"Are you okay?" Dawn asked as she popped her head into his office. "You're staring at that report like it personally offended you."

Jude sighed and set down the security assessment he'd been pretending to read for the last twenty minutes. "I'm fine."

"Right." Dawn leaned against the doorframe, crossing her arms. "That's why you've been scowling for a while now."

"I have not been—" He caught himself. "Is there something you need?"

"Just reminding you that you're scheduled to take the ladies driving at two. Which is in..." She glanced at her watch. "Ten minutes."

Jude nodded. "I haven't forgotten."

"Good." Dawn lingered a moment longer. "You know, whatever's bothering you, it might help to talk about it."

"Nothing's bothering me."

Dawn's knowing look told him she didn't believe him for a second. "If you say so." She pushed off the doorframe. "I'll let you get back to glaring at that report."

After she left, Jude leaned back in his chair and rubbed a hand over his face. He needed to get himself together. This was just a driving lesson—a simple task that required him to be professional and focused. He could manage that.

He stood and grabbed his jacket. After stopping briefly to chat with the guys in front of the monitors, he stepped out into the cold end of January air. The sun was shining brightly, creating a glare off the snow that had him blinking as he pulled his sunglasses from a jacket pocket and slid them on.

Reaching the garage at the main house, he let himself in, then stared at the cars parked there. Most were top of the line and expensive. He wanted a vehicle that wouldn't intimidate Angela and Kiara.

Finally, he settled on a compact sedan that was the cheapest of the vehicles there, even though it was still fully loaded and top of the line. He went to the cabinet that contained all the keys and punched in the code to open it.

After he retrieved the keys to the sedan, he went to the car and unlocked it. He slid behind the wheel, grunting as he had to scrunch his body to fit.

Once he'd adjusted the seat and started it up, he opened the overhead garage door and backed the car out onto the large cement parking pad outside the garage. He parked it so that it pointed in the right direction. He didn't think the ladies were ready to tackle backing up just yet.

As he got out of the car, the door to the house opened, and Angela and Kiara appeared, both wearing jackets and knit caps.

Kiara waved enthusiastically when she spotted him, then she headed in his direction. Angela followed more slowly, her eyes not quite meeting his.

"Ready for your first driving lesson?" he asked, keeping his voice professionally neutral.

"More than ready," Kiara said, practically bouncing with excitement. "I've been watching YouTube tutorials all morning."

"That's... good initiative," Jude said. "But there's a big difference between watching and doing."

"Is this the car we're practicing in?" Kiara asked, looking at the car he stood next to.

"Yes. Which one of you is going first?" he asked.

"Me," Kiara said without hesitation.

Jude motioned to the driver's door. "In you get then. Angela, you can sit in the back, probably behind her because if you sit behind me, you won't have much room."

Kiara was behind the wheel in no time flat. Once both were in their seats and buckled up, Jude slid into his.

For the next couple of minutes, he walked Kiara through adjusting the seat and mirrors. He wasn't a driving instructor, but his goal was to get the two women comfortable with the car and maneuvering it before turning them over to a professional.

"Okay," he said once Kiara had everything adjusted properly. "Before we start moving, let's go over the basics. The brake pedal is on the left, accelerator on the right. Your right foot does all the work—you'll never use your left foot for anything in an automatic transmission vehicle."

Kiara nodded eagerly, her hands gripping the steering wheel.

"The most important thing to remember is that this car is much more responsive than you might expect. A tiny bit of pressure on the gas pedal goes a long way when you're first starting out."

"Got it," Kiara said, though Jude could see her knuckles were white from how tightly she was holding the wheel.

"Relax your grip a little," he instructed. "You want to be firm but not death-gripping it. Now, put your foot on the brake and shift into drive."

The car lurched forward slightly as Kiara released the brake, making her gasp. Angela's hand gripped the back of Kiara's seat, her gasp also audible.

"That's normal," Jude said calmly. "The car wants to move forward when it's in drive. You control that with the brake. Now, very gently press the accelerator."

The car moved forward at a crawl, and Kiara let out a nervous laugh. "I'm doing it! I'm actually driving!"

"You're doing great," Jude said.

Out of the corner of his eye, he could see Angela watching intently. It didn't surprise him at all that Kiara had volunteered to go first. He had a feeling that this was the norm for them. Angela needed to observe first.

For the next half hour, Jude guided Kiara around the roads of the estate. It was actually the perfect place to practice driving, since there was no other traffic and the pattern of the road was a meandering circle, so they could just keep going around and around.

"Okay," Kiara said. "Your turn, Angie."

They'd come back around by the house, and Kiara was doing really well. No real surprise. She'd had confidence even before getting behind the wheel.

"Maybe we should do it another day," Angela said.

"Nope." Kiara turned in her seat to stare at Angela. "It's your turn *now.*"

Jude could see the apprehension on Angela's face. Where Kiara had been eager and excited, Angela looked like she was facing an execution.

"Hey," he said gently, turning in his seat to face her. "We don't have to do this today if you're not ready."

"No, I need to do this," Angela said, her voice barely above a whisper. She took a shaky breath.

Something in her tone made Jude's chest tighten. He wondered what other fears she'd had to overcome since leaving that farm.

They switched places, with Kiara sliding into the back seat and Angela taking the driver's position. Jude watched as she adjusted the seat and mirrors with careful precision, her movements deliberate and controlled.

"Take your time," he said, settling back into the passenger seat. "There's no rush."

Angela's breathing was shallow as she gripped the steering wheel. "What if I crash into something?"

"You won't," Jude said with quiet confidence. "And even if you do, it's just a car. Duncan has plenty of them."

"But what if I hurt someone?"

"Angela." Jude kept his voice firm but kind. "Look around. There's no one here but us, and we're surrounded by open space. The worst thing that could happen is that you drive into a snowbank."

"You've got this," Kiara said from the back, her voice encouraging. "It's actually easier than it looks."

Angela's hands trembled slightly as she gripped the steering wheel. Jude noticed immediately.

"Take a deep breath," he said, his voice softer than he'd intended. "There's no rush."

She followed his instructions, her shoulders relaxing marginally. "Okay. Brake on the left, gas on the right."

"That's right. And remember, gentle pressure on everything. This car responds to the lightest touch."

Angela shifted into drive, and the car lurched forward just as it had with Kiara. But instead of pressing the accelerator, Angela immediately slammed on the brake, sending them all forward into the restraining strap of their seatbelt.

"Ack!" Kiara squawked as she flopped back into the seat once the car settled.

"Sorry!" Angela's knuckles turned white on the steering wheel. "I'm sorry."

"It's okay," Jude said, fighting the urge to reach over and place his hand over hers. "That happens to everyone on their first time. Even Kiara did it. Just ease off the brake slowly."

Angela took another deep breath and did as instructed. The car settled into a gentle forward motion.

"Good," Jude said. "Now, just a little pressure on the gas."

The car inched forward as Angela applied the slightest pressure to the accelerator. Her entire body was rigid with concentration, her eyes wide and fixed on the road ahead.

"You're doing great," Jude encouraged. "Give it a little more gas. Just keep it slow and steady."

As they continued along the winding estate road, Jude noticed Angela gradually relaxing, her death grip on the steering wheel easing slightly.

"How am I doing?" she asked after they'd completed half a circuit.

"Perfectly," Jude said, and he meant it. She was cautious but controlled. "You're a natural."

"I don't feel like a natural," Angela muttered, but he could see a tiny smile tugging at the corner of her mouth.

That small smile made something warm unfurl in Jude's chest. He'd missed seeing her smile over the past couple of days.

"Can I try going a little faster?" she asked.

"Of course. Just ease into it gradually."

Angela pressed the accelerator a bit more, and the car picked up speed.

As they neared the house a short time later, completing the first lap, Kiara spoke up from the back. "Can you please let me off? I need to use the bathroom."

"Oh, we can be done for today," Angela said, glancing into the rearview mirror.

"Nope. Just let me off. You keep going. You need to do at least as many laps as I did."

Frowning, Angela slowed the car to a stop. Kiara reached forward and patted her on the shoulder. "See you in a few."

Once Kiara had shut the door, she hurried toward the house. Jude's gaze returned to Angela, who was still gripping the wheel as she stared straight ahead.

"Sorry," she said. "I didn't know she was going to do that."

Jude knew that was the truth because it was clear she didn't want to be left alone with him.

"We can end the lesson if you want," Jude offered, not wanting to make her more uncomfortable than she already was.

Thanks to Duncan's directive that Jude guard Angela and help her as needed, there was no way for her to avoid him. So, the sooner they could get past this awkwardness, the better.

"No, I should practice," Angela said, her voice soft but determined. "I need to learn this."

She eased the car forward again, her movements more confident than before but still cautious. They drove in silence for several minutes, the only sound being the quiet hum of the engine and the occasional crunch of snow under the tires.

"You're doing really well," Jude said finally, breaking the silence. "Most people aren't this controlled their first time behind the wheel."

"Probably because most people are in their teens when they learn to drive," Angela muttered drily. "And teens aren't known for their controlled behavior."

Jude chuckled. "Well, there is that."

"Although maybe you were," she said. "You seem like someone who has been controlled since birth."

"You're not wrong," Jude conceded. "How about you?"

"Oh, I was definitely an out-of-control teen."

The sarcasm in her voice made Jude grin, if only on the inside. He liked to get these brief flashes of personality. Especially when she was in the middle of something that was stressful for her.

"Being out of control was never allowed," Angela said, her tone more normal. "I think Jim figured that if we had energy to be out of control, we had the energy to be doing more chores."

"Well, you don't have to worry about chores here," Jude reminded her.

"I know," she said. "But we're finding it a bit of a challenge to just sit around with nothing to do. That's not how we've lived our lives."

"Just try to think of this time as a vacation," Jude said. "An extended vacation while you figure out what to do next."

"So we should just sleep late and lounge around the pool reading?"

"Well, since the pool is indoors, you could do that."

"And what a pool it is," she said.

"Duncan doesn't do anything by half measures," Jude told her.

"I'm coming to understand that. I mean, he wants to build us a *house*."

"You do realize that he has an ulterior motive in doing that, right?"

Angela glanced at him as she slowed to take a curve. "He wants to keep us close by?"

"That's part of it," Jude said. "But keeping you here on the estate also means it's easier to keep you safe. The estate is more secure than any other place he lives. So as long as you're on the estate, he doesn't have to worry about your safety."

"And that's why Annie lives here too?"

"It is. She wanted to move out on her own, but Duncan didn't want her to move away from the estate. Her cabin was the compromise."

"Has Duncan made any sort of decision about letting people know about me?" she asked. "So we can go into Serenity instead of having to go to Coeur d'Alene every time we want to buy something?"

"He hasn't let me know anything," Jude said. "I'll talk to him again and see what he's thinking."

He suspected that she wasn't keen to challenge Duncan if he put her off. Annie had no problem challenging her dad on things she didn't like, but he knew that Angela didn't have the same confidence in her relationship with him.

Hopefully, that would come in time.

Jude watched her profile as she concentrated on driving. The afternoon sun caught in her light brown hair, highlighting subtle gold strands he hadn't noticed before. He forced himself to look away.

"You're doing really well," he said as she passed the house again.

He'd thought Kiara might be standing outside waiting, but she wasn't.

"I've always been good at following instructions."

The simple statement carried a weight that made Jude's chest tighten. He wondered how much of her life had been spent following instructions out of fear of punishment.

As they rounded a curve in the road, Angela spoke again. "I'm sorry about how I acted after our shopping trip. It was childish."

Jude hadn't expected an apology. If anyone should be apologizing, it was him. "You have nothing to be sorry for."

"I do though." She glanced at him briefly before returning her attention to the road. "I made things awkward by asking personal questions, and then I got upset when you gave me honest answers."

"Angela—"

"It's okay," she continued. "I understand your position. I just... I need to keep things professional too. I don't want to make your job harder than it needs to be."

The words hit Jude like a physical blow. She was trying to protect him from her own feelings, putting his comfort above her own hurt. It was so typical of what he was coming to know about Angela—selfless even when she was in pain.

"Pull over," he said quietly.

Angela's eyes widened in alarm. "Did I do something wrong?"

"No. Just... please. Pull over."

She guided the car to the side of the road and put it in park, her hands trembling slightly as she released the steering wheel. "I'm sorry if I—"

"Stop apologizing." Jude turned in his seat to face her fully. "You have nothing to apologize for."

Angela stared down at her hands folded in her lap. "I made you uncomfortable. I can tell because things are awkward now."

The vulnerability in her voice undid something inside Jude. He'd been so focused on protecting himself, on maintaining a professional distance, that he'd hurt her in the process.

"Angela, look at me."

She lifted her eyes to his, and the pain he saw there made his chest ache.

"I wasn't uncomfortable because of your questions," he said carefully. "I was uncomfortable because it's very rare that I speak about my private life. I'm not used to it."

Her brow furrowed. "But you wouldn't have had to speak about it if I hadn't asked you those questions."

Jude ran a hand through his hair, knowing he somehow had to get rid of the awkwardness without leading her on. There couldn't be anything between them, regardless of the pull they apparently felt toward each other.

But he needed her to feel comfortable around him since there was no alternative. Until the situation with Jim and Craig was resolved, Duncan wouldn't remove him from his position in Angela's life.

And if he dared to go to Duncan to request the change, the man's suspicions would be roused. He wouldn't agree without a good reason, and Jude didn't have one he felt comfortable giving the man.

If he dared confess that he was feeling drawn to Angela, Duncan probably would agree to his request. But would he lose confidence in Jude's ability to do his job without distractions?

That couldn't happen.

He didn't know what he'd do without his job. Who he'd be.

So somehow, he had to clarify to Angela that there could never be anything between them. All without acknowledging how he might actually feel or how he suspected she might feel.

"Listen," Jude said, choosing his words carefully. "I want you to feel comfortable around me. We're going to be spending a lot of time together, and I don't want things to be awkward between us."

Angela nodded slightly, her eyes still uncertain.

"The truth is, I'm not good at personal conversations. I never have been." He looked out at the snow-covered landscape for a moment, gathering his thoughts. "In my position, I've learned to keep people at a distance. It's safer that way."

"Safer for whom?" she asked softly.

The question caught him off guard. "For everyone involved."

Angela turned slightly in her seat to face him better. "I think I understand. You're worried about crossing some kind of professional line because you work for my father."

Jude felt his pulse quicken. She was getting too close to the truth. "It's more complicated than that."

"Is it?" Her voice was gentle, not challenging. "Because it seems pretty simple to me. You're afraid of losing your job if you show that you're human beneath all that... security guy exterior."

Despite himself, Jude felt the corner of his mouth twitch. "Security guy exterior?"

"You know what I mean." A small smile played across her lips. "All serious and professional all the time."

"That's who I am, Angela."

"I don't think that's all you are." She looked down at her hands again. "But I understand if that's all you want me to see."

The words hung between them, honest and raw. Jude felt something inside him shift, and a door cracked open that he'd kept firmly shut for years.

"It's not about what I want," he said finally. "It's about what's appropriate. What's possible."

Angela's gaze met his again, searching. "And what is possible, Jude? Between us?"

The directness of her question startled him. He hadn't expected her to be so forthright, though perhaps he should have. Everything he'd learned about Angela showed her to be somewhat reserved and tentative until she set her mind to something. Then she could be quite tenacious.

"Friendship," he said after a long moment. "We can be friends."

It was both the truth and a lie. They could be friends, like he was friends with Annie and Benji. However, the way his heart quickened when she looked at him suggested that it would be a challenge to have a simple friendship with her.

"Friends," she repeated, testing the word. "I think I'd like that."

Jude nodded, feeling both relief and an inexplicable disappointment. "Good. Then let's start over. No awkwardness. Just... friends."

Angela smiled, a genuine smile that reached her eyes. "I'd like that."

"Should we continue with the driving lesson now?" Jude asked, injecting a lightness into his tone he didn't entirely feel.

"Yes, please." Angela put her hands back on the steering wheel. "I think I'm getting the hang of it."

Jude thought she was too. The sense of pride that filled him could be how a friend felt, right?

He actually had no idea if that was the case. However, he felt like she deserved to have people proud of her since she'd probably had precious few who had been for most of her life.

CHAPTER FIFTEEN

It was easier said than done to keep control of his feelings, and Jude should have been glad for a break from the estate and the possibility of running into Angela. Except he was surrounded by things that made him see his own life in stark contrast.

He looked around the cozy space, taking in all the little things that made it a home for his best friend, Cooper, his wife Melanie, and their kids.

The framed pictures on the walls and the mantle over the fireplace. The lamps on the end tables. The knitted blankets draped over the back of the couch and the arm of the overstuffed glider. The plants in front of the window.

So many things that this home had that his didn't. He had only one picture in his whole house, and it had been taken shortly before his dad had passed away. They'd been standing side by side, smiles on their faces.

Neither of them were big smilers, but they had gone fishing and managed to catch exactly nothing. Still, it had been the best day of his life because they'd spent time talking and laughing in ways they didn't when they were tied up with work.

But that day, his dad had banned all talk of work. It had meant that for the first hour or so, silence had been more prominent than conversation. Soon enough, however, conversation had begun to flow.

His dad had shared memories of growing up, and the times he'd spent with his dad and older brother out fishing or hunting. His dad—Jude's grandfather—had passed away from cancer shortly before his own dad's heart attack. His grandmother had passed when his dad had been a teen.

So, like Jude, he had been raised by just his dad.

By the time they had returned to shore that day, their cooler empty of the sandwiches and drinks they'd filled it with, Jude had smiled more in those hours on the boat than he had in ages.

It seemed that his dad had cherished the time as well because he'd convinced Jude to set up his phone to take a picture of them together. Though he'd grumbled about it at the time, he was glad he'd done it.

Not long after that, his dad had passed away. The hole he'd left behind was a constant reminder to Jude of his dad's absence, but the memories of that day had sustained him. And he liked to think that his dad would be proud of the man he'd become.

"Did you shoot anyone this week, Uncle Jude?"

Jude smiled down at the eight-year-old boy as he shook his head. "Not this week."

"Dad didn't shoot anyone this week either."

"That's good," Jude told him. "Just the way we like it."

Alex held up his hand, showing Jude what he held. "I made that yesterday."

Jude took the Lego figure and turned it over in his hand. "You did a great job, buddy."

"I didn't even need help." The boy grinned. "Right, Dad?"

Cooper Sullivan walked in carrying his five-year-old daughter. Chloe gave Jude a wide smile and a little wave.

Both children had light caramel-colored skin, a perfect blend of their parents' skin tones. Cooper had lightly tanned skin, and his blond hair was cut short into a crew cut. The kids had loose dark brown curls, and their eyes were a light grey.

"That's right," Cooper said as he set Chloe down. "You did it all by yourself."

"Good job," Jude said as he handed the figure back to the little boy.

"Let's head out onto the back deck," Cooper said with a tilt of his head. "I've got to keep an eye on the steaks."

Jude followed him through the kitchen, where Melanie was prepping some food. She handed Cooper a tray with steaks on it, then told the kids to put on their winter clothes if they wanted to play outside.

The back porch was screened in, so it was still chilly, but Cooper had no problem barbecuing even in the middle of winter.

Jude shoved his hands into the pockets of his coat, watching as steam billowed from the barbecue when Cooper opened the lid. He quickly slapped the steaks onto the grill and closed it.

The back door swung open, and the kids came barreling out. They headed down the steps, then followed a path in the snow to the play structure Jude had helped Cooper assemble the previous summer.

"So how's work?" Cooper asked as he leaned against the railing of the porch.

Jude shifted his weight, his breath forming small clouds in the cold air. "Busy. Duncan's daughter is back."

Cooper's eyebrows shot up. "The one who was kidnapped?"

Jude and Cooper had connected several years earlier when they'd both volunteered to work security at a church Christmas event. Jude hadn't been super involved at the church, but every once in a while, they had need of his particular set of skills. Usually at Christmas and Easter and once during the summer when they had large events open to the public.

He and Cooper had hit it off, and over time, he'd revealed bits and pieces of his life and his job, knowing he could trust the man. Cooper and Melanie had become close friends. The only ones Jude had allowed into his life.

"Yeah. Angela." Jude kept his voice neutral, but something in his tone must have caught Cooper's attention because his friend studied him more closely.

"That's got to be intense for everyone involved," Cooper said carefully. "How's she adjusting?"

"Better than expected, I think. It's overwhelming for her, but she seems resilient." Jude watched Alex push Chloe on the swing, the chains creaking in the cold air. "She and her sister both."

"Sister?"

"The people who abducted her had adopted another girl too. Angela considers her a sister." Jude paused, then added, "Duncan's treating her like family too."

Cooper nodded thoughtfully. "That's good of him. Must be hard for all of them, figuring out how to be a family after all this time."

"It is." Jude watched the kids as they tossed snow at each other. "Duncan's asked me to handle her security."

"Makes sense. You're the best he's got." Cooper glanced at the grill, then back at Jude. "How's that going?"

The question seemed casual, but Jude knew Cooper well enough to recognize the underlying curiosity.

"Pretty well," Jude said, not sure yet if he wanted to share the struggle he was having with his emotions. Cooper might be his best friend, but Jude still kept things pretty close to his chest. "It's been awhile since I've been so involved in hands-on security training."

"Are you out of shape?" Cooper asked. "Getting your butt kicked?"

Jude gave a huff of laughter. "No. I'm not out of shape, though Annie manages to drop me occasionally."

"So you've had to get out from behind your desk," Cooper said. "And you're struggling?"

"Not struggling," Jude told him. "It's just that my days look different now."

Cooper took a minute to flip the steaks. "Is it weird to have someone around who looks like Annie, but isn't her?"

"Not really," Jude said. "Though they are biologically identical, it's not hard to tell them apart. Their hairstyles are different, and their personalities are not the same, which shows up in their mannerisms and such. None of us would ever mix them up."

Jude gave Cooper some details about Jim and Craig. Duncan had contacted someone in the Serenity Point Police Department so that they were aware of what was going on. However, their main interactions with law enforcement had been with the FBI.

All talk of work ceased, however, when they sat down to eat. It was a noisy, somewhat chaotic meal, with the two kids eager to talk about whatever they deemed important in their world.

Jude soaked it all in, having long accepted that something like this would never be his. The homey environment. The cozy warmth of the home. The chatter of children. The home-cooked meal. The love and affection that flowed between Cooper and Melanie.

In the past, he'd appreciated stepping into their home and being part of their small family for a short period of time. But that day, being there made him wonder what his life might have looked like if he had opened himself up to having a family.

Early in their acquaintance, Melanie had tried to set Jude up with people she knew. Cooper's sister. Melanie's older sister. A cousin. A friend from church.

Rather than waste his—and their—time, he'd told Melanie he wasn't interested in blind dates. She'd still tried sporadically since then to set him up, but he'd politely declined.

"I have someone who wants to go on a date with you," Melanie said as she passed him a basket of fresh dinner rolls. "She's sure that you're her soulmate."

Jude lifted his brows. "Say what?"

"She thinks you're her soulmate," Melanie said with a grin.

"Even if I believed in soulmates, it seems a bit weird that some-one who hasn't even had a conversation with me thinks that is what I am to her."

Melanie laughed. "She spotted you at church, and when she saw you talking to me, she figured that getting close to me would mean she could get close to you."

"As a cop who has seen stalker situations, I'd recommend that this be a stern no from you, Jude."

"Even if she weren't delusional, I would have given a stern no."

The idea of dating her twisted his stomach, for some reason. Yeah... for some reason. He knew the reason, but he didn't want to acknowledge it.

"I told her that you were unavailable," Melanie said. "Just be aware and maybe don't make eye contact with her."

"You're going to have to show me her picture so I know who she is."

"I honestly don't think she's harmful," Melanie said as she brought up a social media account with a picture. "She's actually very sweet."

The woman in the photo was attractive enough—blonde, mid-thirties, with a bright smile—but Jude felt nothing as he looked at her image. No spark of interest. No curiosity.

"Thanks for the warning," he said, handing the phone back to Melanie.

"You know," Melanie said, studying him with that perceptive gaze he sometimes found uncomfortable. "You used to at least con-sider these setups. Lately, you've just shut them down immediately."

Jude reached for his water glass. "I'm just busy with work."

"Hmm." Melanie exchanged a look with Cooper. "That's the same excuse you gave last time. And the time before that."

Cooper cleared his throat. "Melly, maybe Jude doesn't want to talk about his love life."

"Or lack thereof," Jude muttered, trying to keep his tone light.

"I just want you to be happy," Melanie said, her voice softening. "You deserve someone special in your life."

The sincerity in her voice made something in Jude's chest tighten. These people genuinely cared about him. They wanted him to have what they had.

"I appreciate that," he said. "But I'm good. Really."

"Uncle Jude doesn't need a girlfriend," Alex announced with the certainty only an eight-year-old could muster. "He has a gun."

The adults burst into laughter, the tension of the moment broken by Alex's matter-of-fact declaration.

"A gun is not the same as having someone to come home to," Melanie said, still smiling.

"I don't know," Cooper teased. "My Glock has never asked me to take out the trash."

Melanie rolled her eyes. "You're not helping."

"I'm not sure those are equivalent, buddy," Cooper said, ruffling his son's hair.

"They're not," Jude agreed, grateful for the child's inadvertent rescue. "But thanks for the support."

Chloe looked up from her plate, her gray eyes serious. "My teacher says everyone needs someone to love them. Even the grumpy ones."

"I'm not grumpy," Jude protested mildly.

"You kinda are," Cooper said with a grin.

Melanie reached over and patted Jude's hand. "It's part of your charm."

The conversation moved on to other topics, but Jude found himself turning the children's words over in his mind. Did he need someone? He'd convinced himself for years that he didn't. That his work was enough. That the occasional dinner with friends like this satisfied any need for human connection.

But lately, there had been moments when he'd caught himself wondering what it would be like to come home to someone. To have a place that felt lived in rather than just occupied.

And those thoughts had started right around the time Angela Burke had entered his life. She was the one who came to mind when his thoughts wandered in the direction of home and hearth.

"Earth to Jude," Cooper's voice broke through his thoughts. "You with us?"

"Sorry," Jude said, shaking his head slightly. "Just thinking about work."

Cooper's expression said he didn't buy that explanation, but he didn't push. Instead, he stood and began clearing plates. "Why don't you help me with the dishes?"

Jude nodded, grateful for the distraction. In the kitchen, he and Cooper worked in comfortable silence for a few minutes, the sound of running water and clinking dishes filling the space.

"You know," Cooper said finally, handing Jude a plate to put in the dishwasher, "I've known you for what, five years now? And I've never seen you this distracted."

Jude focused on organizing the dishes in the rack with more attention than it required. "I told you, work's been busy."

"Right. Work." Cooper shut off the water and turned to face him. "Want to try again?"

Jude reached for another plate. "There's nothing to try again."

"Jude." Cooper's voice was gentle but firm. "I'm a cop. I know when someone's avoiding a subject. And you're avoiding this one like it's radioactive."

For a moment, Jude considered deflecting again. But the weight of keeping everything bottled up was becoming harder to bear. And if he couldn't trust Cooper with this, who could he trust?

"There's someone," he murmured, not looking at his friend.

Cooper's eyebrows rose. "Someone?"

"Yeah." Jude ran a hand through his hair. "Someone I can't have."

"Ah." Cooper leaned against the counter, crossing his arms. "Married?"

"No, of course not." Jude set the plate carefully in the rack. "Worse."

"Worse than married?" Cooper's brow furrowed. "What could be worse than—" His eyes widened. "Wait. You don't mean..."

Jude nodded grimly. "Angela."

Cooper let out a low whistle. "Duncan's daughter."

"The very same." Jude closed the dishwasher door with more force than necessary. "And before you ask, nothing has happened. Nothing will happen."

"But you want it to."

It wasn't a question, and Jude didn't bother denying it. "Doesn't matter what I want."

Cooper was quiet for a moment, studying his friend. "How serious is this? Is it just attraction, or...?"

"I don't know." Jude braced his hands against the counter, staring down at the granite surface. "I've never felt this way before. It's like..." He struggled to find the words. "It's like I can't stop thinking about her. About making her smile. About keeping her safe."

"That last part is literally your job description," Cooper pointed out.

"It's different." Jude shook his head. "With Annie or Benji, I'd take a bullet for them because it's my duty and I care about them. With Angela..." He paused, then shook his head. "She's my responsibility. My job. That's all she can ever be."

Cooper studied him for a long moment. "Is that the only reason? Her being Duncan's daughter?"

Jude wiped his hands on a dishtowel, buying time. "She's also almost twelve years younger than me."

"That's not unheard of."

"She's been through trauma. She's vulnerable."

"All valid concerns," Cooper acknowledged. "But none of that explains why you look like you're carrying the weight of the world on your shoulders."

Jude sighed, leaning back against the counter. "You know what my life is. The estate. The security protocols. And sometimes I still have to guard Duncan when he travels to high-risk areas. What kind of life is that to offer someone? Especially someone who's just getting a taste of freedom for the first time?"

"So this is about protecting her from you?"

"From the life I lead," Jude corrected. "From the risks I still have to take at times."

Cooper was quiet for a moment, then shook his head. "You know what I think? I think you're making excuses."

"Excuses?" Jude's voice sharpened. "Cooper, I could lose my job. Duncan trusts me to protect his daughter, not to—"

"Not to what? Fall in love with her? Care about her as more than just an assignment?" Cooper's voice was gentle but direct. "Jude, you're not some predator taking advantage of a vulnerable woman. You're a good man who's developed feelings for someone. That's not a crime."

"It is when that someone is—"

"Duncan's daughter. Yeah, you mentioned that." Cooper crossed his arms. "But you know what? Duncan's also the man who stepped in when your dad passed away. Who trusts you more than anyone else in his life. Don't you think he'd want his daughter to be with someone he knows will protect her? Someone with integrity?"

Jude felt his chest tighten. "You don't understand. The Burke family means everything to me. They're the only family I've really had since Dad died. If I cross this line and Duncan feels I've betrayed his trust..."

"Then you'd talk to him about it. Man to man. Like an adult."

"I can't." The words came out more forcefully than Jude intended. "I can't risk it."

Cooper studied him with those perceptive cop eyes. "So you'd rather be miserable? Live the rest of your life wondering what might have been?"

"This is my reality. My mother left because she couldn't handle my father's job. She couldn't live with the uncertainty, the danger, the fact that his work always came first."

"Not every woman has that response. Melanie knew the risks when she married me, and she still took the chance."

"Not everyone is as devoted as Melanie," Jude said. "As my dad found out."

"But you're not your father."

"I'm exactly like my father," Jude said firmly. "I've made the same choices he did. Put the job first. Kept people at arm's length. The only difference is I learned from his mistake. Except for once, I have never let anyone get close enough that their leaving would hurt. So, my job is my life. It's all that matters to me."

Cooper frowned. "But now there's Angela."

"Yes. Now there's Angela," Jude agreed quietly. "Which is why I need to put a stop to it before it goes any further."

"Does she feel the same way about you?"

Jude's jaw tightened. "It doesn't matter."

"That's not what I asked."

"Cooper—"

"Does she?"

Jude closed his eyes briefly. "I think so. Maybe. I don't know."

"And that terrifies you."

"Of course it does." Jude's voice was rough.

Cooper was quiet for a long moment, then said, "You won't lose everything, you know. You'll never lose me and Melanie. You'll never lose your integrity. And you'll never lose God. Have you prayed about the situation?"

Jude hesitated, then shook his head. "I'm not even sure what to pray."

"At the very least, you could pray that God would make His will clear. Ask Him to give you clarity about things. There is no moral right or wrong in this situation. I'll just encourage you to search for God's will."

Jude had heard similar words from the pastor of the church over the years. But even though he understood the concept of seeking God's will for his life, he'd never practiced it. He'd never really had a conflicted spirit about any of the decisions he'd made over the years.

He wanted to say that he wasn't confused or conflicted over his burgeoning feelings, but that would be a lie.

His phone chimed with a text message alert, so Jude pulled it out to check. While Sunday was technically a day off for Jude, the team always knew they could get hold of him by phone. It wasn't likely an emergency, or they would have phoned him.

Angela: *I made some cinnamon buns today. Do you want some? I could bring them to your place.*

A smile tipped the corners of his mouth.

"I see that," Cooper said with a laugh. "Text from Angela, huh? I like that smile on you."

Jude rolled his eyes, then considered his response. He didn't generally favor sending text messages since he tended to spend more time correcting the mistakes his fingers made.

Deciding to wait until he was in his vehicle to respond, he said, "Guess I'd better head back to the estate. Thanks for the meal and the advice."

Cooper reached for his hand, then pulled him in for a quick hug, slapping him on the back. "Glad you could spend some time with us. We'll have to do it again soon."

Jude agreed, then went to say goodbye to Melanie and the kids. The hugs they gave him always brought a bit of emotion bubbling to the surface.

He didn't have many affectionate interactions with people. And while he was usually okay with that, it was in those moments when the kids wrapped their tiny arms around his neck that he wondered what it would be like to have kids of his own.

The wonderings never lasted long because he knew that his choice had been made years ago to not take that path. But now...

"But now *nothing*," Jude muttered as he started up his truck.

He lifted his phone to record a quick voice memo to send back to Angela. After it was sent, he set his phone in the holder he had for it, then put the truck in gear to head home.

CHAPTER SIXTEEN

Angela set her phone face down on the counter and returned her attention to the icing she was making to put on the cinnamon rolls.

She shouldn't have sent the text, but they'd agreed to friendship. And in her mind, friends could share cinnamon rolls. And if friendship—and sharing cinnamon rolls—was all she could have, then she would cherish it.

Unfortunately, she wasn't sure exactly what friendship meant to Jude. She assumed that if he wasn't interested in what she'd offered, he'd tell her that it wasn't a good time. Which would be fine.

Earlier in the day, she'd watched the livestream from the church in Briar Hollow. It had made her a little homesick. Not for anything but the church and the people there. She missed the smiles and hugs of the older women who had taken her under their wings. Would she find anything like that in Idaho?

Probably not if she was never allowed off the estate.

Grimacing at the thought, Angela grabbed a spoon from the drawer and began to drizzle the frosting on the cinnamon rolls.

After the livestream, she'd been at a loss for what to do. After discovering the cook was off for the day, she'd decided to make use of the empty kitchen.

Kiara had spent the afternoon looking over schooling options on their laptop. She seemed to have zeroed in on taking some classes online and was actually excited about the possibility.

Angela wasn't sure what she was going to do yet. Her skills seemed useless in this new life on the estate, and she didn't know how to change that.

When her phone let her know she'd received a message, Angela set the bowl of icing aside and picked up her phone.

She was surprised when she didn't see a text message. Instead, there was a voice memo. Smiling at the prospect of hearing Jude's voice, she leaned a hip against the counter and tapped the screen to start the playback and lifted it to her ear.

"Hi Angela. I'm currently not at the estate, but I'll swing by the house when I'm back. Probably in about an hour or so."

The message was short, and before she could think about it, she tapped to replay it. His words made her smile, but also made her wonder where he'd been.

Not that it was any of her business.

Still, she was curious about what he did on his day off. She had a hard time envisioning him with a hobby, but she'd like to know if he had one.

The rest of the house was quiet. Julian had left, and though no one had said where he'd gone, Angela assumed he'd returned to New York, where he lived.

Duncan and Elizabeth were somewhere in the house, and Benji was with Annie. They'd left for church earlier that morning but hadn't returned yet.

Every day, Angela felt a little more lost. She had more money than she knew what to do with, but now she felt like she had no direction. No purpose. Useless.

Which was how she'd ended up making cinnamon rolls again. It was the one thing she knew how to do well, but there was no one clamoring for them here like there had been in Briar Hollow.

She finished slathering the icing on the slightly warm rolls, hoping that whoever ate one would enjoy it.

Though she could have put all the dishes she'd used in the large dishwasher, Angela filled the deep sink with warm, soapy water. It felt lovely to plunge her hands into the warmth as she stared out the large window above the sink at the snow-covered landscape.

She was still trying to get used to the cold. The day before, she and Kiara had placed an order online for some warmer clothes to supplement the clothes they'd brought with them from Briar Hollow. Most of those were purchased at the thrift store in the town.

Finished cleaning the last of the pans she'd used, Angela glanced up in time to see a large dark gray truck drive past. Her hands stilled in the water, tightening around the dishcloth she held.

Was that Jude arriving back on the estate?

Her heart gave a flutter as the vehicle moved out of sight. She hurriedly finished washing the pan, then rinsed it before reaching for the dishtowel she'd been using.

Moving quickly, she set the pan down on the counter, then went to one of the cabinets and pulled out a couple of plates. She had no idea if he'd actually hang around to have a cinnamon bun, or if he would want to just pick some up and take them home to enjoy.

Along with the plates, she also found a container and set it on the counter, ready to fill it if it looked like he was just picking some up. So whatever he decided, she was prepared.

Of course, she knew what she preferred.

She moved one of the cinnamon rolls onto a plate, then hesitated. Would it look too eager if she had two plates ready? Maybe she should wait until he arrived before plating a second one.

The sound of the mudroom door opening sent a ripple of anticipation through her. Angela smoothed her hands down her flour-dusted apron, suddenly wishing she'd taken a moment to check her appearance.

"Something smells amazing," Jude's deep voice carried from the hallway before he appeared in the kitchen doorway.

He looked different somehow—more relaxed in jeans and a dark blue sweater that made his eyes seem even more vivid than usual. His hair was slightly tousled, as if he'd been running his hands through it.

"I hope you're still offering those cinnamon rolls," he said, a hint of warmth in his tone that she wasn't used to hearing.

"I am." Angela gestured to the cooling rack, suddenly finding herself nervous. She gripped her hands tightly together to keep them from fluttering. "I just finished icing them."

Jude came further into the kitchen, his presence filling the space in a way that made it feel both smaller and cozier, even though it was large and sunny.

"You didn't have to go to all this trouble."

"It wasn't any trouble," she said, reaching for a second plate. "You know I enjoy baking. These days, it gives me something to do with my hands when my mind is restless."

"I know that feeling." Jude leaned against the counter, and Angela felt him watching her as she carefully transferred another cinnamon roll to the plate. "Though I tend to take my guns apart and clean them when I need to occupy my hands."

"I'm not sure that would work for me," Angela said with a small smile. She slid one of the plates toward him. "I hope you like it."

Jude picked up the plate and leaned in slightly to breathe in the scent. "This smells incredible. I haven't had homemade cinnamon rolls like these since..."

He paused, and something flickered across his face—a memory, perhaps.

"Since?" Angela prompted gently, still wanting to know more about him.

"Since I was a little kid," he finished. "My mom wasn't much of a baker, though she did make some great chocolate chip cookies. But there was this older woman who lived next door to us—Mrs. Patterson—and sometimes she'd bring us freshly baked cinnamon rolls. Iced, just like these."

Angela felt a small thrill at this glimpse into his past. "You grew up in New York City?"

"Yes. In the Bronx." Jude took a bite of the cinnamon roll and closed his eyes briefly. When he opened them again, he looked almost surprised. "This is amazing."

"Thank you." Angela felt warmth spread through her chest at his approval. She gestured toward the small breakfast nook by the window. "Why don't you sit at the table? Would you like some coffee?"

"Sure. That would be nice."

Angela quickly made Jude a cup of coffee, glad that she'd finally mastered the fancy coffee machine.

"Did you want cream or sugar?" Angela asked, noticing that he'd taken his plate to the table, and judging from the contents of his plate, it looked like he'd helped himself to another cinnamon bun.

"Nope. I just take it black."

It was only as she carried his mug to where he stood by the table that she noticed that he'd also transferred her plate there. It wasn't until she sat down that he took the seat across from her.

He might not have the wealth of Duncan, but Jude Kessler had stellar manners, just like her father. It was an oddity in her world... her old world. Jim and Craig had never shown her and Kiara any level of respect.

As they settled across from each other at the small table, Angela willed herself not to say anything dumb. She'd wanted him to decide to eat there, but now that he had, she didn't know what to say.

The murmur of conversation had her turning toward the entrance to the kitchen. Her heart sank when Duncan and Elizabeth appeared. The couple came to a halt, then exchanged glances before advancing further into the room.

"Hello there, Jude," Duncan said.

Jude had gotten to his feet and greeted his boss with a nod. "Angela invited me over to have a cinnamon roll since I missed out on the last batch, and I thought it would be a good time to review the week ahead."

"Sounds like a plan," Duncan said.

"Would you like some?" Angela asked as she moved to slide from the breakfast nook.

"I can get it, darling," Elizabeth said, waving her off with a smile.

Angela sank back down, then scooted over, knowing someone was going to have to sit beside her. Her eyes widened when Jude shifted his plate and mug over to her side of the nook.

She moved over further to make sure he had the room he needed, but Jude didn't sit back down until Elizabeth and Duncan had joined them. His arm pressed against hers since there wasn't a lot of room in the nook, but Angela didn't mind. His strength and warmth called to her, making her want to lean against his arm. To rest her head on his shoulder.

Sunlight streamed in through the windows next to her, casting them in a softening light as the day inched toward twilight. Outside, the snow-covered landscape gleamed white, and though she hadn't been out in it, so didn't know for sure, it looked cold.

But sitting there next to Jude, she was warm and happy.

"So how are things for this week?" Duncan asked. "Everything ready for Tuesday?"

"Yes. I've made arrangements for a car for Jill, as well as a suite at the resort."

"How long is she staying?" Duncan then shifted his attention to Angela, pointing at the half-eaten cinnamon roll on his plate. "This is very good, by the way."

"Thank you," she said.

"They are very delicious," Elizabeth agreed. "And they're going to be far too tempting."

Jude took a sip of his coffee, then set the mug down. "She's staying through Sunday."

Duncan grimaced. "I have half a mind to fly myself and Liz out of here for that period of time."

"We can't abandon the children," Elizabeth said gently as she rested her hand on Duncan's arm. "As challenging as it is to deal with Jill."

"Well, there's really no reason you should have to deal with her," Jude said. "Will Julian be back?"

"Yes, he'll be flying back here tomorrow night."

Angela was glad for that, though hopefully Julian would be sober for the visit.

"Good," Jude said. "That will make things easier for Angela."

"I'm nervous about meeting her," Angela admitted, then immediately regretted the confession. She didn't want to seem weak or childish.

"That's completely understandable," Elizabeth said warmly. "Meeting a parent for the first time—especially under these circumstances—would be overwhelming for anyone. And having to do it twice is probably double the stress for you."

Duncan's expression softened as he looked at Angela. "If at any point you feel uncomfortable or want to leave, just tell Jude. He'll get you out of there immediately."

"I will," Jude confirmed, his voice steady and reassuring.

Angela felt some of the tension in her shoulders ease. Having Jude there would definitely help. Even with their complicated friendship, she trusted him completely when it came to her safety and well-being.

"What about Annie?" Angela asked. "Will she be meeting with her mom while she's here?"

Duncan and Elizabeth exchanged a look that Angela was beginning to recognize—the kind of silent communication that came from years of marriage.

"That's up to Annie," Duncan said carefully. "Jill will probably ask to see her, but I won't pressure Annie into doing anything she's not ready for."

"She's been doing better lately," Elizabeth added. "More confident in setting boundaries. But the idea of seeing her mother is still difficult."

Angela nodded, understanding more than she wanted to about difficult family dynamics. The irony wasn't lost on her that she was nervous about meeting her biological mother while simultaneously grateful for the distance she'd had from her.

"Any other plans for the week?" Duncan asked.

"We'll continue with the self-defense training and driving lessons as time allows."

"No weapons training yet?"

Jude shook his head. "Once this week is over, we'll start with that."

"Kiara seems to be looking forward to it," Elizabeth said with a smile.

"Oh yes," Angela agreed. "She's been so excited about learning all this new stuff."

"She's definitely been an eager pupil," Jude said.

Angela felt a twinge of insecurity. Would he have preferred her to be more enthusiastic, like Kiara was?

"You're not as eager, Angela?" Duncan asked.

"I, uh... tend to approach things with a bit more caution." Angela gripped the glass of water she'd filled for herself. "But once I feel a little more confident, I enjoy learning new things."

"Caution is good," Duncan said. "Don't let anyone tell you differently. As long as it's not fear that keeps you from ever tackling things."

She'd had a lot of fear in her life, but that had been more about what would result if she didn't learn fast enough. Without that pressure, her caution wasn't completely based in fear. Mainly her normal reluctance to tackle new things.

"I hope you're better with a gun than I was," Elizabeth said with a laugh. "I think I was Jude's worst student ever."

"I'd like to say you are wrong," Jude said. "But sadly, you are quite correct."

"I might take that title," Angela said.

"You haven't practiced in a while, Liz." Duncan glanced at his wife. "Maybe you should spend some time refreshing while the girls are taking lessons."

"I could do that," she replied with a smile. "It will give me something to do while you're gone."

"You're leaving?" Angela asked, the question slipping out before she realized what she was saying.

"Next week, yes. I need to go to New York and then Miami for some meetings."

"Do you have bodyguards when you travel?"

Duncan nodded, then Jude said, "He travels with a team of four. He is well protected."

"I lost my best bodyguard when I promoted you, though."

Jude chuckled. "You didn't get rid of me completely."

"True. You have my back when it's most vulnerable."

"What do you mean by that?" Angela asked.

"I take Jude with me when I go to areas where the risk is higher. I trust him implicitly to keep me safe."

Angela's stomach clenched at the thought of Jude putting his life on the line to protect Duncan.

"But the team you have guarding me right now is great. I trust them without question."

"How do you trust them?" Angela asked. "After what happened to me and Annie, how do you trust them?"

"The main reason I trust *them* is that I trust *Jude*. He has done due diligence in vetting each member of our staff. Whether they are a driver, a gardener, or on the security team."

When Angela looked over at Jude, she saw he was focused on his cinnamon roll.

Duncan chuckled. "Jude doesn't like it when people toot his horn, but someone has to do it as he never will."

It made Angela feel good that her heart had landed on a trustworthy man. An honorable man. At least it proved that she had the ability to discern whether a man was good or bad. Even if he would only ever be her friend.

"Jude has certainly earned our trust over the years," Elizabeth said, her warm gaze settling on him. "He's proven himself time and again."

Jude shifted in his seat, clearly not enjoying being the topic of conversation. "It's just my job."

"It's more than that," Duncan said firmly. "And you know it."

Angela watched as Jude's jaw tightened slightly, a flush of color rising on his neck. She found his humility endearing—another quality that made him different from the men she'd grown up around. Jim and Craig had boasted about even the smallest accomplishments, demanding recognition for everything they did.

"Speaking of your job," Duncan continued, mercifully changing the subject, "how is the plan coming for the new security system at the girls' house?"

"Garrett and I have been exchanging ideas," Jude replied, visibly relieved by the shift in focus. "I think we've landed on something that will provide maximum security without making it feel like a fortress."

"That's important," Elizabeth nodded. "It should feel like a home, not a prison."

The word "prison" made Angela's stomach tighten. She'd felt trapped for so long on that isolated farm—even though she hadn't fully realized it until they'd escaped. The idea of her new home feeling even remotely like that was disturbing.

"It won't," Jude said, as if reading her mind. His eyes met hers briefly. "The security features will be invisible unless they have to be obvious. Hidden exterior cameras, reinforced glass that looks normal, door locks that respond to your fingerprints. Nothing that would make you feel hemmed in."

"That sounds better," Angela said, though she still felt a flutter of anxiety at the thought of needing such extensive security measures.

"The goal is for you to feel safe without feeling trapped," Duncan added gently. "I know that's a delicate balance, especially given what you've been through."

Angela nodded, grateful that he understood without her having to explain. She picked at her cinnamon roll, suddenly not very hungry.

"On a lighter note," Elizabeth said, clearly sensing the need to change the subject again, "have you given any more thought to what you'd like to do? Duncan mentioned you and Kiara were discussing options."

"Kiara's looking into online classes," Angela said. "She's always been good at academics. I'm... still figuring things out."

"What interests you?" Elizabeth asked. "Besides baking, which you're clearly talented at."

Angela felt heat rise in her cheeks. "I don't know. I've never really had the chance to explore different things. On the farm, we just did what needed to be done."

"Well, now you have time to discover what you might enjoy," Duncan said. "There's no rush."

Angela knew there wasn't. But the more time that passed without having a direction, the more worried she became that she wouldn't find something meaningful to do with her life.

But for the next week, her focus was going to be on meeting her mom. Once that was accomplished, she'd get serious about finding something to do with her life.

When they'd finished eating their cinnamon rolls, Jude said that he needed to leave. Angela felt a bit bereft that they hadn't had more time with just each other to talk.

She put a few more cinnamon rolls into a container, then gave it to Jude before he left. Alone in the kitchen, she put away the rest, then headed up to her room.

By the time Wednesday afternoon came, Angela was a ball of nerves. Her anxiety about meeting her mother was even worse than how anxious she'd felt over meeting Duncan.

The clothes they'd ordered had arrived Tuesday morning and, thankfully, they'd fit, and Angela thought they looked okay. She still didn't know how to dress as a rich person since she and Kiara always had to just settle for whatever they found at the thrift store.

Annie seemed to go for comfort over style. Elizabeth, however, tended to dress more stylishly, so Angela had tried to land somewhere in the middle.

Kiara hadn't seemed nearly as worried about what to wear. Though Kiara had always been more confident than her, Angela wasn't sure what to make of her confidence since coming to the estate.

Was she really that confident about everything?

"No time to think about that now," Angela muttered as she slid her feet into the heeled boots she'd ordered. "Let's get this over with."

She swung her door open to find Kiara in the hall.

"Ready to go?" Kiara asked with a smile.

Was she? Not really. But it was time to suck it up and face yet another new challenge.

I can do all things through Christ who strengthens me.

She was once again leaning on that strength to get through a difficult situation. Nerves fluttered wildly in her stomach as they left their rooms.

"Everything is going to be okay, Angie," Kiara said as she looped her arm through Angela's.

"Is it?"

"Duncan has already made it clear that he's not going to force you to have a relationship with Jill," Kiara reminded her. "So go into it hoping for the best, but with the knowledge that if it doesn't go well, you can walk away with Duncan's blessing."

Except that Angela felt like she'd be failing if she couldn't establish a relationship with her mother. Her *real* mother.

"Let's go," Kiara said. "Jude will be waiting for us."

That was the only bright spot in the whole situation. She might be facing something challenging, but at least she'd be doing it with Jude by her side.

CHAPTER SEVENTEEN

Jude poured himself a cup of coffee from the carafe on the buffet in the breakfast room, then took a sip.

"You have my permission to shut the meeting down if things start going south," Duncan said.

Jude nodded. "I'll keep that in mind."

Duncan hadn't defined what *going south* really meant, but Jude had his own definition. Basically, if the meeting with her mother was causing Angela even the smallest amount of distress, it would be over.

Jill would be livid. She'd always had a bit of a temper, and though he hadn't been on the receiving end of it, his dad and Duncan certainly had been. He had a feeling she wasn't going to be a fan of his anymore than she'd been a fan of his dad's.

Her biggest problem with his dad had been his unwavering loyalty to Duncan. As far as Jude's dad had been concerned, Duncan always had the last word, and Jill hadn't always liked that.

Jude operated in the same way. Duncan had tasked him with protecting Angela, and he would do that, regardless of what Jill might think.

"Basically, I don't want Angelica to suffer emotionally. She's already dealing with a lot. I would have preferred that this meeting wait, but I know Jill has been as anxious for this day as I was, and she has a right to reunite with Angelica too. We've been lucky to delay this meeting as much as we have."

"I'll make sure Angela's okay," Jude assured him. "And Kiara will be there for her too."

Duncan took a sip of his coffee. "Julian will be there as well."

Jude wasn't sure how much help that was going to be. The man had been drinking more than usual since Angela had arrived, and Jude couldn't help but wonder what was causing that.

Plus, Julian had taken his mother's side in most things, and Jude wasn't sure that this would be any different.

"Good morning."

Kiara's voice had Jude turning toward the entrance to the breakfast room, which was where they came for coffee throughout the day, especially when the cook was busy in the kitchen.

Angela was at her side, her face pale and tense. Jude wanted to go to her and reassure her that everything was going to be fine.

And everything would be fine because he'd be there to protect her. It would be within his power to remove her from the situation, even if she wasn't being physically threatened.

As the ladies approached them, Jude drank in the sight of Angela.

She was wearing a navy blue sweater dress that brought out the blue-green of her eyes, paired with knee-high brown boots that added to her height. Her hair was styled in soft waves that framed her face, and she'd applied just enough makeup to enhance her natural beauty without looking overdone. She looked elegant and poised, even though he could see the anxiety in her expression.

"You both look lovely," Duncan said, greeting them with a warm smile. "How are you feeling, Angelica?"

"Nervous," she admitted, her voice thin. "But ready, I think."

Jude's protective instincts were heightened as he observed how nervous she was. "We don't have to leave for another twenty minutes. Would you like some coffee? Something to eat?"

Angela shook her head. "I don't think I could keep any food down right now."

"I'll have some coffee," Kiara said, moving toward the sideboard where the coffee service was set up. "Want some, Angie?"

"Maybe just a little," Angela said, though she looked like she might be sick.

Jude watched her carefully, noting the way her hands trembled slightly as she accepted the cup from Kiara. She hadn't seemed this nervous over meeting Duncan, but then, she also hadn't heard negative stories about Duncan the way she had about Jill.

"Would it help if I go over what to expect?" Jude asked gently.

Angela nodded, her fingers wrapped tightly around her coffee cup. "Please."

"Jill has a suite at the resort, but we've reserved one of their small boardrooms for this meeting," Jude told her.

"We needed to have control of the location because Jude is going to stay for the duration of the meeting," Duncan added. "If the meeting had been in her suite, she might have kicked him out."

"And we don't want that," Jude said.

Duncan set down his coffee mug with a slight clink. "Remember, Angelica, you're in control of this situation. If you need a break, take one. If you want to leave, you leave. There's no pressure to make this work if it doesn't feel right."

"What if she asks about Annie?" Angela's question was directed at Duncan. "What should I say?"

"Tell her the truth—that Annie wasn't ready for this meeting yet," Duncan replied. "You don't owe her any explanation beyond that."

Kiara reached over and squeezed Angela's hand. "And I'll be right there with you. If you need me to change the subject or speak up, just give me a signal. Tug your ear or something."

Angela gave a soft huff of laughter, though the color still hadn't returned to her cheeks. Jude found himself wishing he could somehow absorb her anxiety, take it on himself so she wouldn't have to face this meeting feeling so uptight.

"Julian will meet you there," Duncan added. "He's already at the resort with Jill. I just hope they haven't decided to have a pre-meeting drink."

"What if she doesn't like me?" Angela asked after she took a small sip of her coffee.

Jude felt something tighten in his chest at the vulnerability in her voice. "Angela, any mother would be lucky to have you as a daughter."

"But what if she expected someone different? Someone more like Annie?"

"Then that's her loss," Kiara said firmly, settling into the chair beside Angela. "You are exactly who you're supposed to be."

Duncan leaned forward slightly. "Angelica, I want you to remember something. Today is just a chance for you to meet her and see how it goes. You don't owe Jill anything, especially if she starts making you feel bad about yourself."

Angela's eyes widened slightly at Duncan's words. "But she's my mother."

"Biology doesn't automatically grant someone the right to hurt you," Duncan said gently but firmly. "Our situation is very unique, and we all need to approach it with love. Jill may or may not feel the same way."

Jude glanced at his watch. "We need to be going in a couple of minutes."

Angela took a deep breath and then exhaled. She gave her mug to Kiara when she held out her hand for it. Kiara set both of the mugs on the tray where they placed the dirty dishes.

Duncan approached Angela and gently placed his hands on her shoulders. "Just remember that you are enough. You are perfect just how you are, and I love you."

Jude heard Angela's swift intake of breath. "You do?"

"Yes. I love you because you're my daughter, but I also love the woman I've come to know." Duncan smiled down at her. "So you go and stand tall, and I look forward to hearing how it went when you get back."

"Okay."

Kiara led Angela from the room, and after a nod to Duncan, Jude followed them.

The ride to the resort was quiet, with Angela spending most of it staring out the window. Kiara was also looking out the window, but she seemed more interested in the scenery, asking questions about what they passed as Jude drove. Since he had lived in the area for most of his adult life, he was able to satisfy her curiosity.

"Wow," Kiara said as they neared the hotel at the resort. "That is beautiful."

Jude pulled the SUV into the porte-cochère of the hotel. "We can get out here."

He got out and came around to hand the keys to the valet who stood waiting. Before guiding the ladies inside, he glanced around. One of the other security vehicles had pulled in behind them. Two more of the security team got out.

While he was inside the room with Angela and Kiara, they would be keeping an eye outside. Probably overkill, but he and Duncan never wanted to regret not having enough security in place should something happen.

The manager of the resort was waiting for them at the front desk and greeted them with a warm smile.

"Hello," she said, offering him her hand. "I'm Kayleigh St. James. Welcome."

He took her hand. "I'm Jude Kessler. Thank you for setting up the room for us."

"You're welcome." She turned toward Angela and Kiara, her eyes suddenly growing wide. "Annie?"

"Uh." Angela sent Jude a worried look.

Jude had forgotten that one of Cole's sisters worked at the resort. He hadn't thought they'd run into anyone that knew Annie.

"No," Jude said. "This isn't Annie. Rather than explain here, perhaps you should call Cole. Tell him that Jude says it's okay to tell you what's going on."

"Okay. I will *certainly* be doing that." Kayleigh gave Angela a smile and a wink. "It's been a pleasure to meet you, whoever you are."

Angela returned her smile. "You too."

"I'm sure you'll meet again," Jude said. "Maybe once you've spoken with Cole and Annie."

"That would be lovely." Stepping toward a hallway, Kayleigh said, "In the meantime, let me show you to the room we've reserved for you."

They followed her down the hallway to a room that had a cozy vibe to it. There was a gas fireplace at one end of the room that had flames dancing in it. Instead of a large table dominating the room, there was comfortable furniture clustered around the fireplace.

It definitely was better suited for the meeting to come than a space set up as a boardroom.

"Beverages have been set up," Kayleigh said, gesturing to a buffet against the wall. "And there are some snacks as well."

"Thank you," Jude said. "It's more than I expected."

"We try to make sure people feel comfortable here."

"We appreciate it."

She handed Jude a business card. "Give me a call if you need anything."

"Will do."

When Kayleigh left the room, Angela asked, "She knows Annie?"

"Definitely," Jude said. "That's Cole's older sister."

"Oooh. So he didn't tell his family about me and Annie being twins?"

"I guess not," Jude said. "Or if he did, he didn't tell them all."

"Is that going to be a problem?" Angela asked. "If they know?"

Jude shook his head. "They're a trustworthy family. I feel confident that they would keep the secret until your dad decides to go public with it."

He hoped that she might follow that rabbit hole while they waited so that she wouldn't get too nervous. Unfortunately, she didn't. Instead, she just nodded and let the subject drop.

When the door to the room opened, all three of them turned toward it. Julian stepped in first, then held the door for his mother.

Jill stepped through the doorway, her gaze sweeping the room before landing on Angela. Her arms went wide as she headed toward her. Whether Angela wanted a hug or not, she was getting one.

"Oh, look at you," Jill said as she cupped Angela's face after giving her a tight hug. "You're just absolutely adorable."

Jude frowned. *Adorable?* He would have thought she'd say that Angela was beautiful, or even pretty. Isn't that what mothers usually said about their children? That they were beautiful or handsome?

"Mom," Julian said after he'd closed the door. "This is Kiara."

Jill let go of Angela's face and turned toward Kiara. "You're the adopted sister."

"She's my sister," Angela said, moving to Kiara's side.

"Annie is your sister."

Jude placed his hands on his hips, waiting for Angela to say the words that would free them from this awkward situation.

"Mom, I explained the situation," Julian said.

"Of course you did, darling." Jill waved dismissively. "But she'll adjust to the situation more quickly if she accepts some pretty obvious things."

Well, it was clear that Jill was still Jill.

Jude itched to step in and redirect the conversation, but that wasn't his role yet. He was there as a silent witness. A silent protector. Until Angela gave him a sign that she wanted his help.

However, if Jill took one more backhanded swipe at Kiara or Angela, Jude wasn't sure he could hold his tongue. And he didn't think Duncan would get upset with him if he didn't.

Unfortunately, he was drawn into things against his will.

"Well, Jude," Jill said when she spotted him. "You have certainly aged like fine wine."

"Mom!" Julian protested.

"Your services are not required at the moment," Jill said as she walked toward Jude, waving her hand at him dismissively.

"My boss would say otherwise."

"You're saying that Duncan told you to spy on my meeting with my daughter?"

"Mom, just ignore Jude." Julian tried to guide Jill away from him.

Up close, she was as stunning as she'd ever been as a younger woman. It appeared that Duncan's money was being put to good use.

"You tell Duncan that I don't appreciate him trying to manipulate everything. And if he's not careful, people might learn things he doesn't want them to know."

Jude wanted to defend Duncan, but he knew that the man would be upset if he did. Duncan didn't require defending, and there was a zero chance that Jill would ever reveal anything about the family. He knew that Duncan had made sure that Jill signed a document that said that if she ever revealed anything about Duncan, the family, or his business, she would lose all financial support.

"Let's go sit down and have a chat with Angela."

This time, Julian was more successful in moving his mom over to the seating area. Kiara followed with Angela, and the two of them sat down on a loveseat. Jill settled into the armchair closest to Angela, crossing her legs elegantly.

Julian sat on the couch, then got back up and went to the buffet. If he had been hoping for something alcoholic, he was going to be disappointed.

Sure enough, Julian's shoulders dropped, but then he reached out to grab a mug and filled it with coffee. After adding cream and sugar, he returned to his seat.

During this time, Jill had been telling Angela all about her family. Angela wasn't asking any questions, or really interacting at all.

That wasn't a deterrent for Jill, however. The woman had plenty of experience in making small talk.

Jude wanted to tell Jill that if she wanted any chance with her daughters, she needed to show that she was interested in them. That she cared about them.

How things went with Angela might play a role in Annie one day meeting her mom. But judging by how things had progressed so far, Annie wouldn't be changing her mind with help from Angela.

"What are you doing with your time?" Jill asked.

"We are taking some self-defense training, and we're learning how to drive."

"You don't need to know how to drive," she said. "I'm sure Duncan could hire someone to drive you around."

"We want to know how to drive," Angela said.

"It's a good skill to have," Julian said, braving his mother's wrath by siding with the ladies.

"It's a waste of time," Jill told him. "But I suppose it's her time to waste."

Angela shifted on the loveseat, and Kiara reached over and took her hand. Jude could see the tension in Angela's shoulders, the way she was holding herself rigid, like she was bracing for more criticism.

"Learning to drive has been wonderful for us," Kiara said, her voice steady but with an edge that Jude recognized. "And Angela is doing really well at it."

"Oh, I'm sure she is," Jill said, though her tone suggested otherwise. "But I still don't understand why you need to learn to drive."

"Because I want to," Angela said, her voice gaining strength. "I want to be able to go places on my own."

"Oh, darling, you're never going anywhere on your own ever again," Jill said with a laugh, then gestured to where Jude stood. "Even a visit like this, and you have a shadow. I hope you don't plan to get a job because you'll have a shadow there too."

"I'm still figuring out if I'm going to get a job," Angela said quietly.

"Well, you don't need to work. Duncan has plenty of money. Though I suppose you could do something charitable. Maybe volunteer at a well-known charity or something suitable for someone of your position."

Angela's brow furrowed. "My position?"

"As Duncan Burke's daughter, darling. You have a certain status to maintain now." Jill's smile was bright but somehow cold. "You'll need to learn how to dress appropriately, how to speak to the right people, how to carry yourself. It's all quite important."

Jude saw Angela's face pale slightly, and he had to fight the urge to interrupt. This wasn't going well at all.

"No one knows who I am to have those sorts of expectations of me."

"Surely now that you're back, Duncan would be more willing to let everyone know who you and Annie are."

"He hasn't decided yet," Angela said. "We're just taking things one step at a time."

"Probably a good idea so that you can be prepared to face the world. It's very different from what you're used to."

"I think Angela dresses and acts beautifully," Kiara said firmly.

Jill's gaze shifted to Kiara, and her expression cooled. "That's sweet of you to say, my dear. But you wouldn't really know, would you? Coming from where you both did."

The room fell silent. Julian set down his coffee mug with a thud on the end table next to him, and Jude felt his jaw tighten. He'd heard enough.

"Angela," he said quietly.

She looked up at him, staring for a moment before giving a subtle shake of her head. Jude wanted to insist, but it was Angela's choice.

And her determination to push through challenging stuff was one of the things he loved about her. So he just gave her a nod and stayed where he was.

"Oh wow, Jude," Jill said, angling a smirk at him. "I guess you don't have all that much power, do you?"

Jude kept his mouth shut. His instruction had been for it to be Angela's call to end the meeting unless absolutely necessary for him to step in.

It was hard though, and he wished he understood why Jill seemed determined to torpedo a potential relationship with Angela. It was the wildest thing.

Jill had always been a bit pretentious, but this was a lot, even from her. It appeared that even though the years had left her physically untouched, her personality had taken a nosedive.

"I realize you can't do anything about where you grew up, Angela," Jill said. "But you need to accept that things are done differently in this world."

As he stood there, Jude sent up a prayer, asking God for His peace and wisdom for everyone involved in the situation. He didn't think Angela would benefit from having Jill in her life, but it wasn't his decision.

"Why didn't you want Annie?" Angela asked.

Jill's posture straightened even further, her shoulders pulling back as she lifted her chin. "Of course I wanted Annie."

"Then why didn't you want visitation with her like you had with Julian?"

"Oh, they've been filling your ears with gossip, haven't they?"

"How can it be gossip when there's proof? And the people talking about it are the ones most deeply affected by your decision?"

"You wouldn't understand," Jill said, a haughty tone in her voice. "It was hard to look at Annie after I lost you. She was a constant reminder of what had been taken from us."

"But Annie needed her mother," Angela said. "And besides, you weren't the only one I was taken from. Duncan still looked Annie in the face every day and loved her. He did what he could to make her feel safe and protected."

"It's different as a mother," Jill said, her voice tight. "You wouldn't understand."

"It's sad to think that I had a better relationship with the woman who kidnapped me—who I considered a mom—than Annie had with her mother."

Jude's eyebrows rose as he listened to Angela speak to Jill. He had no idea where she had found the courage to say what Jill needed to hear, but he was glad she was doing it. It was too bad he hadn't recorded the meeting because Duncan would have loved to hear Angela stand up for herself and for Annie.

He glanced at Julian to see how he was taking everything. It looked like he wasn't paying attention to anything. He seemed to have checked out, slumped in his chair, staring at the fire in the fireplace.

"I'm not sure why you're talking to me like this," Jill said. "I did the best I could considering the circumstances."

Angela didn't look like she was buying that explanation any more than Jude did.

"I understand it was a difficult time," Angela said. "None of it was easy for any of us. But it makes me sad that because I was kidnapped, Annie was robbed of having a loving mother in her life. She didn't deserve to be punished because she was the one the kidnappers returned."

"I see how this is," Jill said as she got to her feet. "You've let Annie poison your mind against me. Julian. Let's go."

Julian looked up at his mother, gave a sigh, then pushed up to his feet.

Turning to Angela, he said, "I'll see you back at Dad's later."

Jude tracked the man's progress as he followed his mother out of the room.

That had... not gone as he'd thought it would. He'd been sure that Jill would walk all over Angela, and she had, to some extent. But then Angela had stood up for herself and Annie, and Jude was so proud of her.

"I didn't plan to talk to her about that," Angela said when Jude took the seat Jill had vacated.

"I think it was necessary," he said. "Julian has probably never talked honestly to her about it, and Annie has refused to have any communication with her. Perhaps it was time for someone to hold her accountable for what she did."

Angela bent her head and pressed her fingers to her forehead. Jude wanted to go to her and physically comfort her, not just use his words.

In the end, it was Kiara who slipped her arm around Angela. "You did a good thing, Angie. Don't second-guess what you said. I know you're going to, but don't."

Angela looked up and met Jude's gaze. "Is Duncan going to be upset with me?"

Jude couldn't keep his chuckle inside. "Oh, he definitely won't be. In fact, I think he'll congratulate you on it."

"And Julian?"

"He didn't speak up to defend his mom, so he knows that you only spoke the truth." Jude hesitated, then said, "I'm actually really proud of you for standing up for yourself and for Annie. You did great."

Angela's eyes widened as she stared at him. "You're proud of me?"

Jude knew he probably should pull back, but the reality was that he'd told her the truth. He *was* proud of her.

He hoped that she could continue to take a stand for herself and others, like she had for Annie.

"Ready to go home?" he asked.

"Yes, definitely."

CHAPTER EIGHTEEN

Feeling a little numb, Angela put one foot in front of the other, following Kiara out of the room. Jude stayed close to her side, his arm brushing hers as they headed down the hallway.

He touched her hand as he said, "I just want to let them know we're done with the room."

Rather than continue toward the door with Kiara, Angela stuck close to Jude.

"We're finished with the room," Jude said to the woman behind the high, polished wood counter. "Please pass on my thanks to Mrs. St. James."

"I will," the woman said with a smile. "Have a nice day."

"You too." Turning, Jude laid his hand lightly on Angela's back. "Let's go home."

Angela didn't argue. She was so done with that day, yet there were still hours to go.

"The SUV is on its way," the female bodyguard said to Jude as they joined her and Kiara. "I thought your meeting would last longer."

"Me too," Jude said. "But it took as long as was needed."

When the SUVs pulled up outside the doors, Angela followed Kiara out the door that Jude held open for them. The day was warmer than previous ones, but Angela still felt wrapped in a chill.

The previous half hour played over and over in her mind, and she parsed through all the ways she could have approached things differently. She still wasn't sure where the courage to speak up for herself and for Annie had come from.

It was possible Annie wouldn't be happy with what she'd said. And who knew what Julian thought about what had happened.

Jude might feel that it had been a good conversation, but Angela wasn't sure.

"Angela."

She looked up to see Jude holding the passenger door open for her. Gazing at him for a moment, she saw that while he might have said that everything was great, there was concern in his eyes.

Her stomach knotted as she turned to hoist herself into the front seat. When Jude shut the door, Kiara leaned forward and squeezed her shoulders.

"Everything is fine, sis," she said. "Be proud of standing up for yourself and Annie."

"I shouldn't have said any of that yet," Angela said. "Not until I had more of a chance to get to know her."

"I don't agree," Kiara told her. "But regardless, no what-ifs or if-onlys. What's done is done."

Seeing Jude reach for the door, Angela didn't respond. He seemed to think she had been courageous, but she didn't feel that way at all.

The drive back to the estate was made in silence with only the music coming from the radio to keep the mood from becoming too intense. Angela needed time alone with her thoughts, but it seemed that that might not come for a little while.

"Do you want me to come with you?" Kiara asked.

Angela glanced at Jude. She kind of wanted Kiara there. However, her sister hadn't really played a part in what happened during the meeting with Jill, so she didn't need to be there.

"I'm going to go with Angela to speak with Duncan," Jude said to Kiara after they arrived back at the estate. "So you don't need to."

"As long as you're okay with that, Angie," Kiara said, giving her a look.

"Yes, I'm fine with that."

"Everything will be fine," Kiara said as they took off their coats in the mudroom. She gave her a tight hug. "Come find me when you're done."

Angela walked beside Jude toward Duncan's office, her mind still spinning with the confrontation. The plush carpet beneath her boots muffled their footsteps, making their progress through the hallway eerily quiet. She couldn't help but wonder if Julian had already called Duncan to tell him what had happened.

When they reached Duncan's office door, Jude paused and looked at her. "Ready?"

She wasn't. Not even close. But waiting wouldn't make it any easier. She nodded, tucking a strand of hair behind her ear.

Jude knocked, and Duncan's voice called for them to enter. As the door swung open, Angela took a deep breath, steeling herself for whatever reaction might come from her father.

Jude opened the door, allowing Angela to enter first. Duncan was sitting behind his desk, papers spread before him, but he immediately set them aside when he saw them.

"That was quick," he said, rising from his chair. His eyes moved between them, clearly trying to read their expressions.

Angela's throat tightened. What could she say? That she'd confronted his ex-wife about abandoning their daughter? That she'd basically ruined any chance of having a relationship with her biological mother within the first thirty minutes of meeting her?

Duncan gestured toward the sitting area. "Have a seat and tell me all about it."

Angela sank into one of the leather chairs, the material cool against her palms as she gripped the armrests. Jude took the seat beside her rather than standing at attention as he sometimes did, which somehow made her feel both comforted and more nervous.

"How did it go?" Duncan asked, his gaze moving between her and Jude.

Before she could formulate a response, Jude spoke. "Angela was remarkable."

Heat crept up her neck at his words. Remarkable wasn't how she would describe what had happened.

"I..." she began, then faltered. "I'm not sure it went very well."

Duncan's brow furrowed as he sat back down. "What happened?"

Angela twisted her hands in her lap, the silence stretching until it felt oppressive. How could she explain that she'd basically attacked Jill within minutes of meeting her? That she'd let her emotions take control and possibly destroyed any chance of establishing a relationship?

"I confronted her about Annie," she said finally, the words tumbling out in a rush. "About how she abandoned her after I was taken. I shouldn't have—I barely knew her. But she kept making these awful comments about Kiara and about how we needed to change, and then she said it was different for mothers and I just..." She trailed off, pressing her lips together.

Duncan leaned forward, his expression intent but not angry. "What exactly did you say?"

Angela's stomach churned as she replayed the conversation. "I asked why she didn't want Annie. Why she didn't fight for visitation with her like she had with Julian. And I told her it was sad that I had a better relationship with the woman who kidnapped me than Annie had with her own mother."

The words hung in the air, and Angela braced herself for Duncan's reaction. She'd overstepped. She'd spoken out of turn about family dynamics that weren't hers to judge, no matter how much the injustice of it had burned in her chest.

But instead of anger, something that looked almost like pride flickered across Duncan's features. "And what did she say to that?"

"She said I wouldn't understand. That it was hard to look at Annie because she was a reminder of what she'd lost. I told her that you'd managed to do it. That you'd continued to look into Annie's face and love her."

Duncan's expression softened. "And how did she respond?"

Angela shrugged. "She just said that it was different for a mother."

Duncan was quiet for a long moment. Behind him, the fireplace crackled, the soft pops and hisses filling the silence as Angela waited for his judgment. He looked thoughtful rather than upset, his expression unreadable as he studied her.

She glanced at Jude, who sat calm and steady beside her, his presence a quiet reassurance.

"I'm sorry," she added quickly. "I know I should have been more diplomatic. I just—"

"Angela," Duncan interrupted gently. "You have nothing to apologize for."

She blinked, not sure she'd heard him correctly. "But I—"

"You stood up for your sister," he said. "And for yourself. That's not something to be sorry about. I'm proud of you."

Angela blinked, certain she'd misheard him. "What?"

"I'm proud of you," he repeated, his voice firm. "You stood up for yourself and for your sister. That takes courage."

Relief washed through her so suddenly that Angela felt light-headed. She'd been so certain he would be disappointed, would tell her she'd ruined everything before it had a chance to begin.

"I thought you'd be upset," she admitted. "That I'd messed up any chance of having a relationship with her."

Duncan shook his head, a sad smile playing at his lips. "Angela, a relationship with Jill was never going to be simple. She's... complicated. Always has been."

"That's one way to put it," Jude murmured beside her.

Duncan's smile widened slightly at Jude's comment. "The truth is, you said what needed to be said. Maybe not by Annie—she's too close to the situation, too hurt by it. But you spoke from a place of care and concern for your sister."

The knot in her stomach loosened slightly. "Julian left with her. He didn't say much."

"Julian has been caught between his mother and the rest of us for years," Duncan said with a sigh. "It's not a position I envy."

Angela glanced at Jude, remembering how he'd called her remarkable. The word still echoed in her mind, warming something inside her despite the chill that had settled in her bones after the confrontation.

"I didn't go there planning to confront her," Angela said. "But the way she talked about Kiara, like she was just some... inconvenience. That she wasn't my sister. And then implying we needed to change everything about ourselves to fit into her world..." She trailed off, the indignation rising again.

Duncan leaned back in his chair, his expression thoughtful. "Jill isn't wrong about this world being different from what you're used to, but that doesn't mean it's better. And it doesn't mean you have to change to fit into it. Annalisa and Benjamin haven't been part of my world, and you don't have to be either. All of you are fine just as you are. There's no need for any of you to change."

"So you really think I did the right thing?" she asked, still uncertain.

"I do." Duncan leaned forward, his expression earnest. "For too long, Jill has been allowed to rewrite history, to play the victim in a story where she lost one daughter and couldn't bear to face that loss every day with her other one. It's about time someone held her accountable."

Angela's shoulders relaxed slightly. She glanced at Jude, who gave her a small nod of encouragement.

"What happens now?" she asked quietly.

Duncan sighed, running a hand through his silver hair. "That depends on Jill. She might be angry for a little while. She might try to reach out again. Or she might decide this relationship isn't worth the effort if it means facing uncomfortable truths. If you want to try again with Jill, we can arrange another meeting. If you'd rather wait, that's fine too. There's no wrong answer here."

Angela considered his words. The thought of facing Jill again made her stomach tighten, but she also didn't want to give up after one difficult encounter. "I think I need some time to process everything."

"Take all the time you need," Duncan said. "This isn't something that needs to be rushed. If she does reach out, you get to decide what kind of relationship you want—if any. You're under no obligation to pursue one if it doesn't feel right."

Angela nodded, processing his words. The weight of the decision felt both heavy and liberating.

Everything had happened so quickly—the meeting, the confrontation, now this conversation with Duncan. Her emotions felt raw and tangled, like a ball of yarn that had been batted around by a kitten.

"Thank you," she said, the words inadequate for the relief she felt. "For understanding."

"Always," Duncan replied simply.

Angela rose from her chair, suddenly desperate for some quiet space to sort through her thoughts. The emotional whiplash of the day had left her drained.

"If it's okay," Angela said, "I think I'd like to go rest for a while."

"Of course," Duncan said, his voice gentle. "And Angela? You handled yourself beautifully today. Don't let anyone tell you otherwise."

The warmth of his words wrapped around her like a blanket. She'd expected disappointment, maybe even anger, but instead, found understanding and pride. It was more than she'd dared hope for.

Jude rose beside her, his movements fluid and controlled as always. "I'll walk you back to your room."

"Come back when you're done, Jude," Duncan instructed. "I need to address a few things with you."

Jude nodded, then led Angela to the door.

As they left Duncan's office and walked through the quiet hallways of the house, Angela found herself stealing glances at him. His jaw was relaxed, his posture less rigid than it had been at the resort. The tension that had radiated from him during the meeting with Jill had eased.

"Thank you," she said as they reached the staircase leading to the second floor. "For being there today. For... everything."

Jude paused at the bottom of the stairs, turning to face her fully. The afternoon light streaming through the tall windows caught the blue of his eyes, making them shine.

"You don't need to thank me," he said quietly. "That's what friends do."

Friends. The word should have been comforting, but it sent a strange pang through her chest. She wanted to be his friend, truly she did.

But standing there, feeling so vulnerable, Angela felt something deeper stirring—something that made her pulse quicken and her chest tighten with longing.

She nodded, forcing a smile. "Right. Friends."

The word felt hollow on her tongue, but she couldn't take it back now. She'd already made things awkward between them once before. She wouldn't do it again.

"I was there because it was my job," he said. "But I would have wanted to be there for you, regardless."

Angela hated the reminder that any time Jude was with her, it was because of his job. Because Duncan had instructed him to stay close to her. He might say they were friends, but it was hard to dismiss the fact that, first and foremost, he was her dad's trusted employee.

"Get some rest," Jude said, his voice gentler than usual. "Today was a lot."

It had been a lot, and more than anything, right then, she wanted to lean against Jude. She wanted him to wrap his arms around her and just hold her.

She'd never had that before. Never had someone stronger than her standing at her side. And now that she'd had a taste of it, she didn't want to lose it. She also didn't want the person at her side offering her strength and support to be anyone but Jude.

"I guess I'll see you later," Angela said. "Or if not, I'll see you tomorrow for training."

Jude regarded her for a long moment, as if trying to see into her very soul. Finally, he said, "Yep. I'll see you then."

With a final goodbye, Angela climbed the stairs slowly, her legs feeling heavier with each step. The adrenaline from the confrontation with Jill was finally wearing off, leaving her drained and emotionally raw. By the time she reached her room, her hands were trembling slightly as she turned the doorknob.

The familiar sanctuary of her bedroom welcomed her with its soft blue walls and comfortable furnishings. She kicked off her boots and sank onto the edge of the bed, finally allowing herself to truly process what had happened.

She'd stood up to her biological mother. The woman who had given birth to her, who should have loved her unconditionally, and Angela had called her out on abandoning Annie. The memory of Jill's shocked expression when Angela had challenged her still sent a flutter of anxiety through her stomach.

But Duncan had been proud of her. Jude had called her remarkable.

It hurt, though. She had wanted to be able to forge a relationship with her birth mom. The Bible talked about honoring parents, and she didn't know how to reconcile that with a mother who didn't seem very honorable.

She'd spent her life trying to keep the peace. To not upset Jim, Sandra, or Craig. Kiara had been more likely to push back against them, but not Angela.

She'd lived her life in fear of reprisal, and even though people said she'd done well that day, the fear was still there. It seemed very likely that there would be backlash. Whether it was from Julian or Jill, Angela didn't know, but she was convinced she'd be made to pay for the stand she'd taken that day.

Angela pulled her phone from her pocket and stared at the blank screen for a moment before setting it aside. She wasn't ready to talk to anyone yet.

The one person she might want to talk to had been requested by her father to report back to him. Angela wondered if it was a follow-up to the meeting with Jill, or if it was something else.

She flopped back on her bed, then maneuvered her way under the comforter. Lying on her side, she gazed out the window. Only the tops of the trees and the bright blue sky were visible from her vantage point.

When she allowed herself to think about everything that had transpired over the past few weeks, it was hard not to get over-whelmed. She still wasn't sure how she fit into this new life.

She didn't want to go back to Briar Hollow, but she missed parts of it. Her church. The ladies of the knitting circle. And having a purpose.

She needed to have a purpose in her life. There had never been a point in her past when she could live a life of leisure. If Jim had ever caught them sitting around with nothing to do, he'd been quick to find them work.

So, to wake up each day with no real plan beyond training was unsettling for her.

But what could she do about it?

Well, what she could do was make sure she didn't sink into a depression over it. There were so many positives in her life. She needed to focus on those.

Not on the fractured relationship with her birth mother. Not on the fact that she had no job or way to fill her days. Nor on the fact that she loved someone who only wanted to be friends.

Feeling tears sting her eyes, Angela flung the comforter off and sat up. She couldn't wallow.

She wouldn't wallow. She was sure that wouldn't be how God would want her to deal with her situation.

Sliding off the bed, she got to her feet and headed for the walk-in closet to change out of the sweater dress she'd chosen for the day, that hadn't been up to her mother's standards.

Once she was in a pair of leggings and an oversized sweater, she pulled on a pair of thick socks and left her room, grabbing her phone as she went.

"What's up?" Kiara asked when she opened her door in response to Angela's knock, also having changed into comfier clothing.

"Let's do something," she said. "I need a distraction."

"And you don't want to bake?"

"No. Not today."

Kiara leaned a shoulder against the doorjamb. "So what are you thinking?"

"Maybe we can see if Benji and Annie want to watch a movie or something."

Kiara smiled. "That sounds like a plan."

Angela knew all the mess of feelings would still be there later to deal with, but she needed something to buoy her up right then. And spending time with her siblings—minus Julian—seemed the way to do it.

Later, when everything wasn't so fresh, she'd spend some time in prayer asking God to help her figure out how to sort through it all.

CHAPTER NINETEEN

Jude watched as Angela climbed the stairs and disappeared without looking back at him. He wished that he could have gone up with her and just spent some time letting her talk through how she felt.

It was clear that she had mixed feelings about the meeting with Jill. As he'd told her and Duncan, he thought she'd done well. But he understood why she didn't feel the same way.

He put a foot on the lowest step and gripped the railing. The pull to go get her and find a quiet corner in the house to talk was strong.

But it wasn't his place. And if he took the time to do what he wanted, Duncan would wonder why his request that Jude return to the office had been ignored.

Turning from the staircase, Jude told himself he would check on her later. At the very least, he could send her a text to make the offer to talk if she needed it.

With a deep sigh, Jude returned to Duncan's office, his footsteps echoing in the empty hallway. Angela's words still lingered in his mind—her gratitude, her uncertainty. The way her eyes had clouded with something he couldn't quite name when he'd called them friends.

When he entered the office, Duncan was standing by the window, hands clasped behind his back as he gazed out at the estate grounds.

"How is she?" Duncan asked without turning around.

"Processing," Jude replied, closing the door behind him. "It was a lot to take in."

Duncan nodded, finally turning to face him and moving to his imposing chair behind the desk. "Tell me everything that happened. I want to hear the details Angelica might have left out."

Jude moved to the chair he'd occupied earlier, settling in as he recounted the meeting with Jill—her dismissive attitude toward Kiara, her thinly veiled criticisms of Angela, and the remarkable way Angela had stood her ground.

"She didn't mention how Jill tried to dismiss you from the room," Duncan noted when Jude finished.

"It wasn't really a surprise," Jude said. "So it wasn't important."

"It shows Jill's character hasn't changed." Duncan shook his head. "And Julian? How did he handle all this?"

"Mostly stayed silent. He didn't defend his mother, but didn't stand up for Angela either."

Duncan's expression darkened. "That sounds like Julian. Always trying to walk the middle line." He sighed. "Do you feel that I should have a meeting with her myself?"

Jude considered the question for a moment, appreciating that Duncan was interested in his opinion.

"You should probably be open to that," Jude said. "But I'd wait to see how things unfold over the next couple of days before requesting a meeting with her."

"Do you know when she's leaving?" Duncan asked.

"Neither she nor Julian has told me a departure date."

"I'll ask Julian. I've tried not to wade into this because things are already tense between him and me, but I'll do it if necessary."

"I think Angela needs to steer clear of Jill for a little while."

"Do you really want her to have a relationship with Jill?" Jude asked.

"If it's a healthy one," Duncan said. His eyes narrowed slightly. "Would you consider your relationship with your mom to be healthy?"

The question took Jude aback. It was rare that Duncan ventured into the personal with him. And to ask about his mother? That was even more of a rarity.

"I don't know," he admitted. "But it works for us, I guess. I don't really want it to be different."

"That's good," Duncan said. "It's not easy being a parent, especially to grown adults when you can no longer guide them the way you once could through incentives and punishments."

Jude felt like his mom still tried her best to "guide"—also known as manipulate—him into doing what she thought was best for his life. It was only because he'd learned to brush her efforts aside that their relationship had survived.

"Have you thought about starting a family yourself?" Duncan asked.

Jude was sure that he hadn't sufficiently hidden his surprise at the question. It was even more surprising than the question about his mother.

"Uh... maybe when I was younger I thought about it," Jude said.

Duncan leaned back in his chair, steepling his fingers in front of himself. "But not now?"

He took his time answering, uncertain what question might be coming next. Had Duncan sensed that he wasn't viewing Angela in quite the same way he did the rest of the Burke family?

Jude had tried to keep his actions professional when he was with Angela, but it was possible he'd failed.

"I think perhaps my time for considering marriage and a family has passed me by."

Duncan frowned. "Why would you say that? You're not that old. I was older than you when Benjamin was born."

"I'm content with my life. Plus, I don't want to chance leaving a child behind the way my dad did. Being older and in this profession ups the chances of that happening."

Duncan gave him a considering look. "Aren't you a Christian?"

And yet another surprising question. "I am."

"But you don't trust God to protect you?"

"My dad also trusted God, and God ended up taking him. So, I don't know how I feel about that." Jude returned Duncan's gaze. "How do you know about what Christians think?"

"Elizabeth, Annalisa, and Benjamin talk about what they believe around me quite a bit. I think about it."

"But not enough to become a Christian yourself?"

Duncan didn't answer right away, his gaze shifting to the window next to his desk. Finally, he looked back at Jude.

"I'm considering it," Duncan said. "I just... I don't know."

"Don't leave it too late."

"Your dad said the same thing to me before he passed away."

"And yet here we are, so many years later, and you're still thinking about it."

"True." Duncan gave a brief chuckle. "I'm not sure what's holding me back."

Jude had an idea. There was a verse in the Bible he'd heard during a few sermons over the years that spoke of it being easier for a camel to pass through the eye of a needle than for a rich man to enter heaven.

Perhaps that was what Duncan was struggling with. The idea of surrendering his wealth to God was probably daunting considering his substantial worth.

"I've just been thinking a lot about family now that mine is complete once again. More than complete because we've added Kiara, and hopefully Cole one day."

"*Hopefully* Cole?" Jude prodded with a grin. "You've certainly had a change of heart about that man."

Duncan shrugged. "He's proven himself. A lesser man might have run after I threatened him."

A lesser man. Was that what he was? For not being willing to risk it all to be with Angela? That didn't sit well with Jude, and he knew it wouldn't be what his dad would want him to be.

The truth was, he hadn't even given Duncan the chance to threaten him. There was a part of him that wanted to tell Duncan that he had fallen in love with Angela and that he thought Angela might have some feelings for him as well.

But even if he was willing to put his job on the line, did he want to put Angela in a position of having to choose between him and her father?

"I hope you know that I would respect your decision when it comes to a woman. That I would trust that you wouldn't bring anyone into our lives that would negatively affect us."

"I appreciate that," Jude said, because he really did. "But it's not a concern at the moment."

"I just want to make sure you aren't holding back because of your job here," Duncan said. "And I know your salary is more than enough to support a wife and a family."

"It is," Jude said, trying to keep the image of coming home to his cabin to be greeted by Angela out of his mind. But now that the idea had been planted, it played out like a movie, with him even smelling the aromas of vanilla, cinnamon, and baked bread. Scents he'd come to associate with Angela.

"I could always get Elizabeth to set you up with someone," Duncan said. "Just say the word."

"Oh, that will never happen. I have a couple of friends who have tried that, and it's failed. I'd rather not go that route again."

"Well, download one of those apps and start chatting."

The offer to set him up hopefully meant that Duncan really wasn't aware of the current that flowed between him and Angela. Never in his life had he been so conflicted about something.

"I'm not keen on doing that," Jude said. "I think I'm a little old for the people who use those apps."

Duncan nodded. "I hear you. I just hope that you really are happy being single, and not wanting to be married and struggling because you can't find someone."

"I'm very content in my life," Jude assured him. "Don't worry about me."

"Strangely enough," Duncan mused. "I do worry about you. Maybe it's because at one time in my past, your dad asked me to take care of you if anything happened to him. In some ways, you feel like a son."

The words sent an unexpected warmth spiraling through Jude. "I didn't know that, but that sounds like him."

"So if you have any concerns, I hope you feel comfortable coming to me with them. And I don't mean just work concerns. I'm talking about personal concerns too."

Jude wasn't sure what had prompted this conversation, and he wasn't entirely comfortable with it. Still, he nodded because that would be the reaction Duncan expected.

But would he actually follow through and come to Duncan with concerns? Jude wasn't sure he would.

"I would feel comfortable talking to you if I felt the need."

Duncan studied him for a moment longer, then seemed to accept his response. "Good. Now, about security for the rest of the week—"

As Duncan shifted into work mode, Jude found himself only half-listening. His mind kept drifting back to Angela climbing those stairs, the vulnerable set of her shoulders, the way she'd looked at him when he'd called them friends.

The conversation with Duncan about family and marriage had stirred something uncomfortable in his chest. The image Duncan had unknowingly planted—coming home to Angela—felt both impossible and desperately desired.

He forced himself to focus on Duncan's words about patrol schedules and perimeter checks, but the fantasy lingered at the edges of his consciousness like a stubborn shadow.

When the meeting finally came to an end, Jude returned to the security building. After checking in with the people on duty, he continued on to his office.

Though he knew it probably wasn't the best idea, he pulled out his phone and shot a text off to Angela.

Hi Angela ~ How are you doing? Just wanted to make sure that you're okay.

He leaned back in his chair as he waited for Angela to reply. The concern he had for her exceeded anything he'd ever had for anyone except his dad.

That wasn't to say that he didn't have concern for the people around him. The Burkes. Cooper, Mel, and the kids. His security team. But it was different with Angela.

He felt a visceral need to protect her. To use his skills to make sure she was never hurt. To make her happy. To do his best to make sure that she never had to live in fear the way she had with Jim and Sandra.

Previously, he hadn't wanted the responsibility of loving someone. Now, however, whether he wanted it or not, that love was there. And it sparked his desire to do what he could to make Angela happy and to let her know she was important to him.

When she didn't respond right away, he set his phone aside and turned his attention to his email, hoping there was a report from the team he'd left in Briar Hollow.

Seeing one, he clicked to open it and skimmed over it. His stomach clenched as he read what the man had written.

Craig continues to show up at the bar every couple of days, and once he's drunk enough, he starts moaning and groaning about his dad and how obsessed he is with his daughters who left town. Craig couldn't care less about them, and would be happy if they never came home. Last night, he was more upset than usual because he'd been left to do all the heavy lifting at their farm. If I had to guess, I'd say that Jim has left town.

Jude shifted his gaze to stare out the window, trying to imagine what might be going through Jim's mind. And what he might be planning.

There was no doubt in Jude's mind that Jim was a smart man. He'd managed to kidnap two children from a wealthy man and keep one of them hidden for over two decades.

Jim had taken his time to make a move, which concerned Jude. That time had given Jim the opportunity to plan. And Jude had to assume that the man had formulated a plan and was now busy putting it in motion.

Jude glanced at the security monitors. They had a lot of cameras around the property, but did they have enough?

Before he could take the time to devise a plan himself, he needed to alert Duncan to this new turn of events. He placed the call to Duncan and had a brief conversation with him, promising the man that he'd let him know if anything more developed.

In the middle of their conversation, a text came in from Angela. He wanted to read it right away, but he forced himself to focus on what Duncan was saying.

After he ended the call, Jude took a deep breath, mentally switching gears as he pulled up Angela's message.

Angela: *I'm doing fine. Now that I have had a little distance from the meeting, I'm doing better.*

Jude was glad to hear that, but he hoped she was being honest with him. Not just saying she was fine when she really wasn't, because she thought that was what he wanted to hear.

That's good to hear. Just a reminder that we have weapons training tomorrow morning at ten at the security building.

Angela: *Yep. We'll be there.*

Jude stared at the screen of his phone, trying to figure out if he should extend the conversation or put an end to it. Well, he knew what he *should* do, but he didn't want to end it just yet.

He wished that he had called her instead of texting because then continuing the conversation would have been easier.

In the end, he told Angela that he'd see her the next day, then said goodbye.

Jude sat for a moment at his desk, replaying the time they'd spent together earlier. But then, he put aside the emotions of that day and focused on the latest update about Jim.

He got up and went out to where members of his team were monitoring the cameras and let them know that they needed to be on the alert for any anomalies on the cameras.

There was no way he was going to let Jim get close to the family again.

The next morning, Jude was ready for Angela and Kiara when they arrived at the security building. He'd asked Dennis, another member of the security team and a weapons expert, to join them.

When Angela and Kiara appeared in his office doorway, he got up and went around his desk to greet them. "Good morning."

"It is," Kiara agreed. "We get to learn to shoot a gun."

Jude chuckled. "I have a feeling I'm not going to have a problem with you not wanting to be armed when leaving the estate."

"Nope," she agreed. "Are there people who don't like to be armed all the time?"

"Annie doesn't like to wear her gun," Jude said.

"I have a feeling Angela will be the same," Kiara said with a smile at her sister.

Jude knew that was probably true. But now more than ever, he needed her to feel comfortable with a weapon.

"Well, let's get this started," Jude said.

He took the ladies to the elevator that transported them to the basement of the building. The space was divided into several rooms, with the largest being the actual shooting range.

Dennis was already waiting there with the weapons they had decided to have Angela and Kiara start their training with.

"Kiara, Dennis will be training you, while I'll be helping Angela," Jude said.

"Sounds good." Kiara gave him a smile before turning her attention to Dennis. "So, where's my gun and what's the target?"

With a chuckle, Dennis led Kiara to the first lane of the five that were set up for gun practice. Jude took Angela to the one on the opposite end from Dennis and Kiara.

"Before we start, tell me how you're feeling about this," Jude said, taking in the shadow of apprehension on Angela's face.

She was dressed in a pair of jeans and a thick cream-colored sweater. Her hair was pulled back in a ponytail, revealing the fine bone structure of her face.

Letting out a sigh, she said, "I don't know. I realize it's a good thing for me to have the ability to defend myself, but after seeing Jim and Craig with guns, I'm not sure how I feel about it."

"Your reason for this training is different from how Jim and Craig use their weapons. You're not going to be seeking out opportunities to use your gun. You'll only use it as a way to protect yourself if you feel threatened."

Angela crossed her arms. "Have you shot someone?"

Jude shook his head. "No. I've been fortunate that I haven't had to do more than draw my gun. But every time I've drawn it, I've been prepared to use it. And you need to be as well."

There was a reluctance on Angela's face that reminded him of Annie when he'd trained her. He had a feeling that Angela would never feel completely at ease with being armed, and he was okay with that.

As long as she was willing to learn and eventually wear a weapon, he wouldn't press her to enthusiastically embrace guns.

Teaching her how to shoot helped to appease the strong desire Jude had to protect her. If ever he couldn't be there for her, he needed to know that she could protect herself.

It was extremely important to him that nothing happen to her, and that had less to do with his job and more to do with her place in his heart.

CHAPTER TWENTY

Angela watched closely as Jude showed her the different parts of the gun he'd chosen for her. His movements were confident and quick. Clearly, he was very familiar with guns. Meanwhile, she'd already forgotten the name of the gun.

Was there anything he wasn't good at?

His comfort with weapons was yet another reminder that his job required him to be ready and willing to take another person's life—should they be a threat to the ones he was charged with protecting. She wasn't sure she'd ever be comfortable shooting someone.

"First, we're going to go over basic safety. This is the most important part, and I need you to really listen to me."

Angela focused on his words as he explained how to hold the weapon, where to keep her fingers, and how to check if it was loaded. His voice was patient but serious, and she found herself hanging on every instruction, determined to show him she was taking it seriously.

She hoped she could remember everything, because it was a lot. And despite her best efforts, it was hard to completely focus on what he was saying when just being near him was a distraction.

"You'll need to put these on," Jude said, handing her a pair of earmuffs.

He put his on while she adjusted hers over her ears.

"Do they feel okay?" Jude asked.

Angela's eyes widened as she nodded. "I can hear you really well."

"These are electronic and are designed to enhance low-level sounds while dampening loud noises. They make it easier to communicate while we're down here."

When he gave her the gun, he stepped closer to adjust her grip, the warmth of his hands over hers making it difficult to concentrate on anything else.

"Like this?" she asked, trying to ignore the way her pulse quickened.

"Yes. Good."

He circled around her. "Keep your feet shoulder-width apart." His breath stirred the hair near her ear as he helped her position herself correctly. "Now, line up the sights."

She squinted down the barrel, trying to focus on the target at the other end of the range rather than on Jude.

"When you're ready, take a breath, exhale, then squeeze the trigger," he instructed, his voice low and steady.

Angela tried to follow his directions, but her hands trembled slightly as she held the weapon. The gun was heavier than she'd expected, and the weight of it reminded her of the times she'd seen Jim clean his rifle at the kitchen table, the way his eyes had gone cold and distant when he handled it.

"I can't seem to keep it steady," she admitted, frustration creeping into her voice.

"That's normal for your first time." Jude moved behind her again, his chest nearly brushing her back as he reached around to help adjust her stance. "Here, let me help you."

When his hands covered hers, guiding her grip once again, Angela's breath caught. She could feel the solid warmth of him behind her, could smell the clean scent of his soap mixed with something distinctly him. Her heart hammered against her ribs, and she wondered if he could feel how nervous she was—though she wasn't sure if the nerves were from the gun or from his proximity.

"Better?" he asked, his voice close to her ear.

She nodded, not trusting herself to speak. With his hands steadying hers, the weapon felt more manageable, though she was acutely aware of his closeness.

Even though he was well into her personal space, she didn't feel uncomfortable. In fact, she felt safe and protected.

"Now, remember what I said about breathing. Take your time."

Angela inhaled slowly, trying to calm her nerves and focus. She wanted to do this well. She might not have the enthusiasm for it that Kiara did, but she understood the importance of everything they were doing. Because of that, she'd try to do her best to learn what Jude taught her.

She exhaled lightly and squeezed the trigger. The gun kicked back harder than she'd expected, the sharp crack of the gunshot echoing through the range despite her ear protection. The recoil sent a jolt up her arms, and she stumbled back a step, bumping into Jude.

"Easy," he said, his hands coming up to grip her shoulders, steadying her. "You did great on your first shot."

Angela blinked as she looked down the lane at the target. She'd missed it completely, but somehow that didn't matter as much as the fact that she'd actually pulled the trigger.

"I can't believe I did that," she said, surprised by the rush of adrenaline coursing through her.

"How do you feel?" Jude asked. Though he'd released her shoulders and moved around to her side, he was still standing close to her.

She considered the question, taking inventory of her emotions. The fear she'd expected wasn't there—or at least, it wasn't the paralyzing kind she'd felt when watching Jim handle his weapons. This felt different. Controlled.

"Better than I thought I would," she admitted. "It's loud, though."

Jude's mouth curved into a small smile, crinkling the corners of his eyes. "That's why we have ear protection. Ready to try again?"

Angela nodded, raising the gun once more. This time, without Jude's hands guiding hers, she had to concentrate harder to remember everything he'd taught her.

Feet apart, grip firm, sight alignment, breathing. She took her time, blocking out everything but the gun and the target.

The second shot felt more controlled, though her arms still absorbed the recoil with a jolt that traveled up to her shoulders. This time she managed to stay planted, and when she looked downrange, she could see a small hole near the edge of the target.

"Much better," Jude said, and the approval in his voice sent a warm flutter through her chest. "You're getting the hang of it."

Angela lowered the weapon, surprised by the small surge of pride she felt. She'd actually hit the target, even if it was just barely. "I can see why some people find this satisfying."

"It's about control and precision," Jude explained, stepping closer to examine her stance again. "You're doing well for someone who was so nervous about it."

The compliment made her stand a little straighter. She'd spent so many years being told she wasn't quick enough, smart enough, good enough at whatever task Jim or Sandra had assigned her. Having someone like Jude—someone whose opinion she valued more than she should—tell her she was doing well felt like a small victory.

"Let's try a few more rounds," he said. "I want you to get comfortable with the weight and the recoil."

Angela nodded and raised the gun again.

Over the next several minutes, she shot at the target many times. Jude helped her reload, then she tried again. Some of her shots hit the target, though never the bullseye.

"Can you hit the bullseye?" Angela asked after she'd emptied the gun for a second time.

The corner of his mouth tipped up. "Maybe."

"I want to see," Angela told him. "Otherwise, I'll always assume I'm better than you."

Jude chuckled at that. "Well, if you practice enough, you could be better than me."

She set her gun on the shelf that was on the divider next to her. "I think I need some incentive."

"Alright." Jude removed the gun from the shoulder holster he wore. "Let's see how I do."

Angela moved to the side as Jude stepped to where she'd been standing to shoot. He didn't hesitate the way she had.

His movements were fluid and practiced as he raised the weapon, and Angela studied the confident set of his shoulders, the way he seemed to become completely still for a moment before firing.

The gunshot cracked through the air, and Angela's gaze immediately went to the target. A hole had appeared dead center in the bullseye.

"Show off," she muttered, though she couldn't keep the admiration out of her voice.

When Jude glanced over at her and winked, Angela's heart just about stopped. The moment didn't last long, and soon he was focused back on the target.

When he fired again, another hole appeared right next to the first one. Then a third shot, so close to the others that Angela wondered if he'd hit the same spot twice.

Lowering the gun, he turned to face her. His expression was a little smug, but there was a twinkle in his eye that made her smile.

She shook her head in amazement. "That's just not fair. How long have you been shooting?"

"Since I was twelve," he said, ejecting the magazine with practiced ease. "My dad started taking me to the range when I was old enough to hold a gun properly."

"Was he a good shot?"

"The best," Jude said. "My goal from the moment I first held a gun was to be as good as he was."

"And did that happen?"

"Eventually. Once we moved here, where I had more access to this gun range, I improved significantly. I was around seventeen when I finally bested him."

"I bet he was proud of you," Angela said.

Jude didn't talk often about his family, but from the little he'd said about his dad, she felt confident in that statement.

Jude's expression saddened, though he did smile. "He was."

"You and your dad were close?"

"Very. When my mom left, it was just us guys."

"You didn't see your mom again?" Angela asked. "Was she like Jill?"

"No, she's not like Jill at all. While my dad had primary custody because they both felt I'd be better off living with him, she insisted on having visitation. She always made sure she saw me at least once a week when we lived in New York. I would also stay with her on some weekends."

"And do you see her much now?"

"Not much other than video calls or if I happen to be in New York with Duncan. However, we do talk once a week."

Angela knew the purpose of their time together that day was to train her on guns. But they had very little time with just each other, so she wanted to take advantage of it. He knew so much about her that it only seemed fair—at least in her mind—that she know more about him.

"Did she remarry?"

"Yes, and she had two more kids."

"You're a big brother?" For some reason, that fit in well with the protective air he gave off.

"Uh..." His brow furrowed. "Yes?"

"Do you hang out with your siblings much?"

"Pretty much not at all. They're almost twenty years younger than me."

"Really?"

"Yes. My mom was young when she had me—like nineteen years old—and after she left, she decided she wanted to just live her life without any responsibilities beyond me. It took her until she was nearly forty to settle down and get married again. Pretty much right away, she had her son, and a year after, she had her daughter."

"Do you wish you could see them more?"

Jude shrugged. "To be honest, I've never really thought of them as my brother and sister."

"Kind of like how I don't really think of Julian, Benji, and Annie as my brothers and sister?"

Jude gazed at her for a long moment, then nodded. "Though I hope that you will eventually have a good relationship with each of them."

There were times when Angela couldn't imagine being as close to them as she was to Kiara. But she also knew that she needed to give it time and keep an open mind about the relationships they could have.

Jude turned his attention back to his gun, and Angela watched as he reloaded it, fascinated by the efficient economy of his movements. Everything about the way he handled the weapon spoke of years of training and experience. It was both impressive and slightly intimidating.

"You make that look so easy," she said.

"I can't even begin to hazard a guess as to how many times I've done it."

"Have you ever had to shoot someone?"

Jude turned to face the target. "No. I've had to pull my gun a few times. That was enough to get people to back off. My dad had more experience with that as a cop."

"I'm not sure I could shoot someone," Angela confessed.

Jude shifted to look at her. "If you're going to pick up a gun, you have to be prepared to use it."

"But I don't *want* to pick up a gun."

Jude's blue eyes stared intently at her, and Angela struggled to hold his gaze. She felt like she was letting him down by admitting that.

"I think most people don't want to have to pick up a gun because it means a situation is dire. But that is precisely why you need to practice and become comfortable with a weapon in your hand." His gaze hardened briefly. "If someone were to threaten Kiara, wouldn't you want to have the ability to protect her?"

"Of course. I would want to be able to protect her and anyone else I care about."

It was the only reason she'd shown up, but she still didn't have to like it. On this particular point, she and Jude would have to differ.

"And that's why I'm going to train you until you're capable of protecting yourself and others." He hesitated, his gaze going to the target. "Do it for your dad. For Kiara." He glanced at her. "For me."

Hope rocketed through her at those words and his glance. Was it possible he felt as pulled to her as she was to him? Or was it all her imagination?

"I'll try my best to learn everything you want us to know."

Jude nodded, then lifted his gun to aim at the target. He fired off six shots, then lowered his arm.

"Now, it's your turn again," Jude said, any hint of emotion gone. He stepped out of the way, gesturing for Angela to take his place.

She narrowed her eyes at him for a moment, then went through the process of loading her gun, just like he'd shown her. After positioning herself, Angela took a breath and exhaled.

Her first shot missed, but the next three hit the paper, though they were nowhere near where Jude had hit it.

"You're already improving," Jude said.

"Thanks," she said, feeling a small flush of pride at his approval. She emptied the magazine with her final shots, trying to focus on the target rather than on Jude watching her.

Angela set the gun down, her arms slightly sore from the unfamiliar tension of holding the weapon steady. She rolled her shoulders, working out the stiffness.

"We should take a break," Jude suggested. "You don't want to overdo it on your first time."

"I'm fine," she insisted, though the relief in her arms when she'd set the gun down had been immediate. "Just getting used to it."

"Everyone's muscles get tired their first time shooting. It's using a completely different set of muscles than you normally would."

She couldn't argue with that. Her forearms and shoulders ached in places she didn't know could ache. Down at the other end of the range, she could hear Kiara's excited voice as she talked with Dennis. Like everything else they'd done, her sister seemed to be taking to this much more naturally than Angela.

"How's Kiara doing?" she asked, glancing toward them.

"From what I can see, she's doing well. Dennis is one of our best instructors." Jude checked his watch. "Let's take a break."

Angela nodded, grateful to remove the ear protection and leave the shooting lane. Jude led her to a small sitting area just outside the range, where there were tables with two or three chairs clustered around them. There was a glass wall that allowed them to still see the shooting lanes, but the noise was muffled.

A water cooler stood in the corner, and Angela headed straight for it, suddenly realizing how thirsty she was.

The cool water helped ease the dryness in her throat. She filled a second cup and offered it to Jude, who accepted it with a nod of thanks.

"So," she said, settling into one of the chairs, "how often do you come down here to practice?"

"At least twice a week," Jude replied, taking the chair across from her. "Sometimes more. Depends on how my week is going."

Angela tried to imagine him down here alone, methodically working through target after target with that same focused intensity she'd just witnessed. The image fit him perfectly—disciplined, precise, never satisfied with anything less than excellence.

"Do you ever get tired of it?" she asked. "All the training and preparation?"

Jude considered her question, gently rolling the paper cup between his palms. "Sometimes. But then I remember why I do it, and it doesn't feel like a burden anymore."

"Why do you do it?"

His gaze met hers, and something in his expression shifted. "To protect the people who matter to me."

"So for the same reason I'm doing it," Angela said.

"Yep." A quick smile crossed Jude's face. "Although I have to say that for the most part, I do enjoy the training and practice. I'd probably still do it, if slightly less frequently, even if I didn't have to do it for my job."

"How did you do, Angie?" Kiara asked as she and Dennis approached where they sat.

"I did okay," Angela told her. "How about you?"

"Well, I'm in no danger of outperforming my trainer." Kiara dropped down into the chair that Jude had vacated, indicating that she should sit there.

"Neither am I."

"I think I'd like to see Jude and Dennis have a shoot-off," Kiara said with a grin. "See who's better."

Dennis crossed his arms and widened his stance. "I'm up for it."

"Really?" Jude asked. "You think you can out-shoot me?"

"Yep. I think I can."

"Guess we need to see," Kiara said. "My money is on Dennis."

"Well, mine's on Jude," Angela replied.

"Let's get it set up." Dennis turned and headed for one of the center lanes.

Jude let out a sigh and followed the man. Kiara got up and tugged on Angela's arm.

"C'mon. We're the cheerleaders."

Angela allowed Kiara to pull her over to where the men stood discussing the details of the challenge. Once everything was decided, they put their ear protection back on, then the two men took up their positions.

They each took their first shot, then discussed who won that before moving on to the next round. They planned to do a best of seven.

Dennis might have had the bigger ego when it came to believing he was the better shot, but the proof in the pudding—or on the targets—was that Jude held that title. Jude won the first three rounds, then Dennis got two. But in the end, Jude took the sixth round, winning with four shots.

"And that's why I'm the boss," Jude said as he reloaded his gun before slipping it into his shoulder harness. He thumped Dennis on the shoulder. "Keep practicing."

Dennis chuckled. "Maybe I let you win."

"You tell yourself that," Jude drawled.

"My goal is to beat Dennis," Kiara said. "And apparently, you too, Jude."

"It's a good goal to have," Jude told her with a nod.

With their practice session at an end, Dennis and Kiara headed upstairs. Jude had the target from the lane Angela had been using move forward. He pulled the target off.

"We're going to keep this so you can compare it in the future, to see how you improve."

Angela watched as Jude rolled it up into a cylinder. He kept it in his hand as they walked up the stairs to the main floor.

"I'm going to keep this in my office," Jude said. "In a couple of weeks, we'll compare it again."

Angela hoped that she improved enough that it would be evident in that comparison.

"Will you and Kiara be available to go to the DMV to get your learner's permits tomorrow afternoon?"

"Yes, I think so," Angela said. "We've been studying for the written test."

"Good. We have appointments for you both in Coeur d'Alene. After the kidnapping, when Annie had returned and you were still missing, Duncan had your and Annie's last name legally changed from Burke to Turner, so we have a birth certificate in that name for you to use."

"I won't be Reynolds anymore?" Angela asked.

"No, you'll be a Turner, like Annie."

Angela had no problem with that. Being a Reynolds hadn't been a positive thing for her, and she didn't remember being a Burke, so there was no connection there.

She'd always assumed she'd be a Reynolds until she got married. If that ever happened.

"What about Kiara?"

"She'll have to use the name she has on her birth certificate."

In what they'd viewed as a minor miracle at the time, Sandra had handed over what she'd said were their birth certificates shortly before she'd passed away. Now they knew that Angela's, at least, had been faked.

Sandra hadn't revealed that information, even though, shortly before her death, she'd encouraged them to leave the homestead as soon as they could. Unfortunately, it had taken them longer than they'd hoped, but they'd made it off the homestead, eventually. And now they'd made it out of Briar Hollow.

Not that Sandra would be happy they'd ended up with Duncan. But even though there were still times—lots of them—when she felt overwhelmed, Angela was glad they were on the estate.

And only part of that had to do with reconnecting with her birth family.

CHAPTER TWENTY-ONE

Jude pulled the UTV to a stop in front of the rec building and got out. He pulled open the door and stepped into the building, already eager to see Angela. Or rather, to see how she was progressing.

He'd turned over most of the self-defense training to Dawn, but he couldn't seem to stay away. At the time, it had seemed like the right thing to do. Considering the feelings he had for her, keeping a bit more distance between them seemed like a good thing.

Unfortunately, he had needed to do it for the sake of his job too. There were projects that he'd needed to review and sign off on. He wasn't just in charge of security for the estate. Duncan had him overseeing all areas of security for his companies and real estate.

Jude wasn't a pro in every aspect of security—like the tech side of things—but he understood enough to be able to advise Duncan. The biggest thing was that Duncan trusted him. And Jude trusted the people he'd hired, who had the expertise he lacked.

Trust was a huge part of his life. His trust in God and the belief that He had a purpose for him. His trust in Duncan when he'd said he'd always have a home at the estate. And Duncan's trust in Jude that he would keep his family safe.

Trust.

His steps faltered as he considered the word in light of his true motivation for going to the rec center: his desire to see Angela.

It was his job to keep watch over her, but he knew he'd still be there even if it wasn't.

As he stepped into the large gym, his gaze swept the room. He noticed that Annie was there, but he wasn't looking for her.

When he saw Angela, his gaze stayed locked on her. She and Dawn were currently on the mats while Kiara and Annie sat off to the side.

Jude leaned back against the wall, crossing his arms as he observed Angela's moves.

She had definitely gained more confidence since their first day of training, though she still needed more power behind her moves. He was proud of her, though. She was working hard at it, and that was all he asked.

She happened to glance his way, and the moment her eyes landed on him, a beautiful smile enveloped her face. His heart slammed in his chest at that look. Never before had someone looked at him with such unfettered joy, just because they'd seen him.

The thing was, he felt the same way. Just laying eyes on her made him happy. The difference was that he had learned to control his outward expression.

But even so, a smile tugged up the corners of his mouth.

"Hey, boss!"

Dawn's greeting reminded him that they weren't alone. His smile slid away as he gave her his attention.

"Just checking to see how it's going."

Dawn's smile took on a knowing edge as she nodded. "It's going very well. Angela and Kiara have both picked up the moves quickly."

"Do they need practice dropping a bigger target?"

"That wasn't the plan for today," Dawn said. "But since you're here, we might as well take advantage of you."

"I'll go get changed."

He'd taken to leaving a change of clothes at the gym so he was always ready to help during training if needed.

When he returned, he found that Dawn had Kiara on the mat with her, while the twins sat side by side at the edge of the mat. He paused just outside the open doorway, taking in the sight of them.

He knew the sisters had been hanging out together, but probably not as much as Duncan would have wished. But Jude thought that would come in time.

When he walked into the gym, Dawn waved him over. "You get to start with me."

"Feeling the need for some practice, huh?" he asked as Kiara moved over to join Annie and Angela.

"I figured I'd show Kiara and Angela that you aren't breakable," Dawn said.

"What's that supposed to mean?" Jude flexed his hands, preparing for the interaction that was to come.

"They still think they need to take it easy on you."

Jude lifted an eyebrow at her. "Planning to get a few hits in, are you?"

"You bet." Dawn rubbed her hands together. "Let's do this."

Since they'd sparred a lot over the years, Jude knew Dawn would not pull her punches. They'd both be trying to fight off an attacker.

Jude focused in on Dawn, watching for the tells he'd learned about her through their previous sparring sessions. This wasn't something he'd do with any of the other three. At least, not yet.

Dawn came at him fast, her movements fluid and controlled. Jude deflected her first strike and countered with a move designed to test her reflexes. She blocked it easily, then spun away from his follow-up attempt.

The familiar rhythm of sparring settled over him—the focused concentration, the calculated movements, the constant assessment of his opponent's next move. But he was acutely aware of Angela watching from the sidelines, and he found himself wanting to show her how he could handle himself.

Dawn swept his legs, and he rolled out of the way, coming up in a defensive crouch. She was good—better than most of his security team—and she wasn't holding back. That was exactly what he needed the women to see.

"Nice try," he said, circling her with careful steps.

"I'm just getting started," Dawn replied, her eyes gleaming with competitive fire.

She feinted left, then came in from the right with a series of quick strikes that Jude blocked, each impact reverberating up his arms. He caught her wrist on the fourth strike and used her momentum to spin her away from him, but she twisted free with practiced ease.

From the corner of his eye, he caught Angela leaning forward, her attention completely focused on their movements. The knowledge that she was watching sent an unwelcome surge of adrenaline through him that had nothing to do with the sparring match.

Dawn took advantage of his momentary distraction, landing a solid hit to his ribs that drove the air out of his lungs. He staggered back a step, grimacing.

"You're distracted," Dawn said, her voice low enough that only he could hear.

Jude narrowed his eyes and refocused, pushing everything else out of his mind. This was about showing Angela and Kiara what they could do if they took their training seriously, not worrying about impressing anyone.

The next time Dawn came at him, he was ready. He blocked her strike, then countered with a swift movement that caught her off balance. Not enough to take her down—Dawn was too good for that—but enough to put him back in control of the exchange.

They continued trading blows, neither gaining a clear advantage, until Dawn finally signaled for them to stop. Both were breathing hard, with a sheen of sweat on their foreheads.

"See?" Dawn said, turning to the women watching from the side. "Even Jude has to work for it. And I guarantee he's not holding back with me."

Jude rolled his shoulder, feeling where one of Dawn's strikes had connected. "Definitely not holding back," he confirmed, meeting Angela's wide-eyed gaze briefly before looking away.

"Angela, you're up," Dawn said, gesturing to the mat. "Let's see what you've learned so far."

Angela hesitated for a moment before standing and making her way to the center of the mat. Jude moved to the side, crossing his arms as he watched her approach.

There was still a bit of hesitation in her movements that spoke of uncertainty. However, she had a more confident look on her face that told Jude that while she knew she wasn't going to be able to take Dawn down, she was going to at least try.

"Remember what we've practiced," Dawn said, taking a defensive stance. "I'm going to come at you slowly at first, then we'll build up the intensity."

Jude leaned forward slightly, his attention completely focused on Angela's form. He wanted to call out corrections, to guide her through the movements, but he forced himself to stay silent. Dawn was a good instructor—better than he was in some ways—and she'd correct Angela where necessary.

Dawn moved toward Angela with deliberate slowness, telegraphing her approach. Angela reacted exactly as she'd been taught, stepping to the side and bringing her arm up to block. Her form was good, better than it had been even a week ago.

"Good," Dawn said. "Now, counter."

Angela struck out with her palm, aiming for Dawn's solar plexus, but her movement lacked the force it needed to be truly effective. Still, her technique was solid.

They continued through a series of defensive moves, Dawn gradually increasing the speed and intensity of her attacks. Jude watched Angela's confidence grow with each successful block and counter, noting the way her shoulders relaxed and her movements became more fluid.

But then Dawn came at her with a move they hadn't practiced extensively—a grab for her wrist that Angela wasn't quite prepared for. For a split second, panic flashed across Angela's face, and her body tensed.

Jude felt his own muscles tighten in response, fighting the urge to step in and protect her.

But then something shifted in her expression. The fear gave way to determination as she remembered her training. Instead of pulling away—which would have strengthened Dawn's grip—Angela stepped toward her attacker, twisting her arm in the direction of Dawn's thumb, the weakest point of the grip.

Dawn's hold loosened, and Angela used the momentum to break free completely. She didn't stop there, following up with a strike toward Dawn's sternum that, while not powerful enough to do damage, showed she understood the principle of counterattacking.

"Much better," Dawn said, nodding with approval. "You remembered not to pull away."

Angela's chest rose and fell with rapid breaths, but her smile was triumphant. "I almost forgot. For a second, I just wanted to yank my arm back."

"That's normal," Dawn assured her. "The goal is to make the correct response automatic, so you don't have to think about it in the moment."

Angela nodded, pushing a strand of hair back from her flushed face. Her gaze flicked briefly to Jude, and he gave her a small nod of encouragement.

"Let's try it again," Dawn said. "This time, I'm not going to telegraph as much."

For the next ten minutes, Jude watched as Dawn put Angela through her paces, working on escaping from a variety of grips.

"Okay. Let's see how you do against Jude."

Angela looked at him with wide eyes, then nodded.

Jude watched the uncertainty flicker across Angela's face and felt his protective instincts flare. He wanted to reassure her, but he also knew she needed to push through this barrier. Fighting against someone larger and stronger was the whole point of the training.

"I'll start easy," he said, moving onto the mat. "Just like Dawn did with you."

Angela took a deep breath and squared her shoulders. The determination in her stance reminded him of the way she'd confronted her mother at the resort—that same quiet steel beneath the surface.

He approached her slowly, reaching for her wrist with deliberate, telegraphed movements. She responded exactly as she'd been taught, stepping into him and twisting away from his grip. Her technique was solid, but he could feel the hesitation in her movements.

"Good," he said. "But you need to commit to the movement. If you hesitate, you give your attacker time to adjust."

Angela nodded, her jaw set with concentration. "Again?"

This time when he reached for her, she moved with more conviction. Her escape was cleaner, faster, and she followed through with the palm strike Dawn had taught her. The heel of her hand connected with his chest—not hard enough to hurt, but with enough force that he felt it.

"Better," he said, stepping back. "Much better."

The approval in his voice seemed to bolster her confidence. Her shoulders relaxed slightly, and when she looked at him, there was less fear in her eyes.

"Let's try something more challenging," he said, wanting to see how she'd handle a more realistic scenario.

Jude moved toward her again, this time with less telegraphing. He reached for her shoulder, and Angela reacted immediately, ducking under his arm and spinning away. Her movement was fluid, instinctive, and he felt a surge of pride at her progress.

"Excellent," Dawn called from the sidelines. "That was much more natural."

Angela's face lit up at the praise, and Jude had to fight back a smile. The transformation in her confidence over the past few weeks had been remarkable to witness.

"One more," he said, knowing he needed to push her just a little further. "This time, I'm going to grab your wrist and not let go easily."

Angela nodded, though he saw her swallow hard. When he moved toward her this time, he didn't hold back as much. His hand closed around her delicate wrist with firm pressure, the kind of grip that would genuinely require technique to break.

For a moment, Angela froze. He could feel the tension in her arm, the way her muscles locked up in response to being restrained. The fear was back in her eyes, and Jude had to resist the urge to immediately release her.

But then he watched something shift in her expression. Her jaw tightened, and instead of pulling away, she stepped toward him just as Dawn had taught her.

She twisted her wrist toward his thumb, and when his grip loosened slightly, she swept her leg behind his and pushed hard against his chest with her free hand. Jude, caught off guard by the unexpected move, lost his balance and toppled backward, landing on the mat with a solid thud.

For a moment, the gym was completely silent. Then Dawn let out a whoop of triumph.

"That's what I'm talking about!" she exclaimed, clapping her hands together. "Perfect execution, Angela!"

Angela stood frozen, staring down at Jude with wide eyes and parted lips. The realization of what she'd just done seemed to hit her all at once—she'd taken down the head of security, a man with years of training and experience.

He'd learned a couple of valuable lessons in the exchange as well. Being near Angela was a huge distraction. But also, he needed to not underestimate her ability. That combination was going to land him on the floor at her feet again if he didn't get a handle on those things.

"I'm so sorry," she gasped, reaching out a hand to help him up. "I didn't mean to—"

"Don't apologize," Jude said, taking her offered hand, even though he didn't need her help and rose to his feet. His pride in her accomplishment far outweighed any embarrassment he might have felt. "That was exactly what you were supposed to do."

He noticed a flush creeping up her neck as she released his hand. The warmth of her skin lingered on his palm, and he resisted the urge to flex his fingers.

"But I didn't think I'd actually—" She gestured vaguely at the mat where he'd just been sprawled.

"Take me down?" Jude finished for her, the corner of his mouth lifting. "That's the whole point, Angela. The techniques work if you commit to them."

"I'll try to remember that."

"Let's take five," Dawn announced, glancing between them with that knowing look that made Jude want to avert his eyes. "Hydrate, everyone. Then we'll switch partners."

As Angela moved toward the water cooler at the side of the room, Jude followed, suddenly parched. She filled a paper cup and handed it to him before filling one for herself.

"Thanks for not going easy on me," she said, taking a small sip of water. "It helps me understand what I'm actually capable of."

Jude studied her profile as she drank, noting the way strands of her hair had come loose from its ponytail during their sparring session. A few of them clung to her damp neck, and he wondered what it would feel like to brush them away.

"You're stronger than you think," he said, forcing his attention back to her words rather than on the graceful curve of her neck. "You just needed to believe it."

She turned to fully face him, and the proximity hit him like a physical force. They were standing close enough that he could see the flecks of green in her blue eyes.

"I wouldn't have believed it if someone had told me I could do that," she admitted, her voice soft. "Take down someone like you."

The admiration in her tone sent warmth spreading through his chest. He'd been praised by Duncan countless times, had earned the respect of his security team through years of proving himself, but somehow Angela's quiet acknowledgment meant more than all of that combined.

"You did good," he said, his voice gruff.

Something shifted in her expression, a softness that made his pulse quicken. Not much in his world was soft. Yet Angela had come into his life, softness wrapped around strength. It was so appealing to him, and right then, he wanted to pull her into his arms and hold her close.

For a moment, the noise of the gym faded into the background—Dawn's instructions to Kiara, Annie's quiet encouragement—and it felt like they were the only two people in the room.

"Angela." Her name escaped his lips as barely more than a whisper.

She took a small step closer, and Jude felt his resolve wavering like a candle's flame in the wind.

Everything he'd told himself about maintaining professional boundaries, about protecting both their positions within the Burke family—it all seemed suddenly insignificant compared to the pull he felt toward her.

"Jude, I—"

"Alright, everyone!" Dawn's voice cut through the moment like a blade. "Let's switch things up. Kiara, you get Jude."

The spell broke instantly. Angela stepped back, color flooding her cheeks as she looked away. Jude cleared his throat and crushed the paper cup in his hand, the small sound unnaturally loud in his ears.

"Right," he said, his voice carefully neutral as he tossed the cup into the garbage can and turned to face the mat. "Kiara, you ready?"

Kiara bounced to her feet with characteristic enthusiasm. "Absolutely. I've been watching your technique with Angela, and I think I can take you."

The confidence in her voice almost made Jude smile, despite the tension still thrumming through his system. Almost.

He forced himself to move away from Angela, to focus on the task at hand. But as he approached the mat where Kiara waited with that eager gleam in her eyes, he could feel Angela's gaze following him. The awareness of her attention made his movements feel awkward, self-conscious in a way they never had before.

"Ready to see if I can take you down too?" Kiara asked with a grin that reminded him that she and Angela weren't actually sisters by blood. Where Angela approached everything with careful consideration, Kiara dove in headfirst.

"Let's see what you've got," Jude replied, grateful for the distraction of Kiara's competitive energy.

The next fifteen minutes passed in a blur of movement and instruction. Kiara was aggressive in her movements, throwing herself into each technique with an enthusiasm that sometimes worked against her. She tried to muscle through moves that required finesse, and Jude had to remind her repeatedly that technique trumped strength.

But she was learning. Both of them were.

After Dawn put an end to the training time, Jude glanced over to where Angela sat cross-legged on the edge of the mat beside Annie.

They both smiled at him, but only one of the smiles made his heart skip a beat. And that smile tempted him more than ever to throw caution to the wind and follow his heart.

CHAPTER TWENTY-TWO

Angela followed Kiara to the large black SUV that was parked near the back door. Jude stood near the back passenger door, giving them a nod as they approached.

"I'm going to sit in the back," Kiara announced as she climbed into the SUV.

Angela slid into the middle bench seat, a bit surprised when Jude joined her, but then she saw two bodyguards in the front seats.

"Isn't this a bit overkill?" Angela asked.

Jude glanced at her as the SUV moved away from the house. "What do you mean?"

"Three of you for just two of us?"

"Two of us will go in with you and Kiara, while one stays with the vehicle."

It still seemed excessive, but she wasn't up to date on all the procedures being taken for their safety. She hadn't even asked what Jim and Craig were up to.

Maybe she should have wanted more details, but she was going to trust that Jude and his team knew what they were doing and would keep them safe.

Angela pressed a hand to her stomach, trying to quell her nerves. She had studied so much for the driver's written exam, but tests had never been her thing. Sandra had hardly ever tested them, and when she had, if they didn't do well, Jim got involved.

She opened her phone to the trial test she and Kiara had been using to help them study. When Jude reached out and took the phone from her, she let it slip from her hands.

"Let me help you," Jude said when she gave him a questioning look.

Angela shifted on her seat, uneasy about showing Jude that she struggled. Finally, she gave a nod.

Because they were still avoiding Serenity, they were headed to Coeur d'Alene, which gave them plenty of time to study.

Angela tensed when Jude asked her the first question. The words seemed to blur together as she tried to recall what she'd studied. Her mind went blank for a moment, and her heart beat faster as the pressure mounted.

"You can take your time," Jude said, his voice low and calm.

She took a deep breath, focusing on the question again. "B. You should yield to the vehicle on the right."

"Correct." His smile was warm, sending a small flutter through her chest.

They continued through several more questions, and Angela found herself relaxing slightly. Jude's method of questioning was methodical but gentle, nothing like the intimidating way Jim would hover over her shoulder when Sandra had tested them.

"What does a flashing yellow light mean?" Jude asked, his shoulder brushing against hers as the SUV rounded a curve.

"Proceed with caution," Angela answered quickly, growing more confident with each correct response.

Kiara leaned forward from the back seat. "Hey, why don't I get any study help?"

"Because you got every practice question right yesterday," Angela reminded her, glancing back at her sister.

"True." Kiara grinned. "But I wouldn't mind some one-on-one time with the teacher."

Heat crept up Angela's neck at the teasing note in Kiara's voice. She looked down at her hands, suddenly very interested in her fingernails.

"We can switch if you want," she offered, though part of her didn't want to give up this moment with Jude.

"No need," Jude said, his attention remaining on Angela. "You're doing well. Let's keep going."

The warmth in his voice made Angela's pulse quicken. She tried to focus on the next question he asked, but found herself distracted by his proximity—the way his sleeve brushed against her arm when he moved, the faint scent of his cologne mixing with the leather interior of the SUV.

"Angela?" Jude prompted gently.

She realized she'd been staring at his hands as he held her phone, completely missing whatever question he'd asked. "Sorry, could you repeat that?"

"What's the legal blood alcohol limit for drivers under twenty-one?"

"Zero tolerance," she answered quickly, grateful it was an easy one.

"Right." His eyes crinkled slightly at the corners. "You know this material better than you think you do."

Angela wished she felt as confident as he did about her ability to pass the test. The closer they got to Coeur d'Alene, the more her stomach churned with anxiety. What if she failed? What if all this studying hadn't been enough?

"Hey," Jude said softly, and she realized her leg had started bouncing nervously. "You're going to do fine."

"How do you know?" The question slipped out before she could stop it.

Jude's gaze held hers for a moment that felt longer than it probably was.

"Because I've seen how hard you've been studying. And because I believe in you."

His quiet confidence stirred something inside her. Angela wanted to believe him, to borrow some of that certainty for herself.

"Thanks," she murmured.

The SUV slowed as they approached the DMV building, a plain single-story structure with a crowded parking lot. Angela's mouth went dry at the sight of all the cars. So many people. So many potential witnesses if she failed.

"Looks busy," Kiara commented, leaning forward to peer through the windshield.

"We have appointments," Jude reminded them, handing Angela back her phone. "You won't have to wait in the main line."

The driver pulled around to the entrance, and Angela took a deep breath as the engine shut off. Her palms felt clammy as she clutched her phone.

"Ready?" Jude asked.

"As I'll ever be," she replied.

Jude exited first and moved around the vehicle, scanning the area before opening Angela's door. The cold air hit her face as she stepped out, and she tugged her coat tighter around herself. Kiara bounded out behind her, seemingly unfazed by the prospect of the test ahead.

Inside, the DMV was exactly as Angela had imagined—fluorescent lighting, rows of plastic chairs filled with people waiting for their turn. The sound of muffled conversations created a constant hum of background noise.

Angela's steps felt unsteady as she followed Jude toward the information desk. Her heart hammered against her ribs, and she shoved her hands into the pockets of her jacket, hoping no one would notice how nervous she was.

The woman behind the counter looked up with the practiced smile of someone who dealt with impatient people all day. "Can I help you?"

"We have appointments for written tests," Jude said, his voice calm and professional. "Angela Turner and Kiara Reynolds."

Angela startled slightly at hearing her new last name spoken aloud. She was still getting used to the idea that she was no longer Angela Reynolds. That part of her identity had been stripped away, along with everything else from her old life. And she didn't miss it.

"Let me check," the woman said, shifting her attention to her computer screen. "Yes, here you are. You'll need to fill out these forms first, then we'll get you set up for the written portion."

The clipboard felt heavy in Angela's hands as she accepted it, though she knew that was just her nerves making everything seem more difficult than it should be. The words swam briefly before her eyes, but then she blinked and focused on the questions—basic information about her address, her emergency contacts, whether she wore corrective lenses.

Jude guided them to a quiet corner with a few empty chairs. Angela sat down and stared at the form, realizing she didn't know what to put for some of the fields. What was her home address now? The estate? Her future house? She glanced up at Jude, who seemed to anticipate her confusion.

"You'll need to use the business address," he said, his voice low as he sat beside her. He recited it slowly so she could write it out.

Angela filled in the form carefully, methodically printing each letter. When she reached the emergency contact section, her hand hesitated over the blank line. Should she put Kiara, like she usually did? Or should it be Duncan?

Angela wanted to write Jude's name and number, but she wasn't sure she should.

"Who do I put for the emergency contact?" she asked, keeping her voice low.

Jude seemed to consider it for a moment before he said, "You can put Kiara, if you'd like. It's probably best you don't put Duncan. You can put me or Annie."

"You don't mind if I put you?" she asked. "It might be better if you were the one they contacted in an emergency, not Kiara."

Jude nodded. "That's fine."

Angela wrote his name in the emergency contact section, then added his number, which she'd already memorized.

Kiara had finished with her form and was looking around with a smile as she waited. "This is exciting, isn't it? Our first official ID in the real world."

The real world. That's what Kiara had taken to calling everything beyond Briar Hollow. As if their previous life had been some sort of dream—or nightmare.

"I guess," Angela murmured, trying to match her sister's enthusiasm.

When they returned the completed forms to the counter, the woman directed them to where they'd wait to be called for their test.

"You can do this," Jude said.

The chairs were not exactly comfortable, and for someone of Jude's size, it meant he was pressed close to her side. Angela took comfort in his presence, though she knew when it was time to take the test, she'd be on her own.

Or not.

I can do all things through Christ who strengthens me.

She had to remember that she wasn't alone.

Please, God, give me clarity of mind. Keep my nerves from robbing me of the information I've worked so hard to memorize.

A touch on her hand had Angela opening her eyes. Seeing Jude's hand on hers, Angela turned to look at him.

"It's time," he said. "They called your name."

"Oh, I didn't hear."

Jude stood when she did and walked her to where she was to take the test.

"I'll wait here for you."

She heard them call Kiara's name and glanced over to see her sister hurrying over. But before she reached them, Angela was taken to the testing terminal.

After they explained how it worked, they left her to it. Angela took a deep breath and exhaled, then said another prayer before she focused on the test.

While she was confident with most of her answers, there were a few she wasn't sure about. She knew she could only get six wrong if she wanted to pass, so she hoped she'd done okay.

When she completed the test, she held her breath as she waited for the result. Relief flooded her when a DMV employee approached her and informed her that she'd passed.

Getting up, she hurried back to where Jude waited. His brows rose questioningly as she approached him.

Waving the paper the DMV employee had given her, she said, "I passed!"

In her excitement, and without conscious thought of her actions, Angela threw her arms around Jude. For a moment, she worried that he'd push her away. But instead, his arms came around her, gently holding her close. If only time could stand still. She wanted to bask in the moment and commit it to memory.

But even though she wanted to prolong the contact, Angela released Jude and stepped back.

He smiled down at her with a smile that reached his eyes. This wasn't Jude, her bodyguard, smiling at her. This was Jude, her friend... the man her heart longed for.

"I knew you could do it."

"I didn't get a perfect mark, but at least I didn't fail."

"Well, that's all that matters."

Kiara came out then to announce to them that she had also passed. Angela hugged her tight, so glad that the test was over. Of course, an even more difficult test was still to come. But she'd deal with that later.

It took them a while longer to finalize everything that would give them permission to drive off the estate. Angela still didn't have the excitement about driving that Kiara did, but it was probably a good skill to have.

"Will I actually have to drive anywhere?" Angela asked as they got back into the SUV once they'd finished everything at the driver's licensing office.

"What do you mean?" Jude asked.

"Won't I always have to have a bodyguard with me? Like Jill said?"

"Yes. I can't imagine that Duncan would want you going off on your own."

"So I assume the bodyguard can also drive. Right?"

"It's true that they could drive you if you preferred that. Most of the time, Annie prefers to drive her own car, and Dawn follows in one of the estate vehicles."

"I'm sure Kiara will want to drive, even if the bodyguard is in the car with her."

"We'll cross that bridge when we get to it," Jude said. "For now, if you want to practice driving with your bodyguard, you can. Or, you can let them drive if you're more comfortable with that."

"When will we know who our bodyguards are?"

"I think Lucy will become Kiara's full-time guard," Jude said. "We're still working on yours. But for now, it's me."

The joy that information caused her brought a smile to her face. "And I'm fine with that."

After a beat, Jude said, "So am I."

With the stress of the test gone, Angela was able to relax in her seat next to Jude.

The quiet hum of the SUV and the warmth radiating from Jude's presence beside her made Angela's eyelids droop momentarily. The adrenaline from passing her test had faded, revealing the effects of the fractured sleep she'd had the night before.

In her relaxed state, Angela studied Jude's profile as he gazed out the front window—the strong line of his jaw, the scruff on his cheeks, dark lashes that might make a woman jealous.

She blinked and turned her gaze away from him.

When had she started memorizing these details about him? It was as if she wanted to capture every moment they were together to ponder when they weren't.

"Thank you," she said quietly, not wanting to disturb Kiara, who had fallen asleep in the back seat.

Jude turned to look at her, his blue eyes questioning. "For what?"

"For helping me study. For believing I could do it when I didn't believe in myself." She twisted her hands in her lap. "For everything, really."

Something shifted in his expression, a softness that made her breath catch. "You don't need to thank me for that."

"I do, though." The words tumbled out before she could stop them. "I don't know what I would have done without you these past few weeks. You've made everything feel less overwhelming."

Jude's gaze held hers for a moment that stretched longer than it should have. Heat rose up her neck as Angela realized how much she'd revealed. She looked down at her hands, suddenly fascinated by the way her fingers tangled together in her lap.

The silence stretched between them, filled with unspoken words that Angela didn't know how to voice. She could feel Jude's attention on her, could sense the tension radiating from his still form beside her.

A sideways glance revealed his gaze was still fixed on her face with an intensity that made her forget how to breathe. The space between them seemed to shrink, though neither of them had moved. Angela's heart hammered against her ribs as she watched something shift in his expression—a crack in the professional mask he always wore.

The SUV hit a rough patch in the road, jolting them both back to reality.

Jude cleared his throat and looked away, his jaw tightening as he stared out the window with renewed focus.

Angela pressed her back against the seat, trying to create a distance that felt impossible within the confines of the vehicle.

Embarrassment filled her as she realized how close she'd come to... what? Leaning toward him? Closing that gap between them? The thought terrified and thrilled her in equal measure.

She'd been so caught up in the moment that she'd completely forgotten that Jude was on the job. Kiara might be asleep in the back seat, but Lucy and the driver certainly weren't. They could hear everything they said.

"We should be back at the estate in about twenty minutes," Jude said, his voice carefully neutral again.

Angela nodded, not trusting herself to speak. She turned toward her own window, watching the snow-covered landscape blur past as she tried to sort through the tangle of emotions in her chest.

The moment had passed, but the feelings lingered, brightening in her heart. The muted feelings she'd had for Jude had just had their intensity turned way up.

They were no longer something she could easily ignore. But even if she couldn't ignore them, she couldn't do anything about them either.

Jude would keep her even more at arm's length if she had more moments like what they'd just shared. At least she thought they'd shared it. Or had it all been in her mind?

For the rest of the drive back to the estate, Angela kept her gaze fixed on the passing scenery, acutely aware of every shift in Jude's position beside her. The air between them felt charged, like the moments before a thunderstorm when the atmosphere grew heavy with anticipation.

When they finally pulled through the estate gates, Angela felt both relief and disappointment.

Relief that she could escape the confines of the SUV and the intensity of whatever had passed between them. Disappointment that their time together was ending for the time being.

Kiara stirred in the back seat as they came to a stop, blinking sleepily. "Are we home?"

Home. The word still felt foreign on Angela's tongue when it came to the estate, but less so than it had weeks ago.

"We're back," Angela confirmed, already reaching for the door handle before Jude could get out to open it for her.

She welcomed the sharp bite of the air against her heated cheeks as she stepped out of the SUV. She needed something to clear her head, to remind her of the boundaries that existed between her and Jude, no matter what her heart might be telling her.

Duncan was waiting for them in the mud room, his face lighting up when he saw them.

"How did it go?" he asked, his eyes moving between Angela and Kiara.

"We both passed!" Kiara announced, grinning proudly.

"That's wonderful news." Duncan's smile was warm. "I knew you could do it."

"You weren't that happy when I got *my* license," Annie remarked as she appeared beside her—their—father.

Duncan gave a rueful laugh as he slipped his arm around Annie's shoulders and dropped a kiss on her head. "I know. I'm sorry about that. I realize now how important that was to you."

Annie shrugged. "At least you came around eventually."

As Angela watched Annie and Duncan interact, she wondered if she would ever get to the point where she was that comfortable with him.

When they'd first arrived at the estate, she would have said that she'd never be comfortable enough with him for that, and that she didn't really care. But as the weeks had slipped by and he'd continued to demonstrate the kind of man he was, Angela wasn't so sure that she didn't care about a close relationship with Duncan.

Maybe she did want a father in her life. A *good* father, this time around.

Their arrival in Serenity Point had introduced them to many good men. There had been good men in Briar Hollow—she'd met them at the church—but unfortunately, the men she knew the best there had been anything but good.

But now she had Duncan. And Jude. Even the men on the security team seemed to be decent and respectful. Julian... Well, she was reserving judgement on him.

So though she might have at one time resisted the idea of any type of close relationship with a man, that was definitely changing. She was quite sure that Duncan would embrace a closer relationship as father and daughter, but she didn't know for sure how Jude would feel about her desire for something more serious with him.

She needed to find someone to talk to about what she was feeling. Kiara would normally be her first choice. But in this instance, she kind of wanted to speak to someone who knew Jude well, which limited her possibilities to Duncan, Elizabeth, and Annie.

Glancing at Annie, Angela thought maybe it was time she had a conversation with her twin.

CHAPTER TWENTY-THREE

Jude stared out the window of his office, considering that perhaps he shouldn't have arranged a meeting with Duncan. He'd been uncertain how to move forward after that interaction with Angela on the way home from Coeur d'Alene.

He couldn't just ignore it because he doubted that would make it go away. And he wasn't sure that he wanted that anyway.

After a couple of days of thinking and praying about it, he'd decided that he needed to talk to Duncan. He was involved in this, whether Jude wanted him to be or not. As his boss and Angela's father, Duncan would have thoughts, Jude was sure.

And maybe he'd give Jude the clarity he needed about the situation. Hopefully, he wouldn't fire him because of how things had developed. Jude certainly hadn't planned on falling for Angela, but here he was.

Pushing back from his desk, he left his office. He told the security team he was heading to the main house for a meeting and that he'd be back later.

With January behind them, the weather didn't hold quite the chill it had. The day had been cloudy though, and it was possible they might get some snow.

Fragrant warmth greeted him as he stepped through the back door into the mudroom. The smell of sugar and chocolate greeted him, and he couldn't help but veer in the direction of the kitchen. He still had a few minutes before his scheduled time to meet with Duncan.

As he detoured into the kitchen, his gaze immediately landed on Angela. She was standing at the counter, transferring cookies from a baking sheet to a wire rack.

She looked up, her eyes widening before a smile lit up her face. "Hi!"

That smile and the smell of cookies drew Jude further into the kitchen.

"Hey. I wondered what smelled so good."

"Chocolate chip cookies," Angela said, gesturing toward the cooling racks that held dozens of golden cookies. "This is my favorite recipe for them."

Jude moved closer, the warmth from the oven mixing with Angela's presence to create something that felt dangerously like home. He could see flour dusting her apron, and a smudge of it on her cheek made his fingers itch to brush it away.

"They smell incredible," he said. "Mind if I try one?"

"Here you go." Angela selected one from the rack, her fingers brushing his as she handed it to him.

The cookie was still warm, the chocolate chips soft and melting slightly on his tongue. It was perfect—sweet without being cloying, with just the right amount of salt to balance the flavors. But he could barely focus on the taste when Angela was watching him with such a hopeful expression.

"Good?" she asked, and he caught the slight uncertainty in her voice, as if his opinion mattered more than it should.

"Amazing," he said honestly. "Best chocolate chip cookie I've ever had."

Her smile bloomed again, and Jude felt that familiar tightness in his chest that seemed to happen whenever she looked at him like that. Like he was someone worth smiling for.

It made him feel like his heart was too big for his chest.

"I was thinking of taking some to the security building later. For you and the team," she said, then seemed to catch herself. "I mean, if that's okay with you."

The thoughtful gesture touched him. She'd been thinking of him, of his team. The confirmation that he occupied space in her thoughts when they weren't together, the way she did in his, was both thrilling and frightening.

"They'd love that," he said. "We don't get many homemade treats."

Angela's cheeks flushed pink, and she tucked a strand of hair behind her ear in a gesture he'd come to recognize as a nervous habit. "I enjoy baking for people. It makes me feel useful."

The simple statement hit him harder than it should have.

After everything she'd been through, everything she'd been denied, she still wanted to take care of others. Still wanted to contribute, to matter.

"You are useful," he said, the words coming out more intense than he'd planned. "More than useful. You're—"

He caught himself before he could finish the thought, before he could tell her that she was precious, that she mattered more to him than anyone else.

The kitchen suddenly felt too small, too intimate, with just the two of them surrounded by the domestic warmth of her baking.

His heart was far too involved already. Perhaps the upcoming conversation with Duncan about this should have happened sooner.

"I'm what?" she prompted softly, and when he looked at her, he saw something vulnerable and hopeful in her expression that made his resolve crumble a little more.

The sound of footsteps in the hallway broke the moment, and Jude stepped back instinctively, putting distance between himself and Angela just as Duncan appeared in the doorway.

"Jude, perfect timing," Duncan said, though his gaze moved between them with what looked like curiosity. "Ready for our meeting?"

"Yes, sir," Jude replied, grateful his voice came out steady despite the way his pulse was still hammering from the interrupted moment with Angela.

"Actually," Duncan continued, his attention shifting to Angela, "these smell wonderful. Mind if I steal one before we disappear into my office?"

Angela's face lit up again as she selected a cookie for her father. Jude watched the easy interaction between them, noting how Duncan's presence seemed to both relax and energize her. The relationship between them had grown stronger over the past few weeks, and Jude was glad to see it.

"Take some with you," Angela offered, already reaching for a plate. "I made way too many anyway."

"You're spoiling us," Duncan said with a warm smile as he accepted the plate of cookies.

Jude found himself reluctant to leave the warm circle of Angela's attention, but Duncan was already heading toward the door. He forced himself to follow, though not before catching Angela's eye one more time.

"Thank you for the cookies," he said, and the soft smile she gave him in return made his chest tighten all over again.

As they walked through the hallway toward the office, Jude's mind raced with how to begin the conversation he'd requested.

Duncan's office felt smaller than usual as they settled into their chairs, the familiar space suddenly charged with the weight of what Jude was about to confess. Duncan poured himself a cup of coffee from the service on his desk, offering one to Jude, who declined with a shake of his head.

"So what's up?" Duncan asked. "You didn't specify what we need to discuss."

Jude still hadn't figured out how to broach the subject, so he jumped in using a professional perspective.

"I want to pursue assigning Angela a bodyguard."

Duncan frowned. "Why? I thought we were going to wait on that until after the situation with Jim was resolved."

As Jude struggled for an explanation, Duncan continued to regard him with an intense stare. He'd never felt this way in the man's presence before, and he didn't care much for it.

"I think it would be for the best if she had someone else protecting her."

"Best for her or best for you?"

"For us both," Jude said, praying that Duncan would understand without him having to go into detail.

Duncan took a bite out of another cookie, then lifted his mug to take a sip of coffee. All the while, he kept his gaze steady on Jude. It took everything within him not to squirm.

He had *never* squirmed in Duncan's presence, and he didn't want to now. But it was *so* hard not to.

"Well," Duncan finally said. "I'm aware that Angela has some feelings for you."

Jude straightened. He knew?

"The question is, how do you feel about her?" Duncan asked. "Is the request for the bodyguard change because you hope she'll lose interest if you aren't around her as much? Or is it because you're not sure you can do your job well because you also have feelings for her?"

Jude wanted to ask which one was likely to get him fired. But the reality was that his job wasn't as big a consideration as it had been when he'd first started feeling drawn to Angela.

"What do you like about Angelica?" Duncan asked, apparently taking Jude's silence as an answer to his initial questions. "What's drawn you to her?"

The answer to that was pretty easy since he'd spent a lot of time thinking about her.

"From the moment I met her, she has shown how strong she is. How persistent she is. There might be things she isn't sure about doing, but she hasn't backed away from anything yet. Faced with scary situations, she pushes forward."

Duncan nodded. "She is very determined."

"I have so much respect for how she's handled everything. She's faced a lot of difficulties in her life, and I just want to do what I can to make things easier for her."

Duncan regarded him with a steady stare. Jude had no idea what was going through his mind.

"How did you know that she had feelings for me?" Jude asked, hoping Duncan didn't say that he hadn't known for certain but that Jude had confirmed it.

Duncan chuckled. "I just watched one daughter fall in love, so I'm primed to recognize the symptoms in her twin."

Fall in love...

Jude's chest constricted at Duncan's casual use of those words. Love.

Was it that already? The constant pull he felt toward Angela, the way his day brightened when he saw her smile, the fierce protectiveness that surged through him whenever she was threatened or hurt? Was it really love?

"I care about her," he said carefully, testing the waters. "More than I should, given my position."

"Your position." Duncan set down his coffee mug and leaned back in his chair. "Tell me, Jude, what exactly do you think your position is in this family?"

The question caught him off guard. "I'm head of security. I work for you."

"You do work for me, yes. But you're also someone I trust with my life and the lives of my children and the woman I love.

Someone who's been part of this family for over two decades." Duncan's expression softened. "When I told you that you are like a son to me, I meant it."

The words sent an unexpected warmth through Jude's chest, but they also made his situation feel even more complicated. If Duncan saw him as family, how would he feel if a relationship developed between him and Angela?

"That's exactly why this is problematic," Jude said. "Angela is your daughter. She's been through enough without me complicating her life."

"How would you be complicating it?"

Jude ran a hand through his hair, struggling to articulate the tangle of concerns in his mind. "I'm older than she is."

That had definitely weighed on his mind a lot, in addition to everything else.

Duncan apparently didn't have the same concerns because he gave a dismissive wave of his hand. "You are aware that I'm older than Elizabeth by more years than you are older than Angela."

He *was* aware of that, but it felt different when it was his age they were discussing.

"If she were nineteen or twenty, I might feel differently," Duncan said. "But she's almost twenty-eight."

"And probably hasn't dated much, if at all," Jude said. "I'm too old to be a pit-stop on her search to find the man she wants to be with."

"Do you think that's what she's doing?" Duncan asked.

"I don't know," Jude admitted. "But how would she know that I'm the best for her if she doesn't date other guys?"

"How many women have you dated?"

Jude had never discussed his dating life, but he knew Duncan was aware that he'd had one serious girlfriend years ago. "One seriously."

Duncan's brows rose. "Have you gone on any other dates since her?"

"Not many."

"Why not?"

"Because it felt like my life and job were incompatible with dating."

"I never would have wanted you to feel that you couldn't have a personal life."

"I have a personal life. I have friends I spend time with."

"But no romantic life."

"No."

"Until now."

Jude didn't respond because Duncan was right.

"So why shouldn't she be worried that you might not know what you want in a woman and she's just a pit-stop for you?"

Jude knew that she wouldn't be, but in saying that, he was taking away one of his excuses. He wasn't sure why he was trying to talk himself—and Duncan—out of him pursuing a relationship with Angela. That was what he wanted, and yet here he was, giving her father all the reasons why he wasn't a good choice for her.

"Here's what's going to happen," Duncan began. "I'm going to stay out of things between you and Angela. I trust you, and regardless of what you choose to do, you won't lose your job."

Jude really wished he could believe that.

"I'll leave the decision about assigning her a bodyguard in your hands," Duncan said. "Trusting you'll put her wellbeing at the forefront of that decision."

"I would always do that," Jude said.

"I know. You're a good man, Jude. I'm not surprised Angela has seen that in you."

Jude rubbed a hand on the back of his neck. He hoped that his dad would have agreed.

"I'm surprised you're not giving me more of a hassle, considering."

"Considering?" Duncan asked. "Considering what?"

"You threatened Cole's career."

The older man chuckled as he grinned. "I sure did. That might have sent any other number of men running, but Cole proved that Annalisa was important enough to him to give up his career."

The unspoken question was whether Jude was prepared to do the same.

He was. But first, he and Angela needed to have a conversation.

On returning to the kitchen, he found that Angela was no longer there. The housekeeper told him that she'd left with Annie.

That surprised Jude a little, but he wasn't going to interrupt their time together. Thanking the housekeeper for the information, he headed back to the security building, planning to text her later to see if they could talk.

~ * ~

"Something smells good," Annie announced as she came into the kitchen with Benji.

"Cookies!" Benji exclaimed as he hurried toward the counter where they sat.

"Would you like one?" she asked.

"Yes. I definitely would like one, and then two more."

Angela chuckled as she watched Benji grab a paper towel and then pile three cookies on it. He grabbed a fourth and took a bite of it before heading out of the kitchen with a wave.

"Do you want some?"

"Sure," Annie said as she sat on a barstool at the island counter. "They smell delicious."

Angela got a small plate, then set a couple of cookies on it for Annie.

"Thank you."

"I was actually going to text you to see about getting together for a chat," Angela said.

"Really?" Annie took another bite of her cookie. "Did you have something particular in mind you wanted to chat about?"

"Actually, yes," Angela said after a moment's hesitation. "But could we maybe go to your place?"

"Sure. As long as you bring some cookies with you."

Angela laughed. "I can do that."

It didn't take long for her to put away the cookies and clean up the pans and mixing bowl. Soon, she and Annie were heading out, Nyla, Annie's dog, trotting along beside them.

The road was clear of snow, and the weather wasn't as cold as it had been when she and Kiara had first arrived. It was still chillier than she was used to, so she shoved her hands into the pockets of her jacket as they walked.

"What's Kiara up to today?" Annie asked.

"At the moment, she's trying to see if there's a college course she could take remotely."

"What's she most interested in?"

"She's always loved books, and she worked at the library in Briar Hollow, so I think she'd like to get a degree that would allow her to do something with books."

"Work in a library?" Annie asked.

"I imagine so," Angela said. "She figures that she'll be able to do that because she won't have to worry about people thinking she's connected to the Burke family like you and I do."

"I suppose that might be true," Annie said. "But I'm sure Dad would hope that she'd at least keep a bodyguard around."

"I think she'd probably agree to that, depending on what the situation looks like."

As they approached Annie's home, Angela followed her up onto the porch and into the warmth of the cabin.

"So what is it you'd like to talk about?" Annie said after they'd hung up their coats and removed their boots. "Is it Jude, by any chance?"

Heat rushed to Angela's cheeks as she followed Annie into the living room. "Is it that obvious?"

"I've seen the way you look at him." Annie settled onto the couch, tucking one leg beneath her. "And I've definitely noticed how he looks at you when he thinks no one's watching."

Angela's heart skipped. "How does he look at me?"

"Like you're a beautiful sunrise after the longest night." Annie picked up a cookie from the plate Angela had brought. "It's the same way Cole looks at me, which is how I recognized it from Jude."

Angela sank into the armchair across from her twin, trying to process this information. She'd been so uncertain about Jude's feelings, constantly second-guessing every interaction, every lingering glance.

"I don't know what to do," she admitted. "There have been times when I thought maybe he felt something too, but then he's pulled away."

Annie nodded thoughtfully. "Jude takes his responsibilities very seriously. He probably thinks having feelings for you conflicts with his job."

"That's what I was afraid of." Angela twisted her hands in her lap. "I don't want him to feel like he has to choose between me and his work."

"Is that why you wanted to talk to me? For advice about Jude?"

"Partly." Angela took a deep breath. "I also wanted to talk to you about... us. About being sisters. Twins. I feel like we've barely gotten to know each other at all."

Annie's expression softened, and she set her cookie down. "I know. I've felt the same way. It seems like it should be easier. That we should have this instant connection because we're twins, but instead, we're practically strangers."

"Exactly." Relief flooded through Angela at being understood. "Everyone expects us to be close right away, but it's not that simple."

"It's weird, isn't it?" Annie tucked a strand of hair behind her ear—the same nervous gesture Angela often made herself. "Looking at someone who has your face but isn't you."

Angela nodded, studying her twin. It was like looking in a mirror, but not quite. Annie's hair was long and straight, and while her style was mostly casual, her clothes were clearly quality. Her posture was more confident.

They had the same raw materials, but very diverse life experiences had molded them into different people.

"I want to know you," Angela said softly. "The real you, not just what everyone else says about you."

"I want that too." Annie leaned forward. "It's just been... overwhelming. I spent my whole life as an only daughter, and suddenly I have a twin sister. I knew you existed, but having that knowledge is different from facing the reality. Plus, I've been so wrapped up in my relationship with Cole."

"I understand," Angela assured her. "You have your own life. I don't expect you to drop everything for me."

"But I should have made more effort." Annie's voice was tinged with regret. "It's just—I don't always know what to say. What to ask. But right now, I can maybe help you a little with Jude."

"I'd appreciate that," Angela said. "Anything that might give me some insight into who he is."

Annie leaned back against the couch cushions. "Well, I've known Jude since I was a little girl. He's always been... steady. The kind of person who's there when you need him."

Angela nodded, drinking in every detail about the man who occupied so much of her thoughts. "I've definitely gotten that feeling about him."

"He takes his responsibility to our family seriously—maybe too seriously sometimes." Annie's expression grew thoughtful. "After his dad died, Dad made sure that Jude knew he had a home with us. So he was a bodyguard first, then moved into the role of head of security. I'm sure he's felt pressured to fill his dad's shoes."

And that was what worried Angela the most. That his devotion to the Burke family and his job would mean he wouldn't be willing to consider entertaining any sort of personal relationship with her.

"He's only talked a little about his dad."

"That's actually more than I would have thought he would. They were incredibly close. When Mr. Kessler died, Jude shut down for a while. He was barely an adult, but he was determined to follow in his dad's footsteps." Annie brushed some crumbs from her lap. "And he's good at it. Dad trusts him completely."

Angela tried to imagine a younger Jude, grieving but determined, taking on such enormous responsibility. It made his devotion to duty make more sense.

"Has he... been with anyone? He said he didn't have an ex-wife or a current girlfriend, but that doesn't mean he hasn't had an ex-girlfriend." The question felt intimate, almost invasive, but Angela needed to know.

Annie shook her head. "There was someone years ago, but I don't think he's had a serious girlfriend since then. It's possible he's been dating, but if so, he hasn't brought them around or even mentioned them."

"I don't have any experience with boyfriends," Angela admitted, her gaze on her hands.

"You think I've had a lot of experience?" Annie asked. "Cole was my first. My dad is very overprotective, so I knew any guy I wanted to date would have to pass his test."

"Do you think Jude would?"

"Probably more easily than Cole did. Dad knows Jude and trusts him. Those are huge positives."

Angela appreciated all the insights Annie had offered, and she just hoped that they weren't for nothing. If Jude wasn't interested, or refused to act on his interest, it wouldn't matter how much she knew about him.

She just prayed that it was God's will. Her feelings for Jude were already so deep that she knew there would be hurt to heal from if he wasn't romantically interested in her.

CHAPTER TWENTY-FOUR

Jude used his phone to open the garage door at the main house. He'd made arrangements to take Angela out for some driving lessons on the roads off the estate that afternoon.

Kiara had begged to go earlier that day, so Lucy had finally taken her out. Angela hadn't been as excited to go, so Jude had told her they'd go out later, figuring she'd be more likely to go with him than with Lucy.

He figured it would also be a good time for them to have a conversation. It had been a couple of days since he'd talked with Duncan, and he still wasn't sure how to proceed.

He wanted to be with her. His heart told him that his life would be so much better with her by his side.

The thought stopped him in his tracks for a moment. He'd been thinking about Angela so much lately that he'd barely had time to consider the bigger implications of his feelings. But there it was—a simple truth that had been building for weeks. His life would be better with her by his side. Not just as someone to protect, but as someone to share his life with.

As Jude stepped inside the garage, he spotted Angela waiting near one of the less expensive vehicles—a silver sedan that they'd used previously.

She wore a thick blue sweater under a black coat, and her hair was pulled back in a simple ponytail. The sight of her made his heart beat a little faster.

"Ready for your driving lesson?" he asked, keeping his voice casual despite the energy thrumming through him.

Angela nodded, though he noticed her fingers fidgeting with the hem of her sweater. "I guess so. Though I'm still not sure why I need to learn when I'll always have someone with me who can drive."

"Independence," Jude said, moving toward the driver's side. "Even with a bodyguard, there might be times when you want to be the one behind the wheel."

He opened the driver's door and waited for Angela to get behind the wheel. Once she was settled, he shut the door and rounded the hood to get in the passenger side.

The interior of the car felt intimate with just the two of them, her subtle scent of vanilla mingling with the leather seats.

When she reached out to start the engine, he stopped her with a touch of his fingers. She looked over at him, her eyes wide.

"Do you really not want the independence that comes with driving?"

"Honestly, driving has always been more Kiara's dream than mine. I always figured she'd get hers first, and then once we were settled elsewhere, I'd get mine."

"And now you're being pressured to get yours sooner than you're ready," Jude said.

Angela shrugged. "I guess I just don't see the sense when there will always be someone around to drive me."

"That's not necessarily true," Jude said.

She frowned at him. "What do you mean?"

"If you were out and something happened to your bodyguard, you would need to be able to escape on your own. And if that escape is a car, you need to have the ability to drive it."

Angela's brows were arched high as she stared at him. "What might happen to my bodyguard?"

"Anyone who's trying to get to you will take out the bodyguard first," Jude said. He hated the worry that was growing in her expression, but he needed her to be prepared. "That's why we're teaching you self-defense and how to handle a gun. And that's why you need to learn to drive."

"I don't want to think about anything happening to you," Angela said.

"And I don't want anything to happen to you." Jude reached out and took her hand. "You need to promise me that you will do what I say if we're ever faced with that situation. Or if I'm not with you, you listen to whoever is guarding you. We can't do our job if you're trying to keep us from getting hurt."

Angela nodded, then her gaze lowered to their hands, his large and tanned against her smaller, fair one.

The simple contact sent warmth up his arm, and he had to resist the urge to intertwine their fingers. He was supposed to be teaching her to drive, not getting lost in her closeness.

"Angela." He had to clear his throat before he could continue. "We need to talk."

She looked up at him, those blue-green eyes searching his face with an intensity that made his chest tighten. "About what?"

The words he'd been rehearsing for days suddenly felt inadequate. How did he explain that she'd become the center of his world? How did he tell her that he thought about her constantly? That somehow she'd undone his carefully controlled life and made him long for things he'd never seriously wanted before?

"About us," he said finally, his thumb brushing across her knuckles before he could stop himself. A flush crept into Angela's cheeks. The knowledge that he affected her the same way she affected him made him press on. "I think it's time to have a discussion about what's happening between us."

Jude forced himself to release her hand, immediately missing the contact. "But first, let's get out of here. I don't feel like having a conversation in the garage where there are cameras."

"There are cameras in here?" Angela asked, leaning forward to peer out the front windshield.

"There are cameras in all the public areas on the estate."

"It's hard to comprehend."

"Actually, it's not that unusual," Jude said. "Most places out in the world have cameras, so you're being filmed no matter where you go."

"Oh, I suppose that's true."

"For now, why don't you drive us off the estate, and after a little bit, I'll take over."

"Okay." Angela reached out and pressed the button to start the engine, then she put it into gear.

Gripping the wheel with both hands, she slowly accelerated. The car had been backed in the last time it was used, so she could pull straight out of the garage.

Now having a better understanding of why Angela wasn't as gung-ho to get her license as Kiara, Jude decided to just focus on teaching her to drive. The license could wait forever if need be. As long as she became comfortable behind the wheel, he wouldn't press her to get her full license.

He didn't say anything as she carefully guided the car toward the front gate. It opened as they approached, and Jude lifted a hand at the guard who was on duty.

After they'd pulled through the gate, Angela looked at him. "Which way?"

He considered it for a moment, then said, "Turn left."

There wouldn't be a lot of traffic on the portion he was going to have her drive, and since this was her first time driving off the estate, that would be a good thing.

As she drove, he considered yet again what to say to her. He wondered whether Duncan had spoken to her at all about the conversation they'd had.

She drove slowly, her knuckles white from gripping the steering wheel too tightly. Jude resisted the urge to tell her to relax her grip. She needed to find her own comfort level.

"You're doing fine," he said instead, keeping his voice low and calm. "Just keep your speed steady."

The car rounded a gentle curve in the road, tall pines lining both sides. Jude glanced at Angela's profile, noting the slight furrow between her brows as she concentrated.

"There's a turnout about a mile ahead," he said. "We can pull over there."

Angela nodded without taking her eyes off the road. "Is it on the left or right?"

"Right side. You'll see it."

Jude's heart pounded against his ribs as he considered what he was about to do. Nerves weren't foreign to him. Whenever he went into a high-risk situation with Duncan, there had always been nerves.

However, these types of nerves were new to him. It felt like so much was at stake.

He'd spent years maintaining professional boundaries, keeping his feelings carefully controlled. Now he was about to risk everything.

When the turnout came into view, Angela slowed the car carefully and eased into the space. She put the car in park but left the engine running for the heater.

"How did I do?" she asked, finally turning to look at him.

"Perfect." The word came out rougher than he'd intended. He cleared his throat. "You're a natural."

"I wouldn't go that far." A small smile played on her lips, but it quickly faded.

The silence stretched between them, filled with all the things they'd both been avoiding saying. Angela tucked a loose strand of hair behind her ear, then clasped her hands in her lap.

"So," she said, her voice soft. "You wanted to talk?"

Jude shifted in his seat to face her more fully. The winter sunlight filtering through the trees cast dappled shadows across

Angela's face, highlighting the uncertainty in her eyes. The car's heater hummed softly between them, creating a cocoon of warmth against the chill outside.

"Yes." He took a deep breath, steadying himself. "I think we both know there's something happening between us."

Angela's cheeks flushed pink, but she held his gaze. "I wasn't sure if it was just me."

"It's not just you," Jude said, the admission sending equal measures of relief and anxiety coursing through him. "I've been trying to maintain a professional distance, but I've done a poor job of it."

"Why?" she asked. "Why try to keep that distance?"

"Because it's my job to protect you. Because you're Duncan's daughter. Because I'm older than you." He ran a hand through his hair. "Because I didn't want to take advantage of your situation."

Angela's brow furrowed. "My situation?"

"You've been through so much change in such a short time. New family, new home, new life. I didn't want to be one more complication."

A small smile touched her lips. "What if I want that particular complication?"

Angela's words hung in the air between them, vulnerable yet brave. Jude's chest tightened as he searched her face, seeing hope and something deeper in her eyes.

"Are you sure about that?" he asked, his voice rough with emotion. "Are you sure there isn't someone closer to your age and less complicated than me that you'd rather be with?"

Waiting for her answer felt like standing on the edge of a cliff. It was exhilarating and terrifying all at once. He'd never been this open with anyone about his feelings, had never allowed himself to be this vulnerable.

Angela reached across the center console and took his hand. Her touch was warm, her fingers fitting perfectly between his.

"I can't imagine feeling the way I do about anyone else," she said. "I might not have had a lot of experience with men, but I know a good man when I see one. Your strength. Your loyalty. Your commitment. It touches me deep in my heart. You're a man of honor and integrity, and those are very attractive qualities to me. I like how you encourage me without being pushy. Without making me feel stupid for not knowing things or taking longer than others to learn something. You make me want to be a better person."

Jude's heart hammered against his ribs. He gently squeezed her hand, marveling at how something so simple could feel so significant.

"You make me want to be a better man too," he said. "And with you, I find myself thinking and imagining a future I've never given much thought to. I don't know if you've noticed, but I'm not big on emotions."

"I've noticed," she said. "But you smile at me."

And Jude did right then, too. "You make it easy to smile."

She beamed at him then, lifting his hand to press the back of it to her face. "You make me smile too."

Jude turned his hand over to cup her cheek, feeling the satiny softness beneath his fingertips. When his gaze met hers, he saw in her eyes a reflection of what he felt.

"You're beautiful," he murmured. "So beautiful."

A shy smile lifted the corners of her mouth as her cheeks pinked. "You're the beautiful one. Well, I guess it would be handsome."

Jude had always been aware that his looks were something that attracted women, but he hadn't cared about that until now. He liked the idea that she found him attractive.

Lowering his hand, he took hers in his again.

"I talked to your dad," he admitted, wanting to make sure she was aware of what had transpired. "About us."

Angela's eyes widened. "You did? When?"

"A couple of days ago. I needed to know where he stood before..." Jude trailed off, realizing how calculating that might sound. "I mean, I respect him, and you're his daughter. I didn't want to complicate life for either of us."

"What did he say?" Angela leaned forward slightly, her expression a mixture of curiosity and apprehension.

"He said he trusts me. And that he'd stay out of things and let us figure this out for ourselves."

"Wow. That kind of surprises me."

"It did me too," Jude admitted. "But I suppose he learned some things from his dealings with Cole."

"I'm glad that he dealt with them first," Angela said. "So maybe it will be easier for us."

Jude hoped that would be the case, but he wasn't delusional enough to think it would all be sunshine and roses. He wanted to make it as easy as possible for them, but the reality was that they still had hurdles to overcome.

"I did want to let you know that I'll be bringing someone else in to operate as your bodyguard."

"What?" Angela frowned, and her fingers tightened around his. "Why?"

"If we go out together, I want to be able to focus on you without having to be on the alert for security threats. I'll always be armed. I mean, I'm never without a weapon, so I'll always be able to protect you, but I want to have someone else there too."

"Will it ever just be the two of us?" she asked. "Like if we go on a date?"

Jude gave her a smile. "Depends on what we decide to do. If we're going where there are lots of people, we'll have someone with us. But if we go to a quiet place, like on a hike or something, it can be just the two of us."

"Guess I'd better start liking hiking, huh?"

When Jude chuckled, Angela's smile grew.

"I don't mind hiking," he said. "There are some nice beginner trails around here that we can start out on. In fact, we have some on the estate that we can go on once the snow melts."

Jude realized then that he was going to have to get creative. He'd never really planned dates in his last relationship. They'd just kind of decided together what they wanted to do.

With Angela, he wanted to do special things. Memorable things. He wanted to build a sturdy foundation for them because he wasn't just playing around.

If he was going to open his heart and his life to a woman, it was because he wanted everything with her. A family. A home. Children. All of it.

He thought that was what Angela wanted too, but he supposed they'd need to have a conversation about that before too much time passed.

But for right then, he was content to sit with her. Holding her hand. The car creating a cocoon for them.

There were no cameras or people watching them. Just the sparkling snow and towering trees that surrounded the car.

"We can sort of have a first date now, if you want," Jude said.

Angela's eyes widened. "Really?"

"If you don't mind just us driving around. Maybe we could swing into Serenity and get some hot drinks."

"I'd like that," she told him with a smile that let him know that she really meant it.

"Let's switch seats, head into Serenity for the drinks, and then I'll drive us around for a bit."

"That sounds perfect," Angela said.

Jude wasn't sure how many women would actually consider the plan a perfect first date, but all that mattered was that Angela did.

It didn't take long to switch seats, then Jude put the car in gear and guided it back onto the road in the direction of town.

Because he still had to keep Angela's identity on the down-low in Serenity, he had to go to the place that had a drive-thru lane. Once there, Angela chose a mocha latte, while he settled on a large black coffee for himself.

"Do you want something to eat?" he asked. "I'm pretty sure they serve pastries of some kind here."

"I'm actually fine with just the drink."

"I think I'd prefer to eat the pastries you make anyway," Jude told her. "I think you've spoiled me for everyone else's baking."

Angela's laugh was soft. "Well, let me know if there's something specific you'd like. I'm always up for suggestions."

"I'll keep that in mind."

After paying and getting their drinks, Jude drove them out of town, choosing a road that would eventually loop back to the estate, but would be a nice long drive to get there.

He wasn't quite ready to end his impromptu date with Angela because he knew it might be hard to have all the time he wanted with her just yet.

But they'd get there. He felt confident of that.

CHAPTER TWENTY-FIVE

Angela cupped her hands around the disposable cup and lifted it to take a sip of her mocha latte. As the delicious combination of chocolate and coffee slid down her throat, she hummed in appreciation and contentment.

She couldn't believe that Jude had actually acted on the feelings he had for her. Though she'd sensed he might have felt drawn to her, she hadn't been convinced that he'd jeopardize his career for her.

But he had.

And now she was sitting there with him, drinking coffee together, on what he'd called their first date.

The silence between them felt comfortable, like they'd known each other for years instead of weeks. Through the windshield, she watched as the snow-laden pines created a tunnel of green and white along the winding road. The heater hummed quietly, keeping the winter chill at bay.

"What are you thinking about?" Jude asked, his deep voice breaking the silence.

Angela turned to look at him, observing his profile as he drove. The firm line of his jaw, the way his dark hair curled slightly at the nape of his neck, the steady confidence in his hands on the steering wheel.

Her heart did a little flip in her chest.

"I'm thinking that this feels... nice." She hesitated, searching for the right words. "Unexpected, but wonderful."

Jude glanced at her, the corner of his mouth lifting in that small smile that seemed reserved just for her. "Unexpected is one way to put it."

"Did you ever think when you first met me in Briar Hollow that we'd end up here?"

He shook his head, his eyes returning to the road. "Not even close. I was focused on getting you and Kiara safely to the estate. That was all that mattered then."

"And now?" The question slipped out before she could stop it.

Jude was quiet for a moment, and Angela wondered if it was too soon to delve deeply like that.

"Now, all I can think about is how much I enjoy being around you, and it has nothing to do with keeping you safe." He gave a huff of laughter. "Well, not nothing, because I do still want you to be safe."

Angela took another sip of her drink. "And I want to be safe. I also want you to be safe."

They continued to chat as Jude guided the car around curves, pointing out different things they drove by. Interspersed with that they shared personal experiences and opinions. It was the perfect way to learn a bit more about each other.

She'd learned that he did, in fact, have a best friend. For some reason, she'd assumed his focused life had precluded friendships. Especially close ones.

"Cooper and his family would love to meet you," Jude said.

"Really?" Angela asked.

"Of course. Why wouldn't they? You're wonderful."

Angela gave a little laugh as she pressed the rim of her cup against her chin. "I'm glad you think so."

"I'm not the only one who thinks so. I'm sure Kiara does, and Duncan definitely does. You're sweet and generous, which are qualities most people admire." Jude glanced over at her. "I know

Kiara is your best friend, but did you have any other close friends in Briar Hollow?"

Angela gave a little chuckle. "Yep. All the grandmas at church."

"What?"

"After I'd been working at the bakery for a little while, I met an older woman. She'd come in a couple of days a week for a cinnamon bun, and after she ate it, she'd sit at one of the small tables we had and would chat with people as they came in. During lulls, she'd chat with me if I came to the front."

"That sounds pleasantly... small town."

"It was," Angela agreed with a grin. "It was one of the good things about Briar Hollow, and my boss, Patty, couldn't say anything about it because Ida was her aunt. Ida and Patty were night and day in how they treated people, however. Which is why Ida ended up offering the apartment in her basement to us."

"Oh, she was your landlady?" Jude asked.

"Yes. And for the short time we had her, she was wonderful. She was also the reason I began to go to church. After her persistent invitations, I finally caved, figuring if I went once, it would satisfy her."

"Did it?"

"Not really. I went one Sunday, and even though I enjoyed it, I didn't go back. So... the invitations began again. Next time I went, she introduced me to all of her friends, and after that, I just kept going."

"Why haven't you asked about church here?" Jude asked.

"Well, I knew I couldn't go to one in Serenity, and Coeur d'Alene seemed a little far to ask someone to drive me. I've been watching the Briar Hollow church's livestream."

"They have a livestream?"

Angela smiled. "They're surprisingly up to date on technical things there, which I've appreciated since moving here."

"Well, I go to church in Coeur d'Alene, so you're welcome to come with me. Just don't expect a highly social experience since I don't tend to stick around much when the service is over."

"I didn't socialize a lot at church either. That happened if I went to the Wednesday afternoon knitting circle."

"You knit?"

"I do. Sandra had Kiara and I learn that, along with some basic sewing."

"Do you wish you were still there?"

Angela took another sip of her drink as she considered her answer. "There are aspects of life there that I miss—like the church and the people in the knitting circle. But unfortunately, the bad outweighed the good. So, no, I don't wish I was still there. Besides, *there* is not where you are."

A smile lifted the corner of Jude's mouth. "That is true, which is why I'm glad you're here."

After an hour of driving around, they headed back to the estate. It had been the perfect way to spend the afternoon, and Angela hoped they could do it again soon.

"How are we supposed to act around people here?" Angela asked as they pulled up to the gate.

Jude gave the guys at the gate a salute as he drove through the open gate. "I'd prefer that during work hours, we keep things professional when we're around others. After hours, however, we can be more relaxed."

Angela thought it might be a challenge to be completely professional, but she would try. Because Jude had asked it of her. She knew that because his job and personal life were so intertwined, it was important to be respectful of his request.

"Thank you for this time," Angela said as Jude pulled the car into the large garage. "It's been wonderful."

After he'd pulled into one of the spots, he turned the engine off but didn't make a move to exit the car. Instead, he turned to face her, his eyes filled with an emotion she hadn't seen from him before.

Her guess—her hope—was that it was affection. Maybe something more.

"I've gotta get back to the office," he said, reaching out to take her hand. "But I'll give you a call later."

Angela smiled at him as anticipation filled her. "I'll be waiting."

He lifted her hand and kissed the back of it. "I enjoyed our time together, and I can't wait until we can do it again."

"Me too."

As they got out of the car, Angelica wondered if he'd hug or kiss her, but he didn't. She wasn't sure whether she was relieved or disappointed.

Probably relieved, because she didn't want their first kiss to be in a garage with cameras focused on them. She suspected that Jude felt the same way, especially because it was still technically business hours.

After taking the empty cups from the car, she said goodbye to Jude, then headed into the house. She tossed the cups into the trash before heading upstairs to find Kiara. She really needed to talk to her sister.

At Kiara's door, she knocked, then opened it. She found Kiara curled up on the loveseat, her phone in her hand. That was usually how she read, so Angela figured that was what she was doing.

Kiara looked up at her as she approached. "Where have you been?"

She grinned as she dropped down onto the armchair. Pulling her legs up to the seat, she wrapped her arms around them. She rested her chin on her knees. "On a date."

"Say what?" Kiara set her phone aside and turned her full attention on Angela. "With *who*?"

"Jude." A smile came to her face as she said his name.

"I'm so confused. I thought Jude said that relationships were a distraction."

He had definitely said that, but evidently he'd changed his mind. Or maybe he still believed that, but he also wanted to be with her.

"He talked to Duncan about it," Angela said. "And he told Jude that he didn't have a problem with it and would stay out of it, leaving it up to the two of us to figure this out."

"And you think this is a good idea?" Kiara asked.

It was the first time Angela had heard skepticism in her sister's voice. When she'd told Kiara how she felt about Jude, she'd seemed supportive of her feelings. But maybe that had been because Kiara had figured that the possibility of a relationship between the two of them was unlikely. That Jude would never be interested in her.

"I think it's a great idea," Angela said. "Jude is an honorable man. He is strong and protective."

"He's boring," Kiara said.

"He is not," Angela protested.

"So where did you go on your date?"

Angela hesitated, knowing that that information wouldn't change Kiara's mind about Jude being boring.

"We got coffee and went for a drive."

Kiara laughed. "Like I said... boring."

"It wasn't boring," Angela told her, lowering her legs to the floor. She slipped her hands under her thighs and leaned forward. "It was perfect for us."

"It wouldn't be for me," Kiara said.

"Yes, I know. We've always had different ideas of what a perfect date would be."

"And apparently different ideas of who the perfect man is too."

"Jude is a great man," Angela said. "I know he's not perfect, but then neither am I."

Kiara shrugged. "I guess if he makes you happy, that's what matters most."

Angela appreciated the sentiment, but she didn't think Kiara was completely sincere.

"Are you okay?"

"I'm fine," Kiara said. "Just bored. Never would have thought I'd miss working."

"How about college courses?"

"I can't start taking anything yet," she said. "I probably can't start until the fall."

Even though Kiara was an avid reader, she wasn't one to sit around and read for hours on end.

Angela sat back in the chair and crossed her legs and arms. "So what would you like to do?"

"I don't know," Kiara said. "I have all this money, and yet I feel like a prisoner. I want to be able to go into town and do some shopping or pick up a coffee. Maybe walk around and see what the town has to offer. Go to the library."

"There's no reason you can't do that, I wouldn't think," Angela said. "As long as you take Lucy with you."

"And that's another thing. I'm not thrilled that I have to have a guard with me everywhere I go."

Angela tightened her arms around herself. "You don't need to stay here. This doesn't have to be your life."

"Do you want me to leave?"

"Of course not," Angela replied. "But it's not fair to ask you to completely change your life just because I am."

Kiara sighed heavily, shifting on the loveseat to stare out the window. "It's not that I don't want to be here with you. I just need… more."

"Let's ask Duncan about you having a bit more freedom. I know why I have to be limited in being seen around here because I look like Annie, but there's no reason you have to be so restricted."

"I just wish I knew what the future looked like for me. In Briar, we always had a plan. Something we were working towards. Now, it feels like we don't need goals anymore. We're being handed everything on a silver platter. It makes me feel... unanchored, useless."

"We're still working toward things. Getting our licenses. Learning self-defense. Learning to use a gun."

"I know. It just feels different now."

Angela felt helpless to know how to help her sister. Kiara had always taken the lead in their lives, but it felt like that wasn't as necessary now.

This wasn't how she'd expected the conversation to go with Kiara when she'd come to tell her about Jude, but she knew it was important to hear Kiara's thoughts.

Kiara had been there for the worst part of her life. She'd stood by her. Supported her. Helped her get to safety. Angela wouldn't just abandon her now. She needed to help Kiara find peace in her life on the estate.

It might help once they moved into their own place. However, even though they'd broken ground on the site and work was underway, it wasn't going to be ready for awhile.

"Sorry," Kiara murmured. "I'm in a bit of a mood today. Just need to snap out of it."

"You've always told me that my feelings are valid," Angela reminded her. "And so are yours. It's been a big change for us."

"I should be happy," Kiara said. "There's really no reason to be unhappy in this current situation."

Angela didn't know how to respond to that because *she* wasn't unhappy. But it hurt that Kiara was struggling so much.

"I'll be fine," Kiara said after a minute of silence between them. "I just need some time."

Angela got to her feet and went to hug Kiara. "I'll let you be. But remember that I love you."

"I love you too."

Angela left Kiara's room, closing the door softly behind her.

Rather than return to her room, she headed downstairs, hoping that maybe she could have a conversation with Duncan. There was an hour until dinner, and the workday should be over, but Angela had come to realize that Duncan didn't hold to conventional business hours.

As she reached the bottom of the stairs, she spotted Julian coming from the direction of Duncan's office.

"Hey, Julian," she said. "I didn't know you were back."

"I just got here a couple of hours ago."

"Are you here for long?"

"Probably a week or so."

Angela looked at Julian more closely. He didn't look good. Gaunt was the first word that came to mind as she took in his features.

"Are you feeling okay?" she asked.

"Yeah. Why?"

"You look like you haven't slept or eaten in ages."

"I'm fine," Julian said dismissively.

Angela didn't know him well enough to push the subject, so instead, she said, "Is Duncan in his office?"

"Yep."

"Do you think he has time to talk to me?"

"I'm sure he'll make the time. Just knock on his door."

Angela watched as Julian turned and walked up the stairs. Something was wrong with him, she was almost positive. But maybe that was just how he was. Without knowing him better, there was no way for her to be sure.

When she reached Duncan's office, the door was closed. She hesitated for a moment, then knocked. When she heard Duncan respond, Angela opened the door and entered the office.

It was hard not to feel intimidated by the space. But before she could dwell too much on that, Duncan got to his feet, a smile on his face.

"Angela." He came around the desk to greet her. "To what do I owe the pleasure?"

"I wonder if I could chat with you for a few minutes," she said, clasping her hands together tightly.

It was the first time she'd sought him out, let alone initiated a conversation of importance.

"Sure." Duncan motioned to the sitting area in his office. "Why don't we go sit over there by the fireplace?"

Once they were seated, Duncan said, "So what's on your mind? Are you doing okay?"

"I'm fine," she assured him, then smiled. "Better than fine actually."

Duncan returned her smile, a twinkle in his eyes. "Does it have something to do with Jude?"

"It might," Angela said, not sure how much she wanted to talk to him about it.

"Well, I hope this makes you both happy. Jude is a good man. The best."

"Yes. I think he's pretty awesome."

"Though he's not a man of many words, I do believe he thinks you're pretty awesome as well."

Her smile grew at that comment. "I'm glad to hear that."

"Did you want to talk about Jude?"

Angela shook her head. "Actually, I want to talk to you about Kiara."

His expression sobered as he nodded. "Okay. What's on your mind about her?"

"Can you tell me how restricted she is with her movements?" she asked. "Like, could she go into Serenity with her bodyguard?"

"Does she want to leave the estate?"

"Yes. I think she's finding it difficult not having anything to do. I don't think either of us is well-suited to a life of leisure."

"I understand that."

"If you'd asked me if I would like to be able to sleep in every day and live my life with no financial worries, I would have definitely said yes. However, the reality is quite different. We both need a purpose in life."

Duncan had a contemplative look on his face as she spoke. Angela hoped he truly understood and didn't think that she and Kiara were just being difficult.

"Would she have any interest in traveling?" Duncan asked.

"She might."

"I have properties around the world, and she could use the jet to travel to any of them."

Angela wasn't really keen to go traveling when she was just getting used to living there. And she didn't know if Jude would be able to go with them. She wasn't prepared to leave him behind right when they were starting to develop a relationship.

"I'll ask her about it."

"I don't want to make you two prisoners here, and I'm sorry that Kiara feels that perhaps she is. If she has any suggestions of things she'd like to do, we'll certainly consider them. I just want you both to be safe."

"I understand that," Angela said. "This is just new for us. For all of us."

"Yes, it is," Duncan agreed. "But I'd endure anything just to have you back, and I'll do whatever I can to help you make this transition as smooth as possible."

"I appreciate all you've done for us," Angela said. "We are very thankful."

"Do you have any other concerns?" Duncan asked. "Might as well address them while you're here."

Angela hesitated for a moment, then said, "Is Julian okay? I'm worried about him."

Duncan's brows rose at her words. "Julian?"

"Yeah. He just looked exhausted and a bit... gaunt."

Duncan frowned and seemed to be lost in thought for a moment. "He's had a pretty busy schedule since he left, so I suspect he hasn't been sleeping or eating well."

Angela considered that, and she couldn't argue that it wasn't the case because she didn't know how Julian normally reacted to stress and busyness. Still, combined with his obvious need to drink, it felt like something more was troubling him.

She left it alone, though. Even if Duncan hadn't considered Julian's health before, perhaps now that Angela had said something, he'd give it more thought.

"That was all I wanted to talk to you about," Angela said, getting to her feet. "I should probably go get ready for dinner."

"Sounds good. Thank you for coming to talk to me."

Angela gave him a quick smile, then headed for the door. She hurried back upstairs to her room.

She and Kiara didn't exactly dress up for dinner. However, they also didn't rock up to the table in shorts and a tank top. Their days of eating dinner in their pajamas on the couch were in the past until they were living in their own place.

They'd always eaten dinner as a family with Jim and Sandra, but it hadn't exactly been a pleasant experience. The meals with Duncan and the family were much more pleasant. Although Julian's presence might make them a little more tense.

As she switched into a nicer sweater and a pair of black slacks, Angela couldn't help but wish that Jude would be joining them for dinner. She wondered how long it would be before he was welcome at the table with the family.

His absence would be harder to accept if Cole was at the table. But as far as Angela was aware, he was still in California. However, he was likely to show up at some point if he missed Annie the way she missed him.

Once dinner was over, Angela decided that she needed to have a talk with Kiara about the travel idea. Hopefully, Jude would call after that so that they had plenty of time to talk.

CHAPTER TWENTY-SIX

Jude pulled on his leather jacket before proceeding into the garage. After climbing into his truck, he exited the garage, pressing the button to close the overhead door behind him. It was just a short drive to the main house, and within minutes, he pulled up to the back door and got out.

The February day was bright and sunny. Beautiful, he supposed. But now that they'd gotten past the coldest part of winter, he was ready for warmer days.

As he approached the back door, it swung open, and Angela appeared. She wore a long navy blue wool coat and a burgundy scarf. Her face lit up when she saw him.

Jude couldn't help but bend to hug her when she approached him with her arms open. He held her tight for a moment before letting her go.

Looking down at her, he said, "Ready to go?"

"I am."

He helped her into the passenger side of his truck, then slid behind the wheel. "Kiara didn't want to come?"

"No. Not this time."

Selfishly, Jude was glad.

When Angela had mentioned the previous day that she needed to go to the store again, Jude had asked if she would like to combine a trip to Coeur d'Alene for shopping with attending church. She'd quickly agreed.

"Can you tell me a little about your church?" Angela asked. "And how long you've been attending there?"

"It's a large church, which is one of the reasons I like it. Fewer people know who I am that way." He went on to describe what he knew of the pastoral staff and the church itself.

Their conversation turned to spiritual things, which surprised Jude a little. He didn't speak much about spiritual things with anyone except Cooper. His dad had encouraged conversations like that, but once he'd passed, Jude had found it difficult to have spiritual talks with people he didn't know well.

Angela, however, made it easy. She listened in that quietly attentive way of hers, asking questions that weren't too prying. She encouraged him to elaborate on what it had been like to grow up with a dad who'd embraced faith later in his life.

"It was almost like having two different fathers," Jude told her as they merged onto the highway. "He changed a lot after he became a Christian. Not in the way he treated me, that was always consistently loving and caring. But he was... lighter. Like some weight had been lifted off him."

Angela nodded, her lips pursed in thought. "Do you remember how old you were when it happened?"

Jude considered the question. "Ten or so? I just remember that all of a sudden I was being dragged to church each Sunday instead of getting to watch cartoons while I ate my favorite cereal."

She smiled at the image. "Did you like it?"

"At first? Not even a little." Jude let out a small laugh. "But Dad was stubborn, and he persisted. Over time, we made connections in the church, and regular attendance just became normal."

Angela lapsed into silence for a moment, letting the information settle between them. Jude found himself wanting to fill the quiet, to keep her engaged. "He always said faith was the only thing that gave him hope when other things in his life went bad."

He glanced at her to see how his comment landed. She was still watching the trees whip by, but he caught the tilt of her head, the way she tucked her hair behind her ear.

"I think that's true," she said softly. "It's the only thing that makes sense out of all the horrible things that happen. Trusting that God has a purpose and is still in control, regardless of what's happening."

Jude wasn't sure why her words sent a prickle along his shoulders. Maybe because they sounded so certain, when his own faith had begun to feel almost like a habit.

He found that he enjoyed the conversation, and he knew that his dad would have told him that a shared faith was key to building a stable and lasting relationship.

His dad hadn't experienced that himself, since he hadn't become a Christian until after Jude's mom had divorced him. Still, once he'd become a Christian, he'd been committed to learning all he could about living a life that glorified God. And he'd been eager to share all he learned with Jude.

"Here we are," Jude said as he pulled into the parking lot of the church.

It was a large building with a steeple that towered over the neighborhood. The church had two morning services, but he usually attended the second one, since that was the one that Cooper and Melanie attended.

As they walked from the car to the entrance of the church, Jude turned toward Angela and held out his hand. She transferred the Bible she carried to her opposite arm and took his hand with a beaming smile.

Seeing how much joy she got out of just holding hands warmed Jude's heart. Her hand was small in his, but he could feel the strength in it. That strength was no doubt from the work she'd done on the homestead and in the bakery.

Her grip tightened as they walked into the foyer. As usual, the space was filled with people who had been there for the first service and also those who had arrived for the second one.

Keeping hold of Angela, he wove his way among the groups of people who stood together talking and tried to keep out of the way of others who were milling around or making their way to the exit.

Reaching the sanctuary, he guided her to where Cooper and Melanie usually sat. When they reached an empty row in the general area, Jude allowed Angela to go into the row first, then followed her in.

After Angela had settled onto the cushioned pew, placing her Bible in her lap, Jude glanced around, then sat down beside her at the end of the row.

The sanctuary gradually filled around them, the gentle murmur of conversation creating a pleasant background hum. Jude noticed her looking around at the stained glass windows that lined the walls and the wooden cross hanging above the stage.

"It's beautiful," she whispered, leaning closer to him.

He nodded, though in truth, he rarely paid attention to the aesthetics of the building anymore. Seeing it through her eyes made him appreciate it anew.

"Cooper and Melanie should be here soon," he murmured, leaning close enough that his shoulder brushed against hers.

She gave him a smile that made his chest tighten. "I'm a little nervous about meeting them," she admitted.

"Don't be. They're good people."

Before Angela could respond, Jude spotted Cooper's tall frame moving down the aisle. He raised his hand slightly in greeting, and Cooper's face broke into a wide grin when he spotted Jude.

"There they are," Jude said, standing as Cooper and Melanie approached them.

Cooper clapped Jude on the shoulder before turning his attention to Angela. "You must be Angela. We've heard a lot about you."

Melanie, a petite woman with a warm smile, nudged her husband. "Not that much, because Jude barely shares anything." She extended her hand to Angela. "I'm Melanie. It's wonderful to finally meet you."

Jude watched as Angela shook their hands, her initial nervousness giving way to a genuine smile. He was glad that she seemed to quickly relax.

There wasn't time for conversation right then as the worship service began. Jude wondered how similar the service at his church was to the one Angela had attended.

She seemed at ease with everything, though, and when they stood to sing, she clearly knew the lyrics of the songs.

Would she want to come with him every week?

Jude hoped she would because he enjoyed having her there, worshipping with him. It felt like it added another layer to their budding relationship. A layer that would help build a firm foundation.

When the pastor got up to preach the sermon, Angela unzipped the cover of her Bible, revealing a small notebook and a couple of pens. He watched as she flipped through the notebook to an empty page and wrote something on it.

They were going through the book of Philippians, and when Angela opened her Bible, he could see that she'd already highlighted some passages.

When she struggled to hold the Bible and still make notes, Jude took the Bible from her and held it open between them.

She looked over and smiled at him, then mouthed, "Thank you."

Jude was discovering so many little things he hadn't considered he'd appreciate the way he did. The most recent one was sitting next to her in a worship service, listening to the same sermon. Given the conversation they'd had in the truck on the way there, Jude was confident that they'd discuss what they were hearing on the ride back to the estate.

That week, the sermon was on a passage of Philippians he was very familiar with. His dad had talked to him many times about being content in his life, regardless of what was happening. He'd explained that that didn't mean he couldn't seek to make changes in his life, but that if he was seeking God's will, he should be content with where that led him.

It was how he tried to live. It seemed that the older he got, the easier it was for him to be content. Or maybe he was just getting better at ignoring any discontent.

Jude looked down at the Bible in his hands, noting that she'd highlighted the passage the pastor was speaking on. Philippians 4:11-13.

Given what Angela had gone through in her life, he'd be interested to know her thoughts on the passage.

When the pastor gave another scripture reference, Angela leaned toward him and reached out to flip the pages of her Bible to find the verse.

The warmth of Angela's shoulder against his arm as they leaned over the Bible together filled Jude with a quiet contentment. He could smell the faint vanilla of her perfume mixed with a light floral scent that he couldn't quite identify.

He forced himself to focus on the words in front of them, though his awareness of her next to him made concentration a challenge. The pastor was referencing Romans 8:28, and Jude watched as Angela's finger traced along the familiar verse about God working all things together for good.

She glanced up at him, her blue-green eyes thoughtful, and mouthed silently, "Even the bad things."

The comment hit him harder than it should have. He could hear the weight of her past in that simple statement.

Jude held her gaze for a moment, then gave a small nod. "Especially the bad things," he whispered back.

Angela stared at him for a long moment before a small smile turned up the corners of her mouth.

She turned back to her notes, writing something in the margin of her notebook. Jude wondered what thoughts were forming in her mind, what connections she was making between the scripture verses and her own difficult journey.

When the service ended, Angela closed her notebook and slipped it back into her Bible case.

"This was wonderful," she said. "I've been watching the livestreams from my old church in Briar Hollow, but it was nice to be here. The music. The preaching. All of it was a real blessing."

"I hope that means you'll come back again."

She smiled at him as they got to their feet. "I would love to."

"So, would you two like to join us for dinner?" Cooper asked.

"We'd love it if you would," Melanie said, giving Angela a warm smile.

When Jude glanced down at Angela, she was looking at him with lifted brows.

"Would you like that?" he asked.

"Sure. That would be nice."

"We can still go to the store afterward."

"I'll just text Kiara and let her know I won't be back until later."

Looking at Cooper and Melanie, he said, "Well, it looks like we're coming to your house for Sunday dinner."

"Wonderful!" Cooper's smile broadened. "We're just going to grab the kids from the children's service, and we'll meet you at the house."

Cooper and Melanie went ahead of them up the aisle, while Jude and Angela followed more slowly. The foyer was full of people, so Jude held out his hand to Angela again.

She smiled at him as she took it, wrapping her smaller fingers around his in a firm grip. Keeping her close, he guided her through the clusters of people to the large doors that led out of the church.

The crisp February air hit them as they stepped outside, and Jude drew Angela closer to his side. He couldn't remember the last time he'd felt this kind of contentment following a service.

Not that he was discontent after the services. More that he didn't really feel any sort of way.

Usually, he slipped in and out, exchanging brief greetings with Cooper and Melanie before heading back to the estate. Or sometimes, like that day, he'd go to their home for a meal following the service.

Today felt different, however. Richer somehow. He'd shared a spiritual and emotional connection with Angela that added a depth to their budding relationship that he knew would only strengthen the bond that was developing between them.

"So, Cooper and Melanie have children?" Angela asked as they walked toward his truck.

"Two. Alex is eight, and Chloe just turned five." Jude helped her into the passenger seat. "They're good kids. Energetic, but good."

"I'm looking forward to meeting them."

As Jude started the engine, he glanced over at Angela. Her cheeks were flushed from the cold, and her eyes were bright with anticipation. The sight made his chest tighten in that now-familiar way.

He'd never expected to find someone who fit so naturally into his life. Someone who shared not only his faith, but who also seemed to understand what was important to him without him having to explain it in great detail.

"Cooper and Melanie have been my friends for a few years now," Jude said as he pulled out of the parking lot. "They were the only people I got close to at the church after my dad passed away. He was the one who'd brought me to that church, and after he died..." He paused, searching for the right words. "It felt like I'd lost my spiritual compass for a while."

"I'm sure that must have been difficult."

"It was," he said as he pulled out of the parking lot onto the street. "I stopped coming for awhile, but eventually, I found my way back, and it was after that that I met Cooper. Having him, Melanie, and their kids become part of my life has been a real blessing."

"I'm glad you have them," Angela said, resting her hand on his arm for a moment. "I hope they like me."

"Oh, they will," Jude assured her. "I've already spoken to them about you."

"Really?"

He smiled at her. "Yep. Cooper tried to encourage me to pursue you."

Angela leaned over and rested her head on his shoulder. "I guess I owe him a debt of gratitude."

"So do I," Jude said, his voice tight with emotion. "So do I."

After a few moments of silence, Angela asked, ""Do you have a favorite verse?"

"Yep. It was my dad's life verse, and it became mine. It's the second part of First Corinthians ten, verse thirty-one. *Whatever you do, do all to the glory of God.*"

"Oh, I know that one," Angela said. "And I like it too."

"Do you have a favorite verse?"

"Yes, I do. And interestingly enough, it's one of the verses the pastor spoke on today," Angela said. "Philippians four verse thirteen. *I can do all things through Christ who strengthens me.* I know that in its context it is about allowing God to give us strength to be content, regardless of the circumstances in our lives. For me, it's that, but it's also about leaning on His strength in other areas of my life. Particularly when I face things that scare me or that I feel I can't handle."

As soon as she said it, he understood completely why she would choose that verse. "You say it a lot to yourself, don't you?"

She nodded. "I struggle with fear, especially when it comes to trying new or difficult things. That verse is what I cling to in order to face them."

Jude tucked away the insight she'd given him, grateful that she'd opened up the way she had.

When they reached Cooper and Melanie's house, the front door was flung open even before they reached it.

"Uncle Jude!" Alex yelled out as they walked up the sidewalk, hand-in-hand. "Daddy said you have a girlfriend now."

Jude chuckled as they climbed the steps. "Yes. That's true. This is Angela."

Alex peered up at her, his gray eyes sparkling with curiosity. "So now you have a gun *and* a girlfriend. Cool!"

"Alexander Sullivan, let our guests in and close the door," Melanie called from further inside the house. "You're letting cold air in."

Alex stepped back, and Jude let Angela precede him into the house. The boy closed the door behind them.

"Welcome," Cooper said as he stepped into the hall from the kitchen. "You can hang your coats in the closet there."

Jude helped Angela out of hers and hung it up before he did the same with his.

"This is our son, Alex," Cooper said, reaching out to tousle the boy's curls. "And this is Chloe, our daughter, who thinks she's a princess."

Chloe stepped out from behind her dad, showing that she was indeed dressed as a princess that day.

Angela smiled at her and gave a small curtsy. "It's lovely to meet you both, Alex and Princess Chloe."

Chloe beamed at Angela's acknowledgment of her royal status, twirling once to show off her sparkly blue dress.

"I'm a snow princess today," she announced proudly. "Like Elsa."

"The most beautiful snow princess I've ever seen," Angela replied, and Jude could tell by the genuine warmth in her voice that she meant it.

Cooper gestured toward the living room. "Make yourselves comfortable. Lunch is almost ready."

Jude guided Angela into the living room with a light touch on her back. The room was cozy and lived-in, with toys tucked into baskets and family photos covering most of the wall space. He watched Angela take it all in, her eyes lingering on the framed pictures of the Sullivans throughout the years.

"Uncle Jude, do you want to see my new LEGO set?" Alex asked, already bouncing on his toes with excitement.

Jude glanced at Angela, who nodded with an encouraging smile. "Sure, buddy. Let's see what you've built."

Alex grabbed Jude's hand and tugged him toward a corner of the living room where an elaborate LEGO construction covered a low table. Angela followed, settling onto a chair near Alex's creation, while Jude dropped down to one knee next to it.

"It's a space station," Alex explained, his words tumbling over each other in his enthusiasm. "And it has a docking bay for spaceships and a command center and everything. Look, this part moves!" He demonstrated by rotating a section of the structure.

"That's some impressive engineering, buddy," Jude said, genuinely admiring the boy's work.

He didn't have much interaction with children in his day-to-day life. However, the time he spent with Alex and Chloe was a bright spot. They'd welcomed him without hesitation, having adopted him as an uncle.

And it seemed they were just as welcoming of Angela. Alex happily answered the questions she had about his masterpiece, and it warmed Jude's heart.

It made him wonder if she'd ever thought about having children. He hadn't given it a lot of thought himself. But now, watching her with Alex and Chloe, the image of her with a child of her own took root in his mind and wouldn't leave.

"Do you want to see my princess room?" Chloe asked Angela, drawing Jude's attention back to the present moment.

"I would love to," Angela replied, reaching out to tuck a curl behind Chloe's ear. "But maybe after lunch?"

"Okay!" Chloe clapped her hands together, then skipped over to where Jude knelt beside the LEGO creation. "Uncle Jude, will you come see my room too?"

"Of course, " he said as Melanie appeared in the doorway, wiping her hands on a dishtowel.

"Lunch is ready, everyone. Kids, please wash your hands."

Alex groaned dramatically but trudged toward the hallway bathroom. Chloe followed, her princess dress swishing as she skipped after her brother.

"They're so cute," Angela said with a smile that lit up her eyes.

"That they are." Jude got to his feet and held out his hand to her. Angela took it and allowed him to pull her to her feet. "And now we get to endure their parents' curiosity."

Melanie's laugh told Jude she'd heard his comment. "You know us so well."

With a grin at Angela, Jude led her from the living room into the dining room. "Don't worry. I'll protect you."

Angela laid her head against his shoulder. "I know."

Those two words meant the world to Jude, and he prayed God would give him the strength to be worthy of her trust in him.

CHAPTER TWENTY-SEVEN

In other circumstances, Angela might have been worried about spending time with people she didn't know, especially ones who weren't hiding the fact that they were curious about her. However, she was with Jude. She knew that he would make sure she was alright. And that anyone he counted as a friend would be someone she was safe with.

"Jude, you and Angela can sit over there," Melanie said, pointing to the far side of the table that was set for six.

Jude led her around to the seats, and they stood there until everyone had come to the table. Once they were all seated, Cooper said a prayer of thanks for the food.

"I'm sorry it's nothing too fancy, Angela," Melanie said. "But we're a pretty basic food type of family."

"It looks and smells delicious," Angela assured her. "To be honest, I never ate fancy food until recently. My sister and I were on a pretty strict budget, which meant we ate a lot of pasta and whatever meat was on sale."

"And you know I don't go for fancy," Jude added. "As long as food tastes good, I'm all for it. And I've eaten here enough to know that you're an excellent cook, Mel."

"Hey!" Cooper protested. "What about me?"

"Well, your steaks are tasty."

"Thank you for your recognition of my exceptional skills."

"Your exceptional *grilling* skills. Just don't ask him to make anything else," Melanie said with a playful smile. "The man can grill, but that's about it."

Cooper placed a hand over his heart in mock offense. "I'll have you know I've mastered the toaster as well."

Angela laughed, feeling herself relax further. The banter between Cooper and Melanie was lighthearted, and she could tell there was love and affection between them.

"Angela's an amazing baker," Jude said, his voice warm with pride as he passed her the bowl of mashed potatoes. "Her cinnamon rolls are to die for, and the chocolate chip cookies she made the other day were the best I've ever had."

Heat rose to Angela's cheeks at his praise. "I've been baking for as long as I can remember, and my job before coming here was in a bakery."

"Really?" Melanie's eyes lit up with excitement. "The next time you come for dinner, you should bring dessert."

Angela smiled as she nodded. "I can do that."

Surely the fact that they wanted her to come back meant that they liked her. She wanted the approval of the handful of people Jude trusted enough to call friends.

"I love that idea," Cooper chimed in. "Jude's been keeping you all to himself, so we need more opportunities to get to know you."

Under the table, Jude's fingers sought hers, weaving between them with quiet certainty. Warmth bloomed in her chest as she stole a glance his way, finding the corners of his mouth lifted in a small smile. With a gentle pressure from his fingers, he released her hand, returning to his meal as if nothing had happened. Though to her, it felt like everything had.

"So tell us about yourself, Angela," Melanie said, cutting into her chicken. "Jude mentioned you have a sister?"

"Uh, yes. I actually have two. Kiara. She's... well, she's been my best friend my whole life." Angela paused, considering how much to share. Jude had let her know that he'd told the couple pretty much everything about her current circumstances because he trusted them implicitly. "We've been through a lot together. And then there's Annie, who's my twin."

"Does she look the same as you?" Chloe asked, her fork loaded with mashed potatoes.

Angela smiled. "Yes, we look mostly the same since we're identical, but there are a few differences. Annie's hair is longer than mine, and she wears it straight."

"Can you tell them apart, Uncle Jude?" Alex asked.

Jude chuckled. "Yep. Even if they looked exactly the same, I'd be able to tell them apart."

Angela turned to look at him. "Really? You think you could, even if our hair and clothes were identical?"

"Sure."

"How?"

"Well, let's just say that Annie doesn't look at me the way you do," Jude said with a wink. "She looks at Cole that way."

Cooper and Melanie laughed as Angela felt heat creep into her cheeks.

"Don't go embarrassing her, Jude," Melanie admonished.

"It's okay," Angela said, glancing up at Jude with a soft smile. "He's not wrong."

Angela was so glad that Jude was letting her see this lighthearted side of him. She liked his serious, professional side. In fact, it was that protective nature of his that had first drawn her to him.

But now, it was his smiles and occasional teasing that made her feel special. She didn't see him interact with anyone else that way, though he was definitely more relaxed around Cooper and Melanie than the others she'd seen him interact with.

"Oh goodness," Melanie said. "This is just so *sweet!*

"Melanie has been trying to set Jude up with a woman for ages," Cooper explained. "To no avail."

Angela didn't like the thought of Jude dating someone else. It must have shown on her face, because Melanie reached out to touch her arm.

"Don't worry," she said. "He was never interested in any of them. I was beginning to think he'd never find someone to love and settle down with."

"I've always been pretty settled already," Jude said as he cut into the piece of roast chicken he'd taken. "So I didn't really need anyone to settle me down."

"That's true," Cooper agreed. "You do live a pretty boring life."

Jude chuckled. "Well, don't make me sound too unappealing."

"Like anyone would find you unappealing," Cooper scoffed.

"Anyway," Melanie said. "Suffice it to say, we're thrilled that the two of you have found each other. I pray you find much happiness together."

Angela smiled at the woman, grateful for the support of Jude's friends. It would have made their relationship more challenging if Jude's hadn't thought she was good enough for him.

The rest of the meal was spent sharing stories about their lives. Even Alex and Chloe contributed, both of them happy to talk about stuff they'd done at school that week.

By the time they decided to leave, Angela was happier than she'd been in a while. Meeting and spending time with Cooper and Melanie and the kids had made Angela feel like she was finally putting down roots in Idaho.

Now she had friends there who had nothing to do with who her father was. Nothing to do with Kiara. Nothing to do with Annie, Julian, or Benji.

They were in her life now because of Jude, and that made her happy.

"Do you have your list for the store?" Jude asked as he pulled his truck away from the curb in front of Cooper and Melanie's house.

"Yep. Kiara has a few things she wants me to pick up too."

"I'm surprised she hasn't wanted to go shopping herself."

"She probably would have wanted to today, but she isn't inter-ested in going to a new church."

"Did she go to church with you in Briar Hollow?"

"Sometimes," Angela said. "But she wasn't as committed as I was. Not sure why."

"Maybe after she's been here for a bit, she'll feel more comfort-able."

"I'd like that." But she doubted that would be the case.

Kiara had only come to church with Angela when it was a special occasion like Christmas or Easter, with a smattering of other times thrown in.

It didn't take long to get to the store they'd shopped at previ-ously. This time, Jude took the cart right from the start, allowing Angela the opportunity to gather the things on her list.

Now that she had access to more money, it made shopping eas-ier. But she still struggled with spending too much all at once.

"Could we get a laptop here?" she asked as she spotted the elec-tronic section.

"A laptop?"

"Yes. The one that Kiara and I share is really old. We got it cheap secondhand. We've used it mainly to watch videos and stream some movies on the one streaming service we had. But now Kiara is looking at doing online school, and I don't think the one we have is good enough for that."

"Okay. I should have thought about that. I'll talk to our tech guys and get them to set up two laptops. One for each of you."

"Oh, I don't really need one," Angela said.

"Maybe not, but we'll get you one anyway. I'm pretty sure you could find a use for it."

"I do like to look up recipes and watch cooking shows," she admitted. "So maybe a newer one would be good."

"Give me a couple of days, and I'll have them for you."

"Thank you," Angela said with a smile.

"You're welcome. Now, where to next?"

Angela considered it for a moment before she led him to the clothing section again. She wanted to buy some more comfortable clothing.

"No chocolate today?" Jude asked after she'd put her choices into the cart.

Angela grinned. "Well, now that you've mentioned it..."

With a chuckle, Jude turned the cart toward the candy aisle. This time, Angela picked up several bags of Kiara's preferred candy and a few of her own favorite chocolate bars.

"Which ones do you like?" Angela asked. "Since you've admitted to a sweet tooth."

"I like chocolate and caramel."

Angela turned to look over the selection, then picked one up . "Like this?"

"Yep, that's my favorite."

She picked up three of them and added them to the cart with the other candy. "All done."

Jude reached out and wrapped his arm around her, drawing her to his side for a quick hug. "Thanks, babe."

Babe...

Angela couldn't keep the smile from growing on her face as they walked to the front of the store to check out.

As the cashier rang her purchases through, Angela watched the total climb with less trepidation than the previous time, though it was still a little alarming. When it was all rung up, she paid with her debit card while Jude loaded the bags back into the cart.

Throughout their time in the store, she'd noticed him occasionally scanning the area around them. He wasn't off the clock, but he was so subtle in what he did that she tended to forget that he was also her bodyguard and carried a weapon under his jacket.

After they'd put the bags into the back seat of his truck, they climbed into their seats and Jude started it up.

"Would you like to stop for a hot drink?" Jude asked, angling himself to look at her.

"That sounds great."

With a nod, Jude put the truck into drive and pulled out of the parking spot. It didn't take long for them to get to a coffee shop, where Jude went through the drive-thru and ordered them each a drink.

"Here you go," he said, handing her the mocha he'd gotten for her.

"Thank you." Angela wrapped her hands around the cup, appreciating the warmth, but also loving the fact that Jude knew what drink she liked.

That was probably due to his attention to detail as a security person. But still, it made her feel special.

They passed the ride back to the estate talking more about the morning service, then Jude shared a bit more about his friendship with Cooper and Melanie.

It was such a perfect time. The two of them in the warmth of the truck, with no one else to interrupt or distract them.

But all too soon, they reached the estate. Jude pulled his truck up to the back door of the house. He got out and helped her carry her bags up to her room.

Angela found the chocolate bars she'd bought him, then went back down to the mudroom with him.

"Thank you for such a wonderful day," she said. "Church. Friends. Shopping. It was all just what I needed."

"I'm glad. I really enjoyed it too."

"Here." She held out the chocolate bars. "Your chocolate."

There was a smile on Jude's face when he took them from her. "Thank you."

"Will you think of me when you eat them?"

"Oh, that's a guarantee."

"Really?"

Jude chuckled. "To be honest, you're always in my thoughts, so I think it's a given I'll be thinking of you when I eat these."

His words filled Angela with so much emotion that she had to swallow before she could respond. "I think of you lots too."

An alert sounded on Jude's phone, and he frowned as he read it. He glanced back into the house.

"I need to go see Duncan." Jude turned his attention back to her. "Sorry to cut things short."

"It's fine," she assured him. She really couldn't complain because she'd had a lot of time with him that day.

Together, they walked out of the mudroom and toward the stairs.

At the base of the stairs, she said, "Will I talk to you later?"

Jude nodded. "I'll definitely call you."

"Coming to talk to Dad, Jude?" Julian asked as he appeared at the top of the stairs.

"I am."

"Talk to you later," Angela said, then headed up the stairs, passing Julian on the way. He gave her a curious look but didn't say anything.

At the top, she glanced back to see Jude watching her. He gave her a smile, then turned to walk with Julian in the direction of Duncan's office.

It wasn't quite how she'd wanted their time together to end, but she couldn't really complain. Their time together that day had been perfect.

She went to her bedroom and transferred all the bags onto her bed to sort through. As she picked up the last two bags, Kiara appeared in the doorway.

"You're home," she said. "How was your day?"

"It was good," Angela said, tipping her head for Kiara to come into the room. "I got stuff for you."

Kiara flopped onto the bed beside the bags Angela had placed there. She pulled one onto her lap and started to go through it.

"So what all did you do today?" Kiara asked as she sorted the stuff in the bags.

"We went to Jude's church," Angela said, settling on the bed and crossing her legs. "Then we went to the house of a couple of Jude's friends for lunch after the service. When we were done there, we went shopping."

"And you enjoyed all of it?" Kiara asked.

Angela smiled. "Yes, I did."

Kiara just nodded as she set aside the bottles of shampoo and conditioner that she'd asked Angela to get her. Angela sensed that she wasn't very happy.

"What did you do today?"

"Not much. Shot some hoops with Benji. Read for several hours. Did some more searching for school stuff on the laptop."

"Oh, I asked Jude about getting you a new laptop," Angela said.

Kiara perked up at that. "Really?"

"I told him that you were thinking of doing online school and needed a better one."

"What did he say?"

"He said he'd get us each one."

"I'd love a new laptop," Kiara said. "The one we have has served us well, but it really is a piece of junk."

Angela pulled her knees up to her chest, wrapping her arms around her legs. "It's so weird to ask for something—especially an expensive item—and have it be handed over. Just like that."

"I know," Kiara said. "At least you're entitled to it, being Duncan's daughter."

"Duncan apparently feels that you're entitled to it as well."

"I have a feeling he's just throwing money at me to keep me here," Kiara said, her gaze distant as she stared at the window.

Angela didn't know for sure whether that was true or not. But if it was, she thought it was a good thing.

Unfortunately, it didn't seem like Kiara agreed.

"Regardless of his motives, I'm very glad you're here with me."

Kiara smiled at her, but to Angela, it looked forced. "I am too."

In the past, though they'd both had times where they'd felt down, Kiara's had been less frequent. Angela had struggled more with worry and angst. But since coming to the estate, Kiara had had more moments like the one she was currently experiencing.

It worried Angela. Plus, it didn't feel right to be so happy when Kiara was down in the dumps.

Maybe things would even out for Kiara once she had some purpose in her life. Hopefully, the laptop would help with that.

Angela just hoped that Kiara wouldn't feel like she would be better off away from the estate. She was happy with Jude, but that didn't mean she didn't need her sister anymore.

She just didn't want to have to choose between the two.

CHAPTER TWENTY-EIGHT

Jude followed Julian into Duncan's office, then took one of the chairs the man motioned to. The fact they were taking their seats at the desk and not in the sitting area told Jude this was going to be a serious conversation.

Not that he didn't already know that. Duncan rarely, if ever, dealt with business on a Sunday. At least with him.

"What's going on, Dad?" Julian asked from where he sat slumped in his chair.

"I've gotten a call from someone in Dubai that they're having some issues with Jacque Fournier. Following that conversation, I've decided to make a trip there."

Jude felt a sinking in his stomach. If Duncan traveled anywhere in the Middle East, he always took Jude and a larger security team.

"When are we leaving?" Julian asked.

"You're not going." The answer was swift and sharp. "I want you to stay here."

"What do you mean?" Julian demanded. "I always go with you when you travel abroad."

Jude resisted the urge to shift in his chair, sensing an argument between the two was brewing.

"You're drinking far too much," Duncan said. "I can't take you with me when you have such a dependence on alcohol."

"I'm not dependent on alcohol," Julian scoffed.

"Then why are you drinking so much?"

Jude doubted anyone outside of the family but him would be allowed to witness this interaction between father and son. It wasn't the first time he'd been party to one of their heated discussions. And it probably wouldn't be the last.

"Because there's nothing better to do here," Julian responded.

"And yet you're the only one drinking to excess."

Jude wondered when Duncan would finally wise up and just get rid of all the alcohol at the estate. Although that didn't necessarily mean that Julian wouldn't drive into Serenity and get drunk at a bar.

Duncan probably figured it was better that Julian got drunk on the estate than at some random bar in Serenity.

"You're drinking even more, recently," Duncan said. "Is your mother still giving you hassles?"

Julian gave a derisive snort. "My mother is *always* giving me hassles."

Duncan sighed. "Regardless. You're staying here. You can keep an eye on things."

"Not sure why," Julian said with a huff of laughter. "It's not like you trust me."

"I trust you to stay here and watch over your sisters and Benji, since I'll be taking Jude with me."

That got another sharp laugh from Julian. "Like you think I could do Jude's job. At least I'm competent at my own."

"When you're sober."

Julian got to his feet. "Well, if I'm not going with you, I don't need to be present for this meeting."

Duncan didn't say anything as Julian left the office, but his gaze followed his son until the door shut with a resounding *thud*.

The silence that followed felt heavy and charged with the tension of unspoken words and long-standing frustrations.

Duncan rubbed his temples, suddenly looking every one of his nearly seventy years. "That went about as well as I expected. Julian's been spiraling for weeks now, and I can't seem to get through to him."

The admission hung between them, and Jude found himself in the uncomfortable position of witnessing a father's disappointment in his son. He'd seen Duncan handle billion-dollar negotiations with less visible strain than this conversation with Julian had caused.

"He's been looking a bit more gaunt and tired than usual."

"I know." Duncan's expression grew more troubled. "I've been hoping he'd pull himself together, but I can't ignore it anymore. Not when business is involved. I want him with me for trips like this, but I don't think it's wise. Not for this one anyway."

"Do you have any idea what's causing his spiraling?" Jude asked.

"I don't, but there's no denying that his drinking has increased since Angelica and Kiara arrived. I'm not sure why that's the case, but I think we need to get him some help."

"Do you want me to look into treatment programs?" While he and Julian had never been best friends and were different in a lot of ways, Jude still cared about the man beyond just being concerned for his safety.

"Yes. I think it's time to consider something more drastic. I can't let him slip even further away."

The emotion in the man's voice tugged at something inside Jude. Duncan wasn't a man given to much emotion, but when it came to his family—his children—the man was as emotionally invested as Jude's dad had been. It was one of the things Jude appreciated about Duncan.

"We just got Angelica back, but now I feel like I'm losing Julian. I can't let that happen."

Jude nodded. "We'll figure out how to help him. I promise."

It was a promise Jude felt comfortable making because Julian was no longer just the son of Jude's employer, he was the brother of the woman he loved. And Jude knew that Angela would want to help Julian.

"For now, we need to focus on this trip."

"When are we leaving?" Jude asked.

"Tomorrow morning."

Jude's heart sank. For the first time ever in his job, he really didn't want to go. He didn't want to be apart from Angela, right when they were at the start of a relationship, but it was his job, so he had no choice but to go.

Duncan gave him details about the situation they were going into, and after a brief discussion, they'd come up with a plan for the security for the trip.

"Do you have any idea of how long we'll be there?"

"A week, possibly longer depending on what we find." Duncan straightened in his chair. "You'll need to arrange for additional security while we're away. Lucy can handle Kiara, but do you have someone to assign to Angelica?"

Jude had been considering a few people. One was a woman who was based out of New York. He had planned to see if she'd accept a transfer, but there wasn't enough time before they left to get her to the estate.

"I'll ask Dawn to keep an eye on Angela. I doubt she'll want to leave the estate, but if she does, Dawn could go with her. If Annie needs Dawn, I'll have Derek go with Angela."

"Has there been anything more about Jim?"

Jude shook his head. "The last update was the one about Craig saying Jim had left the homestead. There's been no further sightings by our guys. And the authorities haven't had any leads on him either."

"I don't like that. Please impress upon Angelica and Annie the importance of staying on the estate." Jude lifted his brows at the man, and when Duncan saw that, he chuckled. "Yes. Okay. I realize what I'm asking. But at least try."

"I don't have much time to do that, but I'll try my best."

"Thank you," he said. "And I'm sorry I'm asking you to come with me right at this moment. I hope Angelica won't be too upset."

Jude hoped so too, but he supposed it was a good test of how she could handle the riskier parts of his job.

"How is everything going with the two of you?" Duncan asked.

"I thought you were going to stay out of it."

Duncan laughed, the earlier weight of the situation with Julian and the business lifting. "I did, didn't I? Still, I hope that the two of you can make this work."

"That makes two of us," Jude replied. "And to appease your curiosity, everything is going well, considering it's very early days."

"I suppose you probably want to talk to her about this," Duncan said. "So go on. I'll see you in the morning."

"If anything changes with the security personnel, I'll let you know," Jude said as he got to his feet.

Once he stepped outside the office, he quickly headed to the library to see if it was empty. Finding the space free of people, he sent a quick text to Angela.

Can you come meet me in the library?

Angela: *Of course. I'll be right there.*

Jude turned to look out the large window, staring at the outside world that was turning gray as twilight approached. He wasn't sure what to say to Angela to make it easier for her to accept this sudden and potentially dangerous change of plans.

Jude knew he couldn't sugarcoat anything. It was vital that she understand the risks of his job before they got any further into their relationship. If she wasn't able to handle this, then it was better to find out now.

"Jude?"

He turned to see Angela walking toward him. She'd changed out of the clothes she'd worn to church, and now wore a pair of fleecy pants, a long-sleeve T-shirt, and some thick socks. She looked very cozy and huggable, but she had a concerned look on her face.

"Is everything okay?" she asked as she neared him.

"Would you believe me if I said I just wanted to see you again?"

Her eyes widened briefly at the question. "I'm not sure. I mean, we just saw each other thirty minutes ago. I just don't think you'd give in to that urge, even if you had it."

"Well, you'd be wrong," he said. "I would take any opportunity at all—and might even make up a few—to see you again."

"I'm glad." She smiled at him briefly, but then it faded. "Seriously though, is everything okay?"

"Come sit with me," Jude said, motioning to the loveseat near where he stood.

Angela crossed her arms as she walked to the loveseat to join him. He waited for her to sit down before he sank down onto the cushion beside her.

It took a moment for Jude to realize that she was bracing herself for whatever he was going to say.

Reaching out, he touched her hand. She immediately uncrossed her arms and slid her fingers between his.

"It's nothing super serious," he said. "It's just a work thing that has come up."

"A work thing?"

"Duncan needs to fly to Saudi Arabia to deal with a business matter."

"Saudi Arabia?" She frowned. "Is that... is that one of the places you travel to with him?"

"Yes, I'll be leading the security team for this trip."

"Oh." She stared at him. "Is this a dangerous assignment?"

"It has the potential to be," Jude said. "Though in all the times we've traveled there, we haven't experienced any significant security events."

"So why do you have to go?" she asked.

"The further we are from home, the more security Duncan takes. Nowhere is as safe as here. This situation in Dubai is an internal one at the company, but it can quickly turn external if we're not careful. Duncan just doesn't want to take any risks."

"I'll miss you," she said, seeming to accept the inevitable.

"I'll miss you too."

"How long will you be gone?"

"Probably at least a week. And I need to ask you a really big favor."

"What?"

"I need you to stick to the estate while I'm gone. I haven't had the chance to bring in your bodyguard yet, so if I'm not here, I'd rather you stay on the estate unless it's an emergency."

Her fingers tightened around his as she seemed to consider his request, then she nodded. "I don't have any real reason to leave. I don't need anything from the store since we just went, and I'll simply wait until you're back to go to church again."

"Thank you," he said. "I don't want to have to restrict you like this again, so when I get back, we'll look at bringing your bodyguard to the estate."

"Do you know who it is already?"

Jude nodded. "I've been considering someone from New York. But I want you to meet her first. We'll deal with it when I get back, just in case Duncan needs me to go with him somewhere else."

"Will we be able to message or talk while you're gone?"

Jude smiled at her. "Yes. Definitely."

"Good."

"Can you hang out with me for a bit?" Jude asked, not wanting their time together to be over just yet, especially because of his pending departure the next day. "I just need to send a couple of emails first."

"Sure. Are you hungry?" she asked. "We're on our own around here for suppers on Sundays, but I can make us some sandwiches."

"That would be nice." He glanced around. "I'll come with you to the kitchen."

Jude got to his feet, then held out his hand. Angela took it and allowed him to pull her up. He didn't let go of her hand as they left the library and walked down the hall to the kitchen, which was currently empty.

He settled on a stool at the large island counter, while Angela gathered up the fixings for their meal. Jude watched her for a moment, taking in her movements as she began to make their sandwiches.

"Anything you don't like on your sandwich?" she asked, glancing up at him.

"I'm a pretty simple eater, so as long as it doesn't have anything too wild on it, I'm generally pretty good."

"No fancy mustards?"

Jude chuckled. "Nope. I'm good with plain old yellow mustard."

"Me too," Angela said with a smile on her face as she sliced a tomato.

Jude was glad to see that she was starting to feel more comfortable in the home. When she'd first arrived, she wouldn't have dared to come into the kitchen to make herself a meal without being given permission by someone.

His phone dinged, letting him know an email had arrived.

Though he wanted to keep watching Angela, Jude opened his app and found an email from Duncan's assistant in New York, who seemed to work twenty-four/seven. It gave details of flight departure and arrival times and information about where they'd be staying in Dubai.

He sent out emails to all the security team members he wanted with them. Two were already there at the estate, but they'd swing by New York to pick up the rest of the team members.

By the time he was done, Angela had finished the sandwich and slid the plate across the counter to him.

"What would you like to drink?" she asked.

"Just water," Jude said. "But I can get that while you make your sandwich. Do you want water as well?"

"Yes, thanks."

After he'd filled a couple of glasses, he carried them to the breakfast nook, while Angela brought their plates over.

Once they were seated opposite each other, Jude hesitated for a moment before he said, "Do you mind if I say a prayer of thanks for the food?"

Angela's face lit up with a smile as she nodded. He laid his hands on the table, palm up, and without hesitation, Angela placed her hands in his.

He wasn't used to sharing his faith with anyone. Just like he wasn't used to sharing his life with anyone.

But that was changing, and he was fine with it. Wanted it, in fact.

He said a brief prayer of thanks and also added a request for safety for the team as they traveled to Dubai, as well as those left behind on the estate.

"Have you been to Dubai a lot?" Angela asked as she picked up her sandwich following the prayer.

"We go about once a year, but usually only for a couple of days. Duncan likes to touch base with his company headquarters in each location at least once a year."

"Do you enjoy it?" she asked.

"Dubai?" She nodded. "Well, it's a very interesting city. Very modern. Almost futuristic. It's very different from what I'm used to here, but it's a nice place to visit."

"Would you take some video or pictures for me?" she said. "I'm not sure I actually want to visit there, but I'd love to see the parts of the city that interest you."

Jude smiled. "Well, I'm not usually one to take many pictures just for pleasure, but I'll do it for you."

"Thank you," Angela said, her eyes brightening. "I've only seen places like that in movies."

Jude took a bite of his sandwich, savoring the simple combination of flavors. Something about sharing a meal with Angela made even ordinary food taste better. The quiet domesticity of sitting across from her in the kitchen nook felt right in a way he hadn't expected.

"I'll try to get some shots of the Burj Khalifa. It's the tallest building in the world. And maybe the Dubai Mall. It's enormous, with a large aquarium inside."

"An aquarium in a mall?" Angela leaned forward, sandwich momentarily abandoned. "That sounds amazing."

"It is pretty impressive," Jude admitted. "Though I usually don't get much time for sightseeing."

A shadow passed over Angela's face. "Because you're working. Keeping Duncan safe."

"Yes. I am." He paused, then asked, "Are you worried about that?"

"Of course," she said with a nod. "I don't want anything to happen to you. I also don't want anything to happen to Duncan or any member of the security team. So yeah, I worry."

"That was what my mom struggled with. The constant worry about my dad when he was on the job."

"I'm aware of what your job entails. That it can be life-threatening," Angela said as she set her sandwich down on her plate and lowered her hands to the table. She gazed at him, her eyes wide and filled with emotion. "And I know there's a risk I could lose you. But there's also a chance that I won't. The only way I'm guaranteed to lose you is to walk away, and I'm not willing to do that. If I only have a short time with you, then I'll be thankful for every minute."

Emotion filled Jude, and he had to swallow hard in order to be able to respond.

"I want to come home to you."

He reached his hand out and once again laid it palm up on the table, waiting for Angela to take it. She didn't hesitate.

Her hand was smaller than his and soft. Yet he could feel the strength in it. It was just like her—soft and small, but strong. Her strength never ceased to amaze him.

"I'm not going to tell you not to worry," Jude said. "But I want to encourage you to pray for me and to trust that God's will will be done."

"I do pray for you," Angela said, her fingers gripping his more firmly. "And I will definitely be praying for safety for you and the others on this trip."

"Why don't we pray together now?" Jude suggested.

At Angela's nod, Jude once again took her hand. As they bowed their heads together to pray, Jude felt his connection to Angela deepen. This wasn't something he'd done with a woman before, but he was glad he was there with Angela, sharing that spiritual moment with her.

The rest of their meal was spent talking about simple things, like what they preferred to do in their spare time or what sort of movies or TV shows they watched. He enjoyed learning those small things about Angela, and for the first time in his life, he was opening up about things he usually kept to himself.

But finally, the time came for him to head home to pack and prepare for the trip early the next morning.

"Take care of yourself and stay safe," Jude said as they stood together in the mudroom.

"You too," Angela said.

Jude reached out to take her hand and pull her to him. She came willingly and stepped into his embrace.

He held her close, feeling the warmth of her body against his and breathing in the subtle vanilla scent of her hair. Her arms wound around his waist, and he could sense her reluctance to let go in the way she leaned against him.

For a moment, they simply held each other in the quiet of the mudroom. Jude rested his cheek on the top of her head, feeling the silky strands of her hair against his skin. He wanted to freeze the moment and store it away to carry with him across the ocean.

He didn't want to leave her.

The thought hit him with surprising force. In all his years working for Duncan, he'd never felt this pull to stay home. His job had always been his primary focus, his sense of unwavering duty. But now, with Angela in his arms, he wished he could find a way out of the trip.

"I'll call or message you as soon as I can," he murmured.

She pulled back just enough to look up at him, her blue-green eyes searching his face. "Promise me you'll be careful. Don't take any unnecessary risks."

Leaning forward, he pressed a kiss to her forehead. "I promise."

The goodbye he had to say to her was the hardest he'd ever said. And as he drove back to his place, Jude was eager to get the trip underway so that he could get back to Angela. The sooner he left, the sooner he'd be back.

CHAPTER TWENTY-NINE

The week Jude was gone dragged for Angela. She'd tried to keep busy, even going so far as to order yarn online so that she could work on a knitting project.

"I could sell that in my on-line store," Annie said, gesturing to the wool blanket in Angela's lap. "Or if you want, you could make knitted baby things to sell."

Angela ran her hand over the soft wool. "I think I might like to do that. Not for the money, of course. I would just appreciate having something to do."

"I think it would be great," Annie said. "Plus, you could make scarves and mitts for the shelter next winter too."

The idea appealed to Angela quite a bit. Her preference might have been to do something with her baking, but that was a bit more challenging. Knitting things to help raise money or to donate to the shelter was a good second option.

She'd always enjoyed knitting, and if it gave her something to do while supporting a worthy cause, then it was a win-win situation.

"Why don't you do a little research and see what kind of things you might want to make for the store?"

"Sure, I can do that," Angela said, excited also at the prospect of working alongside her sister.

They still weren't as close as she and Kiara were, and they might never be, but they were spending more time together. They were currently commiserating over the fact that neither of their boyfriends were at the estate.

Annie was more experienced in dealing with the separation since she and Cole were apart most of the time. He came to visit periodically, and she had gone to LA to attend some games, so they'd seen each other, but it wasn't very often.

Jude was due back the next day, and Angela could hardly wait. They'd messaged and video chatted during the time he was away, but never for very long.

Her worry about him had abated a bit as the week had progressed. When she'd told Jude that she would be happy for any amount of time they could have together, she hadn't been lying. But that still didn't mean she didn't want to have years and years together. Not just a few weeks.

"So, Jude is due back with Dad this afternoon, huh?" Annie said as she scratched between her dog's ears.

"Yes, and I can't wait."

"No offense, but I find it incredibly weird that you're dating Jude. I mean, I know we talked about it, but now that it's actually happening... weird."

Angela laughed. "Well, it doesn't feel weird to me."

"Jude has always been like that annoying, bossy older brother."

"So you have two of those?"

Annie grinned. "Yeah. Though Julian doesn't try to boss me around as much anymore."

"Jude doesn't really boss me around," Angela said. "And neither does Julian."

"So how does Jude get you to do things?"

"Like what things?"

"The self-defense training. The weapons training. Having to wear a gun."

"Oh. Well, he's always taken the time to explain to me why it's necessary. He encourages me to just do my best."

"I guess you're more responsive to that than I was. Early on, I did what the security people told me to do. But later, as Benji got older, the demands started to feel more restrictive."

"I grew up with restrictions that weren't for my own good," Angela said. "I know that what Jude is asking me to do is for my own benefit. I know what Jim is capable of, so I'd like to have the knowledge to at least give me a fighting chance against him and Craig, should I need it."

Annie's expression sobered. "That's understandable."

A weight settled on Angela's chest at the thought of Jim and Craig and the threat they still presented to her and Kiara. Though she'd had plenty of security around her at the estate, and she hadn't left the grounds at all for the week Jude had been gone, she still felt like she wasn't as protected as she was when he was around.

When Annie's phone chimed with an alert, she looked at the screen and smiled. "It's Cole. I think I'm going to head home and chat with him."

"Thanks for hanging out with me."

"I enjoyed it. We'll talk about the items for the website later."

Angela nodded, then watched as Annie tapped out a message as she left the solarium, Nyla at her heels.

In the silence left behind, Angela picked up the knitting needles from her lap. She continued to work on her project until her own phone let her know she had received a text.

Jude: *Just getting ready to leave NYC. We should be home around five.*

Angela glanced at the time. It was almost eleven, so six hours.

Can't wait to see you! I've missed you so much.

Jude: *I've missed you too. Do you want to get some dinner later?*

Angela smiled as she read his question. *I'd love to.*

She had no idea where they'd go, but most likely, Jude already had a plan in mind.

Jude: *See you soon.*

Angela set her phone down and resumed her knitting, but she couldn't focus on the stitches. Her mind kept wandering to Jude, to the hours that remained before she'd see him again. Six hours. It felt like it might as well be six days.

She'd never felt this way before, this constant ache when someone was absent.

There had been times when Jim had put her or Kiara in punishment for a day, forcing them apart for the duration. That separation had been horrible, and she had felt intense relief when they were reunited.

This separation from Jude had been different. It had been like an ache that nothing eased. However, the anticipation of being reunited had built throughout the week. And now, all she wanted was to see him again.

She'd always heard the saying that absence makes the heart grow fonder, but she'd never understood the full force of those words until now. The ache in her chest since Jude had left was more than mere longing. It was a constant, low-level hum beneath every moment, intensifying the closer she got to seeing Jude again.

Angela tried to distract herself with everything Annie had suggested—researching new knitting patterns, ideas for the website—but none of it dulled the restless anticipation inside of her.

She wondered if Jude missed her with the same intensity.

It was easy to imagine him focused and all-business while he was away, but she hoped there was at least some small space in his mind reserved for her, some private longing that mirrored her own. Maybe he'd never say it—Jude was not the effusive type—but sometimes she caught a softness in his eyes when he looked at her, and it made her hope all the harder.

She'd never been in love before, and the feelings she had for Jude were overwhelming.

She'd read about love in books—the epic, all-consuming kind that upended lives—but somehow she'd never expected to find herself there, sitting in a sun-warmed solarium, her hands stilled over an unfinished knitting project, heart thumping in anticipation of a man's return.

It was simultaneously intoxicating and terrifying.

More than once over the past week, Angela had caught herself spiraling into worry: Did she care more for Jude than he cared for her? Was she too needy, too intense, too eager for the next message or phone call?

The rational part of her knew she was being silly—they had only just begun their relationship, and neither of them was the sort to rush headlong into declarations. Yet the fear persisted, a thin thread through the days since Jude had left.

She wanted to believe she could be loved the way she already loved Jude. But did he feel the same?

He was so contained, so measured in his affections. Sometimes she wondered if she was imagining the tenderness in his voice, or if his texts were short because he was busy or because he didn't know what else to say. Maybe he was just humoring her. Maybe, once the novelty wore off, he'd be indifferent or, worse, disappointed.

The separation had increased those fears, and she'd prayed every day that God would take that fear from her and give her confidence in what she was building with Jude.

She suspected that loving someone would always feel a little scary, and maybe that was okay. Maybe it was supposed to be that way.

Because what she felt for Jude—the love she held in her heart for him—was like nothing she'd felt before.

"What are you doing?"

Kiara's question drew Angela from her musings. She looked over to see her sister walking into the solarium. Or maybe it was more of a shuffle. Kiara looked rough.

"Are you not feeling well?"

Kiara slumped down on the loveseat next to Angela. She wore her comfy oversized clothes, making her look a little sloppy, which wasn't usual for her outside of her bedroom. Her curls were a mess, partly in a ponytail, but also spilling out around her face. Her pale face.

"Just didn't sleep well." She sank down further into the loveseat, wrapping her arms around herself.

"Because you're not feeling well?" Angela asked. "Or is it something else?"

Though Angela had spoken to her about traveling to help fill her time, Kiara hadn't jumped at the opportunity. However, she had gone into Serenity with Lucy, and she'd spent some time at the library and the bookstore.

She'd come home with a stack of books, finally able to buy the books she wanted instead of just getting them from the library. And for a short time, she'd been excited about the books.

However, the excitement hadn't lasted, and whatever Kiara was struggling with had crept back in again.

"So what are you doing here?" Kiara asked, waving her hand at the wool in Angela's lap.

She lifted the needles to show her. "I'm working on a baby blanket. Annie said she could put it up on her website to sell."

Kiara frowned. "But you don't need the money."

"No, and Annie doesn't either," Angela said. "So all the proceeds from the website go to a shelter in Coeur d'Alene. It'll give me something to do that also benefits someone else."

"I suppose that's good."

"I think so. You could knit something too if you wanted."

"I've never been as good at that as you have," Kiara said.

"Only because you haven't wanted to be."

"True." Kiara stared out the large windows of the solarium. "Is Jude coming back today?"

Angela hadn't talked much to Kiara about Jude and how much she missed him. For some reason, Kiara hadn't been very interested in hearing about what was happening between Angela and Jude.

"Yes. He sent a text saying they'd be back around five."

"I suppose you're excited about him coming back."

Angela's heart ached at the distance that seemed to have developed between her and Kiara.

"I am," she agreed.

"Guess you'll have plenty to keep you busy once he's around again."

"Not necessarily. He'll have work during the day, and we'll still have training to do with Dawn and Derek."

Dawn had continued to work with them on self-defense, and Derek had taken over the shooting practice. She had no idea if Jude would take that responsibility back from Derek once he was home.

"Are you really upset that I'm dating Jude?" Angela asked.

She didn't want to have tension between them, but it was apparent that it was already there.

Kiara sighed. "I'm not upset. Just maybe a little jealous that you've found some purpose here."

"Jude isn't my purpose," Angela said.

"But he gives you something to focus on."

"To some extent," Angela agreed. "But I'm still trying to find other things that give me the ability to be productive."

Kiara slid further down, stretching her legs out while she pulled her hands into the sleeves of her large sweatshirt. She stared into the distance, focusing on something inwardly that Angela wasn't privy to.

"I'm sorry," Angela said softly. "I know this is hard for you."

Kiara's mouth twisted. "I just feel so useless here. I should be grateful that we're safe, that we have all this." She gestured at the room around them. "But I feel like I'm just... existing. Not living."

Angela set her knitting aside and moved closer to her sister. "I understand that. I really do."

"Do you?" Kiara's voice wasn't accusatory, just weary. "Because you seem to be adapting so well. You have Jude. You're busy making things. You're finding your place."

Angela couldn't deny any of that, but it hurt her that Kiara was still struggling to adapt.

After sitting in silence for several minutes, Kiara pulled her legs in and got to her feet.

"I didn't mean to bring you down. I'm happy that you've found your place here and that you've found love. Truly I am." She gave Angela a smile that was a weak imitation of her normal one. "I'll be fine. Once I settle on something, I'll be fine."

With that, Kiara headed for the door, leaving Angela staring after her.

Kiara was a problem that she wanted to solve, but Angela knew that she couldn't do that. All she could do was be there for her sister and support her whenever opportunities arose.

With a sigh, Angela gathered up her needles and wool and left the solarium. It was nearly lunchtime, so she went to her room to put her things away and freshen up.

When she got back down to the breakfast room, which was where they ate lunch, Elizabeth was there. Benji was at school, so he wouldn't be home until later.

Kiara came in a few minutes later, having changed into a pair of jeans and a sweater. She'd also taken the time to smooth all her hair back into a ponytail.

She still looked tired, however.

Elizabeth greeted each of them with a warm smile. The woman had been nothing but loving and gracious to them, and Angela was so grateful for that.

They'd all begun eating the salad and soup that were on the menu for the meal when Julian wandered into the room. He was wearing an untucked white button-down shirt and a pair of loose jeans. The shirt looked like maybe it hadn't seen an iron after he'd pulled it out of his suitcase.

"Are you feeling alright, Julian?" Elizabeth asked, concern on her face.

"I'm fine," he said as he sank into the chair beside Annie.

Angela didn't buy that from him any more than she'd bought it from Kiara. The two of them were quite a pair. A miserable pair.

The conversation around the table was mainly carried by Elizabeth and Angela. Elizabeth was clearly looking forward to the return of her husband, and it was a feeling that Angela understood.

Once lunch was over, Kiara and Julian disappeared first. Angela decided to see if she could make some cookies. It would help kill time, though her main motivation was to have some for Jude when he arrived.

Thankfully, Mrs. Stevens had no problem with her being in the kitchen. While she waited for the cookies to bake, Angela also helped out a bit with the preparations for dinner.

She'd just finished putting the cookies into a container for Jude, as well as in the kitchen cookie jar for everyone else, when she received a text alert.

Jude: *Just loading into the helicopter. Should be there in twenty minutes.*

Angela smiled as she answered his text with one of her own.

I can hardly wait!

Jude: *Me too!*

Angela was glad to hear that. It made her feel like she wasn't alone in the desire to be reunited.

She hurried up to her room and grabbed her thick coat, then went back downstairs. Watching the time, she lingered in the mudroom.

When it was five minutes from the estimated arrival time, Angela pulled on her coat and boots and left the house. The air was brisk, but not unbearably cold, so the walk to the helipad wasn't too bad.

Maybe she shouldn't be going to meet Jude there, but she couldn't stay away.

She had just about reached the helipad when she heard the distant whomp-whomp of the helicopter. A black SUV and a large UTV were waiting there, and Derek waved to her when he spotted her.

Angela waved back, then went to stand at the edge of the helipad. She pulled her scarf up over her mouth and nose to keep them warm, then shoved her hands into her pockets.

When her gaze found the approaching helicopter in the sky, she didn't look away, watching as it continued to grow in size until it hovered over the helipad.

Angela ducked her head as the wind whipped up as the machine slowly lowered to rest on the painted H on the helipad. When the propellers slowed, the door opened, and people began to disembark.

She spotted Jude right away, and though she wanted to rush over to him, she stayed glued to the spot. He was probably still on the clock, so she didn't want to overstep more than she already had by showing up there.

As she watched Jude, her heart rate increased. He was followed out of the helicopter by Duncan, who laid his hand on Jude's shoulder.

Jude turned to face him, and the pair appeared to have a brief conversation before Jude spoke to the other men who'd gotten off the helicopter with them.

Suddenly, he swung in her direction and walked toward her. Angela's heart pounded against her ribs as he neared, and she couldn't stop herself from running to him.

He didn't hesitate to enfold her in his arms when they met partway on the helipad. Angela wrapped her arms around him and held him tight.

"I'm so glad you're back," she murmured. "I missed you so much."

"I missed you too." Jude seemed reluctant to let her go, and Angela was just fine with that.

"I hope it was okay that I came out to meet you."

Jude loosened his hold on her enough so that he could look down at her. "Duncan told me I'm off the clock now, so it's fine."

She hugged him tight again, then stepped back. "Do you have to go to the security building?"

"Just to pick up my luggage later," Jude said. "But Duncan said I should come for dinner with the family."

"Oh, I'd like that very much."

Jude bent and pressed a kiss to her forehead. "Me too."

Hand-in-hand, they wandered along the road back to the main house. Angela felt like she was walking on air.

It had been such a long week, but it was finally over. Jude was back, and Angela felt like she could breathe easy again.

CHAPTER THIRTY

For Jude, arriving back at the estate had felt like coming home in a way it never had before. Of course, he'd never had someone waiting for him to return. And he'd certainly never had someone waiting at the edge of the helipad the way Angela had been.

The sight of her there, bundled up against the cold, had settled something inside him. And when Duncan had told him that he was off the clock—essentially freeing him to reunite with Angela the way he wanted to—he'd wasted no time in going to her and taking her in his arms.

They'd ended up sharing dinner with the family, then they'd gone to the library, where Jude had turned the gas-powered fireplace on. In the cozy warmth of the space, they'd talked for a few hours, catching up on all the things that hadn't been easy to discuss over text or during the few calls they'd had.

And every day over the next two weeks, they'd continued to spend time together. Those meet-ups had become the highlight of Jude's day.

On several evenings, Angela had accompanied him when he'd worked out in the gym at the rec center. She'd even exercised herself a couple of times, but she had made it pretty clear that she much preferred to just watch him rather than participate herself.

They'd also watched some movies in the theater room, sometimes joined by Annie, Benji, and Kiara.

No matter what they did, Jude had enjoyed every minute of it because he'd been with Angela. He never would have imagined that someone would come into his life who he would want to spend so much time with.

Apart from it being time they used to get to know each other better, Jude just enjoyed being around Angela. She made him smile and even laugh more than he usually did. And it wasn't that she was super funny or anything like that.

It all came down to the fact that he didn't feel he had to hold his emotions so closely when he was with Angela. His usually tight emotional control loosened because he felt such a level of peace and contentment when she was around.

He'd come to realize that there was more to life than work... but he only wanted that if Angela was part of it.

Jude poured himself a cup of coffee from the carafe in his kitchen, then leaned a hip against the counter as he stared out the window. The snow that had begun the previous day had finally ended that morning, leaving them with bright sparkling snow drifts.

Later that day, he and Angela had plans to go to Coeur d'Alene for dinner and a show at a local theater. He wasn't really a musical sort of person, but Angela had seemed excited about it. And if she wanted something, he'd do what he could to make it happen.

But that wasn't going to be until that evening. He needed to do a few things around the house that he'd been putting off. One of Mrs. Stevens' daughters came to clean his place once a week, but he took care of his own laundry, which was what he needed to focus on that morning.

Setting his mug on the counter, he headed for his room and gathered up all the laundry. He got the first load going, then returned to the kitchen.

Being a Saturday morning, he didn't have to head to the office, though, as usual, he was available for anything that needed his time and attention

When his phone chimed with an incoming video chat, he hoped it would be Angela. A quick glance at the screen, however, showed it was his mom.

He answered the call and set the phone up so that he could make himself breakfast while they chatted. He hadn't told her about Angela yet, but one of these days he would.

They'd been chatting for a few minutes when a call came in from the security office.

"Mom, I have to go," he said. "I'm getting a security call."

She gave a sigh but didn't argue. Just made him promise to call her again in the next day or two for a longer chat.

"What's going on?" Jude said when he accepted the call.

"I'm not sure, but Angela is on her way to you, I think," Dawn said. "She came flying out of the house and ran down the road headed to your place. She's not wearing a coat."

Jude frowned. "Okay. I'll meet her with the UTV."

The bacon still had twelve minutes until it was done, which would be plenty of time to get her and bring her back.

Worry pricked at Jude as he hurried to the UTV in his garage. He didn't bother to close the overhead door behind him since he'd be back soon.

Cranking the heat, he drove down the winding road that led from his place to the main house. It was about a ten-minute walk, but driving was only a minute or so.

That meant he spotted Angela almost immediately. Head down, she was trudging through the snow drifts on the road since it hadn't all been cleared yet.

He pulled to a stop and got out. The minute Angela saw him, she ran toward him and flung herself into his arms.

"What's wrong, love?" Jude asked, needing to know what he was facing in order to help calm her down.

"He's going to be so mad."

She looked up at him, distress clear on her face. Her eyes were puffy and red, and strands of her hair were caught in the dampness of her tear-stained cheeks.

"Who's going to be mad?"

"Duncan," she said. "He's going to be so mad."

"C'mon." Jude put his arm around her shoulders and guided her to the UTV. "Let's go back to my place, and you can tell me what's happened."

She nodded and allowed him to help her into the UTV. For the ride back to the house, she sat in silence, her hands clasped tightly in her lap.

After he pulled into the garage, Jude closed the overhead door, then led Angela into the cabin. She didn't even look around as he took her through the kitchen to the living room.

"Sit here," he said, guiding her to his overstuffed couch.

He took a minute to check on the bacon, then returned to where Angela sat staring dully into the darkened fireplace.

"Are you cold?"

She looked up at him, then down at her hands. "I'm okay."

"Here." He pulled the throw blanket off his recliner and draped it over her shoulders.

Her hands came up to grip it together at the front. "Thank you."

He sat down on the rustic coffee table in front of her. When he held out his hands, she loosened her hold on the blanket to take them.

"Tell me what's going on."

"Kiara's pregnant."

Of all the things that Angela might have said, that was completely unexpected.

"Pregnant?" he asked. "Really?"

She nodded. "And Duncan is going to be so mad."

"I don't think he will be," Jude said. "After all, her personal life isn't really his responsibility."

"Oh, he'll be mad about this," Angela said, conviction strong in her voice.

"Why?"

"Because it's Julian's."

Jude sat back in shock, staring at Angela with wide eyes. "Julian's?"

Angela nodded. "Kiara said it's his."

"What on earth?" Jude shook his head. "I had no idea there was something going on between them."

"I don't think they're dating or in a relationship or anything," Angela said. "From what Kiara said it happened one night when they'd both been drinking."

"I didn't know that Kiara drank."

"She doesn't, but she's been depressed and frustrated lately. I guess maybe she and Julian got drunk together, and things just... happened." Angela's shoulders slumped as her head dipped. "It's all my fault."

"What?" Jude leaned forward, keeping her hands firmly in his. "There's no way this is your fault."

"I knew that she was struggling, but I just didn't know how to help her."

"Which means it's not your fault," Jude told her. "Kiara and Julian are adults, and this decision and its ramifications are their responsibility. Not yours."

"Duncan is going to be so mad at them," Angela said.

Now that he knew the details, Jude couldn't exactly argue against that. "Not at Kiara, though."

"Why not?" Angela asked.

"Because Julian should have known better," Jude said. "And if he was going to make such a bad decision, he didn't need to compound it by being irresponsible and not making sure they were protected."

The timer in the kitchen beeped, so Jude squeezed Angela's hands, then let them go. "I'll be back in a minute."

She nodded, then wrapped her hands in the wool blanket again.

Jude pulled the baking sheet with the bacon on it out of the oven and put it on the hot pads he'd set out on the counter.

His mind was reeling with the news Angela had just revealed. He was actually surprised that it had taken this long for Julian to get into this predicament, given the reckless way he lived his life.

Although, for all he knew, Julian did have other kids, and Duncan had just paid to keep that information under wraps.

Sighing, he returned to where Angela was and sat back down on the coffee table in front of her. "How did Julian react when Kiara told him?"

"She hasn't told anyone," Angela said. "And she probably wouldn't have told me if I hadn't found her throwing up in her bathroom a little while ago."

"Is she sure she's pregnant?"

"Yes. She had a positive pregnancy test." She gave him a helpless look. "I don't know what to do."

"I'll be honest, I'm not sure what to do either. This is a first for me," Jude told her. "But I'm not sure we should do anything."

"Really?" Angela asked.

"The thing is, this situation really only involves Kiara and Julian."

Angela exhaled heavily. "I suppose that's true."

"For now, the best thing you can do is just be there to support Kiara. She's going to need it."

"Do you think Duncan will ask her to leave?"

"Definitely not," Jude said. "Circumstances aside, this baby will be Duncan's first grandchild. And if you haven't figured it out yet, family is everything to Duncan. He won't do anything that will drive Kiara out of his life with his grandchild."

"He won't try to take the baby from her, will he?"

"I think the only way he'd step in is if she didn't want to raise the child herself. If she wants to give the baby up, he'll make sure that it has a good home with him and Elizabeth."

Angela's eyes fluttered closed as she let out another sigh. When she opened them again, Jude could see the turmoil she was dealing with.

"I know you say I'm not, but I still feel responsible for what's happened with Kiara. For how she's been struggling here. If it weren't for me, she wouldn't be here."

"Was she happier in Briar Hollow?"

Angela's expression saddened. "It kind of seems like she was. She liked her job at the library, but she was always working and planning toward our getting out of Briar Hollow. It was our goal. Our purpose."

Jude leaned forward, resting his elbows on his knees. The concern in Angela's eyes made his chest tighten.

"I know a purpose is important," Jude said. "And I think she just needs to be patient. You haven't been here all that long."

"I found my place here more easily than she did," Angela said, tugging the blanket tighter around her shoulders. "I had you."

The simple statement warmed something in Jude. He reached for her hands again, threading his fingers through hers. "You would have found your way, regardless. You're stronger than you give yourself credit for."

Angela shook her head slightly. "I don't know about that."

"I do," Jude said firmly. "You've proven time and again that you're willing to tackle the tough things."

"I just never imagined that having money would make life more difficult."

"Money makes certain things easier in life, but it can't solve all problems."

Angela's head bobbed in agreement. "I should probably go back. I didn't mean to barge in on your morning."

"You think I'm bothered by that?" Jude asked.

She lifted one shoulder in a shrug. "It wasn't the plan."

"Where we're concerned, there never needs to be a plan in order for you to come to me. If you need me, you let me know."

Angela gave him a soft smile. "All I could think of was getting to you. I couldn't figure out what to do."

"I'm sorry if I haven't helped you with that."

"You have though," Angela said, her expression earnest. "You're right that Kiara and Julian made the decision that led to this situation, and it's their responsibility to deal with it. I appreciate you just being here to listen to me as I had a meltdown."

Angela's eyes locked with his, and something shifted in the air between them. Jude felt his heart rate quicken as she leaned toward him, her hands still clasped in his. The blanket slipped from one shoulder, and without thinking, he reached to adjust it over her sweater, his fingers brushing against her neck.

"Jude?" Her voice was barely above a whisper.

"Yeah?" His own voice sounded rough to his ears.

"Thank you for always being there for me."

"I wouldn't want to be anywhere else."

The morning light filtered through the windows, catching in her hair, illuminating her face despite the redness around her eyes.

He lifted his hand to her cheek, his thumb gently wiping away a lingering tear track. Her skin was soft beneath his calloused fingers, and she leaned into his touch.

"I really should go," she murmured.

"Stay for breakfast with me," he urged. "I have bacon."

A smile brightened her face. "Do you think that will entice me?"

"I sure hope so," Jude said with a wink. "It would me."

"So the way to your heart is with bacon?"

"Or cinnamon buns."

"Oh, I've already given you those. Does that mean I've made it to your heart?"

Jude lifted his brows. "Yes, it certainly does."

Angela's cheeks pinked as she gave him a shy smile. "Well, I wish I'd brought some for you this morning."

"That's okay. Let me make you some breakfast this time."

"Okay. You've convinced me."

Jude got to his feet, pulling her up with him. He wrapped his arms around her, cocooning her in the blanket.

For a moment, he just held her, then he placed a kiss on the top of her head. Releasing her, he said, "You can come sit at the counter and watch me cook, if you'd like."

"I would like that," Angela said. She took the blanket off her shoulders and laid it on the arm of the couch before following him to the kitchen area in the large open design.

"I was going to make some scrambled eggs for myself," Jude said as he removed the container of eggs from the fridge. "Would you like some or do you prefer your eggs done another way?"

"Scrambled is fine," she said. "Is there anything I can do to help?"

Jude started to decline her offer, but then he realized she might need the distraction. "Sure. Would you like to make some toast for us?"

"Definitely." Angela came around the island to join him.

He showed her where the bread and toaster were.

For the next several minutes, they worked together to prepare the food. When it was all ready, Jude carried their plates to the table, and Angela followed with mugs of coffee.

As they sat down, Angela let out a sigh. "I know this wasn't planned, but I really needed it. Thank you."

Jude smiled at her as he laid his hand on the table, palm up. "It may have been unexpected, but it's most welcome."

When Angela placed her hand in his, Jude said a brief prayer of thanks for the food and also prayed for wisdom for Kiara and Julian.

It was nice to have her there to share a meal with him, and it reinforced the growing desire within him to share a future with her.

How soon was too soon to broach that discussion?

CHAPTER THIRTY-ONE

Angela finished curling her hair, then turned off the curling iron. She'd already applied a little bit of makeup and had chosen her outfit for her date with Jude.

The plan wasn't anything fancy, and her clothing choices reflected that. She'd chosen them with warmth and comfort in mind since this date involved picking up some food at the diner in Serenity and then going to a location that Jude promised would give her the best view of the sunset.

After the week she'd had, it sounded like the perfect evening.

She'd taken Jude's advice to just leave the situation regarding Kiara's pregnancy in Kiara and Julian's hands. However, it hadn't been easy because she'd wanted to encourage Kiara to tell Julian and Duncan so they could move to the next phase of the situation.

As long as Julian and Duncan didn't know, Angela felt like they were living in limbo, and it was driving her nuts.

But in the end, it was Kiara's decision, and Angela was trying her best to respect that.

She didn't know how long Kiara would be able to keep her secret, though, because the pregnancy was really doing a number on her. Morning sickness wasn't just happening in the morning.

Angela supported her as much as she could, but Kiara seemed to have withdrawn completely from her and everything else. She spent most of her days curled up in bed, reading. Some days she made an appearance for dinner, but most of the time, she ate in her room.

Even the self-defense training, shooting, and driving lessons had fallen by the wayside for her. Jude didn't press, though Dawn expressed concern and frustration over Kiara suddenly not showing up for anything.

All Angela could do was explain that she wasn't feeling well. Thankfully, that was true.

But now, she was going to put it all aside and focus on her time with Jude, and she couldn't wait.

Once she was ready, Angela went to Kiara's room. She poked her head in, unsurprised to find Kiara curled up on the loveseat near the window, a blanket wrapped around her and the tablet she'd recently purchased in her hand.

"How are you feeling, Kiki?" Angela asked as she approached her.

Kiara shrugged. "Managed to keep the sandwich I had at lunch down."

"That's good. Did you want me to get you anything? More ginger ale? Water?"

Kiara seemed to consider the options, then said, "I wouldn't mind some ginger ale. Super cold."

"No food?"

"I don't know," she said.

"Are you planning to go down for dinner?"

"Do you know if Julian is around?"

"I saw him at breakfast, so unless he left this afternoon, I imagine he's here."

"I'll just eat up here then."

"Has Julian said anything to you?" Angela asked. "Has he tried to talk to you after what happened?"

"Honestly, I don't think he remembers. He was drinking a *lot* that night. More than me, for sure."

It bothered Angela that Kiara was bearing the responsibility of that night when Julian was an equal participant in what had happened. He deserved to shoulder some of the stress that Kiara was under.

"You need to talk to him," Angela said, inching over the line she'd been trying to toe over the past week.

"I will." Kiara sighed, then turned to look outside. "Eventually."

Knowing she wouldn't get any more than that from her sister, Angela headed for the door. "I'll get you the ginger ale before I go."

"Thanks."

Downstairs, Angela entered the kitchen, which was busy with dinner prep, and greeted Mrs. Stevens and her daughter, who were working together.

"I'm just getting Kiara some ginger ale. She'd like dinner up in her room again, if possible."

"Is she not feeling any better?" Mrs. Stevens asked, concern in her voice.

"She's been able to keep a bit more food down, but she's still not feeling one hundred percent."

People were going to suspect something more than just illness was at play if Kiara didn't start acting like her old self soon. She might be forced to reveal the pregnancy before she was ready if she didn't start to feel better.

After delivering the large glass of ginger ale with ice, Angela went back down to wait in the mudroom for Jude to arrive. It didn't take long before the back door opened, and he stepped through it.

Angela smiled as she stepped into his arms. His jacket held a hint of the cold air and the scent of his cologne, which Angela loved.

Jude kissed her forehead, then asked, "Are you ready to go?"

"I am."

As they walked out to his truck, Angela wondered if this might be the night they shared their first kiss. Jude often kissed her forehead or the top of her head, sometimes her cheek, but they'd never had a real kiss.

It would be her first kiss, and Angela couldn't imagine sharing it with anyone but Jude.

"I've phoned the order in, so it should be ready for us to pick up," Jude said as he put the truck in gear and guided it away from the house.

"I'm looking forward to the French fries," Angela said. "They have such yummy ones."

"And I like their burgers."

They'd ordered from the restaurant before, so they had a good idea of what they liked.

"How was your day?" Jude asked as he waved at the guards at the gate.

"It was good. I finished a blanket for Annie to put in her shop. If it sells quickly, I'll make more. But if it's slow to sell, there's no sense in wasting my time on more."

"You could knit blankets to give to the NICU at the hospital in Coeur d'Alene. I read an article online somewhere about an NICU that had donations of handmade blankets that they would send home with the babies."

"Oh, that's a good idea," Angela said. "I'm not looking to make money on them, but I'd like them to benefit someone somehow."

It didn't take long to get to the diner, and Jude left the truck running while he went in to get their food. Angela looked around curiously, as she always did when they came into Serenity.

One day, she wanted to explore the town. She understood why she couldn't be seen out and about yet, but she hoped someday soon her presence in the community wouldn't matter.

She wanted to come to the diner with Jude and sit inside at a booth with him. However, Duncan didn't feel it was safe yet.

Mainly because of Jim...

Last she'd heard, he was still on the loose, and no one knew where he was.

When Jude returned, he handed her the bag with the food, which she put down by her feet. He removed their hot drinks from the tray and put them in the drink holders in the center console.

"Was it busy?" Angela asked.

"Fairly. Lots of older people since they have the early bird special on for them."

Since the sun set at around five-thirty, they were also eating early that night. Angela didn't care, though. She just wanted to spend the time with Jude.

As they drove to the spot Jude had chosen, he updated her on the progress of her and Kiara's home. A home that would now include a baby, Angela realized.

She and Kiara didn't know much about the physical construction of the house, but an interior designer had been in contact with them about their choices for things like the cabinets, appliances, and paint colors.

"Oh, this is beautiful," Angela said as Jude pulled into a small parking area off the side of the road that gave them an amazing view of the snow-covered mountains to the west.

She was just so grateful that Jude was willing to figure out dates like this one that fit within the restrictions that existed because of the security needs of her life. He could have decided it was too much of a hassle or too boring, but that didn't seem to be the case.

They sorted out their food, encompassed in the warmth of the cab of the truck with jazz playing softly from the speakers.

Jude said a prayer of thanks for the food, holding her hand as he did. She was reluctant to let go after he said amen, but eating with one hand didn't work when burgers were on the menu.

She'd ordered a chicken burger, and her first bite confirmed it was as good as the last time she'd had it.

"Duncan is concerned about Kiara," Jude said as they ate.

Angela stared at him, eyes wide. "Really?"

"Yes. He called me this morning to see if I knew what might be wrong."

"Oh, boy. What did you say?"

"Just that you had mentioned she was struggling with not having a purpose, and that she hadn't been feeling well."

"I'm sorry that you're not able to be honest with him," she said, lowering her burger to the takeout container in her lap.

Jude shook his head. "Don't be sorry. In asking you to leave the situation in Kiara and Julian's hands, I have to do the same."

Angela so appreciated how Jude handled things, and the maturity he had when it came to situations that seemed overwhelming to her. Like Kiara's pregnancy.

"I hope she tells Julian soon."

Jude's gaze turned out the front window for a moment before he looked back at her. "Duncan has asked me to look into treatment centers for Julian."

"Treatment centers? Is he sick?"

"It's to get him some help with his drinking. It has gone way beyond what's safe. The situation with Kiara just goes to prove that."

"Do you think it would be bad for his mental state to find out she's pregnant?"

"I don't know," Jude said. "It might give him the incentive he needs to get cleaned up."

Angela hoped that was the case, for Julian's sake, as well as for Kiara and their unborn child.

Jude had just leaned forward to pick up his drink when the window beside him exploded. Blood and glass went flying, and Angela screamed as she realized Jude had been hit by something.

"Oh, no. Oh, no." She reached for Jude, where he sat slumped, blood dripping down his neck and soaking into the collar of his shirt. "Jude!"

There was another shot, and Jude jerked. Angela screamed and reached for the watch she wore on her wrist. The watch she'd been given that had a tracker in it.

Fumbling with it, she pressed the button they'd told her to use if she was ever in need of help.

"Please, God. Please, God." She wasn't even sure what she was praying for, but first and foremost, her concern was for Jude.

Suddenly, her door was ripped open, and she was jerked out of the truck.

"Finally." The voice that growled in her ear was so familiar that a chill went through her, right down to her bones.

The light was on inside the cab, illuminating Jude where he was slumped over the center console. Unmoving.

Her heart pounded as fear coursed through her. But close on the heels of the fear was anger. This person... this horrible, horrible person who'd taken her from her family was trying to take the man she loved from her too.

She refused to believe that Jude was dead. That just wasn't possible. She couldn't accept that.

Angela twisted in Jim's grip, her shoulder screaming as he wrenched her arm behind her back. The smell of cigarettes and unwashed clothing filled her nostrils, a scent that transported her back to years in his presence at the homestead.

"Let me go!" She struggled against his hold, but his fingers dug deeper into her arm.

"You're coming with me," Jim snarled, his breath hot against her ear. "Just like old times."

Angela's gaze darted back to the truck where Jude remained motionless. Her chest constricted with panic. He had to be alive. He had to be.

"Please," she gasped, trying to pull away from Jim. "He needs help. He's hurt."

"Should have minded his own business." Jim dragged her backward, away from the truck, and she lost sight of Jude.

Angela knew that if she didn't do something, she'd be gone, and maybe Jude would be too.

She took a deep breath, praying that God would give her strength, then tried to recall everything Jude and Dawn had taught them about self-defense when an attacker had them in a grip the way Jim did.

Angela's heart hammered in her chest as she forced herself to focus through the panic. Jude's voice echoed in her memory: "Use your attacker's strength against them."

She went limp suddenly, dropping her weight and throwing Jim off balance. As he stumbled, she drove her elbow back hard into his ribs. The impact sent a jarring pain up her arm, but Jim's grip loosened with a grunt of surprise.

"You little—" he growled, but Angela was already twisting away.

She stomped down on his instep with everything she had. The crunch under her boot and Jim's howl told her she'd hit her mark. The self-defense training had drilled one thing into her above all else: create distance, then run.

But she couldn't run. Not with Jude bleeding in the truck.

Jim lunged for her again, his face contorted with rage.

Angela spun, her fist connecting with his jaw in a move Dawn had made her practice. It wasn't strong enough to do more than momentarily stun him, but she darted away from him, back toward the truck.

When she spotted Jude, she saw he was struggling to move.

"Jude!" she cried out as she reached the truck.

"Down," he gasped. "Get... down."

Without hesitating, she dropped to the ground. She pressed herself flat against the cold ground, snow seeping through her jeans as she tried to make sense of what was happening.

Angela heard two shots ring out, and when she dared to look up, she saw Jim staggering backward, his hand clutched to his chest, dark wetness spreading between his fingers. His eyes, wide with shock, locked with hers for a moment before he crumpled to the snow.

With her ears ringing from the gunshots, she scrambled to her feet and turned back to the truck. Jude was slumped against the steering wheel, his gun still gripped in his trembling hand.

"Jude!" She scrambled into the truck, her hands shaking as she reached for him. Blood soaked his shirt and jacket, making it impossible to tell where he'd been hit. "Oh God, please."

"You okay?" His voice was barely audible, his breathing labored.

"I'm fine," she said, tears blurring her vision. "But you're hurt. You need help."

"I love you, Angela," he whispered as his eyelids fluttered. "Never forget."

"No! You're not allowed to tell me that like this. I love you too, but this isn't the place."

"Just wanted... you... to know."

Angela tried to find where the blood was coming from so she could try to stem it. Finally, she located one place, and she gently pressed her hand against it.

Jude's pain-filled groan made tears spill down Angela's cheeks. "I'm sorry, my love. I need to stop the bleeding."

Cupping his cheek with her other hand, she looked into his glazed, half-closed eyes. "You are going to live, Jude Kessler. You're going to kiss me, then you're going to propose to me. And I'm going to say yes. We're going to get married and have at least one baby, but hopefully two or three. And we're going to grow old together. That's how this is going to go."

Jude's lips tipped up briefly. "You're my world, love."

Angela couldn't imagine doing any of the things she'd listed without him. Her heart hurt as she tried to keep Jude's life from ebbing away.

Where was the security team? Shouldn't they have been there already?

As if they'd heard her, Angela heard the roar of engines and then headlights flooded the area. There were shouts, but Angela ignored them, keeping her focus on Jude, willing him to live.

"Hang on," she murmured as she leaned close to him. "Help is here. Hang on, my love."

She gently pressed her lips to his. It was a fleeting contact, but it held her hopes of the life to come for them. And a promise to be there for him every step of the way.

"Angela." Dawn's voice was gentle as she gripped Angela's shoulders. "Let them help Jude."

Angela wanted to stay right where she was, but she wouldn't because Jude needed help that she couldn't give him.

"We have medics here," Dawn said. "They'll help him."

Angela allowed the woman to move her out of the cab of the truck. Clutching Dawn's arm, Angela walked on legs that felt like they might give out beneath her at any moment, and her heart pounded so hard it seemed to echo in her ears. Every few seconds, she twisted to look back at Jude, terrified of losing sight of him.

"They're taking care of him," Dawn said, her voice steady but urgent. "Let them work."

In the back of her mind, she registered that the medics were actually some of the security guards. They swarmed around the truck, their voices clipped and professional as they called out medical terms Angela didn't understand. Derek was cutting away Jude's shirt while another prepared what looked like an IV bag.

"Is he going to be okay?" Her voice cracked on the question.

Dawn didn't answer immediately, which made Angela's stomach clench with fear. "They're doing everything they can. He's strong, Angela."

Not a yes. Not the reassurance she desperately needed.

"We've called for a medivac helicopter from Coeur d'Alene, and it's going to pick him up from the estate and take him to the hospital there."

"What about me?" she asked. "I want to go with him."

"You'll be able to go in Mr. Burke's helicopter once the medivac has picked Jude up."

Angela tore her gaze from Jude to see a cluster of people around where Jim lay on the ground. "Is he dead?"

"I'm not sure."

Angela hoped he was so that the constant watch could be over.

The medics had loaded Jude onto a stretcher and were carrying him toward one of the vehicles. She started to follow, but Dawn's hand on her arm stopped her.

"They need to get him to the helipad as quickly as possible," Dawn said. "We'll follow in another vehicle."

Angela watched helplessly as the van carrying Jude disappeared around a bend in the road. The silence that followed felt deafening after all the chaos.

"Do they have the ability to take care of him? They didn't have an ambulance."

"The van they put him in has everything an ambulance has, and two of the security guards have experience as EMTs. One was a medic in the army. He's in good hands."

Angela wanted to believe that, but with him out of her sight, her confidence wavered.

"Come on," Dawn said gently. "Let's get you back to the estate and cleaned up."

Angela looked down at herself for the first time and saw that her hands and clothes were covered in Jude's blood. The sight made her legs wobble, and Dawn steadied her.

"He has to make it," Angela said. "I love him, and I can't lose him. I just can't."

"I understand," Dawn said. "And we'll be praying that God will heal him. But we need to get you back to the estate so you have time to clean up and get on the Burke helicopter. I have a feeling Mr. Burke will be getting on it with you."

Angela climbed into one of the waiting SUVs, and soon they were on their way back to the estate.

"The police will probably have questions for you because we had to call them to the scene."

"But I want to be with Jude," Angela said.

"I know. We'll see if they'll come to the hospital to talk to you."

When they pulled up to the main house, the back door opened, and Duncan stepped out. He looked more disheveled than she'd ever seen him, and worry was painted on his face.

"Are you okay?" he asked, resting his hand on her back to guide her out of the cold and into the mudroom.

"I'm fine. It's Jude. He's badly hurt."

"We're going to get him the help he needs."

"Can I go to Coeur d'Alene too?"

Duncan nodded. "Why don't you get cleaned up, and as soon as the medivac has come and gone, we'll leave in my helicopter."

"Okay." Nothing could have gotten her moving faster than the promise of being near Jude.

She rushed upstairs and into her bathroom. She'd peeled out of her bloody clothes and was standing under the spray in the shower, staring blankly at the blood that swirled down the drain, when she heard Kiara say her name.

"Are you okay?"

"I'm fine," she assured her, jolted out of her trance. "Jude's hurt, though, so I'm going with Duncan into Coeur d'Alene to see him."

"Do you want me to come with you?"

"I don't think you want to be in the hospital with the way you've been feeling."

"No, but if you need me, I'll be there."

"I'll be okay," she assured her as she finished washing away the last of the blood. "Duncan will be there too."

"You'll keep in contact with me?" Kiara asked. "To let me know how everything is going."

"I will."

Angela just hoped that she didn't have to tell Kiara that the worst had happened and her world had been shattered.

CHAPTER THIRTY-TWO

Jude gained a gradual awareness of pain. He couldn't pinpoint its location exactly, but it was a pretty good indication that he was still alive.

He opened his eyes, blinking a few times as he tried to take in his surroundings. The room was dimly lit, and judging from the beeps and hisses he was hearing, he figured he must be in the hospital.

Without moving, he took stock of his body as his mind fed him bits and pieces of what had led to him being in the hospital.

Jim... He'd somehow found them.

Jude remembered telling Angela to drop so that he could shoot the man, but had he been successful in protecting her?

Fear shot through him as he tried to remember if he'd seen Angela hurt. The memories were fragmented—the explosion of glass, the burning pain in his shoulder and side, Angela's screams.

Had she been shot too?

He tried to sit up, but pain lanced through his chest and shoulder, forcing him back against the pillow with a grunt. The movement sent fire down his left arm and made his vision blur at the edges.

"Easy there."

The familiar voice made Jude turn his head, though the motion sent another wave of pain through his skull. Duncan sat in a chair beside the hospital bed, looking like he hadn't slept in days. His usually immaculate appearance was rumpled, his tie loose and his shirt wrinkled.

"Angela," Jude managed, his voice coming out as a rasp. His throat felt like sandpaper. "Is she—"

"She's fine. Thanks to you, she's just fine."

Relief flooded through Jude so powerfully that his eyes slipped closed for a moment.

"Thank you, God," he whispered.

When he opened his eyes again, Duncan was leaning forward in his chair, studying him with the intense focus Jude had seen him use in boardrooms and crisis situations.

"Jim?" Jude's voice sounded foreign to his own ears, hoarse and weak.

"Dead." Duncan's expression was grim but satisfied. "You got him with two shots to the chest. He died at the scene."

The knot of tension in Jude's chest loosened slightly. Jim would never hurt Angela again. Never take her from her family. Never again make her live in fear.

"How long?" Jude tried to shift position and immediately regretted it as pain shot through his shoulder and down his arm.

"Two days. You've been in and out of consciousness, though mostly out. The doctors had to remove a bullet from your shoulder and another from your side. They said you'd lost a lot of blood."

Jude's hand moved instinctively toward his shoulder, but the IV line in his arm pulled taut. The movement sent a sharp reminder through his body that he wasn't going anywhere soon.

"Where is she now?" He needed to see Angela, needed to confirm with his own eyes that she was truly unharmed.

"Getting some coffee. She hasn't left the hospital since we arrived." Duncan's expression softened slightly. "She's been beside herself with worry. I had to practically force her to go eat something."

The thought of Angela sitting vigil beside his bed while he was unconscious made something warm unfold in Jude's chest, despite the pain radiating through his shoulder. She'd stayed. She'd waited for him to wake up.

"The doctors said that if Angela hadn't applied pressure to the wound when she did..."

Duncan didn't finish the sentence, but Jude understood. Angela had saved his life.

The memory came back in fragments—her hands pressed against his chest, her voice fierce and determined as she told him about their future together. The kiss. Brief as it had been, he could still feel the soft warmth of her lips against his.

He was a bit surprised that this event hadn't frightened her off. It was the worst-case scenario.

"Also, I've managed to keep your mom at bay with frequent updates, but she wants to fly out to see you."

Jude nodded, not surprised at all by that. This was his mom's worst fear come to life. He just hoped she didn't blame Angela for what had happened, since he'd been protecting her when the attack had occurred.

Had he been protecting her, though? Or had he been too distracted by her—trusting that being alone with her in nature would be protection enough?

"Everything is fine, Jude," Duncan said, his voice firm but understanding. "You did what you were supposed to do."

"I didn't see him coming," Jude confessed.

"We had no reason to think he was in the area."

"I don't like that he got the jump on us. If he managed to spot me, I should have spotted him."

"We found his vehicle," Duncan said. "He'd parked a little way from where you and Angela were. When they searched it, they found a package of GPS trackers with a couple missing. We searched our vehicles and found two had trackers on them. One of them was the vehicle you were driving."

"How did he get trackers on the vehicles?"

"We think that he may have spotted Kiara or Annie in Serenity and put trackers on the vehicles they were using."

Jude realized that was very possible. When Kiara and Lucy had gone into the library and bookstore in Serenity, Jim might have seen their vehicle and planted something.

It irked Jude that Jim had outsmarted him. At least to the point where he'd managed to shoot Jude twice right off the hop.

Jude wanted to take credit for having killed Jim. But the reality was that he'd struggled to free his gun and then to lift it to aim. Some might say it was a rush of adrenaline that had helped him.

Jude, however, believed his strength had come from God. In that moment, he'd sent up one simple prayer. *Please, God, help me protect Angela.*

And it seemed that God had answered that plea.

The door to the room swung open, and Jude turned his head on the pillow in time to see Angela step into the room, a cup in her hand. Even in the dim light, he could see her face light up.

"Jude!"

She hurried into the room, handing the cup off to Duncan before rushing to Jude's side. "How are you feeling? Are you in pain?"

"A little, but I'm okay, all things considered."

She leaned over and pressed her forehead to his. "I was so worried."

Mindful of the IV, Jude lifted his hand and gripped the back of her neck, holding her close as he breathed in her familiar scent

"Thank God you're alive," she whispered, her breath warm against his cheek. "I don't know what I would have done if—"

"I'm okay," Jude assured her, though the pain radiating through his shoulder and side told a different story. "Thanks to you."

Angela pulled back slightly, her eyes shimmering with unshed tears. She looked exhausted, with dark circles under her eyes, and her normally neat hair was pulled back in a messy ponytail.

Duncan cleared his throat. "I think I'll go make some calls, let everyone know you're awake. I'll also try to keep the nurses out for a few more minutes."

Jude was grateful when his boss stepped out of the room, leaving him alone with Angela.

The moment the door closed, Angela straightened, then carefully perched on the edge of the bed, taking his hand in hers.

"Thank you," she said, giving him a smile that momentarily energized her tired features.

"For what?"

"You saved my life. If you hadn't shot Jim, he would have dragged me off again."

"You did your part though," Jude said. "You used what we taught you, and then you did what I told you to. I said drop, and you dropped. I couldn't have protected you if you hadn't done that."

"I'm just glad it's over," she said, then frowned. "It *is* over, right?"

"I don't have any details on what's happening with Craig, but as far as Jim is concerned, it's over."

Angela's relief was palpable. "I've prayed that the situation would come to a resolution so that we could move forward with our lives, but I didn't imagine this would be the way it ended."

"Me, either," Jude agreed.

"I wish you didn't have to get hurt in order for that to happen."

"I'm glad it was me and not you."

Angela frowned. "Well, I wish it was me and not you."

The very idea made Jude feel sick. In his mind, their roles being reversed would have been the worst possible outcome.

"Let's just accept how it happened and move forward."

He could see that Angela wanted to argue with him. But in the end, she nodded.

His memories from that time in the truck wouldn't leave him alone, but not all of them were bad. Things had been said that couldn't just be ignored.

"So, if I recall, you proposed to me while I was half out of my mind in the truck."

Angela's eyes widened, then narrowed. "No. Something must be wrong with your hearing. I believe I told you that *you'd* be proposing to *me*."

"Are you sure?"

"Very," she said with a decisive nod.

"And you have no part in what's supposed to happen?"

A small smile crossed Angela's face. "I had a small part."

"A *small* part?" he asked. "And what part was that?"

She shrugged a shoulder. "The part where I said yes. So you see, it's a small part. Just one word. You have to say four."

Jude chuckled, then inhaled sharply at the pain that streaked through his chest. "Well, I must say, from my perspective, that even though it's a small role, it's the most important one."

Angela wrapped both hands around his. "I guess we both have an important role to play in that little scene."

"Did you have an idea of when you want this performance to occur?"

Angela's thumbs brushed across his hand. "Sooner rather than later, perhaps."

Jude's heart thumped heavily against his ribs. "Really?"

He wasn't sure that her definition of *sooner* was the same as his. Sooner rather than later to him was more like a matter of weeks, if not days. Given how much younger she was than him, her definition might be in months. If not longer.

"I know that might seem like I'm rushing things, but when you know, you know." She shrugged. "And this whole... incident has shown that life can end at a moment's notice. I already know that I want a life with you. I love you, Jude."

The words she spoke—this time without the pressure of life-threatening circumstances—resonated deep within Jude. He understood what she meant.

Life could be short. His dad should still have been alive. He might not still have the job as head of security. He might have been retired. But he still should have been alive.

His life may have been cut short, but Jude didn't think his dad would have had regrets over anything. Jude didn't want any either.

He wanted to build a life with Angela. To build a family with her.

"Sooner rather than later it is, then," Jude said with a wink. "Because I love you too."

Angela's smile was beaming as she leaned toward him. She brushed her lips across his, but when she went to move back, Jude once again gently cupped the back of her neck.

Jude's memory of their first kiss was fleeting, so he wanted a solid memory of their second one.

That kiss had been a promise of something more, if he should survive. This one... this one held the promise of life. A life spent together. A future of love.

When the kiss ended, Angela moved back slightly and rested her palm on his cheek. However, any further conversation was prevented by the arrival of the nurse.

Angela got off the edge of the bed, but she kept a grip on his hand, as if anchoring herself to him. Which was fine with Jude, because he wanted to be anchored to her.

~ * ~

"Where are we going?" Angela asked as Jude navigated the truck through the front gates of the estate.

"We're going to reclaim a beautiful spot from a terrible memory."

Angela stared at him. "We're going back to watch a sunset?"

"Yes. After we pick up some food," Jude said. "I don't want to have negative memories anywhere around here. So let's go back and make new memories at the spot where that chapter of your life ended."

Angela thought about it for a moment, then said, "It was such a beautiful spot, and I was looking forward to seeing the sunset there with you."

Jude looked over briefly with a smile. "So we'll go pick up food and make our way back there."

Angela wasn't really sure how she felt about returning to the spot, even though a month had passed since that day. She understood what Jude wanted to do, but all she could see in her mind was Jude slumped behind the wheel, bleeding.

Would returning there help to remove those memories?

"If you'd rather not, I'm not going to force you," Jude said, his voice gentle as he reached over to cover her hands with his, easily steering the truck with just one hand. "Just say the word, and we'll go somewhere else."

She knew that Jude would never do anything to hurt her. If he thought this would help them, she was going to trust him.

"No, let's go back. You promised me a sunset."

They picked up the food and drinks that Jude had ordered at the diner, then made the drive up to the lookout spot.

Once there, rather than eat right away, Jude got out and came around the truck to open her door. Angela stepped into the chilly early-spring air, heart fluttering as Jude's hand found hers.

The sky was already beginning to deepen with color, the sun sinking lower toward the snowcapped mountains. Despite the beauty stretching before them, her stomach tightened as memories flickered through her mind—shattered glass, blood, Jim's voice in her ear.

Jude squeezed her hand gently. "You okay?"

She nodded, drawing a deep breath of the crisp mountain air. "Just... processing."

He led her to a small clearing near the edge of the lookout, then gathered her close to his side, his arm around her shoulders.

With her back to the truck and the scene of the attack, Angela was able to fully appreciate the kaleidoscope of pastel shades across the darkening sky. Tucking herself inside the edge of Jude's jacket, she wrapped her arms around his waist and rested her cheek against his chest.

She could hear the beat of his heart, strong and steady beneath her ear. It was a beautiful sound she'd never tire of, because it was one she'd nearly lost.

And before her was a beautiful sight. One that had become obscured in the trauma of the attack.

She wanted God to redeem that beauty for her. The beauty of His creation.

Every sunset was a reminder of what she'd nearly lost, and she'd struggled to be able to see one without remembering that awful day.

"Heavenly Father." Jude's voice rumbled in his chest beneath her ear. "I come before you today, asking for help for Angela and me. Please free us from the chains of what happened here that day. Free us from the terrible memory of the actions of an evil man. I thank you for giving us the strength to fight against his actions and to persevere. I take no joy in having ended the life of a man, but I thank You for sparing ours."

Angela let Jude's words wash over her, sinking deep into her soul. She didn't want the memory of that night to keep her in chains. She didn't want the worry of what had happened to Jude to taint the future they now had a chance to have.

"Please give us the strength to break free of the fear and worry. As the Bible says, we can do all things through Christ who strengthens us. So we claim that strength through Christ to overcome what happened to us."

Angela clung to Jude, her emotions simmering near the surface. She slowly regulated her breathing, bringing it into rhythm with Jude's.

When he ended the prayer, Angela opened her eyes and stared out at the beautiful sky. The view blurred briefly, but she blinked away the tears.

She leaned on Jude's strength as the silence of nature settled around them. In that silence, peace filled her heart.

She'd never forget what had happened that day, but the power of that memory diminished. The image of Jude bleeding in the front seat of the truck slowly faded in intensity. His skin wasn't as pale. The blood wasn't as bright.

It was like a faded photograph.

When Jude removed his arm from her shoulders, Angela felt bereft. However, he moved to stand in front of her, framed by the colorful sky.

Looking down at her, he smiled. It was a gentle smile filled with the love that he freely shared with her each day. He took both of her hands in his, then lowered himself to one knee.

Angela's mouth dropped open as she stared at him. "Jude?"

"It's showtime, baby," he said with a wink. "Are you ready?"

Emotion rushed through her, robbing her of speech for a moment, so she just nodded. She was ready. She'd been ready for what felt like ages.

"Angela, will you marry me?"

The proposal wasn't comprised of flowery speech or pretty words. It was right to the point, right on script, which Angela appreciated, because it made it simple for her.

So there in the snow, with the sun setting behind Jude, Angela gave him the answer he was expecting. The one she'd been waiting to give him. "Yes."

Even though he knew what her response would be, Jude's face softened with emotion. More emotion than he usually showed.

Getting to his feet, he wrapped his arms around her and spun her in a circle.

"I love you, Angela," he said as he set her down. "You've made me the happiest man in the world."

She reached up to cup his face in her hands. "I love you too."

When Jude kissed her this time, it tasted like promises and forever. Angela melted into him, her hands sliding up to tangle in his hair as the last rays of sunlight painted the world golden around them.

This was the kiss she'd been waiting for—not the desperate one in the truck when she'd feared losing him, but this one, full of joy and love and the promise of the future they would build together.

When they finally stepped apart, both breathless in the cold air, Jude rested his forehead against hers.

"I forgot to take the ring out," he said with a soft laugh. Moving back a bit, he reached into his jacket pocket and pulled out a small ring box. "I hope you like it."

"I'll love it because it was something you chose for me," she told him. "Just like I love the perfume and the necklace you brought back for me from Dubai."

Jude opened the ring box, giving Angela a glimpse of a slender gold band and a setting of three diamonds.

"The larger diamond represents God, and the two smaller ones represent us," Jude said as he slid the ring onto her finger. "It's a reminder that we are not alone in our relationship."

"It's beautiful, Jude," Angela said. "So perfect. Thank you."

Jude wrapped his arms around her and held her close in the cold of the twilight evening that was settling around them.

"Now, let's go back to my place and eat our food. I think we might need to heat it up."

They stood in the waning daylight for a couple more minutes, and as Angela leaned against Jude, she thanked God for bringing them through the valley of death into the land of the living once again.

Whatever life might throw at them after the near-death experience, Angela had no doubts that God would give them the strength to handle it.

Angela wrapped her fuzzy robe around her and left the bathroom, her steps slow. In the bedroom, she placed her hands on the bed and blew out a long breath, slowly swaying from side to side.

Inhale.

Exhale.

Inhale.

Exhale.

The pain finally ebbed, and Angela took one more deep inhale, then let it out before straightening.

The pains were still several minutes apart and didn't last too long, but the time for her and Jude to meet their little one was nearing. It was a week before her due date, but at her last appointment, the doctor had said she could deliver any day.

Jude was at the security building, and Angela knew she had to let him know soon. However, she was trying not to ramp up his worry too much.

From the moment she'd shown him the positive pregnancy test, his protectiveness of her had ramped up even further. Thankfully, she'd had a fairly easy pregnancy.

She texted Kiara and Annie to let them know that she was in labor, but she made them promise not to tell Jude yet.

Kiki: *Do you want me to come over?*

No, I'm fine. I'll tell Jude once the contractions get a little closer.

Kiki: *Okay, but let me know if you change your mind.*

She sent back a thumbs up, then tucked her phone into the pocket of her robe. While she waited for the next contraction, she retrieved her hospital bag from the large walk-in closet.

It had been packed—with Jude's help—for almost three weeks. If he'd had his way, they would have moved to Coeur d'Alene two months ago.

Thankfully, Angela had managed to convince him to stay in their home on the estate. She liked the haven they'd created together since their marriage, and it was where she wanted to be as they prepared to welcome a child into their lives.

After doing a final check through the bag, Angela carried it out of the room. She paused in the hallway leading to the large open living area when another contraction crept up on her.

Setting the bag on the floor, she pulled her phone out and opened the app she was using to track the contractions. She started the timer, then put the phone back in her pocket. She pressed her hands against the wall and allowed her head to fall forward as she breathed her way through the pain.

Once it eased, she took a cleansing breath, then picked the bag back up. After setting it by the front door, she went to the kitchen to make herself something to eat.

She wasn't really hungry, but she wanted to make sure she had fuel in her body for what was to come.

The contractions continued to come as she prepared herself some pasta with tomatoes and Parmesan cheese. From the app, she could see they were coming about seven minutes apart.

She settled into her favorite overstuffed rocker with her bowl of pasta balanced on her stomach, and her large water bottle on the end table beside her chair. Tucking one leg under her, she used the other to set the rocker in motion.

She connected her phone to the Bluetooth speakers and brought up her favorite playlist.

Slowly, she ate her pasta, leaning her head back with her eyes closed when a contraction would tighten her stomach.

Though she would have liked to put off contacting Jude to spare him the worry so early in her labor, she knew there were logistics to take into account.

After two contractions that were a bit more intense, she set aside her nearly empty bowl of pasta and sent a text off to Jude.

I'm having contractions. <3

Jude: *OMW*

Knowing the man she loved and who would take care of her was on his way to her side made Angela feel more settled.

It was only a matter of minutes before the front door swung open and Jude walked in. He spotted her immediately and hurried to her, bending down on one knee in front of her.

He cupped her stomach in his hands just as a contraction started. Angela covered his hands with hers and let her head drop back, closing her eyes.

Jude's hands were warm through the fabric of her robe, and Angela found herself focusing on that warmth as the contraction peaked. His presence alone seemed to ease some of the intensity.

"How long?" His voice was steady, but she could hear the underlying tension in it.

"Since around seven this morning," she said as the pain receded. "They're about seven minutes apart now."

Jude's jaw tightened slightly. "You should have called me sooner."

"I wanted to be sure it was the real thing." She smoothed her hands over his, loving the way his calloused fingers felt against her skin. "Besides, I knew you'd want to rush to the hospital the moment I said the word contraction."

"You bet I would." He leaned forward and pressed a gentle kiss to her forehead. "How are you feeling otherwise?"

"Good."

"Well, the helicopter is getting prepped, so whenever we decide to go, it'll be ready."

Angela still didn't love flying in the helicopter, but she'd gotten more used to it over the past year and a half.

"Have you told Annie and Kiara you're in labor?" he asked.

Angela nodded. "But I made them promise not to tell you."

Jude chuckled. "Sneaky girl."

As she gazed at Jude, her heart swelled with the love she had for her husband. There wasn't a day... a moment, really... where he didn't make her feel safe and protected.

His love for her and his faith in God had made him an unmovable rock in her life. One she depended on.

"Is there anything I need to do before we go?" he asked. "Have you got your bag?"

"Yes, it's by the door."

He glanced over his shoulder. "Anything else?"

"I need to get dressed at some point," she said.

"Are you sure?" he asked. "You look pretty comfy."

"I'm not going to show up at the hospital in my robe," Angela told him indignantly.

Jude grinned as he got to his feet and held out his hands to help her up. "Well, let's get you dressed then."

She had another contraction on the way to the bedroom, but this time she leaned on Jude for the duration.

"Have you picked out what you want to wear?" he asked once they reached the bedroom.

"That dress there," she said, pointing to the light pink floral dress with cap sleeves that hung on a hanger on the closet door.

Jude retrieved it for her, then helped her get out of her robe and into the dress. It was loose, which felt good against her swollen abdomen.

Once dressed, Jude helped her brush her hair and get it looking like she wanted, then he retrieved her sandals and knelt to slide her feet into them.

With each contraction, he was there for her to lean on.

"You need to cancel our reservations for tomorrow night," she reminded him.

"Guess we'll be celebrating our first anniversary in the hospital, huh?" he said as he helped her back to her chair.

"But what a lovely anniversary present we'll have," Angela said, running a hand over her bump.

"The best," Jude agreed.

He picked up the bowl of pasta and her large water bottle and took them into the kitchen. After cleaning out the bowl, he put it in the dishwasher and then filled her water bottle with fresh ice and water.

Again, Angela thanked God for Jude. He was a wonderful husband, and she knew he would be an equally wonderful father.

She continued to track her contractions while Jude made a call to the resort to cancel their dinner reservation for the next evening. He followed it up with a call to the helicopter pilot to make sure he would be ready to go when Angela said the word.

"We need to let Duncan know so he doesn't hear about it from someone else," Jude said.

"Go ahead and give him a call."

Both her and Jude's relationship with Duncan had changed over the past year. For Angela, she'd come to view him as her father, and she called him Dad now.

For Jude, though Duncan remained his boss, they now shared a closer relationship outside of work as father and son-in-law.

"I think maybe it's almost time to go," Angela said after the contractions seemed to be stronger and were coming a little closer together and were lasting a little longer.

Jude came to where Angela sat, and once again took a knee in front of her. He put her hands on her belly and covered them with his, then he began to pray.

He prayed for strength for her, and for a safe labor and delivery of their child.

After he ended the prayer, Jude straightened and helped her to her feet. He led the way to the front door and picked up her bag. Angela kept a grip on her water bottle as she waited for him to lock up.

Before he guided her off the porch, he wrapped his arms around her. She looked up at him.

"Ready to meet our child?" he asked.

Angela nodded. "I'm excited to finally meet them."

They didn't know yet whether they were having a girl or a boy. They'd decided to keep that a surprise, though it had been super hard not to ask the ultrasound technician to tell them the gender.

"Then let's go." He bent to brush a quick kiss on her lips, then took her by the hand and led her away from their home. They were leaving as two, and in a few short days, they're return as a family of three.

Angela could hardly wait.

~ * ~

The hours seemed to crawl by, and Jude was struggling. He absolutely hated seeing the woman he loved in pain. It was his job—literally, but also as her husband—to protect her.

He wished he could do more to help her through the contractions, but there was nothing he could do but be at her side and offer his support. She had even refused an epidural so far.

His petite wife was once again showing him that she was a powerhouse of strength. It was what had drawn him to her initially, and it was still one of her most amazing qualities.

"I need some ice chips," she murmured.

Jude immediately picked up the cup and helped her spoon some into her mouth. She leaned back against the elevated bed, her gaze holding his.

"You're beautiful," he said, reaching out to tuck a strand of hair that had stuck to her sweat-dampened cheek behind her ear.

She gave him a weary smile. "I hope that if we have a son, he looks just like you. I hope he *is* just like you."

Before he could respond, another contraction overtook her. She reached for his hands as her eyes slid shut.

Jude watched the monitor that showed the progress of the contraction, wincing as it went on for what seemed like forever. Finally, he could see the line on the monitor begin to drop.

The nurse had come in and approached them once the contraction was over. "Dr. Ellis will be here in a few minutes to check your dilation."

Angela wrinkled her nose but nodded. It was a necessary part of the birthing process.

"Alright, my dear," the middle-aged female doctor said a few minutes later after checking Angela. "You're at ten centimeters and fully effaced, so whenever you feel the urge to push, you can."

Angela's eyes widened. "Really?"

The doctor smiled as she helped put the sheet back into place over Angela's legs. "Really."

Angela turned toward him. "Jude, we're going to meet our baby soon."

"I can't wait."

"And then we're going to have to decide on a name."

"I think, after all you've gone through, I'm going to let you pick the name."

The smile she gave him faded as she once again reached for his hand.

A few contractions later, Angela grimaced. "I think I need to push."

The nurse hadn't left the room since the doctor had last checked her, and she came over to the bed at Angela's words.

Over the next several minutes, the atmosphere in the room changed.

Jude was used to being in control, but he willingly relinquished it in that particular situation.

If he'd thought things were intense up to that point, he was in for a rude awakening. The intensity ramped up as the contractions seemed to come nearly one on top of the other.

"You're doing so great, love," Jude murmured as Angela fell back against the bed after having gone through another pushing contraction.

"It's a lot," she panted as she looked at him, her eyes glazed with pain.

"But it's almost over," he told her, hoping it was the truth. "And you're doing so well. I'm in awe of how you're handling all this. I love you."

"I love you too."

Thankfully, it wasn't long before the doctor said the baby was crowning. From that point, things seemed to go very quickly.

Soon, the doctor lifted the baby out and placed it on the blanket on Angela's stomach. Jude leaned over and pressed his head to Angela's.

"You're amazing."

She was gazing down at the baby, her hand resting on its back. "What is it?"

"Congratulations! You have a beautiful baby girl," the nurse said with a smile.

"Oh, Jude." Angela looked up at him with damp eyes. "We have a daughter."

The joy and wonder in her expression connected with something in Jude, and his own eyes pricked with tears.

The nurse rubbed the baby with a blanket, and soon their little girl let out a squawk. With his head close to Angela's, Jude looked down at their baby, taking in her scrunched-up face and plump little body, along with a shock of brown hair on her head.

"She's beautiful," Angela said. "And I think we should name her Danielle Joy."

The name hadn't been one that she'd mentioned before, but Jude got choked up.

"Danielle?" he asked.

"For your dad," she said, lifting her free hand to touch his cheek. "He raised an amazing man, and I want to honor him for that."

Jude wasn't one to cry, but in the intensity of that moment, he couldn't contain the tear that slid down his cheek. "Thank you. He would be so honored."

It took a little while, but soon, it was just the three of them in the room.

"Welcome to the world, Danielle Joy," Jude murmured as he held her for the first time. "Your mom is amazing, and I hope you grow up to be just like her."

He noticed that Angela had drifted off to sleep, so he pulled a chair over close to the bed and sat down, cradling Dani close to his chest.

As Angela slept, Jude prayed, thanking God for the blessing of Angela and Dani in his life. But he also prayed for wisdom and strength to be the kind of husband and father God would want him to be.

After the incident with Jim, he'd embraced Angela's favorite verse along with his own, and the two of them had worked hard to build a strong foundation for their marriage.

They hadn't dated for long before he'd proposed, and then they'd decided to forgo a big wedding and just get married at the estate with family and close friends witnessing the event.

Angela could now visit Serenity whenever she wanted, as they'd decided that Annie would reveal to her friends and acquaintances that she had a twin who she'd been separated from when they were young.

Annie and Angela still didn't claim the Burke name, which made Duncan—and Jude—very happy. However, it didn't mean they weren't prepared if the connection was made at some point in the future.

"Jude?"

Jude looked up from Dani to find Angela watching him with a sleepy gaze. She had never looked more beautiful.

"Can I get you something?"

"I'm hungry," she said.

"So am I. Let me see what I can get for us."

There was a bodyguard out in the parking lot, so Jude sent them a message with a food order.

"Has anyone responded?" Angela asked.

Dani had been born just after four in the morning. But even though they assumed people would still be sleeping, Jude had sent several pictures and all the information about Dani to the family, as well as to Cooper and Melanie.

"Your dad replied that she was beautiful, and he and Elizabeth can't wait to meet her."

Jude read through the rest of the replies that had come in. Apparently, everyone had been eager for the news.

"Happy anniversary, by the way," Angela said with a smile. "I can't think of a better way to celebrate our marriage than to welcome a baby created through our love for each other."

Jude's heart swelled with gratitude as he gazed at his wife. "Happy anniversary to you too, my love. This past year has been the best."

He carefully shifted Dani in his arms, marveling at how small she felt against his chest. Her tiny face was peaceful in sleep, her rosebud lips occasionally moving in a reflex that made his chest tighten with emotion.

"Can I hold her again?" Angela asked, reaching out her arms.

Jude stood and placed their daughter gently in Angela's waiting embrace. The sight of them together—Angela's tired but radiant face bent over Dani's sleeping form—took his breath away.

"I can't believe she's finally here," Angela whispered, tracing a finger along Dani's cheek. "After everything we've been through to get to this point..."

Jude sat on the edge of the bed, his hand covering Angela's where it rested on top of Dani's tiny body.

"I keep thinking about how different things could have been," he said quietly. "If Jim had succeeded that night..."

Angela looked up at him, her blue-green eyes serious. "But he didn't. And we're here now with our daughter because God protected us."

Jude nodded, remembering the prayer he'd whispered in that truck, begging God to help him protect Angela. The memory of that moment—the desperation, the fear, the surge of strength that had allowed him to fire those shots—still made his chest tight.

"And I'm so grateful for that," Jude said, his voice thick with emotion. "So grateful for the life we've built together."

"This is just the beginning, my love," Angela said with a smile.

"I can't imagine you want to go through this again before you've even had the chance to recover."

She bent to press a kiss to the cap that covered Dani's small head. "I already know that every moment of pain was worth it."

"Let's just enjoy our time with Dani for now," Jude said. "We can have a discussion about baby number two when Dani's a little older. I need time to recover."

Angela chuckled softly, and Dani squirmed, her face scrunching up for a moment. "Okay. I'll give you time."

Contentment filled the room, leaving Jude certain that it wouldn't take much convincing for him to agree to a second child.

The life he'd never planned to have was now all he wanted. And all the things that had once seemed out of reach were now possible with Angela by his side.

The End

ABOUT THE AUTHOR

Kimberly Rae Jordan is a USA Today bestselling author of Christian romances. Many years ago, her love of reading Christian romance morphed into a desire to write stories of love, faith, and family, and thus began a journey that would lead her to places Kimberly never imagined she'd go.

In addition to being a writer, she is also a wife and mother, which means Kimberly spends her days straddling the line between real life in a house on the prairies of Canada and the imaginary world her characters live in. Though caring for her husband and four kids and working on her stories takes up a large portion of her day, Kimberly also enjoys reading and looking at craft ideas that she will likely never attempt to make.

As she continues to pen heartwarming stories of love, faith, and family, Kimberly hopes that readers of all ages will enjoy the journeys her characters take in each book. She has no plan to stop writing the stories God places on her heart and looks forward to where her journey will take her in the years to come.

www.ingramcontent.com/pod-product-compliance
Lightning Source LLC
Chambersburg PA
CBHW020506260626
47156CB00006B/1889